To

MONARCH

Belle Whittington

Copyright © 2014 by **Belle Whittington**

All rights reserved. No part of this publication may be reproduced, distributed or transmitted in any form or by any means, without prior written permission.

www.bellewhittington.com

Publisher's Note: This is a work of fiction. Names, characters, places, and incidents are a product of the author's imagination. Locales and public names are sometimes used for atmospheric purposes. Any resemblance to actual people, living or dead, or to businesses, companies, events, institutions, or locales is completely coincidental.

Book Layout © 2014 BookDesignTemplates.com

Editing by Editorch.com

Monarch/ Belle Whittington. -- 1st ed.
978-1500787745

Praise for

Belle Whittington

"I swear, the creativity behind this trilogy is amazing. I love the unique take on aliens and other worlds. I also really like Belle's writing style and attention to detail ... There are some gorgeous passages that I actually re-read, involving dreams, galaxies, and even descriptions of the changing seasons. I'm really excited to see where the next book goes."

~Jana Waterreus at That Artsy Reader Girl

"I really enjoyed this book & will continue reading the series and also hunt out more books by Belle Whittington."

~John, Bex 'n' Books

"Firefly makes an excellent sequel to Cicada. I was instantly sucked into this book from page one. It took a few days for me to finish reading, but I was always reluctant to put it down every time. This series is just so different from most of the sci-fi books that I have read."

~Traci, The Reading Geek Book Blog

"Belle's writing style completely captivated me. Relaxed, melancholic in some parts and alerted the others, full of visual and auditory images, it represents a delight for the lover of science fiction novels!"

~Laura, Lucky Books Book Blog

"I hereby pledge my undying love for Belle for not only contacting me and letting me read the book, but also for having written it [Cicada] in first place. I'm really fed up with vampires and werewolves, and I can't even tell you how happy I am that I've come across a few YA novels about the extraterrestrial lately. Hooray for new horizons, new ideas, new worlds, new creatures, new books to pine for."

~Ivana, Willing to See Less Book Blog

"I absolutely love Belle Whittington's writing style. She really reels you in to her World."

~Gabby Matlock, What's Beyond Forks? Book Blog

"I found Belle Whittington to be an author who doesn't just spell things out for the reader but makes you search for information in her writing, and I loved that."

~Carole, The Life of Fiction Book Blog

"Belle is definitely one to watch, she's wonderfully imaginative and a good writer."

~Hannah, Once Upon a Time Book Blog

"Belle Whittington pulls you in with the mystery and gives you little bits here and there, just enough to appease you and drive you crazy at the same time and leave your mind reeling with what in the world is going to happen next."

~Ali, My Guilty Obsession Book Blog

"Belle Whittington has created a unique series and I'll look forward to reading more from her in the future."

~Book Passion for Life Book Blog

Acknowledgements

There are so many people to whom I owe gratitude for their parts in the successful completion of this book and this trilogy. Because of them, my characters are able to share their stories and secrets within these pages.

I'd like to thank the organizers of the Montgomery County Book Festival for their undying devotion to promoting local authors. Attending MCBF is the highlight of my events calendar each year! Likewise, I owe appreciation to the organizers of the annual John Cooper School's Signatures Author Series Luncheon and their commitment to literacy in Montgomery County and the promotion of local authors.

I'd be remiss if I didn't mention all the wonderful book bloggers and reviewers who've so graciously promoted my books and me over the past three years. Many thanks to each of you from the bottom of my heart for all you've done for me!

And a special thanks to:

- My wonderful family who have stuck by me, encouraged me, and hauled heavy, book-laden cardboard boxes to book festivals for me. Countless thanks to my sister Juanita who is my business manager and has worked a multitude of signing tables with me. My mother who stuck with me even though these books creeped her out a lot. Thank you, Nunu! To my beautiful daughter LB who I love and adore – thank you for the beautiful book covers and awesome book trailers!

- Many thanks to the awesome musician, Kyler England, who gave me permission to use her beautiful song, *When the World Stops Spinning*, for the MONARCH Book Trailer. Visit her website and get to know more about her and her music: www.KylerEngland.com!

- Much gratitude to my editor – Melissa at editorch.com for editing both FIREFLY and MONARCH. You are a wonderful editor and even better friend!

- These fabulous authors (listed alphabetically), Alexia Purdy, Ali Cross, Heather Lamb, and Nicole Storey. These ladies deserve my heartfelt thanks for reading a very rough draft of MONARCH and sharing their thoughts with me.

- How could I not include my lovely Beta Readers? This book is the best it can be because of these wonderful ladies (listed alphabetically): Amanda Britton, Brandi Peel, Cyndy Andren, Laura Badgett, Nicole Counts, Nila Bartley, Tabatha Pope, and Vicki Bradley. Ladies, I appreciate your input and enthusiasm and I *heart* y'all oodles and gobs!

- Last, but certainly not least, I owe unending gratitude to my readers, fans, and all the lovely book bloggers and reviewers who have stuck with me and promoted my books. Thank you!

For my loyal readers and fans.
Thank you for taking this journey with me!

I've got the best readers and fans in the universe!

—BELLE WHITTINGTON

PREFACE

I was no longer a bystander to this story. I was the story. Every secret interwoven through the tale I'm about to tell you belongs to me. And the summer I graduated from high school was the summer everything came together in a horrible clash of good versus evil.

Packing up and leaving my small, inconsequential, southeast Texas hometown meant leaving part of myself behind. I said goodbye to the human side of me when we piled into David's truck and drove away from our home. And I waved farewell to any hope of ever returning as I watched our home slip into the shades of night.

Everything had been turned upside down, and deciding what was good and what was evil was like looking through sunglasses at night. It all washed together in a murky blend of darkness, shadows, and secrets.

My biggest secret of all was one for which I had no answer: *which one was I – good or evil?* I stuffed that secret deep behind my ribs and swallowed it down.

Some secrets are best kept in the darkness away from prying eyes and those who would seek to face them head-on. Some secrets kill

CHAPTER ONE

SPRINKLES

My mom had owned two bakeries, each named Sprinkles. One burned down the night Everett almost died ... the night he'd become more than human. The other was built on the very same spot where "the building" had once stood. We'd been shocked to find out Mom had decided to build the new Sprinkles where there had once been a torture chamber run by Hunters – the evil aliens we'd killed in a bloodbath of bullets, baseball bats, and a bovine tranquilizer dart.

That Sprinkles was now nothing but a deep pit in the ground, a smoldering inferno of sparks, ash, and flames. Fire trucks from Conroe and Montgomery arrived to assist the Willis Fire Department. No one had ever suspected there was such a massive supply of explosives and weapons hidden below Sprinkles in a secret basement where a man named Luke had claimed to run an architectural business. Luke had turned out to be a hunter of aliens and one in particular.

Me.

People from miles around would drive to Willis for Mom's chicken salad croissant sandwich and baked potato soup. Her cupcakes and cookies had become so popular that she'd been working on a website for online sales and orders. Now, people would be coming from miles around to see the giant crater that three fire departments were trying to extinguish.

All of Sprinkles was lost.

All of Mom's dreams were lost.

And Mom was gone. Taken. We had no idea who the kidnappers were. However, we had several choices to choose from: the Hunters, Luke, The Resistance, or Ash.

Ash. My former Other. The one I'd promised to go to, in exchange for Everett's life, waited for me somewhere in the jungles of Brazil. I'd promised him that I would come to him on my own by the summer solstice. He'd promised that if I didn't, he would follow through on ending Everett's life. That was something I could never allow to happen. I'd chosen Everett to be my Other. And there was no going back from that now. If he died, I'd die. There was no undoing the bond we'd formed the night of the Rodeo Gala.

But that didn't mean I'd get my happily ever after with my true love. I would go to Ash so that Everett could have a long happy life. And I had no idea whether or not the rest of my life would be long or happy. I would just keep a stiff upper lip and do what must be done.

"What's going on in that head of yours?" Everett asked as he stroked my forearm with his fingertips.

I glanced at him and parted my lips to speak but burst into flames instead. This was the third time it had happened since we'd gotten to the house to find it broken into and pillaged.

Blue flames licked around my arms and shoulders, and I tossed my head back, my arms out, and felt my feet lift from the kitchen floor. Everything around me glowed in a blue haze, and I turned to glimpse myself in the dining room mirror.

My hair stretched out in tendrils, as if it had a life of its own, curling, twisting, and reaching among the brilliant blue flames that leapt from my skin and into the air around me.

Immortality, it seemed, replaced mortality in stages. I hoped it would be the last stage of spontaneous combustion. Because each time it happened, my clothing ignited and left me suspended in flames, mid-air, and naked.

Of course, all this activity had delayed us from going to the airport and heading to South America to pursue Mom's kidnappers. Andrew had called the airlines several times to reschedule our flights until he'd finally given up and decided to allow me time to get through my episodes of fire and levitation.

Natalie gasped as she rushed through the kitchen door and saw me hovering several feet above the tile floor, naked, and trying to cover myself as best as I could with my arms. "Get out of here!" she shouted at David, Andrew, and Everett. "Give her some privacy!"

But they'd already seen me naked plenty of times over the past few hours. I was still embarrassed, but what else could I do? The episodes happened at the least expected moment. I had no time to prepare.

"We're just trying to keep her from burning herself and the rest of us to death," David answered. "That's why we called you to come over and help us with her. Everett has had to haul her up to her room a couple times. She was naked and trembling. That's not right for a dude to have to do. Especially for a nerd like him." Poor David was so embarrassed and awkward that I felt sorry for him.

"I don't mind," Everett said quietly. And I knew he didn't. Only he knew what sort of things I was going through. He'd been through a transformation, himself. "I'd carry her up those stairs a million times."

The guys really were trying to protect themselves, and me for that matter, from myself. But it was becoming obvious to me that Everett was one of the catalysts. Each time I'd burst into flames was right after he'd tenderly touched me.

"How long is this going to last?" Andrew asked Everett, hoping he would have been through a similar experience when he'd gone to Brazil to join The Resistance.

"I'm not sure. My transformation was different because my armband was applied by a human." Everett pulled his sleeve up to reveal the band around his left arm, embedded beneath his skin like a raised tattoo. "Hers was properly applied."

I caught a quick glimpse of a frown cross Everett's face. He was thinking about Ash hovering above me, partially-clothed, in my truck bed. I reached my hand out to him and whispered, "Everett …"

But Natalie shooed the guys out of the kitchen one last time and huffed. I could hear her thoughts, too. She was wondering how she was going to get me down and dressed like a proper lady.

With the guys out of the room, and with Natalie holding a sheet up to provide me some privacy, I closed my eyes and finally allowed myself to enjoy the ecstasy of becoming immortal. I hadn't forgotten the severe pain from just a few hours earlier when Ash had slipped the delicate silver loop onto my arm and initiated the process. So, the warm ebbing and flowing of blue flames was soothing me on the outside while my veins felt as if warm sunshine flowed within them.

I slowly spun around and around like my tiny galaxy does at night while I sleep. I was weightless and careless, and I sighed at the bliss of the conversion from mortal to immortal ... human to alien. Before I knew it, I was fully relaxed, eyes closed, and humming a line from Reeve Carney's *New for You*. It seemed oddly fitting, but I wasn't sure who I was becoming new for – Ash or Everett?

I'd die for you a thousand times, Everett's voice whispered in my thoughts.

And I would for you, too, I responded in like kind.

I slowly spun once more, inhaled deeply, and sighed as I exhaled. *Everett, take me to the forest so we can be alone together.* He heard my thoughts loud and clear in his mind.

Where I first kissed you? he asked, his thoughts winding through my mind. I could feel his heartbeat speeding up as if it was beating right next to my own heart.

Yes, I spun once more and bit my bottom lip. He couldn't see me, of course, because he was in the living room with the other guys. But he could see me in his mind's eye.

"Dude, where are you goin'?" David asked.

"Everett, I don't think you should go in there," Andrew said with a little more force. Apparently, he was trying to come to me.

"Nobody's coming in here right now!" Natalie said, still holding the sheet up.

Babe, Everett whispered in my mind again. *I...*

Mmmm... I sighed in my mind and then began humming the chorus of the song again.

The tension between the two of us was so strong that it felt like the others around us were far away … like Everett and I were the only two people in the universe, and we were the only two who mattered.

I started to call him to me once more, but a well of electric warmth grew in a rising crescendo, filling every cell in my body until I was sure the pain was about to return. I tightened my fists and folded my arms and legs so close to my body that I began spinning faster and faster, preparing myself for the torment that never came.

What did happen, though, was the last few moments of my humanity. It crossed through my skin in brilliant sparkles of light swirling away from me in circles among the flames. One last brilliant flash, and then the familiar wave of energy bounded outward from me, pushing the dining chairs and table, pots and pans, dishes, Natalie, and the sheet away from me.

Then I drifted down to the floor and into darkness.

And dreamed of walking through the roaring flames at Sprinkles, searching for Mom and someone else. *Who was it? Oh, yes! Orion, the alien we'd called the Cicada. The one who'd been my son in my previous alien life.*

CHAPTER TWO

IT'S DONE

I came back to consciousness just as someone was tucking the sheet around me, but like the night of the Rodeo Gala when we were attacked, I didn't even have the energy to open my eyes.

"It's done," Everett said, his voice low and somewhere close by. "Natalie, would you please go fill her tub with hot water?"

"What for?" Natalie asked.

"She has to be, well, recharged ... for a lack of a better word." There was that old matter-of-fact tone the old Everett had frequently used. I'd always adored it. I would have smiled if I could have gotten my lips to move. But, as it was, I was trapped inside my own limp body.

"I'm sure we've got some candy or cookies around here." It sounded like Andrew was opening and closing the kitchen cabinets.

"This is different, Andrew," Everett's voice was filled with more force this time. "Natalie, please do as I asked. We don't have much time."

Once he said those last few words, Natalie rushed out of the kitchen and ran up the steps toward my bathroom. Then, someone lifted me into his arms.

"I should do that," Andrew said, sounding a bit unsure. He was my protective big brother, and it was sweet that he still wanted to look out for me even though everything that was happening was ultimately my fault.

"No, you shouldn't. This is something I have to do. Me and me alone." Everett drew me close against his chest and carried me upstairs to my bathroom.

A layer of moisture from a cloud of steam immediately clung to my skin as soon as we crossed the threshold. Natalie must have filled the tub with very hot water. I tried to ask Everett what he was planning on doing, because if he left me there alone, I was sure to drown. I still couldn't move a muscle even if my life depended on it.

Then he asked Natalie to give us some privacy. At first, I expected her to offer some resistance, but I heard a little smile in her voice when she said, "Well, just don't let her drown." For a moment, I wondered if she could read my mind.

"Never," Everett answered, cradling me tenderly in his arms.

After Natalie pulled the door closed behind her, Everett stepped into the garden tub and lowered both of us into the hot water. He was still fully-clothed, and I was still wrapped in the sheet. The water felt wonderful as he pulled me to him and gently laid my cheek against his chest.

And for a split-second, I remembered asking Ash to take me to the water. Somehow, I'd managed to remember that it was part of the transformation process. However, in my human state, I couldn't put the pieces in the correct order. And since it was my science that had ultimately made it possible for me to become an alien-human hybrid, Ash wasn't as knowledgeable on the subject as I'd been in my alien form. He'd been too busy conquering the jungle people, building the Queen's City, and creating Orion and Nyx to know all the details of my experiments.

Everett's arms wrapped around me and drew me back into the present. And I was glad, because that past had been so painful to me that I'd concocted a way for me to forget when I became a hybrid.

Soon, the waves of energy began crossing from his skin into mine. My eyes immediately opened. Orion had given Everett energy much the same way as Everett was transmitting it to me. He'd saved Everett's life, and perhaps Everett had saved me in a different way.

He lifted my hand and held it in his. Droplets fell from our joined hands and splattered across the surface of the steaming water, creating ripples that mirrored the movement of the light that flowed from Everett's hand to mine. He placed my hand against his chest, and wrapped his fingers around mine. And our hearts beat in time with each other.

The waves of light and energy that flowed from his whole body into mine charged every one of my cells. I'd never felt so alive. Everything seemed so vivid and brilliant, like someone had just wiped the fog from a window on a cold, rainy day. Every detail of everything around me seemed crisp and new.

"You're flowing in my veins now," I whispered, pressing myself into Everett. "Look at how you course through me." I lifted my hand to reveal the light coursing in the veins beneath my skin.

He kissed me on the forehead and pulled me close to him and deeper into the tub. The water was quickly cooling now as the heat bled into my body and flowed through me along with Everett's energy.

Nothing's going to be the same ever again, I asked, allowing the words to wind from my mind to his. *Is it?*

No, he responded. *It's done now.*

I inhaled and pulled his arms tighter around me. My future was full of so many unknowns. The comfort of Everett's arms around me was the only thing I felt sure of.

You're in my veins, too, Everett tipped my chin up so that I could look him in the eyes. *And I can't get you out. You're all I think about, dream about.* And then his lips covered mine and I was lost in his kiss.

The dread of saying goodbye to him tried to crawl up my ribs and into my throat. But he kissed me again, and

I pushed it back down. *I'll deal with it some other time,* I thought as I loosened my legs from the sheet and bent my knees around his.

"You're wearing clothes. In a full tub of water," I lifted my head and smiled at him. "With a naked girl."

"A beautiful, naked girl." He slipped his hand beneath the sheet and caressed the full length of my back.

"What's that sound?" I asked, quickly noticing a faint grinding noise.

"You're getting taller just like I did," his voice grew husky as his hand slipped over the curve of my hip.

My hair spilled down over my shoulder and into the tub. It suddenly seemed longer and thicker than it had ever been. It was growing, too.

"I'm not going to fit into any of my clothes," I gasped, thinking about how I'd packed and prepared for my trip to Brazil. Then I became distracted with undoing the buttons on Everett's shirt and making a line of kisses across his chest, stopping at the tattooed heart surrounding my name. He'd called it his 'brand' when he showed it to me on the night of the Rodeo Gala. We'd always belong to one another even if we had to be separated by time and space.

"Damn, you're beautiful," he said just before he growled and leaned over me, looking into my eyes. "Even with your new blue eyes."

"What?" I gasped.

He lifted a mirror from the edge of the tub and held it up for me. *It was true!* My eyes were blue. No. Aquamarine. Just like Ash's. I guessed that was our native eye color. And it was so weird to see myself without the brown eyes I'd inherited from my dad. A frown tugged at my lips and cheeks.

"I think you're gorgeous with them," he set the mirror down, cupped the back of my head in his hand, and kissed me again.

My hands found their way to his chest, and the rest of the buttons fell to the bottom of the tub when I ripped his shirt open and pulled it off. Just as he was about to slip the sheet from around me, Natalie peeked in the door and asked if I was okay. I giggled and pulled the sheet tight around me again while Everett tried to shield me by leaning over me, exposing his back to Natalie.

"Oh, my," Natalie covered her mouth and giggled. "Looks like she's doing just fine."

Andrew pushed through the door when he heard her say that. "Dude, what the hell?"

"It's done," Everett smoothed the sheet around me, making sure I was completely covered.

"What's done? 'Cause from where I stand, that could be any number of things!" My protective big brother's face was flushed red with embarrassment and anger.

"Come on, Andrew," Everett answered. "Calm down."

"Is she going to catch on fire anymore?" Natalie stepped in front of Andrew, hoping to defuse the situation.

"Her transformation is complete," Everett stood in the tub and held his hand out for me. The sheet was soaked with water and so heavy it tugged away from my skin. "And she's going to need more clothes."

"I'll say!" Natalie gasped. "Did you get taller?"

"Yeah," I blushed, "I think certain other things grew, too,"

Andrew gasped and blushed again. All this talk about my body was extremely uncomfortable and embarrassing for him. Natalie shooed him and Everett out of the bathroom and grabbed a measuring tape out of Mom's sewing kit.

"Let's get you measured," she motioned for me to drop the sheet and step out of the tub. Then she gasped again, "Dang, girl! You look like a sex kitten now! No wonder Everett was gettin' all hot and bothered!" she giggled and went about taking my measurements. "He's sure looking fit these days, too, with all those muscles and tattoos."

"Hottest nerd in town," I smiled.

She took down a list of things I would need, and Everett handed her his credit card as she was leaving. "Buy her whatever she needs. I don't care how much you spend."

"Nothing better than new clothes for a new Blair!" Natalie smiled and slipped Everett's card into her wallet.

16 · BELLE WHITTINGTON

CHAPTER THREE

A NEW BLAIR

Andrew called the airlines to reschedule our flights and then made us something to eat. All of my pants were too short and tight in the hips, and all my shirts were too short and too tight across the bust. I really didn't know what to make of any of the changes in my body as I brushed my much longer and thicker hair.

My full-length bedroom mirror proved that Natalie had told the truth. I had changed from small-town cowgirl to bombshell. I'd always had a nice figure, but curves now accentuated my waist and hips. My shoulders were slightly broader now, which kept my larger breasts from looking completely out of proportion.

The band around my left arm caught my eye, and I turned to examine it closely in the mirror. It was similar to Everett's, yet notably different. Mine appeared more organic where Everett's looked man-made. Still, it looked like an intricately-designed, raised tattoo. It was a reminder of who awaited me in the jungles of Brazil. Ash ... with his brilliant eyes, sly smile, and charm that would melt the frosting off any cupcake.

A flutter of butterfly wings rose behind my navel, and I moved my hand instinctively over them to quiet them. Instead, it ignited a faint blue light in the shapes of swirls and symbols across my abdomen. Ash had initiated the mating ritual when he'd administered the serum from the ancient silver vial he wore on one of the many cords that dangled around his neck.

This was something I had to keep to myself. Only two people knew about the mating ritual – Ash and me. I wasn't sure how long I'd be able to keep that secret, but I would harbor it as long as I could. I was going to have to break Everett's heart soon enough, and there was no need to hurt him any more than I was going to by telling him now.

I shook my head to clear that from my thoughts and wrapped Mom's robe around me. It smelled like her and made me feel like she was hugging me. I needed her now more than ever, and yet I had no idea where she was or what was happening to her. She could be terrified and in danger at that very moment.

I'm gonna find you, Mom. Don't worry, I'm coming. I whispered. I hoped she'd hear me, wherever she was. And I hoped she wouldn't be too freaked out by my new appearance when I found her.

Natalie returned in record time with tons of clothes. When it came to shopping, she had it down to a science.

After plopping the loaded shopping bags on my bed, she gave Everett his credit card back along with the receipts.

"I hope you didn't spare any expense," Everett tucked the card into his wallet.

"Of course not," Natalie smiled as she began pulling the clothes out of the bags and arranging them on my bed.

I didn't know how she did it, but every piece of clothing she bought fit perfectly. I pulled on a pair of jeans and a top I would have never chosen for myself. I usually went for items more suited for work on the ranch. But this outfit was form-fitting. The top had tiny buttons up the front and was a bit low-cut. I guessed it would be okay for the plane, but I'd quickly change into the cargo pants and t-shirt she'd bought me when I got to Brazil.

I was so glad to see that all the other clothing items were exactly what I would have purchased for myself. She'd even gotten clothes for both warm and cool weather. I hugged her and noted how much shorter she was now that I'd grown a few inches. Then I wondered if my new boots Grandpa had given me for graduation would still fit.

Natalie handed me a new pair of thin socks, and once I slipped my feet into the supple leather boots, I smiled. They still fit. But I'd never be able to wear thick socks with them, because my feet had grown, but only a little.

A few twirls of the curling iron and a clasp at the crown of my head, and my hair spilled over my shoulders in long, thick curls. I fidgeted while Natalie applied a little bit of make-up.

"Be still! I'm accentuating your new eyes!" She swished a brush loaded with eye shadow over my eye lids. "Cowgirls …" she shook her head and clucked her tongue. "Y'all just don't accentuate your positives enough!"

She was right. Maybe I didn't. And I didn't know if I'd ever get to see her again, so I stopped fidgeting and let her continue making me over. She finished with a flourish and turned me around to look in the mirror.

And I didn't recognize myself.

"Where did I go?" my voice caught in my throat.

She leaned her head on my shoulder while we continued to look into the mirror. The clothes, hair, and makeup made me look like a supermodel. My new aquamarine eyes glistened brightly and seemed a little larger. My lips were fuller. A faint dusting of freckles still spilled across the bridge of my nose. Even my eyebrows looked perfect.

"You're right here," Natalie placed her hand over my heart. I noticed a film of tears threatening to spill over her lashes. "I always thought we get to choose our own fate," she inhaled and leaned her head on my shoulder again. "But maybe it's the other way around."

We stood like that for a little while longer, looking at the new me in the mirror. Then she broke the silence. "Look on the bright side! You could've turned out hideous!" Then she grabbed a stack of my new clothes and packed them into my suitcase.

After everything was neatly and tightly tucked into my luggage, we headed downstairs where the guys were waiting. I stopped on the stairs when I realized they were just standing there looking at me. Andrew's brows were knit together and a frown tugged at the corners of his mouth. The whisper of thoughts I got from his mind revealed that he feared it was going to be even harder to protect me now.

I glanced to David and all that swirled through his mind was, Damn! *Now that nerd's got a really hot girlfriend. Don't stare, don't stare, don't stare. Natalie'll get pissed.* I bit my bottom lip to keep from laughing out loud and quickly glanced toward Everett who was standing there with his mouth open.

"I guess I look like a –" I started to say 'normal girl now.' But Everett interrupted.

"Goddess," he stepped to the bottom of the staircase and looked up at me. "You look like a goddess."

"Oh, my gosh!" Natalie nudged me, breaking the energy welling up between Everett and me. "Your fella approves."

"That's an understatement," Everett looked me over again. My newly-acquired mind-reading skills weren't as honed as Andrew's, but the bits and pieces of images and thoughts I got from Everett's mind made me blush.

He took the luggage from my hand and looked me over from head to toe. And we were instantly drawn together like I had been drawn to Ash in the truck bed. Only, I was the magnet, and Everett was drawn to me. His lips covered mine and the luggage dropped to the floor next to us just before his arms wound around me.

A flurry of energy fluttered between us where our bodies touched. It reminded me of a flurry of butterflies on a summer day. He gasped and pulled his lips from mine. Looking into his eyes was like looking into the depths of the deep blue ocean. In his eyes were all the possibilities I longed for.

David cleared his throat and reminded us that we weren't alone. Andrew's face had grown dark watching us, and Natalie leaned her head against David's chest thinking about how romantic and magical it was.

But Andrew was thinking the exact opposite. He was thinking that there were many horrors coming our way, and my transformation was just the beginning. Our family was falling apart, and he had no idea how he was going to protect me while saving Mom.

Everett was stunned as if he'd been drugged. His heart was pounding hard against his chest … it longed to be close to mine once more. He started to reach for me again, but Andrew stopped him.

"Y'all are going to have to control this or someone's gonna get hurt," Andrew stepped between Everett and me.

"Better get to the airport if you want to make that flight," David misinterpreted Andrew's statement. He thought there was about to be a fight between Everett and Andrew. But that wasn't the case.

My big brother wasn't trying to keep Everett from making out with me. He was trying to figure out how to get us through the next few months and had no idea what had come over us.

Everett wasn't even thinking about why; he just wanted me in his arms. But I knew. It was the pairing ritual Ash had initiated. The longer I was around Everett, the greater the physical pull between us. Controlling it would never be about willpower.

The ritual was an ancient rite of my alien people. It was meant to bind two Others into an inseparable pair. And it was working. But not as it was intended. Ash had intended for it to bind me to him. I wondered if I'd altered some part of the serum in order to forever separate myself from Ash once I'd become a hybrid.

The memories of my former alien life were still blurry like faded black and white photos of a distant past all jumbled up and out of order. I must have been a heck of a scientist to have pulled it off ... to have found a way to make me forget.

I said 'goodbye' to Natalie and hugged her tight, knowing that it could be the last time I'd ever see her. She'd grown from acquaintance to best friend. How could I ever repay her for everything she'd done for me?

"You'll be back in time for my wedding rehearsal, right?" she asked, tears spilling down her cheeks.

All I could do was nod. It was a lie, but I couldn't bring myself to tell her that I wouldn't be there to be her maid-of-honor, because I'd likely be with Ash by then. Everett and Andrew hugged her, too. Both of them wore the same pain on their face that I felt in my heart. Neither of them knew whether or not they'd ever be back, either.

We piled into David's pickup truck and headed toward the airport. I looked back once to watch my home disappear into the distance, behind the oaks and elms. Many memories swept through our home and around the grove of ancient trees in the back yard. I'd had a very happy human childhood with wonderful parents and a loving family.

And I realized at that moment that I didn't get to say 'goodbye' to Grandma and Grandpa. But hadn't they been doing that for me over the past few months? They'd known this day was coming. They'd made it easy for me. And I loved them even more for it.

Natalie followed behind us in her little Volkswagen Bug and honked her horn as she turned the opposite direction toward her house where a normal family and normal life waited for her. I envied her that.

David took a small detour so we could drive past Sprinkles. Fire trucks from Willis, Montgomery, and Conroe were still trying to put out the flames that continued to roar deep within the enormous crater that had once been Mom's shiny new bakery.

"Damn! How many explosives did he have in that basement?" David gasped as we slowly rolled past one of the fire trucks.

"And what was he planning to do with them?" Everett leaned forward to get a better view.

Andrew craned his neck to see. His face turned as dark as his thoughts. If I hadn't been looking directly at him, I would have missed him shaking his head. His nostrils flared, and his lips narrowed. There was a storm brewing inside my brother. I could sense the growing thunder and lightning in his soul. I could hear the angry whispers of revenge in his mind.

Then Everett's hand found its way to mine. My fingers instinctively twined with his. My fate had claimed me, and there was nothing I could do but hang on for dear life and try to make it out alive.

I love you, Blair Reynolds. His words weaved through my mind.

I love you, too. I turned to look into his eyes. In the light of day, he looked much older and wiser ... so much different from the old Everett who'd had so many dreams of adventure. I released his hand and gently stroked the side of his face and then touched the scar that sliced through his eyebrow.

He'd gotten it the night I'd traded myself for his life. Ash had agreed to free him from the rubble that trapped him in The Queen's City beneath the jungles of Brazil. It would always be a reminder to him of what he could never have – me. One day he would go on with his life, maybe meet someone else and marry her. I knew he wanted kids someday. It just wouldn't happen with me.

Your thoughts are dark. He pulled me into his arms thinking that I was worrying about my mother. I would let him keep thinking that. The truth was too painful. I nuzzled my head into his shoulder and relished the feel and smell of him. He'd told me that I was his home, and I felt the same way about him.

I would spend the rest of my life being homesick.

"Have you heard from your dad?" I spoke aloud, because the silence in the truck cabin was getting to be too much to bear.

"He's doing fine. It's a simple concussion. They're sending him home today," he leaned his cheek against the top of my head.

"That's good. I'm so glad he's okay." And I truly was. Mr. Forster had always been very kind to me and, as it turned out, was very much in love with Mom. They'd been seeing each other the last couple of months, and Andrew and I approved. But he'd been injured trying to protect Mom.

"Me, too. I just wish he could have seen who'd attacked them," Everett tensed a bit.

"It's my fault. Maybe if you hadn't been saving me, you might have been able to help him and Mom," I pulled away from him and leaned my forehead against the window. We were driving past the Pizza Shack now … the place I'd shared a pizza with Ash on the day Daisy was murdered.

"Don't be ridiculous," he drew me back into his arms.

"He's right, Blair," David said glancing at me in the rearview mirror. "Don't beat yourself up. Shit happens."

I really wished Andrew would try to console me, but he was immersed in his own thoughts. Or maybe he knew that it really was all my fault … every single bit of it. I knew he loved me and would do anything for me. But the truth was that our mother was missing because of me. And maybe our brother and father were murdered because of me, too.

That thought pierced my heart.

Quiet your thoughts, Babe. Everett kissed my forehead. *It's going to be okay. I've got connections.*

I nuzzled my face into his neck and closed my eyes. It was too painful to watch my hometown disappear as we drove away down I-45 toward Houston. And I didn't have the heart to tell Everett that there were no connections in the world strong enough to get me out of this mess. I'd have to bite the bullet and follow through on my agreement. It was the only way for everyone to be able to go on with their lives.

We made a brief stop at Taco USA in The Woodlands so David could get himself a giant burrito called The Conquistador. Andrew, Everett, and I decided we would eat on the plane, so we stayed in the truck while David went into the restaurant to get his food to go.

And I stayed in Everett's arms until we pulled into the airport where we said 'goodbye' to another member of our group.

"Don't forget everything I taught you," David said as he hugged me.

"Never," I blinked away the tears that welled up behind my eyelids.

"Take care, Bud," David shook Andrew's hand and drew him in to a bro hug.

"Thank you for everything, Dave," Andrew tried to smile, but it wasn't convincing.

"We'll see each other again soon," David answered and turned to Everett. "Well, for a nerd, you've managed to get yourself a really hot girlfriend." He shook Everett's hand. "Take care of her. She's like a little sister to me."

Everett smiled and shook his hand. "Thanks for friending a nerd like me in high school."

"Thanks for helping me pass my classes!" David laughed. "Hey, we'll all see each other soon. Don't forget the wedding. It'll crush Natalie if y'all aren't there."

We all lied and told him we'd be back in time. But it wasn't convincing. Not to ourselves and not to David. But we left it at that and checked in for our flight and then went through security where Andrew was searched like he was a terrorist. Apparently, he was on some sort of watch list, and that fact was no surprise to him.

I watched as they searched every inch of his carry-on luggage and his body. And I wondered what he'd done that had made him be such a suspicious passenger. When they were finally done interrogating him, he looked grumpy and disheveled.

"Everett, you need to keep her close to you. Look at how all the men are watching her," Andrew tipped his head toward a group of guys wearing football jerseys. They'd stopped talking and were gawking at me like I was a piece of meat. Everett tightened his hold on my hand as if that was going to stop them from checking me out.

It was flattering, but I knew not to encourage it. There was more to it than just my newly-acquired supermodel looks. There was pure chemistry screaming to every heterosexual male around me. And there was nothing I could do about it.

So, Andrew insisted that I stay between him and Everett. I nodded and noticed how much more Andrew was looking like Dad. He was beginning to look much older than his age of nineteen. The weight of the world can do that to a person.

Finally, we were able to board the plane, which felt extremely claustrophobic to me. The plane seemed like a small tube with walls that threatened to close in around me. I wanted to run off that plane and drive to Brazil. But that would take too long, and Mom was waiting for help. So I settled down into my seat and tried to fill my mind with thoughts other than the plane crashing into the side of a mountain.

It was going to be a very long flight from Houston to Brazil. The sun was setting at the same time we were lifting off of the runway. We were flying away into the darkness … into the unknown.

Into shadows darker than the edge of night where specters awaited to undo all I'd done to escape them.

CHAPTER FOUR

FLY AWAY INTO DARKNESS

Surprisingly, the jumbo jet wasn't fully booked with passengers. There were plenty of empty seats around us, but the three of us sat next to each other. I sat by the window. I wanted to look out at the night sky as we flew the same path I'd taken when I'd tumbled head over heels across the Gulf of Mexico the night I'd given myself up for Everett's life. It was likely that I'd never pass this way again.

The higher the plane climbed into the sky, the lower the sun sank toward the horizon as if the darkness was chasing the light away. I didn't realize how hard I was gripping the armrests on my seat until Everett covered my hand with his.

"These things are built to stay in the air," he said as he lifted my hand to his lips and kissed each of my fingers.

I smiled an uneasy smile and bit my lip. I wasn't afraid of flying. I wasn't really afraid of what awaited me. It was the dread of losing all I loved that gripped me. And if I were completely honest with myself, I would admit that I really wanted a giant blaze of glory as my goodbye to my human life. Instead, I was serving myself up on a silver platter to Ash by flying straight into his arms.

My stomach was growling with hunger by the time the flight attendant brought the food around, and I ate like it was my last meal. In fact, I ate two sandwiches, chips, two brownies, and washed it down with a coke. Andrew and I both sounded like cave people when we ate, and Everett was stuck between us with his ear buds in.

Apparently, smacking in stereo was too much for him to bear. That sort of encouraged Andrew to eat even louder until the flight attendant politely asked him to stop. I laughed harder than I had in a long time. Even Andrew had a glint of humor in his serious brown eyes as he apologized to the flight attendant with a piece of roast beef hanging from the corner of his mouth.

"I told you that would catch up with you someday," Everett smiled.

He'd picked up a tablet full of games and puzzles when we were passing through the airport. We played tic-tac-toe, hangman, and Mad Libs. The Mad Libs got us to laughing so hard that Everett spewed Dr. Pepper out of his nose. That called for another scolding from the flight attendant.

The seats in front of us had a video screen on the back of each of them. Passengers could purchase videos with the swipe of a credit card. Andrew and Everett were getting tired and wanted to settle down and watch a movie. So we each plugged in our ear buds and searched through the available videos.

I almost chose *The Lucky One*, because Zac Efron reminded me of Andrew. But I settled on *Cowboys and Aliens* instead. We'd missed seeing it at the movie theater, and I'd always intended on renting it. Perhaps this would be my last chance. I raised my card to swipe it, but Everett beat me to the punch by swiping his and charging my movie to his account.

He winked at me, then settled back to watch *The Hunger Games*. I leaned forward to see that Andrew was watching something sports-related. We dimmed the lights above us. Everyone around us had already done the same, and many were tucked beneath blankets, asleep.

My thoughts couldn't settle down so I could watch the movie. I just couldn't get into it. There was something rising in the back of my mind, faint and too far away to figure out what it was for a long while.

Everett lifted the arm rest between us and put his arm around me. I leaned into him and snuggled my head into the bend of his neck. And, still, the sensation was hovering in the recesses of my mind, growing steadily, slowly closer.

I started fidgeting with the buttons on Everett's shirt, and he pulled the blanket up under our chins. I explored the muscles that rippled across his stomach, he leaned his cheek against my forehead. I made a path of little kisses from his collar bone to his ear lobe, and he whispered, "You're killing me," in my ear.

Soon, Andrew was snoring softly, with his head lobbed over onto the small pillow the flight attendant had brought him. Everett carefully took the ear buds that had fallen to Andrew's chest and looped them over the video screen so he wouldn't wake up.

"He's sound asleep," Everett turned to whisper to me, and I grabbed him by the collar and pulled him to me.

His lips covered mine as he drew me close, filling me with his warmth. The alien sensation just beyond the curtain of shadows in my mind grew a bit nearer. Everett kissed me until I was breathless, and he leaned his head back against his seat and whispered, "We've gotta stop before we get arrested."

"I know," I whispered, unable to catch my breath. "I'm sorry."

"Don't say that," he stroked the side of my face with his hand. "I'm never sorry about kissing you. I want to spend my life kissing you."

I nuzzled my face into his shoulder and wished I could spend forever with him, too. He had no idea that soon we'd be separated forever. I pushed that out of my mind and allowed myself to be drawn into the shadows of sleep where the stir of that alien sensation was rising in a crescendo. As I slipped over the edge of consciousness, I realized what it was.

At first, I heard the drums. *Boom, boom-boom, boom ... boom, boom-boom, boom.* Then the other tribal instruments, so cherished in my alien life, joined in the rhythm until I was no longer asleep; I was in the trance of the pairing ritual.

I dream-traveled to where Everett had created a private tropical paradise for the two of us. The hammock still swayed under the lush tropical leaves of the thick jungle trees. Torches still lit the sun-warmed path that soothed the soles of my feet as I twirled and spun to the rhythm of the drums.

The tribal music of my alien people was intoxicating and sensual, and I danced among the flaming torches. I opened my lips to call to Everett to join me, but I knew that would be a mistake. Ash would hear me, too, and that wouldn't end well.

I forced myself wake up, but the drums didn't stop. *Boom, boom-boom, boom ... boom, boom-boom, boom.* My breath quickened. Every atom in me wanted Everett, and wanted him *right now*. A sort of frenzy spread throughout my body. I glanced down and noticed something glowing through the blanket. So I lifted it to see that my entire torso was lit up with symbols and swirls etched like tattoos of green light across my skin.

Then the drums pounded louder, resounding in my head. But Everett was sound asleep, and judging by the sweet look on his face, he was having a peaceful dream. I had to do something to try to snap myself out of it, so I slipped past him and Andrew and headed down the darkened aisle to the bathroom.

Splashing cold water on my face and blotting my neck with cold damp towels didn't faze the desire for Everett that grew deep within me like the wildfire that ravaged the haunted wood the night before.

I looked at myself in the mirror, and light flashed from my eyes. I no longer had full control of myself. The ritual had worked its magic. I unbuttoned my blouse and the waist of my jeans to reveal the rest of the symbols that shined beneath my skin.

Everett, come to me, I whispered in my mind. *Wake up, and come to me.*

And I knew he'd heard them, felt them – the tribal drums. They called to both of us, because he was my chosen Other. The drums worked to draw us together to complete the ritual of pairing. I tossed caution to the wind and pushed any thought or fear of Ash away.

Three faint knocks on the flimsy bathroom door, and I knew he'd come to me. I pulled the door open and saw the same blue light flash behind Everett's irises. The ritual had claimed him for me ... called him to me.

We pressed against each other so he could close the door behind him. He looked as drugged and dazed as I felt, and he immediately noticed the glowing symbols across my torso, engraving a story into my flesh ... a story about a nerd and a cowgirl who fell madly in love one hot, turbulent Texas summer. A story written in my native alien language.

Everett's lips parted as if he'd intended to speak, but I kissed him instead. The rest of the passengers were asleep, and I didn't want the flight attendants to hear us. One rip and the buttons of Everett's shirt pinged against the bathroom walls and floor.

"We both have brands on our flesh now," I held my hand up to reveal that the butterfly ring he'd given me had melted and etched its shape into the skin around the ring finger on my left hand. Then I placed my hand over the heart he'd had tattooed on his chest over his own heart. My name was scrawled across his flesh right in the middle of it. He'd called it his 'brand.'

He drew in a sharp breath as light from my hand passed through his skin and illuminated the heart and my name.

"Inhale me," I whispered. I didn't even have to think about the words; instinct brought them to my lips.

Everett responded by lifting me into his arms and pulling me tight against him. He managed to spin us around in the tiny airplane bathroom and pressed me against the wall as I wrapped myself around him. Then he lowered his lips to mine, and I exhaled just as Ash had done.

Everett inhaled and the universe exploded in brilliant flashes and pinpoints of light and nebulas of rainbow colors. Planets and moons spun in orbits around a brilliant star, and our thoughts echoed in the void of space.

Sparkles of blue light filled the irises of Everett's eyes as I stroked the side of his face. The tiny bathroom disappeared and we floated in and out of time, in and out of space, through nebulous clouds of blues and purples that sparkled with planets and stars.

"We are Others now. It's complete," he whispered. His voice sounded beautiful speaking my native alien language that had become so beloved to me.

"Yes," my answer sent echoes throughout the haze of clouds around us.

He kissed me once more and the brilliant star around which the planets and moons were spinning exploded. Chunks of rock and earth spun through space, tearing through the clouds and muddying their colors. A huge chunk blazed toward us, and we spun just in time to miss it. Then, losing our grip on each other, everything went black. We slammed against the walls of the tiny bathroom.

People were screaming, jet engines were whining, the airplane shuttered and tilted. I gripped tightly against the ceiling of the bathroom, calling for Everett. Suddenly, the bathroom door burst open, and light sliced into the darkness.

"Blair?!" Andrew shouted, holding a bright flashlight in his hand. He was fighting the slope of the floor as the plane continued its sharp descent.

"I'm here," I answered, pressed against the ceiling. And it wasn't the fact that the plane was falling out of the sky that kept me there, but the shock and surprise of the situation.

Everett had fallen back on the sink, gripping a towel bar with one hand, and reaching up for me with the other. His tattoo still glowed as did the symbols across my torso. By the way we were dressed ... or rather, partially dressed, it was clear that we were up to something. Andrew had no idea the extent of what we'd been up to.

He grabbed Everett, jerked him out of the bathroom, and shoved him up the aisle, tossing his shirt at the back of his head. All the other passengers were screaming. Some were praying for God to save them. Most of them were crying. The oxygen masks had deployed and were hanging down from the ceiling. An elderly lady in a seat near the bathroom was gripping a mask to her face and gasping for air.

I struggled with the buttons on my shirt as I stumbled up the sloping floor, holding on to the armrests and backs of seats trying to reach our row. All the lights in the cabin were out making it easy to see the brilliant flashes of lightning and electricity pinging around the outside of the plane among a halo of bright light. Then, as quickly as the plane had plummeted from high above the clouds, the pilot was able to stop the sharp descent and get control once more.

People were wailing, children were crying, and a man three rows in front of us was throwing up in a barf bag. The lady across the aisle from us crossed herself and then tightened her seatbelt.

Andrew refused to let me sit next to Everett, insisting that he sit between us. When I protested, he lost his temper and spoke through gritted teeth, "Look around you, Sis. There's a plane-load of people who just saw their lives flash before their eyes."

"Take it easy. It's not her fault," Everett interjected. Andrew refused to turn around and acknowledge him. I started to protest again, but he cut me off and continued.

"I told you both to control yourselves, didn't I?" His face was flushed with anger, covered in an expression I'd never seen on my brother's face. "You won't be happy until *you kill us all*, will you?"

"That's enough, Andrew!" Everett grabbed him by the shoulder and pulled him out of my face.

But it was too late. The damage had been done. It would have been better if he'd have hit me. Instead, he'd ripped my chest open and tore out my heart. And I knew ... I knew ... my lip quivered as I looked away ... because I knew my brother blamed Dad's and Aaron's deaths on me. He blamed Mom's disappearance on me, too. He'd laid it all on my shoulders.

And I felt the weight drop on me as he spoke those last words.

I was trapped on that plane, with no way to run from the guilt and shame. I stood and looked around for a place to go. Andrew grabbed me by the wrist and ordered me to sit down.

Then something came over me.

Perhaps it was anger at myself or maybe it was because I was mad at him. Perhaps it was the alien side of me. Or maybe it was the voice that had grown stronger within me over the past few hours that had reminded me of who I really was— Queen ... Monarch ... a royal alien princess who was once born to alien parents who'd both inherited their thrones through birthright and royal blood.

I calmly cocked my head to the side, looked my brother in the eyes, and said, "Do you know who you're speaking to?" I felt my nostrils flare and my breath quicken as the words wound their way up my throat and across my tongue, refusing to be silenced by my heart. "I was born to rule worlds. *Don't you ever forget that!*"

I tore away from both of them and headed to the back of the plane where an empty seat sat all by itself against the back wall. No one could sit next to me, and the seats in front of me were all taken by a family who couldn't speak English.

Then I raised my barrier and drowned out Everett's pleas for me to come back and Andrew's guilty apologies screaming that he didn't mean it. I locked my barrier in place and fortified it with a new one that slid up the outside of it and silenced the ceremonial drums that beckoned me to complete the pairing ritual.

And I was alone.

CHAPTER FIVE

ALONE

"Alone is not so bad," Dad had once said to me as he stroked my cheek with his thumb. "So long as you have yourself, you're never *really* alone." He'd smiled and handed me the brush so I could groom Daisy. I'd had a bad day at school, and I had been fretting about going to the 4-H banquet alone.

But my memories were coming in pairs, and I recalled another memory of a different father … my alien father … in a remote past. "I do not wish my only daughter to be alone," he'd taken my hand in his and placed it into the hand of his most trusted general, a brilliant military man who'd never lost a battle. Ash – the stunningly handsome bachelor who'd been known as a favorite of the ladies. "Our enemies grow strong, and there may soon be a day when I will be gone, and you'll ascend the throne. You'll need a consort who can protect you."

I shook my head to clear my thoughts and glanced around me. The other passengers were terrified that the plane might still plummet from the sky and kill us all in a giant fireball. Flight attendants went row-to-row assuring everyone that everything was okay and trying to tuck the oxygen masks back into the compartments overhead.

The plane was a mess. Papers, books, and other miscellaneous items were strewn about the aisles. We might've plunged to the earth if Everett and I hadn't stopped when we had, I knew this. I also realized that what had happened between the two of us in the tiny airplane bathroom had been out of our control.

"Maybe it was the North Koreans blasting us with some sort of death ray," a guy around my age said to the flight attendant as she handed him a soft drink.

"We're nowhere near North Korea," she patted him on the shoulder and continued down the aisle with her drink cart. I wondered if I was the only one who'd noticed her roll her eyes when she'd turned her back to him.

"I think it was static electricity," a balding man with a Cajun accent said to the woman across the aisle from him.

"Could've been aliens," a man with a head of wild, dark brown hair on his head and several strands of colorful beads around his neck spoke with an unfamiliar accent. "Does anyone feel like they've lost some time or passed out?" He glanced around him arousing another round of anxiety among the other passengers.

I shook my head and smirked. He had no idea that there was a real live alien queen only a few seats away from him. But he was onto something, I had to give him that. He continued talking, and I tuned them all out and turned to my window.

On the other side of the glass, the universe seemed quiet and peaceful. Moonlight lined the edges of wispy clouds with a silvery glow. Stars glittered in the sky behind the moon, twinkling and blinking across the blanket of night. I thought about the night I'd flown back home in the bubble Ash had created and how cold I'd gotten as I'd sped across this very same path of sky.

And I felt a cold feeling grow in my bones.

I was about to start another trek alone, and I wasn't quite sure how I was going to be able to separate myself from Everett and Andrew. The thought was a bit frightening, but it was also a bit liberating. I'd been raised, at least in this human life, to be self-reliant and self-sufficient. But the memories from my former alien life filled me with doubt.

Would I be safe if I were alone in the jungles of Brazil? I wondered as I flexed and tightened the fingers on both hands. *I have my powers, my fire and lightning, and other skills that I'd honed over the past few months. And now that I was more than human, who knew what powers would emerge?*

My hand instinctively found its way to the key that dangled from a cord around my neck. I'd found it in an old tobacco box in Dad's study. I'd suspected it had some sort of significance when I'd decided to keep it. Now, I was sure of it. I just had no idea what it was yet.

Then I thought of Nyx. *"They've taken the key!"* he'd shouted, and we'd all heard him in our minds as we faced Ash, surrounded in the circle of blue flames out in the pasture next to the haunted wood.

What key was he talking about? I wondered as I scooted down in my chair and braced my knees against the back of the seat in front of me. I pulled the cord over my head and examined Dad's bronze key. The number '273' was engraved on one side of it. I still had no idea what the key opened or why I suspected it had some significance. But I knew deep in my bones that whatever the key opened was important. I wrapped the cord around my wrist several times and let the key dangle like a charm on a bracelet.

"We'll be landing shortly," the captain's voice sounded over the plane's intercom. "It seems we must have flown through an electrical storm earlier. We've been routed to a different airport that's smaller than our original destination, so please be prepared for a bit of a rough landing."

The flight attendants began moving up and down the aisles making sure everyone was buckled in and all the trays were up. I tightened my seatbelt around me and briefly wished that I was sitting with Everett and

Andrew. But when I glanced toward them, I saw they were having a heated discussion, so I turned back to my window. The sky was brighter now. It would be daylight soon, and we'd be on the ground in Brazil.

My journey was about to begin.

CHAPTER SIX

THE JOURNEY BEGINS

The moment the wheels touched down on the landing strip, the pilot hit the brakes. All the stray items lying throughout the plane flew forward in a barrage of brain-bashing books and carry-on luggage and a flurry of random papers and magazines.

Inertia forced us forward, causing many to bump their heads on the seats in front of them. The cacophony of screeching tires, whining engines, and screaming passengers was deafening. I reinforced my shield around me, hoping to block out some of the noise. It worked to buffer the louder sounds, but not enough to drown out the terror from those around me.

Instinctively, I turned my head to look out the window again. Black smoke from the burning rubber of the tires billowed past the window, and a battered fire truck sped alongside the plane and bumped along the patchwork landing strip. We definitely weren't in Texas anymore.

What they say is true. Everything is bigger in Texas. That includes landing strips. This one was short, narrow, and sorely in need of repair. Not to mention that it was obviously designed with much smaller aircraft in mind.

The plane began to shimmy, and I had the distinct feeling we weren't going to stop before we reached the end of the runway. I glanced toward Everett and Andrew. Andrew was looking out the window just like I'd been. Everett was bracing himself with his forearms against the seat in front of him and looking over his shoulder at me.

I immediately lowered my shields so I could hear his thoughts.

We aren't going to stop, his voice echoed in my mind. *You've got to do something.*

I love you, I answered in my thoughts.

I know. I love you, too. A small kind of resigned smile crossed his lips. He thought we were going to die. That this was it … the end.

I quickly turned back toward the window, placed my hands against the window pane, and shouted, "Stop!" at the top of my lungs. Everything turned to slow motion just like in the movies. The window glass blew outward sending glistening shards of various shapes and sizes skipping along the ragged landing strip.

The billows of black smoke from the burning tires turned to slow-boiling columns flowing past the windows. I strained with all my might and focused my thoughts on stopping the plane. All the sounds around me were garbled and deep, papers and magazines were suspended mid-air, and Everett was still looking at me with that expression on his face.

Clamping my eyes closed, I imagined the plane catching in a giant net like a monarch butterfly. I felt my hair whipping around me as my powers grew. My heart pounded in my ears, and I chanted in my native tongue, "I command you to halt."

The plane lurched backward and then forward before it stopped abruptly at the very edge of the old asphalt landing strip. Flight attendants rushed to the doors, flung them open, and inflated giant yellow slides. We were instructed to remain calm and exit the plane.

I stood and looked for Andrew and Everett in the crowd of terrified faces of passengers filing down the aisles. Andrew had a small gash on his forehead and he'd smeared the blood trying to wipe it off. Everett was pushing through the crowd trying to reach me, and I held my hand out for his when he got close.

He took my hand in his and we leapt out into the balmy jungle air and onto the yellow slide together. It was like the giant slide at the Montgomery County Fair we'd always stood in line for. But there were no balloons or carnival games at the bottom of this slide.

Our feet landed on the sweltering airstrip. Clumps of grass emerged between the patchwork maze of asphalt and gravel, and a battered railing just in front of the plane was all that stood between the front tire and the edge of a steep cliff. Far below, the tips of the jungle canopy hid a myriad of secrets beneath its shady reaches. I was immediately thankful that the plane hadn't become one of them.

"Damn, that was close," Andrew stepped next to me and peered over the edge of the cliff.

I didn't reply.

"Sis, I'm sorry. I didn't mean it …" Andrew put his hand on my shoulder.

I continued surveying the jungle below for a few moments, then nodded, "I am, too." I turned to look at him. He was much shorter now that I'd gained a few inches. He'd always seemed so big and strong. Now he seemed mortal and unsure. "But you're right. It's all my fault. I know that now. I've known it for a while."

"Stop it," Everett put his arm around my shoulders. "That's not true."

I looked up into Everett's blue eyes, "Yes, it is, Bug Boy."

He started to say something else, but one of the flight attendants called for everyone to form a group. A passenger bus had arrived, and I was sure I'd heard a couple of chickens clucking behind the battered sides of the old rusty bus. I thought of movie night with Mom when we'd watched *Romancing the Stone*, and I hoped the bus ride would be a lot better than the one Kathleen Turner's character experienced.

It turned out to be quite similar, actually. There was no air conditioning, and the ragged windows banged and squeaked in their loose casings. There was a goat tethered to the bus driver's seat and a small coop with two chickens and a rooster was tucked beneath the dash. The bus driver made sure the luggage was secured to the tops and sides of the bus with ropes, bungee cords, and a few lengths of rusty chains.

"Looks like the canthaspis petax," Everett said matter-of-factly as he slid his finger up the bridge of his nose, forgetting he no longer wore glasses.

"Huh?" I grunted, half-smiling at his charming, leftover habit. Oh, what I would've given to have had those days back again when he was the old Everett, and I was the old Blair ... when he wore black-rimmed glasses, and I wore cowgirl boots and worked the ranch.

"Canthaspis Petax is an assassin bug. He kills, say, twenty ants, sucks out their insides, and glues them all over his back," he smiled broadly and pointed to all the mounds of luggage clinging to the bus.

"Ewww ..." I wrinkled my nose.

"Dude, that's gross," Andrew said.

"I think it's cool," Everett shrugged.

As if on cue, the goat that had been tied inside the bus gained its freedom and came bounding out of the bus just in time to butt the driver in the rear, sending him head over heels and into some bushes on the side of the road. The three of us burst out laughing, and I was so overcome with giggling that both of my invisible barriers slid away.

I hadn't seen Andrew laugh like that since before Dad and Aaron died. I sensed the momentary relief from his burden of grief and responsibility roll off of him like he was molting to become something new. And perhaps he was.

Everett tenderly grasped my hand in his and ...

Boom, boom-boom, boom. Boom, boom-boom, boom.

The tribal drums of the pairing ritual picked up where they'd left off in the airplane bathroom. I quickly released his hand and stepped away, feeling the smile leave my face. And, still, they rang in my head and heart. *Boom, boom-boom, boom.*

"Blair, your barrier," Andrew stepped between us. Everett reached for me again, the sparkles of light beginning to form behind his blue irises again.

"Ugh!" I growled and raised both of my protective barriers once more, locking them in place and hoping they'd stay. The last thing we needed was to cause the rickety bus to plunge off the road and into the jungle.

Everett shook his head and took a deep breath. "What happened?" his voice cracked the way it used to.

"I let my shields fall while we were laughing at that goat," I stuffed my hands into my back pockets.

"Oh," Everett mumbled, still looking confused.

And I realized that he wasn't as aware as I was when he was under the spell of the tribal drums. It was just another reason that I needed to find a way to separate from Everett and Andrew and find my own way to save Mom ... and perhaps everyone else I loved. If I stayed on my current course, I was sure the opposite would happen.

Finally, we were able to board the passenger bus. It took the driver a while to catch the goat, but after a wild chase, he was able to secure it to his seat on the bus. I sat in the seat in front of Everett and Andrew. Everett had wanted to sit next to me, but I'd told him I was okay in the seat next to the lady with the fussy baby.

Once we were all settled, the captain assured us that the driver would take us to our original destination, which would probably take eighteen hours. The flight attendants loaded several coolers full of food and drinks into the rear of the bus, but that didn't calm down the tempers that flared around us.

"We'll stop and reload onto a newer bus in a few hours," the bus driver said, which brought a little calm to the situation. However, it didn't calm the poor baby next to me. He fussed and cried for the next hour until he finally gave up and fell asleep.

I wished I could forget my cares and fall asleep like that, but that wasn't likely to happen for a long time. Instead, I pulled my hair up and tried to fan myself with a tattered magazine I found under the seat. My thicker, longer hair was much hotter than the way my hair used to be, and it clung to my scalp and neck as the heat and humidity filled the wobbly old bus.

The bumpy road wound around the high plateau where we'd left the plane and sliced into the jungle-laden mountain side. I gripped the seat in front of me as the bus bolted to the right and then left to avoid a deep rut. Andrew commented about it being a 'jarring situation' and Everett snorted.

I wanted to escape into memories of good times back home when everything seemed possible, and all my dreams seemed to be within my reach. But I couldn't. I knew I needed to observe the jungles around us, because soon, very soon, I'd be traveling them on my own. So I took in the sights, sounds, and earthy smells of the jungle just on the other side of the clanking window.

A monkey followed the bus along for a while, swinging among the lush vines and branches. Most of the passengers snapped pictures of him and thought the curious monkey was funny. A few others were terrified of him.

"There's no phone service out here," Andrew spoke low so only Everett and I could hear. "Anything could happen, and no one would ever know what became of all of us."

"Don't worry, I've got a satellite phone in my backpack," Everett answered. He'd kept his backpack close to him the whole trip, and I immediately wondered what other sort of equipment he carried in there. No doubt there was some high-tech stuff from The Resistance. "If we have any trouble, I'll get us help."

So he'd kept his connections with The Resistance, the thought wound its way through my mind. *What would happen to me if they showed up here right now?* I chewed my bottom lip and shuddered at the thought of being strapped down to a gurney to be experimented on by scientists. *Why is he still a member of The Resistance, anyway?* And then I had a momentary lapse in trust, and, perhaps, judgment. *Was he secretly reeling me in to be captured, so he wouldn't look guilty?*

"No," I said aloud and shook my head.

Just then the jungle monkey leapt against the side of the bus and reached through the window toward me. In its hand was a piece of fruit, and it held it out to me. Its golden eyes looked deep into mine, and I was reminded of a different past when offerings were left at the base of a shining gold pyramid both by my own people and those from the jungle. *Does this little monkey know who I am? If so, how?* I wondered as I held out my hand.

The lady with the baby had dosed off, but awoke and immediately began screaming when she saw the monkey reaching over her. That awoke her baby who started crying. And that startled the monkey, which caused it to bare its sharp teeth and screech at the top of its lungs. It glanced at me once more, then lunged back into the safety of the jungle.

"It was trying to get my baby!" the lady wailed next to me.

"No he wasn't. He was reaching for me. He was harmless," I brushed her off and looked away. Frankly, I was growing tired of her and her crying child.

"I know what I saw!" she yelled over the creaks and groans of the clunky old bus.

"Look, lady, I've about had it with you. We're all stuck here together, so suck it up!" I hissed through my teeth just before I noticed that things around me were taking on a tint of blue.

"Hey, sis, why don't you trade places with Everett," Andrew interrupted.

"Yeah, come sit back here for a while," Everett stood, making room for me.

I quickly switched seats knowing that if I didn't, I would probably do something I would regret for the rest of my life.

"Are you okay?" Andrew whispered.

I nodded and took a deep breath. Then I handed him the jungle fruit the monkey had given me. He turned it over in his hand and examined the plump orange fruit. The skin was the color of a ripe tangerine, but it was translucent. The juicy flesh was visible just below the skin in between spiny prickles that poked outward like a blowfish.

Andrew lifted it to his nose and sniffed the syrupy sweet smell of the delicate prickly fruit. Then he grew a little limp and slouched back in his seat, his hand falling onto his knee, still holding the fruit.

"What's wrong with his eyes?" Everett gasped, reaching for the fruit before it fell to the floor.

My brother looked dazed, almost drunk. His pupils were dilated, and his head lobbed against the window with a sharp *bump*. He groaned a little and smiled like it felt good that he'd just hit his head on the same spot where there was already a bloody gash.

My eyes flashed back at the fruit in Everett's hand. He was about to raise it to his nose, and in that instant a flood of alien memories of my former life flashed past my mind like a movie across the silver screen at The Grand Theatre back home. The bus seat fell from under me, and I tumbled into the past.

This was the fleshy fruit we'd used to create a neuro-tranquilizer. We'd been short on our own supplies due to our hasty retreat across the universe, and it had taken me time to find just the right potion to safely tranquilize the new species we'd encountered ... humans.

Monkeys, of course, had been the ones who had first proven beneficial in the study, but I'd never had much interest in using them in my experiments. After all, my plan had been to find a way to create Others who could survive apart from one another ... so that I could find a way to separate myself from a binding promise my alien father had forced upon me for my own protection.

One of my first human trials had been on a beautiful young woman we'd captured in the jungles. There'd been many humans to choose from, but she was kind.

She had a softness in her heart. I could envision myself as having a part of her within me.

And so I tranquilized her with my newly-developed drug and took her, with the help of Orion, to the pyramid where I examined her DNA to see if it was compatible with my own. It was the beginning of a three-generation process. And I left her on the banks of the Amazon to be found by her own people. Little did she know that she'd carried a small part of me with her when her fiancé rescued her and took her home.

Ash had no idea what I'd been planning. He'd only known it was something to do with the prolongation of our species. Of course, we'd been on this new planet for decades upon decades, but it had taken a long while for me to come to terms with what I must do to regain my freedom.

And, so, he helped me years later when the daughter of the first woman had come to the jungles. We'd strapped her down to the gurney. I'd climbed into the chamber, and he'd reluctantly said 'goodbye.' And my alien essence bound itself to my mother's DNA.

With a bounding *whoosh* I was back in the present, on the bumpy, noisy bus, and Everett was lifting the fruit to his nose. I reached out and snatched it from his hand. At first, he thought it was a joke, but I tossed it out the window as hard as I could, and it splattered against the trunk of an ancient jungle tree.

"It's dangerous," I said as I examined Andrew. He hadn't inhaled too much. His eyes were back to normal, and he shook his head.

"What happened?" he ran a hand through his hair, making it obvious that his haircut was growing out fast.

"I think that monkey tried to kill you," Everett joked.

Andrew bantered back, and they both laughed, but I paid no attention to what they were saying. All I could think about, all I could do, was sit back into the tattered bus seat and remember what I'd done to the two most important women in my life.

I reached into my own backpack, which I'd kept as close to me as Everett had done with his. I might not have had a bundle of high-tech gadgets in mine, but I felt the things in mine were just as valuable.

The silvery platinum necklace Grandma had given me the day we bought my gown for the Rodeo Gala was tucked safely inside a zipper pocket. I retrieved the necklace and looped it around my neck, feeling the weight of the round charm fall against my skin. A butterfly was engraved into the charm, which was rimmed in small diamonds. Grandma had said Grandpa had given it to her. I clasped the charm in my hand and desperately wished I could erase the new memories that flooded my head.

But my alien side was quickly melding with my human half, and there wasn't a thing I could do about it. The alien form of me had failed to erase the possibility of past-life memories ... if that's what you could call them. I had no other words to describe it.

Andrew and Everett continued talking to each other, but their words were muted and distant. I couldn't make them out. I merely leaned back in my seat and allowed my fingertip to trace the engraved butterfly over and over.

And I realized it was time for me to fly, to escape, to disappear into the jungle before anything happened to my brother and my true love because of me.

CHAPTER SEVEN

FLY AWAY

After the sandwiches and drinks in the coolers were consumed, and the sun made its way across the sky toward the west, exhausted passengers settled down into naps, or books, or simply staring out the window at the jungle.

Different scenarios of my escape into the jungle played through my mind, but none of them seemed feasible. Neither Andrew nor Everett would give me up so easily as to allow me to merely wave 'goodbye' and disappear.

I braced my knees against the back of Everett's seat and pretended to sleep. Andrew escaped into his own dark thoughts, and Everett turned in his seat so that his back was to the cranky mother and child next to him.

In the dim light of the early evening, I opened my eyes just enough to watch as he arranged several high-tech devices inside his backpack. Finally, he found what he'd been searching for – a book of jungle insects. Then he rested his forearm over my knees and gently wrapped his hand around mine as he lost himself in his favorite sort of book. And I loved him even more for it. And my heart broke, because I would soon be parted from him … perhaps forever.

We rode like that for an hour or so before the bus came to a halt in the gravel parking lot of a remote bus station. As promised, the airline had provided a new bus to carry the passengers on to our original destination. But something deep within me whispered that wasn't going to be the route I took … that this old bus stop would be the fork in the road where I parted ways with Everett and Andrew.

"Wake up, sleepyhead," Everett squeezed my hand. "It's time to switch busses."

"Man, I'm thirsty!" Andrew stood, bumping his head on the ceiling of the old, raggedy bus. "That monkey fruit knocked me out. I slept like a baby," he glanced at the woman next to Everett. She was pushing past Everett and rushing off the bus, her baby crying the whole time. "Well, not that baby, but most babies," he smiled and yawned.

I giggled and stood, realizing that my legs were stiff from having stayed in the same position for a long time. But having Everett's arm resting across my knees and his fingers laced between mine kept me from moving. It was probably the last time we'd be together as boyfriend and girlfriend, and I'd wanted to relish it as long as I could.

"Feels great to stretch my legs," I smiled and tossed my backpack over my shoulder. "Sure hope there's a working bathroom inside."

"No, kidding!" Everett snorted and grabbed my hand once more. He led me off the bus, Andrew close behind, and out into the balmy air. "I could use something to drink, too. Thirsty?" he asked, looking me in the eyes as if he knew what I was planning ... as if he wasn't about to let me out of his sight so I could escape.

"I'd do anything for a cold coke," I glanced around for a coke machine.

"I'll see what I can find while you're in the ladies' room," he kissed me on the cheek and headed toward the group of airline employees standing near the new bus.

"Let's find the bathrooms," Andrew wrapped his arm around my shoulders.

I still loved my big brother more than anything, but his words on the plane were still seared across my heart. No matter how many times he apologized, they would remain raw and painful because they were true. My thoughts were interrupted by the bus driver chasing his goat across the gravel parking lot.

"There he goes again!" I giggled. "That's something you won't see on a normal day back home."

"Nope!" Andrew agreed and then started laughing out loud. The goat apparently loved butting the driver in the rump. If we'd have been in a movie, Danny DeVito would've been the perfect person to play that bus driver.

There were groups of people milling around the parking lot. Some of them were the people who'd just gotten off the bus with us. Some of them were waiting to board the old bus we'd just exited. But most of them were locals who were merely there to people-watch or to sell their wares.

The jungle threatened to overtake the aging bus station and its gravel parking lot. A dense wall of lush vegetation separated the small bus station from the shadowy reaches of the jungle.

This is my chance to part ways with Andrew and Everett, I swallowed down the flutter of fear that spun behind my ribs. I'd never slept in the jungle before—not in my human life, anyway. The daylight was almost gone, and the jungle was sure to be pitch dark at night. I had the tiny flashlight on the side pocket of my new boots Grandpa had given me for graduation. But that would be like a tiny firefly in the vast darkness of the jungle forest. Then I thought about the orbs of fire I'd practiced making, and I knew I'd be able to light my way in the darkness. I settled on my freaky alien night vision Everett had taught me how to use.

There was no air conditioning inside the old bus station. Rows of plastic chairs lined the large window panes and the open area near the ticket desk. There was a sort of chaos inside the station, and a few chickens clucked in a wire basket carried by a little girl with the dark skin and hair of the jungle people I'd known in my past alien life.

She watched me for a while, her round eyes fixed on me as if she knew who I was. Then she whispered something to an old lady in a colorful dress who sat next to her. The old lady turned to look at me. Shock filled her wrinkled, weatherworn face and she hurried the girl with the chickens out the door.

"That was weird," Andrew mumbled.

"What's not weird about this place?" I looked around and saw a sign that had an image of a man and a woman on it. "Oh, I think the bathrooms are that way," I pointed toward the back corner of the bus station.

"You go ahead. I'll wait here for Everett," Andrew looked like his radar was on full-blast. Ever since the birthday he'd turned seventeen, he'd been cursed with the ability to read minds. It was so bad at first that it seemed like he was going crazy.

"I'll just go freshen up a little. I think I need to change out of these clothes and into something cooler." I tugged at my shirt, which was soaked with sweat from the hot ride on the worn-out bus. Texas summers were nothing compared to the balmy humid heat of the jungle.

"Good idea," he nodded, still immersed in his own thoughts. I wondered whose mind he was reading and why. "Just be aware of your surroundings."

"Ok," was what I said, but I really wanted to say 'duh, no kidding!'

On the other side of a wall that separated the main room from the hall to the bathroom were rows of rusty, beat-up lockers. They were fairly large, and I wondered who would use them and why. I was surprised that there wasn't a line for the bathroom, and I hurried up in case there was a stampede. Most of the people were probably busy tending to their luggage and would probably come looking for the bathroom when they were through.

There were tall lockers along the narrow hallway to the bathroom, and I started looking at the numbers engraved on each 268 ... 269 ... 270. I felt a pang of recognition of some sort of significance to these numbers. 271 ... 272 ... were the last two on the left hand side of the hall.

I shoved an overflowing trashcan out of the way, tipping it over and spilling wads of paper and other things across the cracked tile floor. And there it was – locker number 273.

"Two seventy-three!" I gasped and pulled the cord from around my wrist. I wished I had someone to share this moment with. I wished I could jump up and down and scream '273!' at the top of my lungs.

Those three little numbers were engraved on one side of Dad's old bronze key. They'd plagued me for months and months. My hands shook as I gripped the key and slid it into the lock. *It fits!* I wanted to squeal, but bit my lip instead. I took a deep breath, swallowed hard, and turned the key.

Click! And the locker door popped open an inch. I covered my mouth with my hand to keep from whooping out loud. *This was Dad's locker*, I paused a moment as if I was sitting in front of something very precious and almost holy. I was kneeling in the same spot he'd kneeled at this random bus station in the middle of the Brazilian jungle.

With a quick glance over my shoulder to make sure no one was watching, I paused once more, and then opened the door. It creaked as if it had been closed for years, and a spider web stretched until part of it tore away from the side of the locker and floated briefly in the air before it fell softly against the door like gossamer threads.

The scent of time and stale air filled my nostrils … and something as faint and familiar as a far-off memory – Dad's cologne. "Oh," I whispered as my fingertips brushed across a dusty backpack that hung on one of the locker hooks. It still had the safety pin with beads threaded on it that spelled 'Daddy.' I'd made it for him one summer at Vacation Bible School. He'd said it was his good luck charm. I smiled at the bitter-sweet memory. The charm wasn't lucky enough, because my dad was gone.

Behind Dad's old backpack was another one that looked like it had never been used. Only it wasn't a backpack at all. According to the tag still dangling from the zipper, it was some sort of camping tent called a cocoon.

I rolled my eyes and thought of the irony. Then I flipped the tag over and saw printed in Dad's neat handwriting: 'For Blair, thought you'd find it handy and a bit funny.' I could hear Dad's voice speak those words in my mind as if he were kneeling next to me. He'd had a wicked sense of humor.

I wondered if he was looking down on me at that very moment, watching me pour over that one sentence again and again, willing him to appear and help me out of this mess I'd created myself ... a mess he'd obviously figured out on his own. And, yet he'd never stopped loving me.

The cocoon pouch tipped forward, revealing three envelopes taped to the back of the locker. Each of the envelopes had a name printed across the front. One had 'Andrew' on it, one had 'Aaron' on it, and the third one had 'Blair' on it. I traced the letters of Aaron's name with my fingertips.

He and Dad had died together in an unsolved homicide. Well, it was unsolved as far as the Willis Sheriff's Department was concerned, but Andrew, Everett, and I knew who'd killed them. The Hunters. A chill ran through my bones, which was chased out by the fires of vengeance. I'd get my revenge and settle that score, even if it meant enlisting Ash to do it.

I tugged the envelopes free from the locker wall. The glue on the tape had begun to disintegrate, so they were easily removed. On the back of each of them, Dad had written 'for your eyes only.' I'd wanted to read all three, but a sudden rush of guilt stayed my hand. I returned Aaron's and Andrew's letters to the back of the locker, and stuffed mine in my pocket, realizing that I was lingering too long at the locker.

I swung Dad's backpack over my shoulder and grabbed the cocoon pouch by the handle, then closed the locker. The sound of a small stampede echoed across the cracked tile floor and down the narrow locker-lined hallway. I knew if I didn't get into the bathroom, I might not get a chance. So, I did the only thing I could, I rolled the tipped-over trashcan out into the middle of the hall, hoping it would slow them down while I locked myself in the bathroom.

The ruse worked! I thanked my lucky stars that no one saw me block the hallway with the rusty old trashcan while looking around the bathroom for a place to set my things as I changed clothes and freshened up.

There were two bathroom stalls that were painted pink. Two sinks with rust stains hung side-by-side on the wall underneath two mirrors. In the corner was a trashcan, and on the wall across from the sinks was a shelf.

I placed Dad's backpack and the cocoon pouch on the shelf, then opened my own back pack. It was a relief that I'd put a change of clothes and my toiletries inside. A few minutes later, I was freshened up and wearing clean clothes. I had to braid my hair and wind it into a thick bun on the back of my head, because it had grown even longer since we'd left home. I wondered how much it would grow before it stopped.

A strange memory flickered across my mind. I recalled how my alien mother had styled my hair for my unwanted pairing ceremony. I'd worn it so long that it reached the bend of my knees with precious stones woven throughout its wavy locks. Ash had loved it.

Even though our pairing ceremony had been arranged at the last minute, it had been very elaborate, filled with hastily-prepared offerings and a bridal trousseau unrivaled in its extravagance. I'd barely known him except for his service to my alien father, and I'd never become infatuated with him like so many other females had. However, we'd developed an amicable relationship. With his charm and my loneliness, it was inevitable. Then I'd discovered he hadn't given up his ways of wooing and bedding other females despite our bond as Others. And I'd cut off all my beautiful hair.

Ash pleaded with me, tried bribing me with expensive gifts to allow it to grow long again. When I hadn't relented, he tried threatening me, though I knew he'd never harm me. Still, I responded by blasting him through the wall and setting our marriage bed on fire while reminding him who I was.

It had been very satisfying.

One simply cannot bribe an intelligent woman with shiny things. Therefore, my hair had remained short for decades until I'd discovered how I could regain my freedom. When I'd grown it long again, he'd thought I'd finally forgiven him.

I shook my head to clear my thoughts. Two lives worth of memories, worlds apart, were almost dizzying.

My reflection in the mirror revealed that both versions of me were becoming one very quickly. One day soon, I'd have to choose which role I would take: human cowgirl or alien queen. A frown crossed my lips. I hadn't planned on any of this ... I hadn't realized that humans had such depth of soul.

A knock on the door snapped me back to my senses, and I realized that there was a crowd of women in the hallway waiting for the bathroom. I turned to Dad's backpack, quickly unzipped it, and looked inside.

There were three separate pouches inside, each bearing a label for the three of his kids: Andrew, Aaron, and me. I grabbed mine and quickly looked inside. It was a photo album full of pictures of Dad and me. I had only a moment to flip through the pages and fight back a flood of tears that threatened to overtake me. Before that could happen, I shoved it into my backpack, which I tossed over my back. Then took Dad's backpack and the cocoon pouch and opened the door, letting in the horde of tired, angry women who shoved me aside and nearly trampled me.

After making my way back out into the hall, I quickly tucked Dad's backpack into the locker and secured it closed. I heard the guys calling for me over the growing din in the hallway, so I made a quick dash to find them standing by the first row of lockers where they were safe from the stampede.

"There she is!" Everett gasped, relief flooding his face.

Andrew's shoulders slumped with fatigue of worry and stress. I could tell that being on constant guard for my safety was taking its toll on my big brother. He should be following his own dreams, finding a nice girl, and exploring the world. Instead, he was in constant fear of losing the rest of his family … he was hunting aliens trying to make it all stop.

But he didn't have that power in his hands. Only I did.

"Don't scare us like that, Sis," Andrew sounded weary. I noticed that the stubble on his upper lip and chin was growing. Soon, I was sure, he'd have a furry face and wild hair again.

"I'm a big girl, Andrew. Don't worry about me so much," I hugged him tight and kissed him on the cheek.

"Easier said than done," he half-smiled.

"Go freshen up before they use all the water," I was hoping for a clean escape. I simply could not bear running off with Andrew and Everett calling after me.

Andrew headed for the men's room. When I turned to urge Everett to go before more people got ahead of him, he took me in his arms and twirled me around, pressing my back against the lockers.

"No way you're kissing him and not me," he smiled.

"Silly Bug Boy," I giggled. "He's my brother!"

MONARCH · 75

"And what am I?" he pulled me closer to him.

"You're …" My voice cracked. I didn't want to say it right before I left him and broke his heart. "You're my …"

He kissed me on my neck, then just below my earlobe. "I'm waiting," he whispered.

"You're my Other." My heart sank to my feet. "The other half of me."

And then his lips covered mine with kisses so sweet that I lifted myself up on my tip toes and swore I heard fireworks going off somewhere outside. He pulled his lips away and looked into my eyes. "I love you, Blair. I'll love you 'til the day I die."

"How much do you love me?" the words spilled out as if someone else was saying them for me … as if someone was helping me free myself from the pain of goodbye.

"More than anything on earth," he answered.

I paused a moment, playing with a lock of his hair at the nape of his neck.

"What's wrong, Babe?" his brows knit together.

"Promise me something?" I continued toying with the lock of hair.

"Anything for you," he pulled me close against him in a protective embrace.

"If something happens to me, don't stop looking for Mom. If you love me, you'll do this for me." I nuzzled my face into his shoulder, feeling his heart beat in tandem with mine, and fighting to keep both of my barriers in place.

"Nothing's gonna happen to you," he hugged me tight.

"Promise me. I won't believe you if you don't promise," I pushed away from him so I could look into his eyes. "Promise me that if we're separated from each other, you'll continue to look for Mom."

"Blair," he sighed. I knew it was a struggle for him. It went against everything he was raised to be, what most young men in my small Texas hometown were raised to be— chivalrous.

"Do it. For me," I batted my new, longer eyelashes and pouted my new, fuller lips. He melted like butter.

"Alright, you win. I promise to keep looking for your Mom in the unlikely and impossible event that anything happens to cause us to become separated or in the event of any disastrous situation, which would possibly cause the world to end or even to bring about the zombie apocalypse. Happy now, Miss Reynolds?" he lifted his eyebrow again.

"Yep," I nodded, smiling on the outside. On the inside, I was on the verge of tears. "Now, Mr. Fancy Talk, better get to the men's room before it's time to leave!"

He planted a quick kiss on my lips, then jogged toward the bathrooms. There was a crowd filling the hall, so it would be a while before he and Andrew made it out. *It's my chance to escape! But how can I slip away and still make sure Andrew knows about the locker?* I bit my lip and glanced around for ideas. I spotted our luggage sitting in the growing shadows near some lockers a few feet away.

As quick as I could, I unzipped my suitcase and removed some items I knew I'd need, and a couple I didn't want to lose. Natalie had neatly packed everything in little tight rolls, which made it really easy to stuff some clothes into my backpack. I also removed the scrapbook Grandma and I had made. I may need those memories in the months ... years ... decades to come, so I wouldn't lose my humanity.

One last thing was removed from the inside pocket of my suitcase before I zipped it up. A small box with a latch. Inside of it was my miniature galaxy. It was a token of my love for Everett, created the night of the Rodeo Gala. Everett had once said that it would ensure that he'd always be able to find me, but I'd always had a small question in the back of my mind about how that could be.

Soon the guys would return from the bathroom. I was running out of time, so I quickly removed the leather cord and key from around my wrist and looped it around the handle of Andrew's suitcase. Then I looked for something to write with and found a white eyeliner pencil Natalie had gotten me. Why she thought I'd even know how to use it was beyond me, but it was perfect for this situation.

I wrote '213' in bold writing near the handle on his suitcase and placed the key on top of my writing. If Andrew didn't figure it out, Everett surely would. He'd always been a whiz at all types of puzzles and secret codes. Andrew would be able to retrieve the things meant for him and Aaron from Dad's old locker. And I hoped he'd shove my suitcase inside of there for safekeeping.

And that was it. With a quick raid of the vending machine, stuffing the snacks and drinks into my full backpack, I grabbed the cocoon pouch and stepped outside. Night had filled the gravel parking lot and the surrounding jungle with a blanket of darkness. Strange, yet familiar sounds echoed on the other side of the wall of jungle that lay just beyond the edge of the dim light from the bus station.

All my childhood fears reared up and screamed for me to go back inside and wait for Andrew and Everett. But my heart screamed louder. It said that if I stayed, it would be the end for Andrew and Everett. And Mom. Especially Mom.

You've got to do this, I told myself. *Just do it!*

I took a few steps toward the black barricade of trees and thick undergrowth, and then a feeling of peace came over me as if I were coming home. It was my alien side, the original me who had faint memories of happy times in these jungles.

Perhaps I really will be okay, I inhaled a deep breath. Without any more hesitation, I took off running for the unending blackness of the jungle. Behind me, airline employees called for me to come back to the bus.

But I kept running, quickening my pace, and kicking up gravel behind me. When I reached the edge of the gravel lot, I leapt through the air toward the jungle edge as if I were flying away.

With one gulp, the undergrowth swallowed me up like a black hole.

And I was gone.

CHAPTER EIGHT

GONE

The soles of my boots landed firmly in the leafy loam of the jungle floor. Inside the realm of trees, the air was thicker and filled with the musky odor of decay coupled with the fresh smell of new birth and life.

I paused a moment to allow my night vision to focus then took off running through the dense undergrowth of vines, bushes, and giant tree trunks. This forest was nothing like what I'd known back home in Texas. And, come to think of it, nothing like I'd known in the vast past of my original home light years away.

A drop of sweet rain water dripped onto my bottom lip from somewhere above me, and I remembered that the jungle was a microcosm all its own where the trees themselves made their own rain.

My cell phone ringtone cut through the sounds of the jungle. Florence + the Machine's *Cosmic Love* hushed the sounds of wildlife in the tree canopy high above me.

I leapt upon a mossy trunk of a fallen tree and fished around in my pockets to find my phone. Everett was calling.

"Shoot!" I whispered. I thought I wouldn't have gotten phone reception in the jungle, so I hadn't turned my phone off. The call went to voicemail, then my phone lit up once more. Andrew was calling and his ring tone was the theme song to that really old TV show called *Bonanza*.

They know I'm gone, a frown tugged at my bottom lip.

They'd surely be in a panic. Andrew would be instinctively blaming himself, and Everett would be getting ready to come find me despite his promise. He'd be pulling high-tech gadgets from his backpack and tracking my phone signal.

Why hadn't I thought of that before? I gasped.

As quick as my fingers could move, I sent a text message to both of them. 'If you love me, find Mom. Don't waste time looking for me. I'll be fine.' Then I turned off my phone and removed the battery in hopes it would keep Everett from tracking me.

Then I turned and continued my journey through the tangles and obstacles of the tropical forest. I would need to rest, but not until I knew I was far enough away that they wouldn't find me.

I felt eyes, though. Eyes watching me as I trotted along through the jungle, pacing myself so I wouldn't burn out too soon. It was an odd sensation knowing that

I was being watched, but not knowing who or what was doing the watching. I remained on guard and continued my trek through the undergrowth, pretending I couldn't feel the eyes following me as I trotted by.

My energy level was much higher than it was before my change in the bathtub with Everett ... before Ash placed the silvery loop around my arm and started the process. Now that the silvery band was embedded beneath my skin on my upper arm, I would not require a constant supply of sugar to keep my energy up.

I counted my lucky stars for that and continued moving as quickly and quietly through the brambles as possible. Instinctively, both my barriers slipped away, allowing me to hear and sense my surroundings more acutely.

The change was nearly deafening. Outside of my barriers, the jungle was alive with life and music of tree frogs, night birds, and insects that Everett would've loved to study. There were other things as well, whispers of thoughts from nearby jungle people.

They were very aware of the shift occurring in the depths of their home. A change was coming, and they'd grown up on the legends of the fabled fair-haired god who'd built the tunnels far beneath the earth in Brazil for his queen bride.

He'd returned as was foretold and was bringing his bride home to him. His people would soon awaken, and the drums of his tribe would echo through the jungles once more. The jungle people trembled inside at the thought.

For Ash was a ruthless ruler. He was a god of war intended for things other than sitting on a throne.

I hadn't realized that I'd stopped to listen to the fears of the jungle people in their village obscured by the dense undergrowth. There was nothing I could do for them, so I tuned them out and allowed my mind to roam other parts of the jungle while I took a break from running.

Most of the other things I picked up were the buzzing energy of higher animal life and the hum from the earth, plants, and the nearby Amazon River. For a moment, I was assured that the night was quiet, and I'd be able to journey ahead, unhindered.

Until I felt the tension from behind me.

First the low, deep growl. Then the flex of energy from sheer brute strength. I turned in my tracks to see a jaguar, gleaming teeth bared, emerald eyes blazing, ready to pounce. I was so startled that my aim was a bit off.

The bolt of lightning that left my hand struck the loamy earth just next to its front paw. The ebony beast leapt to the left and its piercing roar cut through my chest. I could see it wasn't going to give up very easily.

My human side took over, and I turned and ran for my life. I ran harder and faster than I could've ever imagined. Still, the hungry hunter stalked behind me, no longer attempting to remain silent. It had locked onto its prey, and it must have thought I'd make a tasty midnight snack.

I needed to find a way to turn and make a stand without being attacked and mauled. I knew it would keep hunting me; I could sense that energy flowing through its veins. It was going to be me or this jaguar.

And I wasn't a quitter.

Ahead, a great constant rush of water drowned out the frightened screaming monkeys and birds in the canopy overhead. A waterfall ... there had to be some sort of way to manage to lose the beast there.

I reached the edge of the jungle where deep clumps of moss and fern gripped tightly between round slippery rocks. One wrong step, and I'd lose my footing and tumble hundreds of feet into the misty depths of the fathomless gorge below.

My boots dug into the spongy moss as I turned to face down the jaguar. It stalked out of the shadows of the jungle and into the moonlight. It was a gorgeous beast, and I hated to do it. But I was not going to be the one to die ... not tonight, anyway.

"Here, kitty kitty kitty!" I called to the giant cat. The jaguar's unnerving roar was a growl mixed with the blood-curdling scream of a woman.

My breath quickened, and I had to force myself to tempt the animal again. "Come on, you jerk! What are you waiting for?" I shouted a little louder than I'd intended.

The beast reared back on its haunches, tensing its muscles and baring its teeth once more before it lunged for me. Muscles flexed beneath silky black fur, eyes glistened, teeth readied for the kill. I forced myself to remain still until the jaguar was just inches from my throat. Then I knelt, clutching the thick moss with both hands.

The animal bounded just over my head and back, grazing my backpack with one of its claws before it landed on the slick rocks at the edge of the cliff. It clambered momentarily, then the weight of its body pulled it over the edge into the abyss where it disappeared into the mist rising from the enormous waterfall.

I realized I'd been holding my breath. I gulped for air, feeling the innate desperation of my own body needing oxygen. When I'd left the bus station, I hadn't anticipated being a possible dinner for a giant cat. Now, I realized any number of things could happen ... especially those I've never dreamed of.

My knees quivered as I gingerly stepped away from the plunging edge of the cliff. The dark wall of jungle no longer looked welcoming. It looked frightening. I needed to rest, and I didn't dare sleep on the ground.

"I should've thought this through," I mumbled to myself as I looked around for shelter. There were no noticeable caves or other places to set up camp for the night.

Then I thought of the cocoon Dad had left for me in the locker. I'd strapped it across my shoulder before I left the bus station. I'd have to climb a tree to use the thing, though I wasn't exactly positive about how it worked.

A thick tangle of black ink blotched against the moonlit sky was all I could make out of the edge of the jungle canopy. I searched for a tree with a large trunk with smaller limbs. It had been a long while since I'd climbed a tree, but I knew it was my best chance for surviving my first night in the unknown alone.

I finally found one that seemed climbable. It had to be extremely old. Its trunk was enormous, with roots stretching out at least eight feet before plunging deep into the fertile soil below. I hopped up on one of the roots and looked up the long trunk. The bark was firm and rough to the touch, and there were plenty of smaller branches to use for climbing.

They were perfect for climbing, as it turned out. I was making good time when I reached about midway up the tree. *Snap!* The branch on which I was standing broke. My stomach lurched up into my throat when I fell backward, tumbling toward the earth. I scrambled to grab a hold of something ... anything. But I was falling too fast.

"Stop!" I croaked, just before my head hit the largest of the roots at the bottom of the tree. Time stopped, everything around me stopped, gravity seemed to stop.

However, I was able to flip over and brace for the rest of the fall, which was only a foot beyond my arm length.

Then I plopped to the ground and lay there a few moments catching my breath. I was exhausted and needed rest. But I knew I needed to find a way to get back up the tree and into the safety of the canopy.

I stood and brushed myself off and wondered if I could sort of float or levitate up the side of the tree. It sounded dumb, because I didn't know what to call it, and I knew it wasn't one of my best strengths. But I'd awoken several times in the past with my body pressed against the ceiling. Surely, I'd be able to figure out a way to do it and get it over with.

That's when I sensed it – Andrew's thoughts searching for any sign of me. Several months earlier, he'd shown me how to search our house by having me envision a giant hand going room to room, searching for anyone who may be hiding. It had worked, and I'd gotten good at it. He was an expert at it. And he was getting really close to finding me.

So, without thinking it over any longer, I focused on the largest limb near the top of the tree. "Up!" I said, pointing at the limb and jumping into the air. The leaves brushed against my face and hands as I whooshed by. A flurry of energy fluttered in my stomach while I rushed upward toward the outstretched branch.

"Stop," I wrapped my arms and legs around the thick branch and steadied myself. *It worked! I can't believe it worked!* I wanted to scream it out at the top of my lungs. I wanted to whoop and holler and let the whole world know that Blair Reynolds can fly!

But I couldn't give myself away. Andrew and Everett might not have been the only ones hunting me, and I had to remember that. After all, I was almost dinner for a jaguar, and I had no idea how long the animal had been stalking me.

I struggled to right myself on the limb, hoping my backpack wouldn't slip off and plummet to the ground. Finally, I was able to straddle the large branch and lean back against the trunk. My heart was pounding against my ribs like a ferocious monster. I closed my eyes and steadied my breath. Beat-by-beat, my heart slowed its pace until I no longer felt as if I was about to die.

My eyelids fluttered open, and I gasped at the quiet beauty of the night. From where I perched, I surveyed the tops of the trees in the valley beyond the waterfall. The mist that plumed up from the depths of the canyon glimmered like clouds of magic in the moonlight. A sprinkle of fireflies, somewhat different from those back home, danced among a patch of shadows to my far left. And overhead, the silvery moon glided across a sapphire sea sprinkled with diamonds. Looking down from such a height created an illusion of a peaceful calm below.

But that was a lie. Danger and other things wove their way through the brambles and vines of the jungle. I stilled my breathing and listened. Andrew was close. He was tracking me. I wasn't sure whether or not he and

Everett were together or if they'd separated. I needed to find a way to hide myself.

The first thing to do was to raise both of my barriers and lock them in place. The second thing to do was to remove the cocoon from the pouch around my shoulder. I unzipped the pouch and slipped my hand into the opening. Just inside was a sturdy metallic ring of some sort. I looped my fingers around it and tugged. Without much of a struggle the cocoon slid out of the pouch and popped open on its own, almost knocking me off the limb.

I steadied myself once more and examined the odd cocoon tent. It really *did* look like a cocoon and turned out to be much larger than I'd imagined. In fact, it looked large enough to hold two people, though they wouldn't be able to stretch out ... they'd have to sleep curled up.

Somehow, the bottom of the cocoon was firm and felt steady enough to hold my weight. Folds of fabric were strategically placed around the outside of the cocoon to give the illusion of leaves. This thing was designed to blend in, and it was a work of camouflaged art. I had to wonder where Dad had gotten it.

The metal ring I'd used to pull it out of the pouch was meant to attach the top of the cocoon to a limb. An extendable belt with a snap buckle was attached to both sides; it was intended to fasten the cocoon to the trunk.

I decided it would be best to face the cocoon toward the jungle so that it would be hidden in the shadows.

Besides, there were two perfect limbs on the other side of the trunk – one for the metal ring, and one to rest the bottom of the cocoon on ... just for safety's sake in case the bottom of the cocoon gave way.

I attached the belt around the tree and tugged until the cocoon slid around to the other side. Then I swung around the tree and steadied myself once more before attaching the metal loop to the upper limb. I wiggled it to make sure it was secure. Then I unzipped the cocoon and looked inside.

What an amazing thing, I thought as I tested the strength of the cocoon with my knee against the floor of the contraption. *Surely this thing is safe. Dad would never have gotten it if it weren't.*

At that thought, I slipped into the cocoon and zipped the opening closed. And felt completely safe and comfortable ... and exhausted. I removed my backpack and unzipped the side pocket. The little box with the latch tumbled out into my hands, and I released my tiny galaxy.

Faint sparkles of light glimmered against the sides of the cocoon, revealing a few more features I hadn't noticed. Three cords dangled from the ceiling. There were tiny labels on each. Two of them opened small flaps on each side so that air could flow through triangle-shaped windows. The flaps formed little covers that kept the rain from coming in, too. When the third one was pulled, another little triangle-shaped cover popped up over the door to protect it from rain.

I was instantly in love with my new little habitat. It was a gift from Dad, and it was perfect for me. I wanted to read his letter and think about everything that had happened during the day that brought me into the depths of the jungle. But I was too weary. So, I kicked my boots off and snuggled down to watch my tiny galaxy spin lazily around, bumping off the fabric walls of my safe cocoon until I slipped over the edge of sleep.

And dreamed of things to come and things that had passed.

I dreamed of battle scars.

CHAPTER NINE

BATTLE SCARS

I slept through the next day, soaking up the solitude of the surrounding jungle. It seemed that my new hybrid body drew on the energy of the earth. I could even sense the energy pulse through the tree I was sleeping in. It was odd and surreal, and I didn't fully understand it.

When I finally awoke, it was growing dark outside the walls of my cocoon. My tiny galaxy bounced against one of the small screen windows as if it wished to escape into the early evening sky where stars were emerging from the darkening firmament. I gently tapped it with my index finger, and the sparkling galaxy spun across to the other window where nothing but the darkness of the jungle greeted it.

My throat was parched. I hadn't even bothered taking a drink of anything after spending a couple of hours running through the tangles of the jungle the night before. I emptied my backpack out and sorted all the food and drinks, placing them into the small pouches sewn into the sides of my cocoon. And smiled. *This could be my home for a little while, at least,* I shrugged and wondered just how little that while would be before I twisted the cap off a bottle of water and drank it down.

My legs were cramped and sore. I needed to stand and stretch, but that wasn't really possible in my cocoon tent. I slipped my disabled cell phone into one pocket on my shorts, and the small box containing my tiny galaxy into the other pocket. I didn't want to risk losing either of them in case I couldn't make it back to the cocoon for some reason.

Carefully, I stepped out of the cocoon and secured the zipper closed behind me. Standing on the limb with my legs quivering was unnerving, and I wondered how I would make it down to the ground without killing myself. *Hope this doesn't end badly,* I bit my lip and started my descent.

One limb at a time, careful not to look down, I moved as quickly as I could despite the fact that I was barefoot. Hanging on the side of the tree made me feel vulnerable and visible to anyone or anything who might be hunting me.

When the ground was close enough, I released my hold and dropped, stopping my fall just a few inches above the loamy forest floor. I was getting better at freezing motion and time, and I had the distinct feeling I would get more practice doing it.

It had grown darker while I'd made my way down from the soaring height of the tree canopy. I craned my neck to see my cocoon, but it was hidden among the shadows and branches above. I smiled. My little home would be safe awaiting my return. Until then, I wanted to explore my surroundings and get my bearings.

This night was darker than the previous one. There was no moon in the sky to line everything in silver. Only an endless expanse of stars hung overhead. So I focused my night vision the way Everett had taught me and then lowered my shields.

I was immediately bombarded with the pulse of the jungle night life. It was both invigorating and a bit scary. I wasn't accustomed to feeling as if I was connected to the energy flowing through the jungle and its inhabitants ... it was an alien sensation to my human side.

Still, part of me reveled in the feeling of my inner battery recharging. Which is why I did what I did next ... I dug my feet into the loamy soil. It still radiated the heat of the day as if the sun itself had left it for me as a gift, an offering.

The constant whoosh of the waterfall beckoned me to make my way down to the river, but something different called me back into the depths of the jungle behind me.

This energy was intense and raw. I cringed at the thought of another giant animal looking for dinner, so I immediately charged up my hands and got ready to blast whatever it was. A sudden snap of a limb sent me rushing into the shadows. I tiptoed behind a large tree and peeked around it in time to see a small campfire ignite about thirty feet into the dark forest.

My breath caught in my throat, and I raised my barriers. As they locked into place, the constant stab of emotional energy ceased. *It was coming from the person who'd just lit that fire!* I swallowed the lump in my throat.

Someone knelt next to the fire and placed something over the flames to cook. It was impossible to make out who the person was. So, I took the safest route and leapt up, up, up into the tree next to me. *Maybe I can leap from limb to limb until I get closer,* I thought as I steadied myself against the tree trunk.

And so I did. One tree … another … then another … until I landed on a large bough stretched out far above the campfire. The aroma of roasting meat made my stomach growl. I hadn't realized how hungry I'd become. It had, after all, been a long time since I'd eaten.

I pushed the thought of food out of my mind and crouched on the branch, resting one knee against the smooth bark. Movement below caught my eye. The camper removed his shirt. Light from the flames danced across his skin in hues of golden yellow, revealing a nasty diagonal scar of three slashes like a monstrous claw mark.

Then Andrew turned to face the fire, fury and aguish filling his face with emotions too deep and raw for someone his age. I nearly slipped from my perch, but caught myself. It was my brother! *When did he get that scar?* My bottom lip quivered, and I wanted to leap down and comfort him.

He began pacing, cursing to himself, and then he knelt and clutched two fistfuls of his hair. But that was only for a moment. As quick as he'd knelt, he was back on his feet. He retrieved a machete from a canvas backpack and paced once more.

Without warning, he laid into a nearby small tree, chopping … cursing … swinging relentlessly. The blade must have been extremely sharp, because limbs, leaves, and long slivers of bark shaved off the tree as one stroke after another flayed the plant like it was the enemy.

And he cursed. Words I'd never heard in my life left my brother's mouth as he continued butchering the tree in an unrelenting tirade. Heat flushed across my cheeks. I had no idea words like that even existed. This was no ordinary cursing, it was something else.

He stopped a moment to catch his breath, then bellowed into the darkness … this time with no words, only a desperate growl of anger … of anguish … of hate and helplessness.

Of lost hopes and dreams.

Pausing only to take in a deep breath, he continued his battle with the helpless tree. Watery sap oozed down the battered tree trunk and glistened in the firelight.

And the muscles on my brother's back moved beneath the enormous battle scar across his flesh as stroke after stroke, the machete did its worst.

And tears rolled down my cheeks and evaporated in the rising heat from the fire below.

And just as I was about to leap down to comfort him, a rustle of leaves caught both his and my attention.

Quickly, Andrew wiped the sweat from his face and sidestepped into the shadows of a large bush. I powered up my hands, and he wielded his machete like a sword. Another rustle of leaves and a snap of a twig. Something or someone was coming closer.

"Andrew?" she emerged from the heavy-laden undergrowth and into the golden firelight. Her long red hair was caught to the side in a thick braid that fell over her shoulder. She wore khaki shorts, lace-up boots, and a t-shirt. A camouflage backpack clung to her shoulders, and a silver cross dangled from the chain around her neck.

"Angelica?" he gasped, released his grip on the machete, and let it tumble to the ground.

She went to him, dropping her backpack and cupping his sweaty face in her hands. "What are you doing?" Her voice sounded so small in the vastness of the dark jungle forest.

"I don't know," he shrugged. "I feel so hopeless."

"Hush, now," she placed a small kiss on his lips. "None of that."

He pulled her to him, wrapping his arms around her and melting into her. They stayed like that for a while. She cooed to him and comforted him. She was perfect for him. I thought back to the night of the Rodeo Gala when Andrew had mentioned how he'd like to bring her home to meet the family. She would've been the perfect fit with us.

A quick flood of wishes flowed across my mind of family Christmases and Easters with Mom doting on grandchildren ... with Grandma and Grandpa watching mine and Andrew's children making memories.

And the emotion sliced through me the way Andrew's machete had flayed the dying tree below.

They were kissing now, the passion and emotion of Andrew's tirade had refocused itself. He held Angelica tight against him, and she clung to him as if she were saving him from drowning. And perhaps she was.

She was to him what Everett was to me.

She was his Other.

And I felt a sharp pang for my own Other.

"Everett," I whispered.

I dropped my barriers. The pull was instantaneous. My hands and feet lifted off the bough, and I was drawn out of the tree canopy and into the starlit sky like a lassoed lamb.

Tumbling head over heels, I glimpsed bits and pieces of the glimmering stars above and the dark tree tops below. The alien side of me must have known where I was going, so I didn't even try to right myself. I managed to twist myself around and stop the tumbling motion in time to see the spark of a campfire glimmer through the tree canopy below.

The wind whipped around my ears as I quickly started my descent, blowing my hair above me in long tendrils reaching for the stars. I slowed just before I met the leaves at the very tops of the trees, and then I could hear it.

The oddest thing in the world was to hear *Battle Scars* by Lupe Fiasco and Guy Sebastian echo through the jungle night.

At first I smiled. The branches and leaves caressed my skin as I slowed my journey toward Everett, looking for the perfect limb to light upon. I found it just in time to land on it and kneel into the shadows.

Everett's camp was much different from Andrew's. He'd set up tiny sensors in a wide circle surrounding his campsite. No doubt, they'd set off an alarm of some sort should they detect motion.

Andrew had camped near me, because he was searching for me. My big brother wasn't about to leave me alone in the jungle. He must have sensed me nearby. But because of my barriers, he couldn't pinpoint my exact location. I bit my lip and wondered if he would find my cocoon while I was away. And I also wondered where he'd gotten that machete. I shrugged. *Maybe he keeps a stash hidden in the woods like Dad had done at his camping lease.*

That was possible. Aaron and Andrew had been no strangers to hunting, camping, and roughing it in the wild thanks to Dad. In retrospect, I realized he'd been preparing them for what lay ahead. He'd been such a good father.

Ash had been right ... we'd chosen wisely when we picked this ... my ... family for hybridization.

I glanced back down at Everett's campsite. He'd built his fire in the center of a small clearing. To the left, an enormous log lay flat on the ground. He was using it as some sort of command center. Small gadgets and computerized equipment perched on the log like a row of birds.

To the right was a tent almost as cool as my cocoon. It looked big enough for one or two people. Triangular in shape, it was suspended about ten feet off the ground and was attached to three trees. I could see the bottom rungs of a small rope ladder that dangled from beneath the bottom of the tent. I smiled at the irony. Everett's tent looked like a one-man UFO and mine was like a cocoon.

Everett knelt on one knee, eating some sort of MRE while tapping on the screen of a small hand-held device. Mom's picture appeared in mid-air above the gadget. *What sort of high-tech stuff does he have?* I wondered as I watched him move his fingertips across the screen of another device. An image of a map with blinking dots on it appeared next to Mom's picture. This technology seemed like something from a sci-fi movie.

He examined the map and then tapped the picture of Mom twice and dragged it onto the map. A moment later, three of the dots changed color and the words "possible locations" scrolled across the bottom of the holographic map.

He tapped the screen on the device, and the map disappeared. Then he tossed the empty food tray into the fire and set the device on the log next to the other gadgets.

I couldn't tell which of the devices was playing the music, but *Battle Scars* was definitely playing in surround sound. Everett stood and ran a hand through his dark hair. His t-shirt was clinging to the sweaty lines of his shoulders and back. He pulled it over his head and tossed it onto a nearby bush to dry.

Butterflies fluttered behind my ribs, and I bit my bottom lip when he dropped to the ground and did a few push-ups. He may've still been a nerd on the inside, but he was definitely something different on the outside.

The muscles in his upper arms and shoulders flexed and bulged as he pushed his weight up and lowered it down, never touching the jungle floor with his chest. His shoulders had gotten stronger and broader; his waist was muscular, yet slim.

I sighed and lowered myself down onto the moss-covered tree bough, resting my chin on the back of my hand. Watching Everett was very entertaining.

He stood, shook the dirt off the tip of his boots and then unbuttoned the waist of his cargo pants. I immediately perked up. He unzipped the zipper. I inched farther down the tree limb. He kicked off both boots, slipped both legs out of his pants, and tossed them next to his t-shirt. His socks were off in a flash and dangling next to his pants.

Holy mother of all things hot! How can a pair of Superman boxer briefs look that good on anyone? I almost fell of the limb.

He knelt next to one of the other devices and tapped a screen, replaying *Battle Scars*. Evidently, it was his theme song for how he was feeling. He tapped an icon on one of the other gadgets and a three-dimensional, life-sized hologram of the picture of us kissing at the Rodeo Gala appeared in front of him.

He circled it, inspecting it closely, cocking his head to the side, focusing on where our lips met. Then he stepped into the hologram, filling in the place where he'd stood, holding me in his arms. And I felt his heartache ... his longing ... his desperation for setting everything right so we could go on with our lives together.

I had no idea how painful his battle scars had been all this time.

He lifted his hand to the hologram of my face and lowered his lips to the image of mine. Then he frowned. I heard ... felt his thoughts. The frustration, the need, the yearning ... the searing pain of separation ripped through him like a flaming blade.

The hologram dispersed into a million tiny bits of light when he growled and waved them away. With one leap, he grasped a limb and started doing pull-ups, strengthening himself for the war to come.

Before that moment, I hadn't noticed what was hidden beneath the swirl of tattoos around his arm. It was a fine line that ran from his bicep to his wrist – the scar from when the Hunters had tortured him in the building, searching for bones that were the color of coal instead of ivory.

Three small white marks along his ribcage peeked between loops of ink in the light of the campfire. They were from broken ribs that had found their way through his skin the night he'd almost died.

Another line slashed through his eyebrow from the night I'd traded myself to Ash in return for Everett's life. And a finely-woven band of raised ink circled is left bicep. The band that matched mine … the band that replaced mortality with immortality, humanity with my kind, forever removing him from his own race.

A frown crossed my face to match his. We were Others forever separated by duty.

The song was perfect for what he … we were feeling.

They'd never go away, the scars we'd gotten.

I drew in a sudden breath. *Why had I come here? What had I hoped to accomplish?* I knew I couldn't be with Everett, couldn't complete the pairing ritual. He was obviously following through on his promise. He wasn't searching for me, he was searching for Mom.

And I loved him even more fiercely at that moment. Yet, my heart sank into darkness, and I lifted my barriers before he sensed me. Tears rolled down my cheeks and sprinkled across his t-shirt below, leaving little dark marks of salt and water.

I needed to go lick my own wounds. There's no moving forward until wounds become scars.

Salt and water are perfect for that.

CHAPTER TEN

SALT AND WATER

"Do you know what's best for healing a festering wound?" Mom had once asked me when I was in third grade. I'd cut my foot while swimming in the lake, and a red streak had begun snaking up my leg before I'd ever told Mom I'd been hurt.

"A shot?" I'd asked, smearing my tears away with the back of my hand.

"Well, that works, too," Mom said while pouring a pitcher of steaming water into a small, plastic tub. "But salt and water will do in a pinch."

I watched as the glistening salt broke the surface of the steaming water and settled into a thick layer on the bottom like sand in the sea.

"Dip your toe in and see if you can stand the heat," Mom patted me on the shoulder and returned the box of salt to the cabinet next to the sink. But I saw her peek over her shoulder to see if I was doing as I was told.

"It's hot!" I whined.

"Too hot to keep your foot in it?" Mom asked.

"Well, no. But it's hotter than my bath," I answered, still feeling sorry for myself.

She knelt next to me and brushed my bangs off my forehead. "I tested it before I asked you to put your foot in it, so I know it won't hurt you."

I winced as I slipped my throbbing foot into the tub of water, feeling it rest on the thick layer of salt at the bottom. Tears rolled down my cheeks, covering my freckles in a waterfall of salty water.

"The trick is to get what hurts you on the outside of you, so your inside can heal," she hugged me gently. "It's the same with crying. Sometimes, when you're feeling bad or sad, you've got to get your crying over in order to clear your mind."

"Kinda like when it rains until all the clouds go away. Then the sun comes out?" I asked.

"Yep, just like that," Mom's voice was so comforting. "Now, you sit here and soak your foot." She placed a saucer with several cookies and a glass of milk on the table. "By the time you're through with these, you'll be done," she smiled.

The memory hit me so hard that it knocked me back into the night sky on a bumpy trip back to my cocoon. I slammed onto the limb in front of my tent, jarring me back to reality – the reality where I was alone, trying to accomplish something I didn't fully understand.

Inky clouds rolled and boiled, covering the night sky with a thick blanket. I slumped into my cocoon, closing the zipper just before a downpour of rain pummeled the sides of my tiny refuge as tears poured down my cheeks and tinted my lips with their salt and water. Winds blew against the walls of the cocoon tent, and I cursed my former alien self and all that had gone on before I was born a human hybrid.

Outside, lightning cracked and thunder followed, and I sank into a black hole of despair.

It was all my fault ... it is all my fault ... it will always be my fault ... I curled into a tight ball and clenched my eyes closed, hoping the lightning would take out the top of the tree, and I and my cocoon would tumble down into nothingness so that everyone I loved would be free.

The storm howled on for most of the night, mirroring the turmoil inside of me. Only when I slipped over the edge into sleep did the winds calm down and the fierce, pelting downpour slow to a mild rain that lulled me deeper into dreams and recollections of my past life.

A memory unwound itself in the middle of the night.

I was walking with my alien father, my arm looped through his. He was speaking to me about my safety and the safety of my birth Other. My original people were born as twins, unable to live without each other until the bond was severed during the pairing ceremony when our chosen Others were bound to us. It was supposed to be a beautiful thing. But for my birth Other and me, it was a different story.

We were the only offspring of a royal marriage, the only ones who would carry on the bloodline of two royal families who'd ruled our world for so long that even the historians could find no records of any other rulers.

Our world was at war with *them*, the ones in the building who'd tried to kill Everett … the Hunters. They'd declared unending vengeance on my people until the very last one of us was dead. And, I realized, as I tossed and turned in the night, it was my fault.

We'd known for a while that our DNA was growing old, and we'd needed to evolve as we'd done every few millennia by mixing trace amounts of DNA of other beings with our own. It was how we'd developed the ability to clone others the way Orion, the one we'd named the Cicada, had cloned Everett.

I was the lead bioengineer. I was the one who'd sent the royal guard to procure several species from a nearby galaxy so that I could test their DNA with ours. My loyal captain, Xi, had been my personal bodyguard my whole life. He'd tried to convince me it was a bad idea to enter the forbidden zone. But I'd been headstrong and foolish. I'd been dead-set on proving my worth to my truest love.

We'd worked side-by-side in the laboratory, my truest love and I. Ky had been my confidant, my best of friends, my lover. He was of high birth, and he'd planned to approach my father and stake his claim to become my chosen Other. My father and mother had been expecting it. Indeed, all of the royal court had been abuzz with the rumors. Since my birth Other had also bonded with a member of the royal guard, the timing couldn't have been more perfect.

Until Xi and the guard returned with the specimens.

The first three perished during the early trials. The fourth was one of the Hunters. We couldn't have known at the time that the hunter they'd captured was the last existing prince of a royal family. The specimen had been so savage and hostile that there was no way to communicate with him. I was not surprised that his DNA failed to mesh with our own.

He'd managed to escape his chains when my back was to him. He'd grabbed a scalpel and lunged at me. But Ky was quicker. He'd intercepted the beast but was no match for his brute strength. Before I could call the guard, the hunter had plunged the instrument deep into Ky's chest.

My screams brought Xi and his men, but Ky lay in a growing pool of his own blood. The injury was too devastating for me to heal. So, I did the only thing I could do. I captured his essence in a vial so that one day he might live again in an alien body. As he took his last breath, I promised him I'd find a way for us to be together again.

Out of desperation, my alien father did the only thing he could do as he walked with me, comforting me in my grief over the loss of my truest love and discussing mine and my sister's safety. We crossed through the gardens and up the stairs that curved around the garden wall to the parapets where my alien father often stood, overlooking the kingdom.

Ash was standing, his back to us. As he turned, a gust of wind whipped his hair about his face and shoulders, revealing a furrowed brow and firmly-set determination on his handsome features.

He bowed to both of us, and when he rose, my father placed my hand in his, binding them together with the chain and vial that Ash still wore around his neck.

"What is this, father?" I stammered.

"This is for your protection, dearest one. Ash is my most trusted general. He has sworn to keep you safe no matter what."

"Safe from what?" I glanced down at the silver chain binding us together.

"From the war to come. The monster who murdered Ky was their future ruler. Ash has discovered an approaching armada of their ships. We had no idea there were so many of them," my father's voice broke. "Many of our people will die. So, I'm sending you and your sister away to start life again where the Hunters won't find you."

I shook my head as tears poured down my face. The taste of salt filled my mouth and washed across my heart. I was sure I would die. *How could I leave my home world with its fluorescent blue seas, its brilliant skies of red, orange, and white? How could I ever call an alien world my home?*

"Why must I pair with someone I do not love? Can't Xi protect me as he always has?" I pleaded with my father.

"If you and your sister do not separate by choosing a mate, I risk losing the both of you. If the Hunters kill one, then the both of you will die," my alien father's eyes welled up with tears.

"But if I pair with Ash, then how can he do battle for you? If he dies, I will die." In my mind, the logic seemed irrefutable.

"He will not do battle for me. He will take you far away just as your sister's chosen Other will do with her. Separate, you both may yet live to rule. Together, here on our small world, you do not stand a chance," his face turned dark as he glanced out over the kingdom. "The royal guard is readying ships. We will send you and your sister in opposite directions with enough of our people to begin anew. Perhaps, one day, our people can return to rebuild our world. For now, there is only looming destruction."

"Please, father, no. I don't even know this man. How am I to pair with him for the rest of my long life?" I pleaded as my father turned his back to me.

Ash kissed my hand, his lips tenderly brushing my skin. "It won't be so bad being paired with me, my love."

My sobs echoed over the railing of the parapets and down the winding steps. I cried for what seemed like forever, clutching the vial around my neck that contained the essence of the one I loved most.

I awoke with a start, my heart pounding against my ribs. My tiny galaxy had cowered in the corner of the cocoon behind my boots. I slipped it back into its tiny box and snapped the lid closed.

It was still night, and I felt as though I'd just lived a whole other life in the span of a dream. I no longer even felt like Blair Reynolds. I no longer felt human. I felt lost at sea, surrounded by miles of endless salt and water.

Sheets of rain began pummeling the sides of my cocoon once more, and for the first time I realized the connection between my moods and the weather. *How could I have not noticed before?* I allowed the realization to sink in. Outside, the storm began growing again, and I wished it would drown the whole world in the sorrows of a lost alien princess.

My eyes instinctively turned to night vision, everything around me switched to shades of gray and green. I fished around for a candy bar and retrieved the note Dad had left for me in the locker at the bus station.

I tore the end of the candy wrapper open with my teeth and then devoured it while opening the envelope. Dad had written the letter on a piece of lined notebook paper. As soon as I laid eyes on the first word, I heard his voice in my heart as if he were speaking the words to me.

My Dear Blair,

If you are reading this letter, then I am long gone. My hope is that you are grown by now, that you had a happy childhood, and that I lived to see you graduate from high school and college. I hope I got to walk you down the aisle at your wedding, too.

Your Mom and I love you very much. After having two boys, we both wanted a girl. You were our dream come true. The moment I laid eyes on you, I knew you were special. I knew you were meant for greatness. Hopefully, by now you know that, too.

Since you've found this letter, you must know about what I've been doing all these years. Hunting aliens is a savage business, and a complicated life. But I've learned a lot, and I've protected a lot of people ... mainly my family. So far, I've kept you all safe. I'm hoping I was able to do so all the way up to the time of you reading these words. Heck, I'm even hoping that I've died of old age!

Well, enough with all the small talk. Now it's time to get down to it. And I want you to understand what I'm about to say.

I know what you are. I know who you are. And I know why you are here.

I stopped a moment to digest what he'd written. My heart was pounding in my chest as if I were about to get into trouble. *How could he have been sure of who I am and why I'm here?* I wiped a tear from my eye and went back to reading.

Stay with me now, don't freak out on me like you did that time a bee got caught in your hair! I want you to know that I'm not upset with you. You did what you had to do in order to survive. Mom is not mad either. No matter what, you are our daughter and always will be. If that means that one day our daughter will be sitting on a throne on an alien planet, well so be it. All-in-all, you are still our flesh and blood. And family never abandons family.

If you haven't already, you will discover a message you left for yourself. Since you've found this letter, you are nearly there. Yes, I found it and listened to it. I'm sorry, I know it wasn't for me, but these are extenuating circumstances and you are, after all, my little girl. I had to know what to expect. And so do you.

And the one thing you need to expect is that you will change quickly, and that is okay. This thing is bigger than any of us now. It encompasses beings from three different worlds. And you came here to become human, so you must do whatever it takes to protect this planet. At all costs. Did you get what I just said? You must protect this planet AT ALL COSTS. It is the one thing you owe us for giving you the means to save your people.

Enough of that. I want to address the Blair who is my little girl, my little darling princess. Your birthday is coming soon, and I've got a special surprise for you. Since you're likely grown by the time you're reading this, you know by now that I got you a horse. She's a mild little filly. I know you'll love her, and I can't wait to see your face light up when you see her.

Take care of your brothers and your mother for me. And never, ever forget that you were raised to be an independent woman. Times will be hard, but you must pull yourself up by your bootstraps and carry on. God gave you two feet to stand on, and that's what I expect you to do.

Love Always and Forever,

Dad

I wanted to crater. The mention of Daisy and then the fact that he'd thought that Aaron would still be alive was like a knife to the heart. But I wouldn't crater. I would do my best to pull myself up by the bootstraps. Tomorrow. Yes ... maybe. Or, the next day, after I'd eaten the rest of the candy and cried a little more trying to drown the world in my tears.

I carefully folded Dad's letter and slipped it inside my backpack. So many revelations in one night, and the night wasn't even over. In the span of a few hours, I'd transformed in some intangible way.

I wondered as I turned over on my side, *What ever happened to the vial of Ky's essence? Was it lost some place out among the stars?* I felt an immediate sadness and deep loss. Not only over the memory of losing my truest love, but also because I wanted to fully remember the real me.

After a little more chocolate, I closed my eyes and fell backwards into the world of dreams.

CHAPTER ELEVEN

THE REAL ME

Cool grass on the bottoms of my feet startled me awake. I'd totally forgotten to protect myself from dream-traveling. But it was too late. By the looks of the terrain surrounding me, I was far from my cocoon.

It was still late at night, and the world of humans was quiet. I focused my night vision, and realized I was standing on the edge of the main street of a small jungle town. And I'd been here before. It was all so familiar, yet I had no idea where I was.

"This way," I started at the sound of a female's voice. She held her finger to her lips and pointed toward the forest at the edge of town.

I knew it was probably the stupidest thing I could ever do, but I followed as she led the way. She was so far ahead of me, that I couldn't make out any defining features. So, I continued my course behind her. Soon, I was stepping over fallen branches and stumbling through vines and brambles trying to catch up.

Every so often, she would glance back to see if I was still behind her. Several times, the moonlight shone between the parting clouds overhead and flashed across her features, revealing a reflective property within her skin.

Whoever she was, she wasn't human ... that much was certain. I hoped I wasn't walking straight into the trap of the Hunters, and I tried taking deep breaths to quiet the panic in my chest.

She stopped, pointed to an opening in a huge pile of ancient stones, and motioned for me to enter.

I shook my head no, but she persisted, smiling as if to ensure me it was safe. A few steps closer, and I could see that her eyes were solid black and much larger than human eyes. Her hair was long enough to reach the bends of her knees. She wore a wide swath of fabric tied with intricate knots to create a dress.

And I was sure I knew her.

She pointed to the opening once more, and I motioned for her to go first. *Might as well play it safe, right?* I thought, remembering Dad's letter and the faith he'd had in my being an independent woman.

She pulled strands of overgrown ivy back and stepped into the dark opening. I followed, powering up my hands and hoping for the best. Damp, stale air tickled my nose, and I sneezed several times. Ahead of me, my companion's skin glowed iridescent and lit the dark, narrow tunnel. We stopped a few times to clear away walls of spider webs, and I had to bite my lip to stop my skin from crawling.

After a short while, we reached a rusty metal door that looked ages old. The lock was damaged, and the only things that kept it closed were the rusted hinges. The stranger blasted the hinges with light from her hands and shoved the door aside. It groaned as if unwilling to reveal the secrets that lay just beyond its threshold.

"What is this place?" I whispered, squinting into the darkness beyond the door.

She motioned again, smiling as if to show that it was safe to enter. I gestured for her to go first and wondered if she could understand English, because she'd only spoken once since she'd gotten my attention an hour earlier.

Several lights flickered on, revealing a dusty, long-abandoned laboratory. Although the place looked old, all the instruments and paraphernalia looked to be of space-age technology. A fine layer of dust covered the microscopes, laboratory counters, high-tech computer screens, and medical instruments that lay neatly in a row next to a surgical table.

"I know this place," the words escaped my lips. My brows furrowed. I was in a dejá-vù, and I strained to recall the details of why it was all so familiar yet alien to me.

My companion motioned for me to sit in front of a computer screen, the monitor of which seemed to be merely a thick piece of glass. I didn't bother wiping the layer of dust and webs off the stainless steel seat. I merely complied without hesitation. She pressed a button, and the screen flickered on, straining against age and having been dormant for so many years.

The images on the screen were three-dimensional, and I didn't even need special glasses to view them properly. It was fantastic technology for something so old and forgotten.

My companion's face flashed across the screen. I glanced at her. She was sitting in a seat next to me now, and she motioned for me to begin the video, or whatever the thing was, she'd brought me there to see. I instinctively tapped a button on the screen, and the video began playing.

"This is my story so that I won't forget and lose my way," she spoke in my native alien language. "Don't forget why you are doing this. Don't be fooled into going back to him and forsaking the one you'd chosen in the beginning."

I paused the video and examined the image. A silver chain dangled around her neck, weighted in the front by a vial. I glanced at my companion, but she was engrossed in the image in front of us.

The video had been recorded with her sitting in the very chair in which I now sat. She was wearing a sort of lab coat, and the laboratory behind her was gleaming and pristine. I had to wonder how long ago she'd made the recording.

I began the video again, and another person walked behind her. All I could see was another lab coat similar to hers and that its wearer appeared to be a male. But when he crossed the laboratory further behind her, I paused the recording and gasped.

"That's Orion!" I looked at her, and she nodded and smiled. "Why? How?"

She just sat there, smiling a peaceful smile. I could see my own reflection in her large, solid black, slanted eyes. My own were wild with shock.

"Who are you?" I asked, and she simultaneously mouthed the same words. "How are you doing that? Answer me!" Again, she mouthed the same words in unison. I stared into her large eyes until she smiled and pointed back at the screen, motioning for me to continue watching.

As soon as I started the video again, the face staring back at me said, "I am the real you."

I stumbled backward out of my chair and smashed against the dusty surgical gurney behind me. A metal tray of instruments crashed to the floor and clattered across the dull, cracked tile.

But when I looked back to where my companion had been sitting, I discovered she was gone. The door was closed. I was alone in the ancient laboratory. And there was no trace of proof that the other woman had even been there ... not even a mark on the dust-covered chair she'd sat on next to me.

Shaking and confused, I sat back down and looked at the face frozen on the computer screen, waiting for me to hear her out. This is what I'd really looked like, what I looked like on the inside of me now.

She ... I was beautiful, in an alien way, with a narrow nose, a bottom lip thicker than the top one, wide slanted black eyes, and iridescent skin. My alien hair had been the same color as my human hair, but it had an opalescent quality, lending a hint of magic to it.

My face had been oval, my neck long and narrow, my fingers long and thin. I'd looked much like my alien mother, and I realized that it was really strange that I'd suddenly remembered that.

I traced the silver vial on the computer screen with my fingertip, removing a fine layer of dust. *What had ever happened* to Ky's essence? I wondered, then I began the video again in hopes I would find out.

"I met Ky when I was young. We'd started out as friends, collecting specimens for our studies at the academy," she ... I softened my voice as I spoke of Ky. Images of two young alien lovers flashed across the screen. "He was my truest love, my confidant. I couldn't imagine spending my life with anyone else but him."

Ky had black hair, the color of jet. He had a broad, sort of goofy smile. In the daylight, their eyes weren't solid black, but had irises and pupils similar to human eyes. Their appearance was almost elf-like.

I felt an immediate rush of sadness as I gazed at the image of Ky. He was very similar to Everett, and I felt a longing and deep dread as if I knew what the video would show next.

"Remember him?" the alien version of me asked. "My one true love, my heart and soul. I've mourned for him for centuries, searching for a way to fulfill my promise to him."

"You found a way!" I gasped, looking into the alien eyes on the computer screen.

"Yes! I found a way," the alien lips parted in a smile. "But first you need to remember other things, then I will show you."

The alien me didn't narrate the images that followed. They needed no narration. I knew them, felt them, remembered them as if they'd been some far-off, distant dream I'd nearly forgotten.

Drums pounded. *Boom. Boom-boom. Boom.* They were the tribal drums of the pairing ritual. The Great Hall was decked with the colors of the king. Black, red, purple, and gold adorned every banner, every robe worn by the Holy Men and Women, and my sister and me.

Two pairs of people sat side-by-side in chairs on the raised dais at the end of the Great Hall. I sat next to Ash, tears streaming down my face and dropping across my bare upper chest. Our hands were bound together with the chain and vial my father had bound us with only an hour earlier.

Ash's face still bore the determined expression he'd had in my dream. His jaw was set, his brow was furrowed, his eyes ablaze with the flames of war. He'd been the most powerful warrior and general in a hundred generations. He was feared by all the soldiers, respected by all the men, and loved by all the ladies. He was, by all accounts, a gorgeous man and had a way with women and a reputation to prove it.

His birth Other was not so fortunate in those same areas. But he was known to be a good man and a loyal member of the Royal Guard. I'd forgotten that my birth Other, my sister, had chosen to pair with Ash's brother. She sat, beaming, next to him on the other end of the dais, her hand bound to his with a similar chain and vial. This was her dream wedding to her true love.

And it was my nightmare.

I tried to subdue the sobs that escaped my chest, but it was impossible. Ky had been murdered only hours earlier, and I wanted to be next to him on the funeral pyre they were building outside at that very moment.

But I wasn't the only one weeping in the Great Hall. Tears were streaming down the faces of both young and old men and women. Some wept for my loss, some because they were Ky's family members, and some because they wished they were pairing with Ash.

A Holy Woman struck the gong, and the drums ceased. Ash stood, helping me to stand next to him, steadying my trembling with his strong arms. He unwound the long chain that bound our hands together and, as was tradition, wrapped it around his neck and stretched his cloak out to cover my shoulders. It was a gesture that meant I was under his protection.

I closed my eyes and tried to imagine that I was standing with Ky and that it was he who was about to complete the last part of the pairing ceremony. But all I'd been able to see was the image of him broken and dying in a pool of his own blood.

"It's okay, my love," Ash whispered. "I will be a kind husband and generous lover."

That had the opposite effect than he'd hoped, for my sobs filled the Great Hall and echoed across the floor, out into the royal gardens, and wound around Ky's and his brother's funeral pyres. Without speaking anymore, Ash uncorked the vial, emptied its contents into his palm, and waited for me to bare my stomach for him. I couldn't do it. All I could do was bury my head into his chest and sob as he gently slipped his hand inside my gown and applied the icy cold liquid that penetrated my skin and made my knees buckle.

He was quick and caught me before I collapsed and held me tight against him, protectively cradling his cheek against the top of my head as I buried my face into his neck and cried even more.

Once my sister and Ash's brother had completed the same part of the ceremony, I immediately felt the tie between my sister and me sever. It was unsettling and left me feeling even more alone.

Then the Holy Men began beating the drums again. *Boom. Boom-boom. Boom.* Over and over, the rhythm pounded, drowning out my tears. Then the energy between Ash and me grew and grew into a whirlwind of light and sparkles surrounded us, binding us together forever.

In my despair, I hadn't noticed that my parents' faces were stained with tears and wore masks of mourning for my plight. I searched the video screen and found Xi, my life-long loyal body guard, standing in the corner of the Great Hall. A tear trickled down one of his cheeks, and the corners of his lips turned down in a frown. He'd been very fond of Ky and had known we'd planned to marry.

One last resounding ring of the gong, and the ceremony was over. All that was left was to complete the pairing ritual. It was the equivalent to the wedding night in the human tradition.

"I will take care of the pairing ritual. All you need to do is relax. It will be over quickly." Ash whispered to me as he carried me away to his chambers.

The image on the screen flickered and then revealed the Great Hall the following morning. As was tradition on my home world, the wedding banquet was held the day after the pairing ceremony. But the hall was not decked for a wedding banquet. It was decked with black banners, drapes, carpets. It was prepared for a funeral banquet.

It was dark out when the torches were lit, and the bodies were brought through the Great Hall one last time to be blessed by the Holy Men and Women. Flowers were placed around the bodies of Ky and his brother. And I, crying hysterically, threw myself onto Ky's body and begged to be burned with him.

Ash gently pulled me away and handed me a flower to honor Ky with. I placed it in his cold hands and bent to kiss his lips. But Ash stopped me, gently pulling me away and wrapping his cloak around my shoulders.

"I cannot live without my Other!" I cried aloud. "I will die without him!"

"Remember yourself, Princess!" my mother called to me from her throne next to my father.

I wanted to shout that this was not my choice, but hers and father's. But it would have been nearly blasphemy, and it wouldn't have honored Ky. So, I folded my arms and hugged myself and allowed Ash to draw me tight in his arms. He was, after all, the only one trying to comfort my sadness.

They were taken to their pyres outside, Ky and his brother, and placed high in the night sky so that the ancestors among the stars would reach down to take them in their arms. I gripped the vial around my neck and hoped that Ky was not really leaving me, that I'd managed to save him in some small way.

The flying lanterns were released into the night sky, alerting the ancestors of two new arrivals. It was something I'd always thought of as beautiful. That night, I'd thought it was the most dreadful thing I'd ever soon. And little did any of us know just how dreadful it would soon become.

Flames ignited beneath the two pyres, and within minutes, my beautiful love and his brother were gone from our world. Sparks of fire carried their ashes high into the night sky to their forefathers and foremothers. And I hid myself beneath Ash's cloak and allowed him to wrap his arms around me, steadying me from crumpling to the ground.

He knew, as well as I, that I now carried his offspring. He would protect me even more fiercely than before, because of what grew inside me. He would never let me leave him, because I would be the mother of his children.

I held the vial close to my heart, because I knew one day I'd find a way to be with my true love again no matter what. I could not live without my Other. It was his children I wished to carry and no one else's.

The screen flickered again, and I remembered the scene well. Ships of the Hunters broke through the night sky and rained down destruction. The pyres were knocked to the ground by blasts from overhead. Fire ignited homes and buildings all around, and sirens alerted our own pilots to take to the sky.

Ash pulled me inside the palace and down into the underground tunnels that led to the royal hangar where escape ships had already been prepared and equipped for a long journey through space. Over a thousand of our kind rested in cocoons aboard our ship and awaited a new home far away through time and space. Even the Royal Guard had gone into stasis overnight. Xi and his men and women were frozen in sleep aboard our ship.

My sister and her new Other entered the other side of the cavernous hangar. We waved goodbye to each other as our husbands rushed us aboard the ships. Explosions outside rocked the hangar, causing chunks of the domed ceiling to fall and ping off the sides of the enormous vessels bound to carry us light years away.

"What about father and mother?" I cried as Ash forced me into a seat and strapped me in.

"They wouldn't leave," he answered, strapping himself in and powering up the engines.

"We can't leave them!" I yelled, unwilling to lose anymore loved ones and struggling to unbuckle my restraints.

"There must be someone here to command the armies, Lore!" Ash shouted. It was the first time I'd heard my alien name spoken in years. "If the king leaves, then the kingdom will fall!"

I started to say something, but there was nothing to be said. Ash was right, and my father was no coward. He was, after all, the one who'd trained my new husband in the arts of war. So, I bit my lip, and gripped the arms of my seat as the ceiling of the enormous hangar slid away, revealing the night sky littered with fire and falling battleships.

"I don't want to leave any more than you do," Ash spoke through gritted teeth. "I want to stand and fight, but I'm ordered by the king to run. It goes against everything inside of me." He clenched his jaws tight and powered up the boosters.

In a split-second, our ship was in orbit. Massive enemy vessels were closing in on our small world, and there was nothing we could do about it. Ash managed to take out several ships to make way for my sister's vessel.

Our ship lurched sideways from an enormous blast. A missile from one of the enemy ships missed our ship's hull and exploded nearby, sending our vessel spinning just in time to see my sister's vessel make it out of the fray, the front-end smashed in and billows of smoke and gas pouring into the vacuum of space.

It lurched momentarily, the autopilot kicking in, and disappeared into the vastness of space beyond. My sister and her husband were dead, and their vessel would soon awake their platoon of the Royal Guard who would then command and repair the ship.

Ash cursed, and then ignited the engines taking us far enough away that we could still see our tiny planet as it crumbled into a cloud of meteorites and shooting stars. I sank into darkness, welcoming the bliss of unconsciousness.

I had to pause the video. It was almost too painful to watch any more of it. I remembered it all now. Every sensation, touch, smell, taste, and sound. Every alien childhood memory now resided among my human ones.

Centuries ago, I'd lost everything except for a husband I did not know or love.

My mouth was dry, and I wished I had something cold to drink. But I'd dream-traveled to my abandoned secret laboratory, so I swallowed hard and tried to moisten my mouth and throat. I had to finish this, no matter how long it took. No matter how painful it was, I had to do it.

I thought back to the letter Dad had left for me and realized he'd watched this same video. It must have been both shocking and heart-breaking for him to see and realize who and what I am and was. He wanted me to watch this video and protect our family and this planet from the Hunters. I was resolved to do just that, even though I wasn't quite sure how to do it yet.

After a few more moments, I tapped the button on the screen and the video continued. I was looking into my alien eyes again.

"You remember now, don't you?" my alien self said. It really wasn't a question, but a statement.

"Yes," I whispered, "I remember."

Then the video changed back to the ship where Ash and I were the only ones awake. All the other passengers were either resting in their cocoons or in stasis. Many weeks had passed since we'd fled into space, and Ash had been careful to make sure we weren't being followed by the Hunters. But we couldn't be a hundred percent sure. However, it had been quiet, and we'd both felt we'd made a clean getaway.

For a few weeks, we hadn't even spoken to one another. He'd been busy scanning space for any sign of Hunters, and I was busy with my scientific experiments. It was getting more and more difficult to keep my energy level up with twins growing inside of me, but I managed to take regular naps so as not to interrupt my work.

"What are you working on?" Ash leaned in the doorway of the laboratory.

I was shocked that the silence had been finally broken, and I dropped an empty beaker. Shards of glass scattered across the floor. I shrugged, looked up at Ash, and stroked my round stomach. "I can't bend over to clean it up."

"I guess not!" he chuckled. It was the first time I'd ever seen him laugh. He scooped up the broken pieces and disposed of them, cleaning his hands in the sink and quickly drying them.

"They're growing fast now," I cradled my belly in my arms, wishing I was carrying Ky's children. It felt so strange speaking to him in such an intimate way, or even speaking to him at all. We'd both been so quiet for so long that I'd been sure he'd regretted following father's orders and pairing with me.

"I never thought I would be a father," he said, placing his hands on my bulging stomach. "I think I just felt one of them move!" he gasped.

"They move all of the time now," I smiled.

"Do you know whether they are boys or girls?" he asked, continuing to cradle my stomach in his hands.

"I think they are girls," I tried to smile, but I wanted to cry. I was lonely and alone and I had no idea how to raise children.

"Lore, I know how hard this has been for you. I've tried to leave you alone so you could deal with your losses in your own way," Ash stepped closer to me. "But I was hoping we could at least be friends, if not more. We've got a lot of years ahead of us."

I swallowed hard but didn't answer as I processed his words through the filter of my broken, lonely heart.

"But I will leave you alone if that's your wish," he stepped away, but I sensed he didn't want to.

"No," my voice broke. "No more silence, please. I've almost gone mad with my own thoughts. I don't want to be alone anymore." I motioned to my bulging belly. "I can't do this by myself."

He rushed to me, pulling me into his arms, and resting his chin on my head. "You aren't alone in this. We can do this together, although I know nothing about birthing children."

"Neither do I, and I'm terrified. I wasn't ready to be a mother," I rested my head on his chest.

"It's my fault. I should have been more careful, but I wanted to comfort you on our wedding night, and ..." his voice trailed off.

"There's nothing to do but plan for the future now," I said, pulling out of his embrace and looking into his eyes. "You know, there were a lot of ladies crying because you weren't going to be single anymore." I tried to break the tension with joking.

He merely cocked a crooked smile and shook his head, then changed the subject. "So, what have you been up to in here all these weeks?"

"Do you really want to know?" I asked.

"Yes, really," he glanced at all the tubes and beakers and fluids boiling over open flames.

"I think our people are too easy to kill. Our population dies in twos, and we must do something about it." I spoke matter-of-factly as if I was speaking to Ky, and I felt a quick pang to my heart.

"You speak sacrilege, Princess," Ash said, then clucked his tongue.

"I was afraid you would say that," my hopes were dashed.

"Oh, come now," he smiled. "Surely, you know I'm joking."

I stared at him for a moment and realized that I was seeing this formidable general in an all new light.

"Well, I agree with you," he said crossing his arms over his chest and leaning against the counter. "I've brought this very idea before the king and the Royal Court, but I was run out by the Holy Men and Women for threatening our holy unions."

"Are you serious?" I asked, not able to tell because I really did not know my new husband.

"Yes, very serious. I was scolded by the king, as well, though he told me in private chambers that he agreed with me." He looked away. It was painful for us both to speak of the dead in such a way, and Ash had truly loved my father as much as if he'd been his own.

"Who's to stop us now from developing a way to sever the bonds without killing a pair of Others?" I asked.

"No one. You are supreme ruler now. I'm merely your consort. I'm here to plant these in there," he pointed to my stomach. "And to keep you all alive." He looked a bit sad at that prospect.

"You don't believe in the marriage bond, do you?" I asked, hoping he'd give me up easily when the time came.

"Not without love," he shook his head.

"Did you give up a true love to bind with me?" I asked. The hope was growing. Perhaps she was even resting in her cocoon on this very ship.

"I've loved many women, Princess." He cocked a smile again. "But I've only ever resolved to marry one. I don't go back on promises."

"Good," I'd let him figure out what I'd meant by that one word.

"Good? That I've loved many women? Or that I've only ever resolved to marry one? Or that I don't go back on my promises? Which one is good?" he teased.

"Good that you haven't forgotten that I'm the princess." I turned back to my work and hoped he'd leave.

He did, but glanced back at me once before he left.

Another flicker of the screen, and the video revealed that time had advanced a few months. My belly was swollen much larger, and I had trouble standing at my lab tables for long periods of time. Ash had moved several stools into the lab for me and had become very interested and supportive of my experiments.

"Is it possible to try it on our first-born?" Ash asked, his expression serious.

"It's dangerous to do it without trials first," I shook my head and continued making notes in my small notebook.

I stopped the video and managed to zoom in on the notebook, gasping at the realization that it was the very same notebook Mr. Forster had given to Mom … the one I now had. Grandma would've said, "wonders never cease." And she would have been right.

Tapping on the screen again, I zoomed back out and pressed play. Ash was persistent in wanting to try the experiment on our first-born.

"What if it kills them, Ash?" I asked. "What if it kills me?"

"Don't be ridiculous!" he scolded me, causing me to tense and move away from him.

"Why do you insist?" my voice sounded small.

"Because I don't want both of my children to die because something happens to one of them," he was exasperated, and I realized for the first time that he loved our children.

"Nothing will happen to our babies," I reached out and touched his arm. "We will keep them safe."

"Could you've kept Ky safe? Look at what happened to his brother because Ky died." His words pierced my heart.

I covered my mouth with my hand to stifle my sobs and rushed out of the lab. If I could have, I would've run to the Royal Guard's chamber, awoken Xi, and ordered him to kill Ash. And he would have done it.

Ash caught me, wrapping his arms around me from behind. "Why can't you love me the way you loved him?"

"Don't!" I cried.

"At least let me comfort you," he scooped me up in his arms. "I am your husband, after all."

"Put me down, Ash, or I'll…" I kicked my swollen feet trying to free myself.

"Or you'll what? Awaken your guard dog and order him to attack?" he laughed.

"Yes," I sounded pathetic. "I will."

"No you won't, Princess," he smiled as he closed the door of the captain's chamber behind us. "And you'll enjoy my comforting you."

I paused the video again. I was ashamed to admit that I did enjoy it. Ash knew women well, and I guessed I was no different from any of the others. But he never found his way into my heart. We were merely two lonely souls needing comfort in the vast coldness of space. Although, his heart had other plans …

One particularly painful day, I stood in front of one of the large round windows looking out at the brilliant nebula we were hiding in. Ash had discovered one of the Hunters' probes following us, so he decided to send out a destruction probe to find it and destroy it. In the meantime, we would hide the ship in the nebula.

Pink, purple, and blue gasses were alight with fire from thousands of stars as we slowly cruised through the enormous gas formation. I was sure my time of delivery was getting close. My belly was bigger than I'd ever imagined it could be, and my back ached constantly. I'd had to give up on my experiments for a while, but I was sure that the serum I'd created would work on our species. I'd just have to wait until I had volunteers to try it on.

Ash had grown more insistent that we try it on our babies, because he simply could not face the prospect of losing them both at once. I'd been shocked at how attached he'd grown to them, for he and I weren't really in love, though we'd developed an affectionate relationship. He hadn't lied when he'd said that he would be a generous lover.

A pair of strong arms wrapped around me and cradled my belly in a protective embrace. I turned and looked up into Ash's eyes. It really was no wonder why so many women had been in love with him. But my heart still loved another … would always love another.

"It won't be long until you'll be holding them in your arms," I leaned my head back against his chest and sighed.

He lifted me up and carried me to my stasis pod. I hadn't been able to sleep in our bed for weeks because of my back.

"Get some rest," he kissed me gently on my lips and lowered me into the pod. Then I felt a small sting on my neck, and I was out.

He'd sedated me without my permission! I gasped, staring at the computer screen. I'd had dreams and recollections of that moment of him placing me in the pod, my belly swollen with his children, and my body exhausted. But until now, I hadn't recalled that he'd sedated me.

He left my pod and returned with the serum I'd developed.

"No!" I shouted at the screen, but I knew what came next. He administered it and slid the pod closed, thinking he was saving his children's lives.

Hours later, I awoke screaming and lying in a puddle of blood. My insides felt as if they were being ripped out of my body. I pounded on the sides of my pod, leaving bloody handprints and smears across the glass covering.

Ash rushed into the room, his face pale. He opened the pod and blood gushed out and covered the floor.

"I'm dying!" I screamed, clutching my stomach. I was trembling from the pain and felt the life ebbing from me. "Take me to the emergency surgery pod!"

He pounded the panel of buttons on the wall, and the emergency surgery pod emerged from a cabinet and presented itself ready for use. A half hour later, I was unconscious, and he was holding our two lifeless daughters in his arms, grief and disbelief covering his face. "Wake up, my children!" tears streamed down his cheeks as he tried to revive them. "Hear your father's voice and wake up."

He'd never told me that it had been his fault. He'd never admitted to sedating me and using me and our two royal children as an experiment.

"I can't go on," I moaned, hiding under the covers of Ash's bed. "I want to go to the ancestors." I simply could not go on breathing and thinking and working.

"No, Princess," Ash's voice was muffled through the thick layer of blankets. "Your people need you. You are the last of your family." He pulled me close to him, but I pushed away.

"Did you send out two lanterns so the ancestors would know our daughters were coming to them?" I'd hidden under the covers, unable to say goodbye to the two babies I'd never gotten to cradle in my arms.

"Yes," Ash's voice broke. He paused, then, "We can have more children …"

"No, we can't," I pulled myself tighter in a ball and wished for darkness. I knew I'd be unable to conceive again, and a family that had ruled a people for as long as history would no longer have any descendants.

My alien face flashed on the screen again. "He'd used the serum incorrectly."

"Yes," I responded, nodding. "It was meant to be used prior to conception."

"And it was first used correctly in this laboratory with the help of my adopted son, Orion," my alien self said, motioning to Orion who waved at me through the computer screen. "We used it many times, creating a village of human twins."

I felt as if I'd been slapped across the face, and I sat aghast staring at the video. After all this time, I finally discovered the connection to ...

"Cândido Godói," the alien me said. "We are just on the outskirts of the village right now, and so are you."

The video flickered once more and cut to a bit of commotion. Orion was carrying someone into the lab. It was an unconscious woman who he carefully placed on the surgical gurney.

"After all this time ..." the alien version of me said, voice full of wonder, as she placed a surgical mask over her face. "Orion, it is important for you to remember how to do this."

"Yes, mother. I will not forget," he forced his hands into a pair of rubber gloves.

The alien me lifted the vial from around her neck and uncorked the lid. A sparkle of light flashed inside the vial as she poured its contents into a glass tube containing the serum. Meanwhile, Orion prepped the subject, baring her stomach and applying antiseptic.

"I hand-chose this woman, because she is loving and kind and has a good husband. They will make excellent parents," the alien me said and then completed the procedure.

The woman on the gurney awoke, screaming in agony, her dark hair damp with sweat and her blue eyes wild with pain and fear. She looked very familiar to me, more familiar than just this distant memory.

Orion sedated her once more, and the alien me did a few more tests, finally removing the mask from her delicate alien face. "It is successful!" tears filled the large, slanted eyes on the screen. "She has been impregnated with Ky's essence. Once she and her husband conceive, Ky will be reborn. I will begin preparations for the same to be done for me next year. This is the only way to create Others who can live apart."

The screen flashed black for a few seconds, and then the alien version of me appeared once more. "I did this to escape the prison I was in so that I could be free once more to love who I choose to love, to be who I choose to be. Ash protected me, but he was also unfaithful with many women—human and our kind, alike.

After so many years, I grew cold to his touch. It only made him more determined to own me. But how can anyone own a queen?" My alien lips turned down in a frown. "We have found a suitable host for me now, and Orion will watch over both Ky and me until we find each other. It's my only chance to be happy and to protect my people."

She turned and called Orion to the screen.

"Yes, mother?" he sat in the chair next to her.

"This box must be given to Ky at just the right time. You must tell him that I have created this from the vial. He needs to save it for when my time comes to be changed. He will have already received his by that time." She placed the silver loop into the box and closed the lid.

"This, you will wear around your neck until it is time. It completes the loop. Do not lose it, son." She placed the same silver necklace and moon-shaped pendant around his neck that Ash had given to me.

"I will guard it with my life," Orion clutched it in his hand, holding it close to his chest.

"Not with your life, son. But keep it safe. Hide it if you need to. Your life is too precious to give up for anything," the alien me stroked Orion's cheek.

And the screen went black. The video was over, and there was nothing more. I didn't need anything more, though. I remembered it all. I'd even dreamed about the night my own essence had been injected into Mom. It had taken a lot of persuasion for Ash to allow me to undergo the experiment.

However, since I was the last remaining member of the royal family, and since I could not continue the bloodline, he'd finally relented thinking that once I was a completed hybrid we would have more children together.

Thinking back to the early trials of the armband, I thought of how excited both Ash and I had been when I'd finally been able to create a device that could allow our alien skeletons to harness the energy of this planet the way we'd been adapted to do on our home planet. It was one of the reasons our people had enjoyed extremely long lives.

Ash had insisted on being the first specimen to try the armband. He'd wanted to experience, first hand, the science behind the creation so he could tell me whether or not it was successful. We'd stood at the top of the temple pyramid. Ash had adorned himself with plumes of long, fine feathers and rubbed his skin with gold dust. His eyes shone even brighter surrounded by the gold, and even I had to admit that he was glorious.

Our people gathered around the base of the pyramid, all eager to see whether or not the armband would work. I carefully slid the braided silver loop up Ash's arm until it came to rest around his left bicep. A moment later, lighting was shooting from his fingertips and a whirlwind of gold dust blew around him and me, catching us both up in a storm of energy.

Electricity flowed from the earth, up the steps at the front of the pyramid, through his skin, and into his veins. Blue light pulsed beneath his skin, and he looked fierce like an alien warrior god. I knew then that I would need one of my own, for I would not, could not allow him to possess greater power than me.

His reaction had been much milder than the one I'd experienced when he'd applied the pairing serum and arm band to me in the back of my pickup truck. At first, I'd thought it was because the two elements had been applied at the same time. But I realized, standing in my old stomping ground, that it had been because I was a human hybrid.

I looked around the ancient laboratory. *This is really happening,* I thought, sliding my hand over the gurney where the woman had been. *The pieces are finally coming together and creating the big picture.*

Turning the lights out, I closed the rusty door behind me and looked down. The thick layer of dust and sand on the tunnel floor was imprinted with several sets of boot tracks. One set wasn't fresh by any means. Spider webs and other things gave away their age. Dad, I knelt and touched the edge of one of the boot prints.

The other set was more recent. Perhaps a few months old or a little more given how insects and other things had made their own markings across the imprints. *Who else could have been here?* I touched the edge of one of the footprints. They weren't the footprints of a female, unless she wore large-sized boots. I shook my head and wondered who all knew the secrets about me that I was only just now discovering.

Walking away from the boot prints and out into the growing morning light left me feeling extremely sentimental. I finally knew where all those old feelings of dread had come from. I'd been afraid of losing Ky all over again. Now, I felt free.

Now I could visit Cândido Godói knowing exactly how the village was linked to me.

CHAPTER TWELVE

CÂNDIDO GODÓI

The village of twins was just waking up. I walked barefoot down the narrow walk along the main street of the tiny Brazilian town. Shop owners were just beginning to open their doors as the sun peeked over the horizon, casting glittery shards of morning light across the glass pane windows on the front of the town café.

My stomach growled as soon as I inhaled the aroma of fresh bread and coffee. I walked into the café and stood at the counter expecting to order breakfast. The old woman who emerged from behind the kitchen door stopped in her tracks, covering her wrinkled face with her hands and shaking her head no.

"Are you okay?" I asked.

"Get out!" she shouted, her accent thick. A man around Mom's age emerged behind her and started shouting at me until I left. They locked the doors behind me and pulled the shades closed over the windows.

The same thing happened at the tiny coffee shop on the corner and every other place I passed along the main street in town. They knew who I was. I could hear their thoughts as I passed by the storefronts. They'd been expecting my return, thinking I would come back to experiment on them. They knew I wasn't human.

I gave them what they wanted – I left their town in peace and disappeared into the forest outside of town. It was peaceful there, anyway, and I allowed my body to absorb the energy from the earth and the trees around me. It would sustain me until I could find food.

A smile covered my face as I picked up my pace, running north toward my cocoon tent. I'd dream-traveled miles the night before, but it didn't matter how far I had to run. "I'm free!" I shouted, stretching my arms over my head and running faster than I'd ever imagined I could run. The brambles and tree roots didn't even bruise my feet, because I was running so fast. And it wouldn't have mattered if my feet were sore, I remembered everything, and I was so glad to be free … to know that all my years of hard work had finally paid off. *I'm free!* rang out in my mind.

After a long while of running, the farmlands turned back into jungle forests, and the position of the sun proved it must be sometime in the afternoon. I was glad when I leapt through an opening in the jungle. The thick vines and shady canopy provided covering and protection.

I stopped on the edge of a wide rushing river. *The Amazon!* I gasped. I'd loved studying the exotic river and the animals around it in school. And there I was standing on the mossy riverbank.

Treading along the cool bank, I traveled upstream until I came to an inlet where water had flowed over into a shady pool. It was the perfect place to take a break. I took off my shorts and shirt and dove into the cool water, plunging beneath the surface and feeling the rush of underwater grasses brush against my skin.

Tiny fish darted away from me in a hurried cloud of silver circles. I tried swimming behind them, but they hid among thick mosses on an old rotting log under the water. As I broke through the glimmering surface, a frog leapt into the pool from a large mossy stone and splashed water in my face. I began giggling, which turned into laughter that echoed through the jungle forest.

I looked down to see streaks of electrical currents flowing from the water, through my skin, and into my veins. Tossing my head back, I drew in more energy until my body lifted out of the water, leaving only the tips of my toes touching the surface.

Spinning and whirling like an ice-skater, I made wide circles across the surface of the pool with the tips of my toes and smiled broadly. My arms stretched out wide as I turned the circles into a giant figure eight.

Light flashed from my fingertips, up my shoulders and neck, across my torso, and lighting up the symbols on my stomach and abdomen. I spun in a circle, faster and faster, and then came to a quick stop.

I'd intended to begin the wide figure eight again but saw two jungle people standing at the edge of the forest near a tree. The man was standing with a spear, and the woman held a basket of fruit, which she placed at the edge of the pool. They backed away and disappeared into the jungle foliage.

The basket held an offering to an alien goddess. Inside were several types of jungle fruits and nuts and a small clay figurine of my former alien self. I ate a piece of the fruit as I sat on the large mossy rock and watched a couple of butterflies flutter among the undergrowth at the other end of the pool.

Once my bra and underwear had dried out enough, I slipped my shirt and shorts back on and stuffed a couple of the other pieces of fruit into the pockets on my shorts and tossed the figurine of me into the pool. It seemed like a good-luck thing to do.

Then, I continued on my way toward my cocoon hoping for a nap and change of clothes. We don't always get what we hope for, though, do we?

CHAPTER THIRTEEN

NYX

I made it back to the enormous tree near the edge of the gushing waterfall just after dark. The night sky was full of stars, and there wasn't a cloud anywhere. I was happy. All my long centuries of work had finally produced viable results. I'd not only found a way to gain my freedom and revive my loved one, I'd also found a way to save my people.

With a big leap, I floated up, up, up toward the top of the tree where I'd left my cocoon. I lit upon the large limb and realized my cocoon wasn't there. All of my belongings were gone ... even the box containing my tiny galaxy.

My hands powered up as I eased my back against the trunk of the tree. I searched my surroundings, but there was no one in sight. I thought about the possible thieves. Andrew wouldn't have taken my things and left me without shelter. Neither would've Everett. My heart leapt a beat at the thought of Everett's name, and I smiled. But then I frowned, because now I was bound to find Ky.

I'll think about that tomorrow, I thought as I shook my head and refocused on the current situation.

A slight movement higher up in a nearby tree caught my attention. I squinted, focusing my night vision to see if the thief was hiding among the branches. A clear patch of stars, shining and brilliant, peeked through the boughs of the tree.

Then the oddest thing happened.

The patch of stars moved ever so slightly. Then two eyes appeared suspended among those stars, and I gasped. It sort of reminded me of a Cheshire cat, but only in real life. Then a smile appeared, and I had to wonder if some of the fruit in the offering basket back at the pool had some hallucinogenic properties to it.

I released a globe of fire, allowing it to tumble off my fingertips. A quick flick of my wrist sent it hovering in a circle around the eyes and smile suspended in midair.

"Put it out!" the mouth hissed, keeping the tone to a whisper.

My mind went back to the night of the Rodeo Gala when Everett and I were attacked by Ash who'd camouflaged himself with the night sky.

"Ash? Is that you?" I hissed back, wondering why we were whispering.

"No, mother," the mouth smiled again. "It's me. Phoenix."

"Show yourself to me and prove it. Then I'll put out the light," I answered. With all the people and things prowling the jungles, I wasn't about to make myself vulnerable in the dark.

The night sky camouflage faded away to reveal my other beautiful adopted son, Phoenix. Ash had given him that name, because as a toddler he'd set things on fire when he'd have a tantrum. We'd called him Nyx for short. He was Orion's birth Other, his twin brother. Neither of them had any relation to me, except for my love for them.

Ash had fathered them with a jungle woman who'd died giving birth to them … or so he'd said. I'd always suspected that he'd killed her and brought them to me in hopes that I'd forget about my plans of leaving him and becoming a hybrid. He'd always thought the main reason I'd planned to do it was so I could have children of my own.

The alien me had loved both Orion and Nyx very much, and they had helped fill the void that the loss of my own babies had created in my heart. But not fully. I would always know they weren't mine, and they'd never be able to ascend to my throne. Nonetheless, Orion loved me best while Nyx preferred his father.

"See? It's me!" Nyx smiled, his dark hair spilling over his shoulder and bare chest. Looking at him now, from my perspective as a human, he bore the intensity of his father with the dark hair and olive skin of the jungle people.

"Nyx, it's so good to see you," I whispered, smiling back at him. It was a very strange sensation actually seeing him, because he seemed sort of like a very distant memory to me, and I no longer had the intense connection to him I'd once had. It was difficult grappling with the chasm between my past and present selves.

"I've missed you, mother," he leapt over onto the limb next to me.

"I've missed you, too, son," I stammered on 'son', because technically he was centuries older than me, though he appeared to be my age. "How have you been?"

"Fine. Busy helping father," he smiled awkwardly at me, and I realized how weird it must be for him to see an eighteen-year-old human female as his mother.

"I know this has to be weird for you," I said, unsure of what else to say. "It's sure weird for me," I chuckled, but it sounded feeble. I was sucking at comforting my adopted son.

"Do you remember me?" he asked, cocking his head over to the side and examining my face.

"Yes," I smiled.

"How well do you remember things?" he asked, seeming a bit skeptical. Yep, he was a lot like his father.

"Like a distant memory … sort of detached from my present self, if that makes any sense." Might as well be honest.

"I was afraid of that," he frowned.

I allowed the flaming orb to fizzle out so I didn't have to watch the sadness creep across his beautiful face. There was really nothing I could do for him. I simply was not the exact same person I'd once been. I was a hybrid now with closer memories of other loved ones that now meant more to me than the ones from my distant past. Maybe that was a good thing.

"What are you doing here?" I asked, changing the subject.

"Father sent me. He wants you to come home. There are Hunters looking for you now, both enemy and human. Orion calls the human 'Luke' and says he and his men want to do experiments on you and then kill you." Nyx held out his hand. I took it.

"I can't come back right now. I have things to do first," I stroked his fingers with my thumb and had the vague recollection of doing that same thing when his hand was much smaller. We were sitting at the top of a stone temple pyramid, and he was cranky and tired. But the people were bringing their offerings, so I could not leave with him right then.

"Please, mother, come home. Father wanted to come get you, but he can't leave right now. He's protecting those in the cocoons," Nyx pleaded, his hand tightening around mine.

"I'm sorry, I can't. Not yet," I slipped my hand out of his.

"Father said you promised him you'd return to him," his brow furrowed.

"Yes, I did promise him that," it was my turn to frown. "But I've got to find my mother first and then … maybe …"

"He should've sent Orion," Nyx looked away. "You could never tell him no."

I rolled my eyes. I remembered the rivalry between them, pitting Ash and me against each other during their teen years. It had caused many arguments with me finally having to lower the boom and remind all of them who was the highest ruler of our people.

Truthfully, I was ticked off that Ash had sent one of his children to come fetch me knowing that he'd murdered mine. Just thinking about it at that very moment made me want to light the whole jungle on fire. Nyx must have seen the rage cross my face, and he softened his attitude.

"I put your things in your backpack and hung it over there," he pointed to where he'd been perched waiting for me.

"Thank you," I answered, glad that my few belongings weren't lost.

"I hope you don't mind that I looked through the photo album," he blushed, glancing at me out of the corner of his eye.

"No, of course I don't mind," I reached out and touched him on his arm, hoping to somehow comfort him.

"With memories like those, why would you want to remember us?" he frowned. "Father wanted me to warn you to be careful about using your powers. The human Hunters have developed devices to detect alien energy." He paused, then, "Orion isn't the only one who's been doing things to protect you. I've been very busy with a project of my own."

"I'd like to hear about it," I answered, genuinely interested.

"You'll find out first hand, and then you'll see that I love you as much as my brother does." He sat there a moment as if he wanted to say something else, but changed his mind before he leapt out of the tree and disappeared into the shadows.

It was definitely time for me to move on and try to locate Mom. I hated leaving the spot where I'd gotten comfortable. But I remembered what Grandpa used to say – "Sometimes life gives you a nudge to get you out of your comfort zone so you can grow."

I was definitely way out of my comfort zone knowing that there were Hunters on my trail. It was time to stretch my wings and jump into the fray.

CHAPTER FOURTEEN

HUNTERS

"I should've asked Nyx if he knew where Mom was," I mumbled to myself as I made my way through the edge of the forest along the ridge above the canyon. "He probably would've just said, 'You should ask Orion, since he's your favorite.'" I rolled my eyes again. *Grandpa would've taken a belt to both of those boys' backsides,* I thought as I continued on, wishing for some moonlight to light my path.

I thought about lots of things as I gingerly made my way through the darkness, too wary to release a globe of fire to light my way. The constant rush of the waterfall was farther away now, but I could still hear the calming sound of water.

I could also hear other jungle sounds now. The canyon was deep and dark, though, and I stayed far enough from the edge to keep from slipping on the mossy rocks and tumbling over.

A man's sudden burst of laughter echoed up out of the gulch. It was so eerie and out of place that it creeped me out enough to stop me in my tracks. Another burst of laughter, and I lowered myself down on all fours and crawled across the mossy rocks to peek over the edge, thanking my lucky stars that I'd put my boots on after Nyx had left.

Far below, a small campfire was surrounded by a ring of men sitting and talking. Though it was difficult to be for sure, they seemed to be dressed in some sort of military fatigues. I strained my eyes to see and inched forward a bit, clinging to the thick moss between the rocks and hoping I wouldn't slip over the edge.

"There's a cluster of some sort of special guard hidden somewhere around here," one of the men said, ignoring the others who were warning him to lower his voice. He sounded like he was drunk. "I say we go crush in their skulls before they wake up."

He was talking about the Royal Guard! Xi and his men and women answered only to me as he'd been my bodyguard since my alien birth. They were a special breed of our kind who dedicated their lives solely to the service of the royal family.

Even their appearance was different from the rest of our kind. Their shoulders were broader, muscles stronger, skeletons larger, and in the place of scalp hair, each of them had the coat of arms of the royal family tattooed on their heads. Some of them had special tattoos on their necks, faces, and bodies depending on their specialty.

They'd been in stasis for so long that it would take them a while to fully awaken. I decided the time had come to do so for their own protection. It was up to me to awaken them. Not even Ash would be able to do it.

"Is that what we're in this part of the jungle for?" another guy asked while taking a leak in some bushes near the campfire.

It was difficult to focus in on all they were saying due to distance and the constant rush of water. So, I anchored the toes of my boots between two large rocks and inched forward, straining to hear whether or not they knew the exact location of the Royal Guard. If they did, I'd have to do something to stop them ... even if that meant calling Ash to help me.

One of the men around the campfire was saying he'd heard there were female aliens among them and he'd like to be the one to introduce them to human men. It made me sick to my stomach, and I felt a snarl cross my face.

The man was an idiot. Even the smallest of one of the females in the Royal Guard could disembowel him with one hand. The thought of that made me happy, and I made a mistake.

I forgot to be careful near the slippery edge and lost my anchor between the rocks. The weight of my backpack slipped forward over my head and pulled me over the edge. I scrambled, trying to keep from falling and landing right in the middle of the men below.

My fingers dug deep into the rich soil. I searched furiously with my boots to find a good foothold. The joints in my shoulders felt as though they'd come out of their sockets, and I had the innate need to scream for help.

But I couldn't.

Finally, I reached over to my right. My hand landed on a root. I grasped it, and letting go with my other hand, swung to my right, gripping the root with all my might. But I was tugged backward. My backpack was caught on something. I couldn't turn my head far enough to see what it was, and I couldn't move forward because whatever had snagged it had a firm grip on it.

And I couldn't use my powers, because the human alien Hunters below would detect my alien energy with their gadgets.

I cursed under my breath and took a quick note of what I would lose if I had to leave the backpack behind. *My tiny galaxy is in my pocket. I'm glad I put it in there after Nyx left. My other pocket has a couple of packets of trail mix in it. The pockets on my boots have a tiny flashlight in one and a small Swiss Army Knife in the other. I had Grandma's necklace around my neck.* I sighed, because I had the feeling I was about to lose the memory album Grandma and I'd made together and Dad's photo album.

Dammit! I mouthed the curse and began working my arms out of my backpack. It swung free from my shoulders and dangled at the end of a knobby root that had worked its way around the loop at the top of the backpack. I wished I could light that root up and burn it to cinders. But I couldn't, so I just hoped my backpack would hang there safely until I could come back for it.

The root I was hanging from started coming loose from the soil, so I began scrambling to get myself up over the edge of the overhang. I dug the toes of my boots into the rocks, soil, and moss, struggling to get a firm foothold.

I managed to find a rock jutting out far enough to step on and lift myself up over the edge. But the rock was loose, and as soon as I slipped over the top of the cliff to safety, it followed the pull of gravity down, down, down hitting one of the men below square on the head.

I wanted to shout, "Bull's-eye!" But I didn't dare. I dipped back into the shadows at the edge of the jungle and hoped they wouldn't see my backpack dangling from the root, that it would be well-hidden among the clumps of heavy vines and ferns. There was nothing I could do at that point but put some distance between me and the Hunters below.

However, a soft neighing stopped me in my tracks. I was sure I'd heard a horse. Another neigh, and I got up the nerve to inch back over the edge of the cliff just enough to see what was going on down there.

I'd made some distance between where I'd fallen over the edge and where I was at that moment. There was a flurry of activity in the camp. Several of the men were trying to help the unconscious man who'd just been clobbered with that huge rock. I bit my lip and stifled a giggle. A couple of others were shining lights up, unable to see past the thick vapor of mist from the waterfall. That gave me a lot of comfort. That meant they probably wouldn't find my backpack.

Then, I saw the horses. They were quite a ways downstream from the camp. There was a narrow path nearby that would take me down into the riverbed, and, from my new position, I could see a way out on the other side where the wall of the river bed gave way to a smooth slope out of the gorge.

Very carefully, I made my way down the narrow trail, slipping a couple of times and catching myself on vines and roots. I suspected that the jungle people used this steep trail to make their way down to spear fish in the rushing stream below. It would be more difficult for predators to hunt them on such a steep trail.

I was glad when my feet finally landed on the smooth stones at the foot of the narrow path. And I was also glad that Grandpa had made sure my boots were water proof. Because a moment later, I was hopping across the rushing stream on large stones and my boots were definitely going under the surface.

On the other side of the stream, I leapt into the shadows relieved that the Hunters were distracted back at their camp. I tiptoed through some thick underbrush, pausing only momentarily to keep from being discovered.

The horses were tied to a rope which was tied between two trees some distance apart from each other. I had my sights on the strongest of the six. It was evident that she had not been properly taken care of by whoever currently claimed her, and I was sure that she had, at one time, been prized by someone who must be missing her now. For I had the distinct feeling she'd been stolen.

She was the only one of the six horses who was still wearing her saddle. It had been a long day for her, no doubt. Any other time I would have been livid that someone had put a horse away for the night without proper care. But not this time. I was extremely delighted to see that she was still wearing her saddle.

As I inched closer to the beautiful chestnut brown animal, she turned and looked at me. I paused again, not knowing whether or not she would stir and bring attention. She didn't. So I reached into my pocket and pulled out a packet of trail mix. I poured a few pieces of it into my palm and held it to her mouth.

"If you get me out of here alive, I promise to take you with me," I whispered to her as I patted her neck. She gently nodded as if to agree.

I climbed into the saddle and tugged the horse's reins. She followed my direction without any complaint. Slowly, I steered the horse away from the camp. Only a few men sat talking around the camp fire. The rest had either helped get the unconscious drunk man into his tent or had gone to their own beds for the night.

When we got a few more yards away from the camp, I bent down to ask the horse to give me all of her speed. She nodded once more as if she understood. *Smart horse.* I wished I could take her back to Grandpa's ranch and let her roam free on the grassy pastures. But I had no hope that I would ever get to go home, so how was there any hope in that for her. Just then I heard voices rise in alarm back at the camp.

"Go, girl! Go!" I dug my heels into her sides as I whirled the end of the long, leather reins over my head and brought them down on her rump in a sharp snap.

The horse whinnied once and tore off into the thick forest. Her strength and speed quickly became evident. She was fast. Faster than Daisy, my heart pained at that thought. Faster than Andrew's wild horse, Spider. I leaned forward in the saddle, gripping the reins and hugging her strong ribs with my knees.

They were following us. Their shouts echoed through the jungle. I snapped the reins again, and the horse lunged forward even faster. She was faster than lightning, and I would have given anything to be back in Texas racing Andrew across the lush green pasture of Grandpa's ranch.

I was now an official horse thief, something that had once been a crime punishable by death. *Well, I'll come to terms with that another day. Right now, I need to escape. Besides, I've saved this poor horse from a life of abuse and neglect,* I assured myself as I dug my heels into her sides. By the time I'd lost my pursuers, I'd practically gone from a saint who'd risked her life to save a horse to an alien queen who deserved to take the beautiful mare. And that was where I left it.

The jungle terrain had changed so much since Ash and I had hidden the Royal Guard. Before we'd landed our ship and camouflaged it within the jungle, we'd jettisoned the Royal Guard's vessel and buried it in the side of a very steep rise along the side of a valley.

Every so often, I would stop the horse and listen for sounds of followers, but the night was quiet except for the usual jungle sounds. It's amazing how loud the jungle is at night. Not only is it alive with nocturnal creatures, it's also alive with dreams and nightmares of the jungle people whose huts are hidden in the depths of the forest.

I followed the river a while longer, straining my night vision to keep the horse on track along-side the riverbank. But the thicker the forest grew, the darker it became. The thought of another jaguar attacking us and maybe killing the horse was what finally drove me to finding a cave to camp in for the night.

Quickly gathering a mound of dry wood, I led the horse into the cave and, only then, felt free to light the cave with a globe of fire. She seemed content to be inside the cavern and away from the dangers of the jungle night. Especially when the distant cry of a large cat echoed through the tangles of the forest.

The cave was just a foot or two above the river, and thick strands of vines and ivy draped over part of the narrow entrance. At first, I'd been wary that it may have been the lair of some large animal, but there were no signs of anyone or anything having been in there for a very long time.

"I've gotta give you a name, girl," I patted the horse on the neck. She nudged me and nibbled at my ponytail. I secured her reins around a large rock and then removed her saddle. The immediate relief of having it off her back was evident in the playful manner she stamped her hooves.

The thief had emptied the saddlebags of everything but a brush. So I gave the beautiful horse a good once-over. Then I gathered an armful of grasses from outside the cave entrance and placed them where she could nibble them. After that, I whittled the end of a narrow stick to a sharp point and stifled a cheer when I managed to spear a fish for my dinner.

Back in the cave, I started a fire and cooked the fish. It smelled amazing, which was a sign of how hungry I really was. After devouring dinner, I leaned back on the saddle and let my mind wander over things I'd discovered and remembered. I'd come a long way from the girl I'd once been who'd wanted nothing more than to be a large animal vet and have a bunch of kids.

There were faint drawings on the walls of the cave. Ancient sketches of sloths, monkeys, and people overlapped each other under a fine layer of dust and spider webs. There were stars drawn across the curved ceiling of the cave, and on the back wall there was a sketch of a stone temple pyramid.

At the top was a man and a woman. Judging from the fire coming from the mouth of the small boy at the man's side, it was a drawing of Ash, Nyx, and me. The sketch of the boy sitting on the steps and pouring rain out of a clay jar surely depicted Orion. While Nyx had set things on fire while in the throes of a temper tantrum, Orion had brought on monsoons. I realized at that moment that Orion and Nyx were the twin sons in the legend of Cloud in the book I'd found in Dad's study.

It's amazing what you experience if you live long enough, I thought while examining the ancient drawing. The jungle people had long thought of Ash as a god and me as his queen. They'd never really known what to make of me, but Ash was a warrior down to the very fiber of his being. And he could be ruthless.

No doubt he would be ruthless again ... very soon.

I could be ruthless, too, if pushed to it. I'd done a lot to escape the heartbreak and pain of my former life. Anyone who tried to put those shackles on me again would see that I possess greater power than even Ash the warrior god.

Surely, it wouldn't come down to that. The world had changed dramatically since our arrival centuries earlier. Ash could find a suitable mate and have a proper marriage with her. I shook my head to clear my thoughts.

Eventually, my thoughts flowed from one subject to another. I wondered what Natalie and David were doing at that moment in time. No doubt the wedding plans were coming along. I missed Natalie and wished I could call her up and tell her everything I'd recalled about being forced to marry Ash and losing my own babies on the long voyage here.

I wanted to talk to her about Everett and how much I missed him. I wanted to tell her I saw Angelica and how glad I was that Andrew had someone to help him and comfort him. Natalie would've wanted to know all the details about Angelica. Most of all, I needed to vent the worry I had deep inside about Mom. I'd locked it up and refused to think about it. But that night, alone in that cave, it crawled out of my chest and looked me straight in the eyes.

I quickly made a mental note of the resources I had at hand for finding Mom. My disabled cell phone was inside my backpack, which was dangling from the side of a deep ravine. That ruled out any chance of me calling or texting anyone. I had a horse, which I stole for no real reason. I had my powers, but they could now be detected by Hunters. So, I had to be careful using them.

Then I thought about the Royal Guard who would carry out any order I issued to them. No matter how big or how small, my Royal Guard would follow through without question or trepidation. Bringing them up to speed on everything that had happened since they'd last been awake would be the problem.

Simply entering the alert sequence into their stasis pod control mainframe and giving them time to wake up was not enough. I would have to leave a message for Xi so he would know what to expect.

I made a mental note of that and rolled over on my side. The campfire lit the walls of the cavern in warm golden hues, bringing back memories of the fireplace back home. My eyelids began feeling heavy, and I realized how tired I was just before I tumbled over into sleep.

And dream-traveled again …

Tumbling across the sky, I made a sharp descent into the canopy as if the mission I was on was urgent. Judging by the nightmare I'd just had, I knew where I was going. And, yes, the mission was *very* urgent.

I hit the ground in haste, out of breath, and running. The slope was steep, but that didn't matter. What mattered was finding the door to the airlock. Years of rubble and erosion had done their job well, and the trees we'd planted had grown enormous and wrapped their roots around the steep hill that camouflaged the Royal Guard's pod. Finally, I located the door and ripped away masses of vines and roots to reveal the security panel.

I wiped centuries of layers of dirt away from the panel and placed my hand over the sensor. Then, I focused my energy until a computerized voice in my native language spoke, "Pressurized air warning." The voice echoed through the jungle, and I scrambled to shut it off, punching in the codes only I knew and silencing the alarm.

Gears groaned into motion on the other side of the metal wall, and a sudden rush of air blew me backward. I steadied myself against the stone precipice behind me and waited for the door to open.

How many decades, centuries, had it been since I'd inhaled the air from my alien home planet? Although the atmosphere inside the ship was ancient, I could still detect what the hangar beneath the palace had smelled like. There was even a faint odor of smoke from the funeral pyres on that fateful night.

I stepped inside. The ship was dark, lit only by the light from the pods containing my Royal Guard. They slept in stasis, their pods lining the walls and ceiling of the domed vessel. I walked across the metal grated floor and stood in front of the stasis pod of my loyal body guard, Xi.

The domed glass cover of his stasis pod had fogged over from the jungle humidity that had followed me into the vessel. I swiped my hand across the glass, revealing the face of my beloved body guard who'd followed me across the universe to keep me safe.

"Will you recognize me, old friend?" I asked, looking up into his sleeping face. Frost lined his eyelashes and his arms were crossed over his chest. He was enormous, standing at least six-and-a-half feet tall. He was a handsome male and was covered in bulky muscles and tattoos commemorating victories he'd won. I knew he'd be stiff when he emerged from his stasis pod. It had been centuries since he'd moved.

I turned and gazed at all the other pods filled with those who'd vowed to protect and defend me with their lives. *How would they recognize me now?* I walked back down the metal grated floor between them, stretching my arms out and leaving marks across their fogged surfaces with my fingertips. *These are my own soldiers. They'll know me.*

The control panel was slow to warm up. It had been dormant for so long that the circuits were cold and sluggish. At last, it came online, casting a welcomed glow across my face. I accessed the vessel's log and made an entry.

"Many things have happened since you entered stasis," I began, looking into the tiny camera on the control panel. "Even I, your queen, am different," I held my hand against the security panel and released my energy into the sensors proving my identity. "Yes, I am Lore – your princess. Our planet was destroyed not long after our ship entered space. We have been on an alien planet for centuries now. And I have found a way to separate Others so that our people are not so easy to kill."

That would give them a lot to think about as they recuperate, I nodded to myself, then said, "I will share more as I am able. Until then, awake and arm yourselves. We are in enemy territory," my brows drew together, and a frown tugged at the corners of my mouth. I paused a moment, then said, "Thank you" before ending my log entry.

I wanted to thank them for being willing to die for me, for leaving their home for me, for staying asleep for centuries, waiting for me. But the Royal Guard is not known for being emotional, and that would have, perhaps, been a bit much.

A light on the control panel began blinking. Xi would notice it and see that a log entry had been made. I would come back in a few days and they would be awake and ready. Then, finding Mom would be a piece of cake.

With a few taps of my fingertips, I entered the code to awaken the Royal Guard. The ship responded by raising the lights a little. Warm air began pulsing into the pods. It was time for me to seal them in and head back to the cave.

I yawned as I locked the door behind me and camouflaged it with the heavy clumps of vines and roots. I thanked my lucky stars that the ground cover had been thick enough to hide my tracks. But any skilled tracker would be able to follow my path right to the door of my Royal Guard who wouldn't be able to defend themselves for the next twenty-four hours.

Maybe I should make it rain, I thought as I looked up at the clear night sky. Focusing my thoughts and envisioning a roaring thunderstorm, I willed the clouds to come and fill the night sky. Soon, it was raining, and I was laughing. I'd never made it rain on purpose. It was incredible!

Rain poured down the side of the hill as I made my way down to my landing spot. I needed to travel back to the cave before the storm got any worse. Just as I was lifting off the ground, something sent me reeling backwards, slamming into a tree.

There had been a sudden flash, and then the loud crack, and then the searing pain to my right shoulder. Something warm flowed down my arm. It smelled of iron and salt, and I knew the odor well. Blood.

I'd been shot.

CHAPTER FIFTEEN

THE SHOT HEARD AROUND THE WORLD

Searing pain stabbed through my shoulder and radiated down my right arm. I managed to shrink back into the shadows to give myself a moment to calm down and assess the situation.

Rain poured down my face, blurring my vision, and hiding the shooter. It took a moment or two, but I managed to focus my thoughts on stopping the rain. It came to an immediate halt like someone had just turned off the shower.

I winced at the pain and felt lightheaded. I was losing blood fast, and I had to do something before I passed out and became completely vulnerable. Carefully, I reached out with my thoughts and searched the surrounding area and sensed someone about twenty feet ahead. There were no other humans or aliens in the vicinity, though I did detect some jungle animals.

"Might as well surrender while you can," the shooter broke the silence. His voice was rough and deep.

My hands were shaking, my knees were trembling, and I was getting light headed from the blood loss. I could call Ash, and he would incinerate my would-be captor. But that would mean that I would be forced to return to him before I finished everything I needed to accomplish.

The thought of that really ticked me off. I'd just recently realized I'd won my freedom, brought back my true love from my past alien life, and a whole lot of other things I'd accomplished as an alien scientist. A fire began growing in the pit of my stomach. I'd come all the way across the universe and waited centuries to gain my freedom. There was no way in hell I was about to give up now.

"You can go straight to hell," I spoke loud enough for him to hear me.

"Your choice," I heard him cock his rifle. A twig snapped, and I saw him emerge from behind a large tree. "I'm gettin' the same amount of money whether or not you put up a fight."

I realized I was going to have to kill him. There was no way around it. It would just be another thing I'd have to put off thinking about until another day.

The fire inside me grew up my throat and behind my eyes. I stepped out from behind the tree to face him head-on. Suddenly, my feet were no longer on the ground. I was suspended mid-air, the maelstrom inside of me glowing through my skin and shining through my eyes. My hair slipped loose from my ponytail and whipped around like tentacles of fire.

"Bow to me, you maggot!" I shouted in my native language. He had no idea what I'd said, and I didn't care.

"What are you, some kind of demon witch?" he aimed his rifle at me and started to pull the trigger.

But I was quicker. "I'm your worst nightmare!" my voice was loud and strange. It resonated out of my chest and off the tip of my tongue.

A lightning bolt spewed out of my mouth, blasting the shooter backwards and knocking the gun out of his hands. I leapt forward and released fire from my hands, incinerating him to a pile of ashes.

"How dare you shoot me," I spoke to the pile of ashes as my feet touched back down to the ground. "I've never done anything to you." I picked up the rifle and staggered. I was growing weaker and weaker and needed to get back to the cave to rest and rejuvenate.

Again my feet lifted off the ground, and I tumbled back across the sky until I landed face-first in the river in front of the cave where the horse was awaiting my return. I was extremely weak and needed to do something to stop the bleeding. It took every ounce of energy to drag myself out of the water and into the shelter. Stumbling a few times, I finally made it inside.

The coals in the fire were still burning hot when I entered the cave. I placed the shotgun near the saddle and pulled my bloody shirt off. Wincing as I craned my neck to look at the back of my shoulder, I realized that the bullet hadn't gone all the way through. It was likely lodged in my shoulder, and I was sure I could feel it.

I was going to have to dig it out with my own fingers.

Before I did anything, I said the Lord's Prayer and then wished Everett was there to help me. He'd surely know how to remove the bullet. No doubt he'd learned all sorts of things like that in The Resistance. I would have called him on my cell phone, but it was in my back pack. And I knew I was being too much of a sissy to do myself or anyone else any good.

So, I took a deep breath and forced my finger deep into the bullet wound. Without looking away, I screamed through gritted teeth, fighting to stay conscious. The horse whinnied and stamped her hooves. Tears and sweat rolled down my face and blood poured out of the bullet wound in gushes.

Still, I probed the wound until I found the bullet embedded deep in my flesh creating a sickening contrast of metal and slippery, wet flesh. I managed to edge the tip of my finger behind it. After several painful attempts, I worked it out, casting the lump of metal into the fire and cursing it.

Then I quickly grabbed a rock from the edge of the fire. Half of it glowed red like burning coals. Without thinking it over or even giving myself a chance to chicken out, I slammed the molten rock against the open bullet wound, cauterizing it and stopping the blood flow.

I screamed and said every cuss word I'd ever heard in one long stream of profanities. When I was sure the wound was melted closed, I tossed the rock out into the river. The smell of scorching flesh sickened me, and I stumbled outside and vomited.

The rains came again as I stumbled back into the cave and passed out.

Lightning pounded the earth somewhere outside the cave and startled me awake. I groaned and winced at the pain, but it wasn't as bad as it had been when I'd blacked out. *How long ago had that been?* I had no idea.

It was dark when I'd returned to the cave with the gunshot wound. Then, I'd had a vague recollection of waking up to daylight streaming in through the vines at the opening to the cave. Now it was pitch black outside, and an angry storm was raging.

Ash must be looking for me, I blinked my eyes and realized how thirsty I was. Inch by inch, I managed to lift myself into a sitting position. The fire had long since died out, but there were streams of energy flowing in lines through the sand on the floor of the cavern.

I glanced down at my fingers on my left hand. Streaks of electrical currents flowed through them in lines of glowing light, forming a golden butterfly where Everett's ring had melted off my finger. The streaks of light continued their course, stopping at the band around my arm and flowing around the braided loop. It was harnessing the energy and speeding up the healing process. A slight smile crossed my dry, cracked lips. *My science was brilliant,* I had to admit.

But I was still weak and needed to rest a little while longer. Not only that, but I needed to lay low. The storm outside wasn't my doing, and neither was it Mother Nature's. I was sure it was Ash's. He must have sensed that I'd been injured at the hands of a human. The justice I'd dealt the man was mild compared to what Ash would've done. Still, I knew the jungles wouldn't be safe tonight for any human.

The horse whinnied, and I realized she needed tending. It took every ounce of energy I had to take her to the river to get a drink and then gather a couple of bunches of grass for her. It was storming even worse, and the jungle canopy creaked and moaned under the twisting, angry winds.

I tossed my bloody shirt into the edge of the stream and weighed it with a rock, hoping the rushing current would wash the blood away. I didn't have any other clothes to wear and didn't know when I'd manage to find some.

Ringing wet and shivering, I lit the fire once more, using my last bit of energy on a flaming globe. Then I passed out again, but not before one last worry about the Royal Guard. They'd surely have been awake for a while now and wondering when I'd return to greet them.

CHAPTER SIXTEEN

THE ROYAL GUARD

"My lady," Xi spoke in our native language. He bowed his head, then raised it again to face the tiny camera on the control panel. "We expected your return nights ago," worry furrowed his brow, accentuating the tattoo across his forehead.

"I have sent out scouts to patrol the nearby terrain and bring back reconnaissance." Three Royal Guard members stepped behind him – two males, Mal and Jex, and a female, Rake, who stood the same height as her male counterparts.

"This is a strange world we've awoken to," Xi shook his head, incredulity crossing his features. "Rake found this," he held my backpack in front of the camera. "She found items inside that led me to believe this belongs to you." He held up the scrapbook with my picture on the front.

I'd gotten almost all of my strength back, thanks to the offerings left at the cave by the jungle people. It had turned out to be a good thing that I'd randomly stolen the horse. Riding her to the Royal Guard's vessel certainly made things easier. However, my knees were still a bit weak, and they buckled a few times as I watched Xi's log entry.

"My lady, I do not know what has happened to keep you from returning to us, but you awoke us and left a message stating we are in enemy territory. I can only assume that you have fallen into the hands of whatever enemy you have discovered."

Oh, no! I gasped and covered my mouth with my hand. *What have I done?*

"We are fully-armed," Xi straightened his broad muscular shoulders. The tattoo around his neck was the mark of his rank. "We will find you and destroy whoever or whatever has taken you."

Uh, oh. I knew what that meant. They would annihilate everyone and everything in search of me.

"Guard!" Xi called, still looking into the camera. If I'd have been there, he would have been looking me in the eyes as a show of respect. "Who do you serve?"

"The Queen!" the rest of the Royal Guard shouted in unison. "Long live the Queen!"

Their voices resonated in the closed space of the pod vessel. It must have been deafening to have been present when they'd shouted those words. I recalled parades back on my alien home planet when the Royal Guard would present themselves before the king in the same manner.

They'd made a more than impressive display. Their uniforms were made especially for ease of movement. Their weapons were unlike any other. They moved as one, trained as one, lived as one organism with nothing but the welfare of the ruler in mind.

"My lady," Xi stepped closer to the camera standing in the same place where I now stood "if you are able to return and retrieve this message, please seal yourself within this vessel." He turned and motioned toward a panel door behind him. "We have all saved part of our rations and stored them here for your use."

They've gone hungry, so I'd have something to eat, I frowned.

"You will also find medical supplies and medicines for your use," he turned back to the camera. "One of us will return periodically to see if you are here."

The screen went black, and I thought about all that could possibly happen now that the Royal Guard had been loosed. It didn't matter whether or not they encountered Ash. He had no authority over them. Besides, Xi would be so angry that Ash had not protected me that he may kill him.

I sank back onto a small bench near the supply panel. The weight of the situation was bearing down too heavily on me at the moment, and I needed some food. I bumped the door with my elbow and it swung open. Stowed neatly inside were ancient dried foods the Guard had placed in the vessel before they'd entered stasis. I tore one of the packages open with my teeth and bit into a stick of dried meat. Surprisingly, it was tasty despite its age.

The flavor of the meat brought back a rush of alien memories of a picnic on the beach under the scarlet sky. The ocean was blue and glowed with fluorescent minerals, and its waves lapped the shimmering sand on the beach and scented the air with spice. It was a distant memory of Ky roasting a wild bird over an open fire for our dinner. He'd placed a flower behind my ear and kissed me for the first time.

Even the distant memory of that kiss left me breathless. The love I'd had for him was deeper than the ocean. I felt a sharp pang of sadness in my chest. I'd been kissed in this life just like that on the night of the Rodeo Gala when Everett and I were on the trampoline swing. My heart skipped a beat, and I snapped into the present.

I finished off the meat stick and ate a package of very old fruit. I could taste the sun from my alien home planet in its tangy flesh. Things were so mixed up and discombobulated. I was two people in one. A human-alien hybrid. A weirdo.

The medicines were sealed in a black package. I found a syringe labeled "antibiotic" and jabbed it into my leg, wincing as the serum entered my bloodstream. It burned and tingled, but I knew it would work. Then I retrieved the syringe labeled "accelerator." It would boost my healing rate. I jabbed it into my other thigh and cried out. The serum was much more painful, like an ice pick stabbing into my leg.

However, in a matter of minutes I was feeling so much better that I was sure I could conquer the world or, at least, the jungle. I stuffed the pockets of my cargo shorts with more of the rations and searched for a clean shirt among the uniforms.

The smallest of the Royal Guard was a female named Max. Her shirt nearly swallowed me whole, but I made a knot at the back and cut its sleeves off with my Swiss Army knife. Then I looped the strips of fabric from the sleeves through the neck and arm holes, pulling up the slack so the shoulders of the shirt didn't hang down to the middle of my forearms.

"Thank you, Mrs. Stanley," I said under my breath. My high school homemaking teacher had taught me how to sew. She would've been proud of my creation. It didn't look too bad even if I said so myself.

I was ready to head back into the jungles to see if I could meet up with Xi. We'd be able to locate Mom in no time at all if I could find him. The best I could do at the moment was leave him another message.

"I was detained and unable to return until now," I spoke into the camera on the control panel. "I've taken one of Max's uniform shirts. Mine was damaged and covered in dried blood," I probably shouldn't have said that last part, but I didn't know how to rewind and erase it, so I plowed forward. "I've also taken one of Max's raincoats," I held it up briefly. It was more like a poncho with a hood and was made of a material with the ability to match its surroundings, offering the perfect camouflage.

Ky had designed the material that the Guard's camouflaged uniforms were made of. He'd managed to clone the camouflaging elements of Guard's skin and embedded it into fabrics and other materials so that when the Royal Guard needed to camouflage themselves, they could do it head-to-toe.

"There is a picture in the photo album found by Rake. It is labeled 'Mom.' I need you to help me find her before she comes to harm. She was taken, and I haven't been able to locate her." I refused to let any tears well up behind my eyes.

"Find her and protect her even if it means bringing her back here and sealing her in." It was a direct order. "Thank you for the food and the medicines," I softened my tone. "I look forward to standing before you and greeting you all in person."

Then I created an encrypted message meant only for Xi, my loyal body guard. "That day ... you remember ... I was successful in capturing Ky's essence, and I found a way for him to be a hybrid as I am now. He is alive, Xi! I need to find him, and I need your help. You will know him ... I know you will." This time I couldn't stop the tears from flowing down my face. They were Lore's tears, and if I were honest, I'd admit they were mine, too. I smiled and pressed the button on the control panel ending the recording.

Sealing the airlock behind me, I tugged the vines over the door of the pod vessel and retrieved my horse. I'd hidden her in a thick grove of underbrush and was glad she was there when I came back to get her. I simply wasn't up to running through the jungle.

She bumped me on my shoulder as if she was as glad to see me as I was her. I climbed into her saddle and nudged her forward.

"We need to find Xi, girl," I patted her shoulder. "And I need to give you a name."

She neighed in return as if she agreed.

"How about Lightning?" I asked, thinking it was the perfect name for a horse as fast as her.

Lightning nodded her head, and I promised to tell her about Daisy one day.

"Let's go find Xi," I said, feeling a mixture of anxiety and excitement. "It's time to tie up all these loose ends."

CHAPTER SEVENTEEN

XI

The rains came again. It wasn't my doing; it was Mother Nature's. Lightning made her way along a path through the jungle as I bowed my head against the onslaught of the downpour. Rivulets poured down my legs, but at least the top part of me was dry thanks to Max's poncho.

I thought about a lot of things as Lightning and I slowly made our way through the jungle. My human memories took me back to a night when we'd all waited in line at the Grand Theater to see the midnight premiere of one of the Harry Potter movies.

Everett had managed to get a pair of Harry Potter glasses and had drawn a scar on his forehead. We'd had so much fun that night, even though we'd stood in line for hours. He would've thought the poncho I was wearing was like an invisibility cloak.

And it was. If anyone were to see me riding Lightning through the jungle, they would've only seen my legs from the knees down and been totally freaked out. I giggled a bit at that thought.

Evening was setting in, and I had no idea where we'd rest our heads for the night. My cocoon tent was inside my backpack. I wouldn't have climbed a tree and left the horse alone in the jungle anyway. Somehow, some way, we'd find a place to rest.

A streak of lightning flashed across the darkening sky, and I saw a flurry of movement and some lights ahead. The horse must have seen it at the same time, because she'd come to a halt. I steered her into the shadows and peered between the tree trunks.

It was weird to see some sort of cantina out in the middle of the jungle. But maybe we were near a small village of some sort. A couple of other horses were tied outside the place, and a muddy road crossed in front of the shabby building.

A group of men tromped out of the jungle and onto the path a good ways ahead of us. Lightning's ears perked up as if she recognized them. And, I had to admit that there was something familiar about them, even though they were wearing rain gear.

They entered the raggedy old cantina, and I felt like I needed to follow them in. I slipped out of the saddle and stretched. I'd regained my strength, thanks to the medicines, but I was stiff from being in the saddle for so long.

I led Lightning into a grove of trees and vines so thick that even the rain couldn't make its way in. Patting her on the shoulder, I assured her I'd return for her and hoped she's stay quiet and safe.

Then I walked into the dim light cast by the battered lanterns hanging at intervals around the old cantina. Rain poured off the tin roof, and there was no paint on the wooden planks along its sides. But there were signs of various shapes and sizes nailed all over the front of the place, and I couldn't read any of them. Although, I could make out that most of them pertained to beer and alcohol.

Maybe it'll at least be dry inside, I thought as I ran my thumb across the sensor inside my poncho, shutting off the camouflage mode. It shimmered to dark grey, which shouldn't stand out too much in a place like this.

I searched my zipper pocket on my shorts and was surprised to find some money still there. We'd exchanged US money for Brazilian currency before we'd left Texas. I had no idea how much things cost in Brazil, but I was willing to wash dishes if I couldn't afford a cup of something warm to drink.

The place was more inviting than I'd imagined. I quietly slipped through the door and made my way to a back corner table. I sat down on the old wooden chair in the darkened corner and almost giggled out loud at the thought that I looked like Strider in the pub in the *Lord of the Rings* movie, minus the pipe.

A short, dark-haired waitress with the looks of the jungle people asked me what I wanted to order ... I think. I wasn't quite sure, because she wasn't speaking English. So, I pointed to a cup of coffee on the menu, which was glued to the top of the table. She nodded and left, and I was glad she didn't ask any more questions.

There was a jukebox just past the end of the bar, and to my left was a table surrounded by the men who I'd followed into the place. They were huddled around the table, speaking in low tones. I couldn't help but notice they were wearing military fatigues. After a little while, another man entered the bar and joined them. He had a massive bruise and cut on the side of his head and he had a black eye.

Those are the men I stole the horse from! I ducked back into the shadows and stifled a giggle at the thought of that rock hitting that man on the head. He'd wanted to kill my Royal Guard while they slept in stasis. Now he'd never get the chance. They'd rip him to shreds.

"Douglas!" one of the men slapped him on the back and pulled a chair out for him. He sort of winced like he was afraid the man would slap him again. There was something very cowardly about him.

"Living and breathing," he turned the chair around and straddled it.

They weren't in The Resistance, that much was sure. They just weren't sophisticated enough for that. But they looked a lot like some mercenaries I'd seen on a documentary once, and I was sure I'd hit the nail on the head.

"What brings you out into the storm tonight?" a man with a shaven head asked. He looked more calculating than the others he was with, and an air of untrustworthiness oozed off him.

"Well, Gordo, we've managed to catch one of 'em," Douglas lowered his voice.

"How?" Gordo leaned closer.

"The boss man provided us with some new high-tech electronics," a creepy smile crossed Douglas's face. "We caught him in a high-voltage web. He's a scary looking mother-fu …"

"Where is he now?" Gordo interrupted.

"Back at the main camp," Douglas motioned for the waitress. He pointed at the guy's drink next to him, and she nodded. "We'll be 'interrogating' him later tonight," he made quotation marks with his fingers when he said *interrogating* and chuckled, exposing some nasty teeth.

Finally, the waitress brought my coffee. It was much better than I'd imagined it would be. She smiled at me and placed a pastry coated with colored sugar on the table next to my coffee.

I smiled and held the wad of money out to her, unsure of how to make change with it. But she refused to take it. She was giving me an offering. I smiled and nodded to her, and she returned to waiting on the other tables.

The sugar coating on the pastry crunched against my teeth and filled my mouth with its sweetness. My mind suddenly rushed back to when I'd first tasted sugar in my former alien life. Ash had introduced me to it. He'd been scouting with some of his soldiers and came back with some from the sugar cane fields.

It was long before Nyx and Orion were born, and during a time when I'd grown complacent and thought I could grow to love Ash. He'd dipped his finger into the burlap sack of sugar and placed it on my tongue. Then he'd kissed me deeply and ardently as if he'd missed me while he was away. And perhaps he had. He'd picked me up and carried me to our chambers in the Queen's City far beneath the jungles.

I shook my head to clear my thoughts just as the door swung open. As if on their own, both my barriers raised themselves and locked into place. He swaggered in, completely comfortable in his own skin.

Ash. The alien warrior god. I hadn't seen him since he'd placed the armband on me and held me, engulfed in flames, as I fought to keep from burning alive.

He looked good.

He dropped a coin in the jukebox and pressed a button. Immediately Lana Del Rey began singing *Blue Jeans* as he casually walked over to sit on a barstool with his back against the bar. *Dayum. No matter what he did, he looked like sex on a stick.*

Ash leaned back, resting his elbows on the bar and his knees spread wide. Everything about him spoke domination. His white t-shirt was purposely ripped so that the tattoos across his chest showed. The silver chain and vial still hung from his neck – a sign of marriage on our home world.

His jeans fit oh-so-nice, and his boots were loosely-laced. His hair had grown quickly as mine had. It flowed down over his shoulders and framed his gorgeous face perfectly. Seriously, he could make a million as a male model. But he wasn't interested in such insignificant things.

I bit into the pastry once more and looked him over head-to-toe. I knew him better than anyone on this planet. He could be kind and protective, and he could be the god of destruction.

I'd never feared him, because my alien powers as a daughter of the royal house had always been more potent than his. Besides, he was never a threat to me. He was loyal to my father and intended on following through on the promise he'd made of protecting me. But others feared him with good reason.

He regarded the group of men at the table with an air of indifference, but I knew he was watching and listening. If he was doing reconnaissance, which I was sure he was, he'd have all the information he needed in the blink of an eye. The men had a map out now and were speaking in whispers. I couldn't hear them over the jukebox. Ash could, though.

The waitress approached him, and I was surprised that he could speak her language. He looked her over as if she was what he was there for. She leaned in to take his order, holding a menu close enough that she could rest her elbow on his shoulder while they discussed what he wanted.

I knew what he wanted though. An ancient flame lit inside of me. *Was it jealousy after all these centuries? Or was it a certain sense of betrayal?* I couldn't pinpoint it. *And why did it even matter anymore?* I sipped my coffee and reminded myself that I'd managed to win my freedom and revive Ky.

Charm rolled off him. He'd completely ensnared his prey. It was always too easy for him to get whatever girl he'd wanted ... all except for me. He could never quite have me, because my heart and soul had always belonged to another – my chosen Other. And that made him even more determined to own me. He wasn't thinking about me tonight, though.

He whispered something into the girl's ear, and she giggled and nodded.

"You'll do," he spoke in our alien language. She didn't understand, but she didn't seem to care. He tossed her over his shoulder and carried her out into the rain, her giggling all the while, and the bartender shouting behind them.

I looked down to see that I'd crushed the pastry in my fist, and it was smoking. I quickly patted out the embers and stuffed the mound of crumbs into my coffee cup.

The memory of him emerging from the jungles carrying twin babies, Orion and Phoenix, would never leave me. By the time he'd paired with the jungle woman and had children of his own with her, I'd discovered that he'd inadvertently murdered my royal babies.

It was an unforgivable betrayal.

A loud round of laughter from the men at the table snapped me out of my brooding over Ash and reminded me what I'd heard before. *They've caught one of my kind. I just know it.* As Queen, I would never let them harm one of my people.

"Let's go see it then," Gordo said, standing up and revealing a grotesque beer belly. The man was so gross, in fact, that I was quite sure that only a mother could love such a monstrosity. I shivered to calm down my gag reflex.

"I've never seen one like this one," the coward named Douglas turned pale.

"We thought you'd done the catching," one of the other guys taunted him.

"I never said that! I said we caught it," Douglas almost whined like a scared little boy.

These guys look like mercenaries, but they sure don't act the part, I snarled in disgust.

The coward folded up the map and tucked it into his pocket despite Gordo trying to reach for it. I counted to fifteen after they exited the cantina before I followed them out. The horses out in front of the bar had, indeed, belonged to them.

They turned their poor horses out onto the muddy road that crossed in front of the old cantina. Gordo's horse strained under his enormous weight, and I thought about stealing all the horses and setting them free.

I sprinted as quickly as I could into the shadows of the jungle to get Lightning. She'd managed to stay quiet and dry, but she was very pleased to see me. The time it took to retrieve her and get back out onto the muddy road provided a safe distance between the mercenaries and me.

I ran my thumb over the sensor inside my poncho, turning on the camouflage mode. *Thank you, Max,* I thought as the image of the jungle wrapped around me, making me invisible.

After a while of riding on the mud road, the mercenaries turned off into a freshly-made path into the thick brambles of the jungle. They had to dismount in order to lead their horses through. I waited a while and then slid out of Lightning's saddle and led her into the dark path.

Ahead, the beams of the mercenaries' flashlights sliced through the dark jungle night. A thick fog was rolling off the warm forest floor and thickening the air with its mist. Good, I thought, glad for the extra cover. *I may need it if I rescue one of my people.* Hmmm... one of my people, I cocked my head to the side. *I could say that about both humans and alien-kind alike.*

Gordo's boisterous laughter yanked me out of my reverie. He was telling some sort of story about how much smarter he was than anyone he'd ever met. Douglas' sniveling chuckle echoed down the path toward me in response.

I threw up a little in my mouth.

These guys were so gross that I decided no matter who their captive was, I was going to save the poor soul from them. That would mean I'd need a surprise attack. I decided to stow Lightning in the safety of the jungle once more so she wouldn't fall back into the hands of the mercenaries. Once she was safely deposited among a thick tangle of vines and brush, I risked being discovered by the Hunters by leaping up, up, up into the canopy overhead, hoping their alien-detecting gadgets weren't on.

From there, I traveled through the trees quite easily, despite the patches of thick fog that drifted among the tree limbs. There were several bright lights ahead, like camping lanterns strung among the trees. I could tell by the change in their tone, the mercenaries had made it to where the captive was.

I hurried, leaping from slick limb to mossy bough, from tangled vine to narrow branch. I slipped several times, but caught myself. The jungle was silent tonight. Something bad was about to happen.

The mercenaries had a large camp with seven tents in a circle around a campfire. Some sort of meat was roasting over the fire, and a younger man with slanted eyes, olive skin, and short black hair knelt, turning the meat over and over.

"Lee!" Gordo called, pointing at the roasting meat. "When's that going to be ready?"

"Soon, boss," Lee answered. When Gordo turned away, Lee's contempt showed in a grimace across his round face. I figured he'd just thrown up in his mouth a little, too.

"Where is it?" one of the other mercenaries asked.

"Are you sure you're up to this, boys?" Douglas looked a little pale. Maybe it was him who wasn't ready.

"Let's see it," Gordo's voice boomed.

"Lee!" Douglas shouted and motioned toward a tarp that looked like it had been tossed over a pole, creating a teepee effect. "You do the honors." The coward couldn't even bring himself to do it. "Step back, guys. The bastard is dangerous," he murmured, moving back behind the rest of the men who crowded around for the freak show.

Lee grabbed the tarp and jerked it hard, in a very circus-like display, revealing a pole and nothing else.

"Where is it?" one of the men asked, looking around as if whatever it was had escaped.

Lee grabbed a hot poker from the fire and jabbed it at the pole. Immediately, a body materialized from nowhere. Not just anybody, either. Xi, my loyal bodyguard, had been in full camouflage.

There was some sort of cuff around his neck, binding him to the pole, and his hands were bound behind his back. He was on his knees, and his ankles appeared to be bound together, as well.

My heart was pounding like crazy against my ribs, and my lungs struggled to keep up. There was no way on this earth I would allow any harm to come to the one who'd pledged his life to protect me. Xi had been with me from my alien birth. He'd carried me on his shoulders and taught me how to fight, to defend myself.

"Can it speak?" Gordo asked. "Perhaps I can communicate with it. I've studied many languages."

I rolled my eyes so hard that I nearly fell from my perch. *Good luck communicating with him, Gordo-the-Magnificent.* I felt the snarl of disgust cross my face, and I wanted to jump down right then and there and flay them all alive.

Lee jabbed Xi again with the hot poker and ordered him to speak, as if Xi could understand a word of English. A dangerous expression darkened Xi's face as another man shouted that they'd captured a second one, and it was a female. I looked around wildly, my eyes scanning the campsite.

"Bring her out, boys," the man motioned toward the tent. Four men exited the tent, all of them gripping various restraints. One had a pole with a metal cable looped around her neck like dog-catchers use. The others were holding onto restraints attached to her wrists and ankles.

Even though she was the smallest of the Royal Guard, Max stood head and shoulders above all the human men in the camp. She really was beautiful, her shimmery skin catching and deflecting the light from the fire. Her head was clean shaven, and my family's crest was tattooed on the top of her scalp.

Max's wide, slanted eyes were wary. She scanned the mercenaries' faces as she was led past them to stand next to where Xi knelt. One of her captors struck her in the back of her knees, and she fell to a kneeling position.

I was puzzled that these two members of the Royal Guard, above all the others, would have been captured by such bumbling fools. And I was angry. A raging fire had grown inside of me while I'd watched them display my very own soldiers like monkeys in a cage.

Lowering both my barriers, I focused on Xi and spoke in my thoughts, "Xi, I am here."

Judging by the faintest change in his facial expression, he'd heard me. He slowly began scanning the trees for me, moving only his eyes.

"Up here," I spoke again, aiming only for his thoughts. "To your right. Look up."

I slipped the hood of my poncho back ever so slightly so that my face would be visible. It would freak out any of the mercenaries if they saw me, because all they would see would be a face floating in the trees.

Xi's eyes met mine, and he blinked in relief. He'd finally laid eyes on his Queen, and I was alive.

"I'm going to set everything on fire. You take Max and run," I spoke into his thoughts.

Without taking his eyes off mine, he shook his head no. It was an infinitesimal motion, and no one else would have noticed. Except for Max, whose eyes found mine just before I slipped the hood back over my face.

"No, my lady," Xi answered, his voice ringing in my thoughts. "This is a trap. As soon as they detect you, this whole area will be enclosed in an electromagnetic cage. You will be ensnared."

"Max," I spoke into her thoughts. "I will find a way to free you both."

"You mustn't, my lady ..." but her words were interrupted by the man who'd captured her.

"Now that we've got them, we'll be able to catch our prey and get a big reward!" the man gloated. "But I'll have a little fun with the bitch before I turn her over, if you know what I mean!" his laughter riled up the other men.

"So, who's this 'prey' you're trying to catch?" Gordo asked, still laughing along with the rest of the men.

"Supposedly some type of alien queen," the man scratched his beard and straightened his shoulders. "Look at me, fellas! I'll be bedding a queen!" He burst out laughing again, revealing a missing tooth behind his scraggly beard. "I might share, but it'll cost ya!"

I felt sick. Very sick deep in my gut. The thought of that man or any of the others touching me made me want to vomit.

Xi was angry, too. His jaw was set, his eyes straight forward, his muscles tense. Max was alert, as always, and sensed the change in her leader. They'd been so in-tune with my thoughts that somehow I'd translated the conversation into our alien language.

"What else are women good for?" Douglas interjected as he elbowed Gordo. "It's not like they've got any other use."

"I'll pay good money for a piece of that," Gordo-the-grotesque boomed, his voice dominating everyone else's. "Let me show you my hip action."

At that, both Xi and Max broke free of their restraints, the metal melting in their hands like butter. Lee dropped the poker and ran into the woods. Some of the other men scattered. But the others weren't fast enough.

Yes, my Royal Guard is deadly.

Xi was enormous compared to the humans. Several tried to restrain him again. But he ripped them in two, blood gushing everywhere, spewing across his face and body, making him appear even more terrifying than he already was.

I covered my mouth with my hand, and quivered. Not even on my alien planet had I ever seen them in real battle situations. I'd only ever seen the Royal Guard practice war games.

Max was, first and foremost, an expert at disembowelment. She opened up the stomach wall of her captor, revealing his entrails to him before lifting him off the ground by the neck and dropping him into the fire. He did not die immediately; he scrambled out of the fire, trying to stuff his bowels back into his torso and moaning for help. I gripped the tree trunk as tight as possible to steady myself to keep from fainting and plunging into the fray.

"You want to do what to my queen?" Xi's voice rang above the screams of horror. Of course, Gordo-the-Magnificent couldn't understand a word Xi said. He merely screamed in horror as Xi gripped Gordo's throat with his massive hand.

At the same time, I heard a woman's scream. It rang out loud and terrified. But it wasn't a woman. It was Douglas. Max had torn one of his arms off at the elbow and had used his blood as war paint across her face.

"No, please! I'll do *anything!*" he begged, sobbing and screaming. Max was enjoying this. He'd said there was no other use for women, but she would be the one to show him what women could really do.

A wicked, bloody smile crossed her face, and with a quick flick of her wrist, she was holding Douglas's bloody nose in her hand. He gripped his face, screaming, and choking on his own blood.

Piece by piece, she dismantled him until he was nothing but a bloody torso and head on two legs, begging for mercy. She opened up the wall of his gut with an enormous gash, and forced him to watch as she removed his organs and entrails one at a time.

Xi had held Gordo still by his throat, allowing only enough breath to keep him conscious and alive. Gordo had watched everything that Max had done to the coward. And now it was his turn. He was shaking so hard it was visible all the way up where I was in the tree canopy. Then, Gordo wet his pants, and disgust crossed Xi's face.

"Tell me now," Xi lifted Gordo off the ground by his neck. "What was it you were going to do to my queen?"

Gordo choked and sputtered. Tears rolled down his face. He gripped Xi's arm to keep from choking to death. "I. Don't. Understand," he whined.

Xi body-slammed him on the ground, and for a moment, I was expecting to see the People's Elbow the way The Rock had done in so many wrestling matches I'd watched with Andrew and Aaron. Max crouched nearby, her head cocked to the side, blood painted across her face, and smiling as Xi stepped on one of Gordo's legs, crunching the bones.

Everything that was in my stomach came up and showered down, pouring across Gordo's neck and chest.

"Go back to the pod vessel, my lady," Xi spoke aloud in our alien language, looking up at me. "You should not see such things."

I didn't answer. I just turned and fled, leaping through the tree canopy.

"Now, I will eat your heart, and you will watch," Xi's voice was less clear now that I'd put some distance between us.

Gordo's screams filled the jungle when I reached Lightning. Then there was silence. I mounted her and dug my heels into her ribs, steering her out into the narrow jungle path.

"Get us outta here, girl! Anywhere but here!" I whispered and tucked myself low in the saddle to avoid the vines and branches overhead.

Lightning was as fast as her name. When we got to the muddy road, we took a right, and the horse proved she was scared, too. I was shaking to my bones. *No, don't think 'bones,'* I thought, and my stomach lurched.

The night was black as pitch, and my human side had taken over. Terror reigned inside my chest and tears streamed down my face. What have I done? I bit my lip and whimpered. *This is too big for one person to handle.*

Mom's voice spoke in my heart, *There's safety in numbers.* She'd always told us that as we were heading out to football games or other activities.

"Mom," I sobbed, feeling lost and scared in the darkness. I couldn't get my night vision to work, because my human side was in override.

I longed to be held and comforted. I needed to feel strong arms around me. "Everett, I need you!" I shouted into the darkness. "I'm lost, and I need you!"

CHAPTER EIGHTEEN

LOST

It's never a good idea to give yourself away by screaming at the top of your lungs into the night. I should have known not to do it. Quite frankly, I was traumatized by what I'd just seen. In my mind, I'd thought I'd like to flay the mercenaries alive for capturing Xi and Max.

Reality is always a different story.

The terror that gripped me, keeping me from focusing my night vision, and making me so scared I couldn't set orbs of fire to light the way, also kept me from seeing the cable that was stretched across the muddy road.

It caught me across the chest, and Lightning kept running. The air was knocked out of my lungs, and I heard and felt a snap in my side as I was jerked backwards out of the saddle. I landed face-down in the mud, unable to catch my breath.

There was an immediate stab in my side, and I was sure the cable had broken a rib. My knees shook as I forced myself to stand, wincing against the pain in my side. *Could this night get any worse?* The thought screamed out in my brain.

I spit, clearing the mud from my mouth. My breath was returning by degrees, but I still wasn't able to focus my night vision. *Where is Lightning?* I scanned the darkness, hoping she'd come back for me.

Rain pelted down in sheets, clouding my vision even further. I backed into the edge of the jungle and searched for any sign of the horse. But I couldn't even see a few inches in front of my face.

"Are you sure you heard something?" a familiar voice startled me, causing me to hold my breath and kneel onto the wet jungle floor.

I closed my eyes and recalled how Everett had taught me to focus my night vision. We were in one of the rooms in the Queen's City the night I'd dream-traveled to the jungle … the night I'd promised myself to Ash in exchange for Everett's life.

"Thought I did," another man answered.

My eyes opened, and I could finally see. Two men in military fatigues stood in the middle of the road. But these two men were not bumbling fools like the ones who'd just been dismantled and partially devoured by Xi and Max. These two men were all spit and shine, and I squinted a bit to make out their facial features through the heavy downpour.

Water flowed down the muddy roadway and washed away Lightning's hoof prints. I thanked my lucky stars and hoped I'd find the horse soon. If I didn't, I'd proceed on as planned and try to find Mom.

Surely, there was still enough accelerator in my bloodstream to help my broken rib heal quickly. I was simply too disoriented to find my way back to the pod vessel, and I had no idea where Max and Xi had gone.

For all I knew, they were still devouring the remains of the Gordo and Douglas. I cringed and put that thought out of my mind. The last thing I needed to do with a broken rib was vomit.

"Probably a jaguar or something," the familiar-sounding man said. He seemed to be in charge. "Let's get to camp and see what the men have caught. Douglas seemed to think it was an alien."

"That man's an idiot," the other guy said. "And a coward. Makes my skin crawl." He turned his flashlight toward the path back to the camp, and for a split second the beam of light flashed across Mr. Familiar's face.

It's Luke! I gasped, wincing at the pain in my side.

The very same man who'd pretended to be an architect and had dated Mom before she'd come to her senses. It was his fault that the new Sprinkles was now a crater in the ground. And now it all made sense.

I'd known for a while that he'd been hunting me. I'd thought he was in The Resistance, but now I realized that he was somehow linked to the mercenaries. *Was he one of them, too? Or was he the one paying them? And why?*

"Let's get back to camp and make sure the key is safe and sound," Luke turned back toward the path into the jungle.

"You've got a point. We need to get rid of some of those guys, Luke. Some of 'em are pervs," the other guy said.

Did he say he had "the key"? That's what we'd heard Nyx shout the night Ash had placed the silver band around my arm. He'd said they'd taken the key. And when we'd gotten to Sprinkles, Mr. Forster was lying prone on the ground, and Mom was gone.

The weight of the realization fell onto my shoulders. *Mom is the key! I remember now! She was the one we'd chosen specifically for our use of making me a hybrid.* I covered my mouth with my muddy hand. We'd cultivated her with our experiments on my own grandmother years earlier. Then, when she was ready, we'd even marked her with the symbol of a key in case the first experiment hadn't worked. Orion and Ash had promised to find her and try the experiment again if something had gone wrong.

But it hadn't. Mom and Dad had Andrew and Aaron and then they'd had Brooke and me. I'd lost my human twin not long after birth, and Aaron had been murdered with Dad.

How much trauma had my plans caused? I frowned.

Slowly, I raised myself to my feet, hugging my side with my arm and stepping out into the muddy road to follow the men back to the bloody camp of horror and see if Mom was still there. But a soft stamping of hooves to my left caught my attention.

I turned and saw Lightning inching from the dark jungle forest on the other side of the road. She shook her head and snorted as if to warn me away from going back to the mercenaries' camp.

Taking her reins in hand, I led her in the opposite direction. She was right. It wasn't safe to go back to that camp tonight. I'd left a message for Xi at the pod vessel and asked him to help me find Mom. Maybe that was the reason he was at the camp to begin with. And Max, being the alien feminist that she is, would not leave a female behind. *Would she?* I wondered ... hoping, praying I was right.

After I'd put some distance between the camp and me, I realized I was feeling weak and shaky. The armband began burning under my skin, and I knew I needed to pause for a while and draw some energy from the earth.

A small opening in the jungle formed an alcove the perfect size for Lightning and me and kept the rain off of us while I knelt, digging my fingers into the loamy earth and relishing the healing energy that flowed into my veins.

Lines of golden light traveled through the rich, wet soil and crossed over into my veins, and up to circle the braided loop beneath the skin on my upper arm. My strength quickly returned, and I stifled a yelp when my broken rib snapped itself back into place. I'd been right – there was still a lot of the accelerator in my bloodstream.

Before long, I was standing next to Lightning with only a slight bruise over my ribcage. But I was too wary to ride her on the road. If there was one cable stretched across the road, there'd likely be more.

"Let's keep off the road, girl," I whispered. "They've likely found all that … gore … and I don't want to be around when they call for help."

Lightning snorted in agreement.

We traveled through dense undergrowth until we reached an enormous break in the trees where clearing had been done. I'd remembered reading about the devastation of the rainforests in school, and I knew Everett would be enraged at the thought of all those squashed insects never to be studied. The alien side of me thought of Ky and how he, also, would have been angered over the loss of so many valuable specimens.

The clouds had finally cleared away, and a crescent moon shone down on the surrounding jungle. Everything around glimmered with an outline of silver, and I was engulfed in the clean scent of ozone left by the lightning storm. On the other side of the clearing, a large white structure punctured a hole in the shimmering canopy and stood like a beacon in the night.

I led the horse across the clearing, aware that we were exposing ourselves. But I was sleepy, and I knew she was too. "The shortest distance between point A and point B is a straight line," I assured Lightning. It was something I'd heard Dad repeat over and over when he was helping Andrew and Aaron with geometry.

Whispers of thoughts and dreams wound around the vines and trees of the jungle on either side of the clearing. The jungle people had heard murmurs of new alien gods among them that ate the hearts of men. *Soon,* they thought with deep dread, *the sacrifices would resume.*

My gasp echoed in the wide open space of the moonlit clearing. The jungle people thought we'd returned to bring back the old ways. It couldn't be further from the truth. Of course, Xi and the Royal Guard would terrorize the jungle until they found me. I frowned at that thought, thinking of the children of the jungle who played along the banks of the rivers. Then I turned my thoughts to the present. I'd have to think about that another day. My mind was too boggled with images of what I'd just witnessed back at that camp site.

The strange structure was much closer now, its white stones gleamed in the moonlight. I hoped it would provide some sort of shelter for Lightning and me. We needed to rest, and I needed to think. Besides, I hoped Everett had heard me calling for him and would track and find me.

Lightning was tired, too. I could feel the fatigue radiating through the horse's body. I pulled her to a stop and slid out of her saddle. We walked together through the vast clearing until we came to stop at the foot of the massive structure.

It was an ancient stone pyramid, made of gleaming white stones and wrapped in vines where the jungle had begun its work of reclaiming. This was not a structure I was familiar with in my past alien life. I had no recollection of it at all. It was one erected by humans. This was where many poor jungle people had lost their lives as sacrifices.

A cringe jolted through me, and Lightning stamped her hooves. I patted her neck and assured her we'd be safe there for the night. The structure was in the edge of the jungle, and there were plenty of shadows to hide behind if the need arose.

On the left side of the pyramid base, I discovered a deep indention in the stone that was the perfect size to house Lightning for the night. I was able to create a sort of make-shift stable using a few large limbs that had fallen onto the jungle floor.

Once I was sure she would be safe, I removed her saddle and brushed her down before barricading her in with the remaining limbs. Then, it was time to find my resting spot for the night.

I climbed the ancient, worn steps to the top of the pyramid where a stone pavilion had been built for the ruler to sit in while the sacrifices were presented to the gods. I felt nauseated at the thought of any ruler thinking that the murder of his own people was an appropriate offering.

There had been a time that Ash had decimated several places in the jungle for such acts. He'd found them vile and offensive, and I'd supported his attacks on those that murdered the innocent jungle people who'd been so generous to us with their offerings of food, textiles, and other things.

Ash had been cruel in some of the attacks. Several rulers and their families were taken to the tops of their stone pyramids where Ash had ordered his own military guard to sacrifice them to him. It had been a bloody end to bloody deeds. And it had instilled such terror in the hearts of the jungle people that they'd feared Ash would begin his own cycle of human sacrifices that I'd ordered him to stop.

After several heated arguments, he'd done so, but unwillingly.

I sat down at the top of the steps and leaned back to look at the stars. The night sky was alive with a meteor shower. Streaks of glitter sputtered out among the constellations overhead, and I thought about how many times in my past life I'd looked into the night sky.

In an instant, I felt her there with me. Lore, my former self. The one who'd set this whole story into motion just to reunite with a long-lost love.

Just? her voice rang in my thoughts as I leaned back on my elbows. *Would you not have done the same to be with your chosen Other?*

I thought of Everett cradling my head in his hand, holding me close, and kissing me for the first time while hundreds of twinkling fireflies surrounded us in the haunted forest. It seemed like it was centuries ago.

Yes. I answered, thinking in our native language. *I would.*

You did, Lore answered. *We are one and the same.*

I nodded, remembering the video I'd left for my human hybrid self.

Remember Ky ... how gentle he was? Remember the night he'd said he was going to ask for Father's permission for us to commit the pairing ceremony? In my mind's eye, Lore was leaning forward, looking into my eyes, imploring me to remember. Her wide, slanted eyes glistened in the moonlight.

Yes, I answered and glanced back up at the stars. *The night sky had looked much like this one.*

He'd placed the vial in my hand and wrapped the chain around my wrist, I imagined Lore leaning back on her elbows next to me.

I'd carried his essence in that vial for centuries, I responded, feeling the deepest, darkest pang of loneliness in my chest. It was the old feeling of dread that had once been my constant companion. *It was the only thing that kept me going.*

You will not forsake him? I imagined Lore taking my hand in hers. *You will choose him over any other?*

I will choose him over anyone, my bottom lip quivered. *I've already reconciled myself to the fact that I cannot have Everett.*

Lore smiled. At least she did in my mind's eye.

But I can't do this all alone. There's strength in numbers, the words wound through my consciousness.

You aren't alone, I imagined her squeezing my hand. *You've got the Royal Guard. You've got your human family. You've got your people, awaiting your return.*

That's true, I replied, watching another meteor skid across the night sky.

And Ky! I imagined Lore's eyes bright with hope.

I nodded, feeling her enthusiasm flow into my chest. Her memories of Ky filled my mind and heart until they were equal to my human memories of Everett. I didn't know how it was possible to love two men with an equal passion. That night at the top of the ancient pyramid, alone with my former alien self, it became a reality.

Lore burst into a million sparkles of light and whirled around me in ribbons of nebulous light. I gasped as the spirals of color and swirls of glittering bits of light crossed through my skin and pulsed through my veins.

I was no longer lost. I was Lore, and I knew what I needed to do.

All I needed now was the safety of numbers.

CHAPTER NINETEEN

SAFETY IN NUMBERS

Movement in the jungle clearing caught my attention. One lone darkened silhouette moved along the same path Lightning and I had traveled to reach the pyramid. Someone was coming. I couldn't make out who it was, but I'd had the distinct feeling whoever was coming was not a foe.

Just in case I was wrong, I quickly hid in the shadows of the stone pavilion and watched as the silhouette grew closer until the sound of footsteps on stone echoed up the side of the pyramid. I flattened myself against a crumpling column and powered up my hands.

And there he was, standing only feet away, his silhouette rimmed in silver moonlight. Even from my place in the shadows, I could make out the windswept swirls of tousled hair, his broad shoulders, and strong arms ... a handsome form of a man.

"Are you here?" his smooth voice sounded small in the darkness of the night.

I relaxed a little, cooled down my hands, and quietly inhaled a calming breath.

"I tracked you here. It's okay to come out. It's only me …" as he turned, the moonlight caught the side of his face, highlighting the handsome lines of his features. "You remember me now, don't you?" A hint of sadness tinted his words.

"I am here," I answered, stepping out of the shadows and into the moonlight.

A broad smile crossed Orion's handsome face. He held out his arms for me, and I allowed my adopted son to wrap me in his strong embrace. He twirled me around and set me back down.

"Mother," he stepped back and slightly bowed his head out of respect. "You finally remember me. The last time I saw you, you had no recollection of who either of us were."

"The last time I saw you …" I had to think for a moment. It felt like it had been centuries since I'd seen him. "You'd saved Everett's life." I took his hand in mine. "We'd thought you'd died that night."

"But now you remember the way of our people, right?" he smiled an uncertain smile. "As long as this remains unbroken, we will not die." He pointed to a raised tattoo that looped around his left bicep, much like mine and Everett's. Almost identical to Ash's. "You developed it before I was born."

"I created yours from one of my own pieces of royal jewelry." I placed my hand atop his tattoo, feeling the braided loop beneath his skin.

He smiled and said, "And you've recalled our language. It sounds much better on your tongue than English."

The crossover of languages was becoming increasingly unnoticeable to me. One moment, I'd be speaking or thinking in English, the next, my native language. I sighed.

"Well, I have two native languages now," I shrugged.

He nodded again, then asked, "Are you hungry?"

As if on cue, my stomach rumbled, and I smiled.

"I thought so. You've always had a certain look in your eyes when you're hungry," he said as he dropped his backpack onto the stone seat in the pavilion. "Stay here, and I'll go find us something to eat."

"I'm sure there'll be offerings soon … from the jungle people, I mean." I stammered. "They seem to show up with food whenever I need it."

"Of course they do," Orion smiled. "You're a goddess." He walked to the edge and turned to me once more, moonlight shimmering against the black curls and waves of his windswept hair. "I won't be long."

By the time I got to the edge of the pyramid platform, he was halfway down the long, narrow staircase. "Orion!" I called after him, my voice echoing down the steps behind him.

"Yes, mother?" he stopped and turned to look up at me.

"I'm not a goddess," I said, sounding slightly defeated and not quite sure that I believed what I was saying.

"Saying the opposite of a thing does not always make it so." He turned and disappeared into the shadows below.

Of course, I smirked and put my hands on my hips. He'd just turned my words around on me. *How many times had I repeated that to him as a child whenever he'd shouted "no!" in the midst of a tantrum?* I shook my head at the absurdity of eighteen-year-old me with my centuries-year-old son.

"They're coming," Orion said, finishing off the last piece of roasted meat. The campfire I'd built on top of the pyramid was beginning to wane. It was late, and a chill had moved into the night air.

"Who?" I tossed a bone over the edge of the pyramid platform.

"I'm not sure." Orion leaned back against his backpack and folded his hands behind his head. "But they're coming from different directions, and they aren't all friendly."

Chill bumps rolled up my legs and arms, and I wished I had my own backpack so I could change clothes. I leaned back against a crumpled stone pillar, glad it still radiated heat from the day before, and pulled Max's poncho around me.

"So, it comes down to it," I shuddered and hugged myself. Not out of fear, but out of sheer exhaustion ... both physical and mental. I'd known centuries ago that all of my plans would lead me to an all-out war. It seemed the clock was winding down, and the time was drawing close.

"Yes. It does," Orion answered, matter-of-factly.

"You sound like someone else I know." A small smile tugged at the corners of my lips.

"Everett ..." he couldn't hide the smile in his voice. "You were very fond of him last summer. It's why I cloned him instead of you. I knew you'd want me to protect him even if it meant risking your own safety." He paused a minute, then, "Father was angry."

"What did he do to you?" I asked, unsure if I really wanted to know.

"He banished me ... ordered me to stay under the soil and sleep where the one named David had buried me." Sadness tainted his voice, and it pierced my heart. Everett and I had visited the place he'd been buried beneath the cement slab in the forest. I'd thought it was a grave. However, Everett had insisted on burying the box near the cement slab and had ordered me not to return to retrieve it.

"Everett *knew* you weren't dead." The words came out sort of mumbled as if I were speaking only to myself.

"He knew a lot of things, Mother," Orion confessed, looking at me out of the corner of his eye.

"The notebook!" I gasped. I'd forgotten it over the course of the last months. I recalled the day I'd tried to get it out of Everett's hand, but he'd clutched it tight and had said he'd let me read it one day. "He put it all down in his notebook, didn't he?"

Orion merely chuckled and nodded.

"What does *that* mean?" I asked.

"Let's just say that he knows everything." He smiled and rested his head back on his hands again.

"Care to enlighten me?" I felt the instant urge to ground him for sassing me.

"I can't." he shook his head. "Everett swore me to silence."

I crossed my arms over my chest and wondered what all the secrecy was about between those two. There were suddenly so many questions I wanted to ask. *Was it Orion who'd applied the band to Everett's arm? If so, where had he gotten the band? Had he made it himself?*

"Are you cold, Mother?" Orion tossed another piece of wood onto the fire, sending glowing sparks into the night air.

"A little chilly." I scooted closer to the fire.

"I can remedy that," he said, while opening his backpack. After a few moments, he tossed me a woven blanket.

"Thank you," I wrapped it around me and rolled over onto my side away from the fire. "Orion?"

"Yes?" he yawned.

"Please don't call me Mother anymore." I winced a tiny bit, knowing those words would stab him in the heart.

"Why? It's what you are to me. The only mother I've ever known. The only mother I've ever loved," pain etched his voice.

"I know all those things," I answered, searching for words to explain. "And I love you, too, Son." I turned back over to face him. "But it would feel more natural to me if you would call me Blair or Lore, your choice... just take some time to think it over. Okay?"

He nodded, and I held out my hand for his. We stayed like that, hand-in-hand, until we fell asleep in the glow of the fire at the top of an ancient ceremonial temple, under a canopy of stars.

A commotion jolted me awake. Dizzy and disoriented, I leapt from my makeshift bed, tripped over the blanket, and stumbled toward the edge of the pyramid platform. I'd been in such a deep sleep, that my reactions were slow and clumsy. All I could think, as I lurched toward the edge was *this is really going to hurt!* Then a strong arm grasped me around the waist, pulled me away from the ledge, and steadied me before releasing me. I turned to thank Orion, but it wasn't him.

"My lady," Max bowed her tattooed head and retreated a few steps. "Forgive me. I had to touch you in order to keep you from falling."

It took a moment to catch my breath and get myself grounded. "No need to apologize," I said between hurried breaths. My heart pounded against my ribs, and my knees quivered from the adrenaline rush.

"Moth— I mean, Blair," Orion stepped carefully around Max. "Are you okay?" He touched my arm, and Max produced a long, silvery blade at his throat.

"Max! Lower your blade at once!" I ordered, anger ripping across my lips. This was Lore's voice, her presence as Queen.

She sheathed her blade and bowed her head again to apologize. "My lady, I beg your pardon once more. I wished only to protect you."

"This man is my ..." I glanced at Orion, his gaze trained on Max. I detected admiration and excitement in the glint of his aquamarine eyes. "Well, it doesn't matter who he is. You can trust him with my safety."

"Yes, my lady," Max raised her head once more, her eyes flickering from Orion's to mine. She was a beautiful and imposing image against the red glow of the coming dawn in the early morning sky. With her fitted uniform, her weapons strapped to various parts of her body for ease of movement, her swirls of tattoos beneath her shimmering skin, she was an image straight out of the movies.

"You've awoken the Royal Guard." Orion's voice was full of wonder, and quite honestly, admiration of Max's appearance. He turned to me, and a light filled his face that I hadn't seen in many years.

"Max, this is Orion," I nodded toward my gawking adopted son. "He can help my Royal Guard as a scout and many other things you'll find useful and informative. He has lived in these jungles for many years."

Her face lit up much like Orion's, and suddenly I felt like an interloper. There was a strong energy between them, and I felt a glint of happiness at the thought of Orion forming a friendship with Max. But I needed to know where the others were, so I had to interrupt.

"Where are Xi and the others?" I softened my voice.

"Xi wanted me to relay a message to you and only you, my lady," Max tore her gaze from Orion's. "A moment alone with you will suffice."

I motioned for her to come sit by the smoldering embers of the campfire then turned to Orion. "My horse will be needing water and fresh grass. Would you please tend to her?"

Orion merely nodded and smiled then managed to tear his gaze from Max who turned to watch him descend the narrow stone steps. She cocked her head to the side and bit her bottom lip.

"Forgive my impertinence, but we are far from home," Max quickly turned to me, her wide eyes bright, her face hopeful. "Has he chosen to pair yet?"

I smiled and shook my head. "No. He's still bound to his birth Other."

She nodded, and a knowing smile grew across her shimmering face, causing her to appear even more beautiful yet lethal. "I shall pursue this."

There was really nothing I could say in objection to her stating her intentions. My hopes as an alien queen had always been to repopulate our people. *Maybe,* I thought as I returned Max's smile, *everything will turn out okay after all.*

"Orion is a good choice," I replied. "He has a good heart and is loyal. Most of all, he is very special to me."

"Do I have your approval to proceed, my lady?" Max leaned forward a bit, her hands clasped together in her lap.

"With one exception— that you always treat him with love and respect. As I have already stated, he is very special to me." I held her gaze and attempted to look serious, which was difficult with that love-struck look on Max's face.

She nodded then bowed her head. "Following my lady's orders is the blood of my life."

"Good. That's settled. Now tell me Xi's message," I said, glad to change the subject before she had a chance to inquire about the names of Orion's parents.

Everything about Max's composure changed. She was back to her mission of relaying her Commander's message to the Queen. She straightened her back, leveled her shoulders, and looked me in the eye.

"The Commander says to inform the Queen that he received her coded message and requests that she remain at her current encampment where he will bring to her what she requested within forty-eight hours' time." She bowed once more, indicating the end of Xi's very formal message.

"Thank you, Max." I smiled and tried to swallow down the flurry of butterflies in my stomach at the thought of seeing Ky. "Oh, and thank you for the use of your raincoat and shirt. I'm sure you need them back." I started to remove them, but Max objected.

"My lady!" she exclaimed. "No. It is my greatest honor to provide you with anything you need. Please do not insist that I take them back."

"As you wish," I smiled at the most dangerous female I'd ever known in either of my lives.

"With your permission, I would like to speak with Orion now," Max stood.

"Strike a trot!" I couldn't hide the broad smile that crossed my face as I borrowed one of Grandpa's phrases.

Quick as a flash, she disappeared down the pyramid steps. I was glad. I needed time to sort out my thoughts. Soon, I'd be reunited with Ky, the whole reason I'd set this chain of events in motion in my past life.

But, now, I found myself conflicted. I loved two men equally, yet separately. Lore loved Ky, and I loved Everett. I'd never bargained on falling in love as a human.

I stood and surveyed the vast clearing below and thought of my past life here with Ash, and then I realized that I may very well have to contend with three different men vying for my affections.

Only one would win. *Who would it be?* I bit my lip and watched as Max and Orion walked side-by-side. I'd married Ash once, but only at the order of my alien father and very much against my own will. I'd promised my entire existence to Ky, risking everything to bring him back to life here on this planet.

But I, Blair Reynolds, loved Everett Forster.

None of those men would give me up easily. Of the three of them, Ash would raise the biggest ruckus. This was going to be even worse than I'd imagined in the beginning. It could very well lead to the alien apocalypse.

I was immediately snapped out of my dark thoughts by movement at the edge of the jungle on the opposite side of the pyramid from Max and Orion. Several figures appeared at the edge of the forest. I squinted against the rays of the morning sun as they stepped out of the shadows and into the morning light.

Rake, the only other female in my Royal Guard, scanned the clearing as she walked ahead of a group of her peers, most of whom were carrying weapons and equipment on their backs and shoulders.

Staying in formation, they crossed the clearing, reminding me of the Roman soldiers I'd seen in a movie once. My deadly Royal Guard was regrouping. They'd found their Queen. Nothing would stop them, save death, which would be more than most could dole out to them.

Rake was the first to approach the base of the steps, kneeling, and bowing her head. The others followed suit. Fifteen loyal soldiers knelt at the bottom of the pyramid, honoring me by bowing their heads, all of which were adorned with my family crest. Each of these elite soldiers would give his or her life in my service. *I hope it never happens*, I thought as I appreciated their display of service.

"Rise and carry on with your orders!" I called, descending the steps to meet with Rake, leader of her platoon.

"My lady," she bowed her head to me once more as I approached her. She stood shoulder-to-shoulder with her male counterparts, which made her much taller than her Queen. "The Commander sent me ahead to prepare an encampment for you." She motioned to her platoon. Several soldiers were already marking a safety perimeter for motion alarms.

"Thank you, Rake. It's good to see you again," I smiled. It had been a very long time since I'd seen her face-to-face. She had a quiet spirit and was a much less flamboyant killer than Max. My alien father had once said she preferred to blast the enemy to bits with a large weapon she carried strapped across her chest, while Max preferred to flay them alive, wearing their blood as battle paint.

"I speak for my entire platoon when I say that it is very good to find you well, my lady," she bowed her head once more. "We have brought medicines and food supplies."

"Thank you, Rake. The medicine and food came in handy to me not long ago," I answered, thinking back to the accelerator and the ancient food I'd eaten in the Royal Guard's pod. My hand immediately found its way to my side where my rib was now healed completely.

"Were you injured, my lady?" alarm crossed her face.

"Yes, several times, actually. But the supplies I found in the pod fixed me right up," I smiled, hoping to ease the tension.

"I will destroy whoever has injured you," her voice deepened just a bit, reminding me that she was not human.

"Don't worry. I already did," I held out my hands and allowed them to power up. Two orbs of fire leapt from my fingertips and swirled above Rake's head.

"You have developed new powers!" Rake gasped. "It must be this strange planet."

"Yes. I think it is." I motioned for the orbs to spin faster around her head until they were moving so quickly, it looked like she had a golden halo. "It took us a few decades to adjust to it when we first arrived."

The rest of the Royal Guard gathered nearby, watching the spectacle. Mal and Jex stood side-by-side, their mouths wide with wonder. Not only were they a set of birth Others, they were also the youngest of the group. The pair had replaced two older soldiers who'd fallen while helping Xi capture the Hunter who'd killed Ky.

At that thought, the orbs exploded, sending glowing embers showering down on the soldiers like fireworks. They cheered, smiling and whooping. Then, they went back to their duties of securing the encampment and setting up shelter.

By mid-day, tents made of camouflage material like Max's poncho, were placed at the base of the pyramid. A wild boar was roasting over a fire at the center of the camp, reminding me of barbeques back home at the ranch. Lightning was safely installed inside of her own corral erected by Max and Orion. In case of rain, they'd attached the makeshift fencing to the pyramid base so that she could seek shelter where she'd spent the previous night.

Max and Rake, the only other set of birth Others in my Royal Guard, tried to convince me to allow my tent to be set up top of the pyramid. They'd insisted I'd be safer there in case of an attack. But I'd refused, saying that I'd missed my Royal Guard and wanted to camp among them. So my tent was placed in the middle of camp.

By nightfall, the soldiers had quieted down, speaking in low tones about this strange planet, its odd inhabitants, and the bizarre animals of the jungle. *Just wait until they've seen the rest of what this planet has to offer,* I smiled to myself. Then my smile quickly vanished as I thought about the Guard being loosed to roam free.

Orion had become popular with the soldiers. They'd quizzed him about the jungle people, the animals, and even asked where the others of our kind were. They'd become edgy and alarmed when he'd told them that many had been lost due to human and alien Hunters. But he assured them that most of our people had rested safely below ground in their cocoons.

Jex's aquamarine eyes sparkled when he asked me about where the ship had been docked. I could read from his young, enthusiastic mind that he'd imagined this planet to have a docking station in orbit like our home planet had.

"We are not in the position to ask the Queen such questions!" Max's voice rang out. She stood and paced the band of soldiers sitting around the fire. "We are in enemy territory, and our Queen answers to no one." Max stopped next to Jex, who lowered his head in submission to Max's rank.

"I meant no disrespect, my lady," Jex softened his enthusiasm.

"I perceived none," I responded, motioning to Max that all was well. "When the time is right, I will reveal everything to you all. I'll withhold no information. You have my complete trust as I know I have your complete allegiance."

"Yes, my lady," they answered in unison, and I could sense pride growing in each of their hearts and minds.

Pride in being the elite, pride in being trusted, pride in being who they were— The Royal Guard.

I rested well with the Royal Guard encamped around me. Inside my tent at night, my tiny galaxy twirled and spun as if it was adapting to the changes just as I was ... with dizzying reality. I watched as the dim sparkles of light reflected against the shimmery fabric of the tent and thought of how different things were than I'd once imagined they would be ... as a normal human girl and as a royal alien princess. None of this was what I'd once envisioned for myself.

"Adaptation is the way of our people," my alien mother had said while brushing my long hair, getting me ready for my forced marriage to Ash. "We sometimes must do the difficult thing in order to survive."

It was one of the rare clear memories I had of my alien mother. She had not been warm like Mom. *Yes, Mom is the mother I would choose to think of – the mother who'd nurtured me when sick, the one who'd taught me how to bake, had laughed and cried with me, had been taken from me. Hopefully, Xi would find her soon.*

The following day was a whirlwind of watching the soldiers practicing war games in the clearing. I sat on the stone seat atop the pyramid and watched as weapon clanked against weapon and soldiers wrestled and practiced battle techniques. Orion joined in the fray and practiced things he'd learned from his father, Ash. He also learned things only the Royal Guard knew ... and he was allowed this because he was held as special by the Queen.

Queen, I thought as I pulled my hair over my shoulder and twisted it into a thick, tight rope. *I want to be more than just a queen upon a throne. I want to be a hands-on leader like my alien father had been. The people had loved him for it.*

However, there were other more pressing matters to attend to. Some things were taking care of themselves, like the Royal Guard rallying for their Queen. But there were pressing matters such as dealing with Ash and figuring out whether or not the summer solstice had come and gone.

I shook my head to clear my thoughts. There were even more pressing matters at hand than failing to turn myself over to Ash before the agreed date ... I'd begun sensing what Orion had mentioned.

They were coming. And they weren't all friendly.

CHAPTER TWENTY

THEY ARE COMING

The Guard halted war games and turned toward the jungle on the right. My heart skipped a beat. *Maybe this is it,* I drew in a deep breath. I squinted and focused on a particular part of the jungle wall where the clearing met the shady reaches of branches and vines.

Something wasn't right about the way a patch of jungle looked slightly blurred and shimmery. I descended the temple steps and powered up my hands. Whatever was coming, wasn't taking me without a fight.

Max was suddenly at my side, pushing me to stand behind her. And then she disappeared, cloaking us both with her camouflaged uniform and skin. I quickly scanned the clearing for Orion and saw him behind Mal and Jex, both of whom had taken a liking to him.

The entire platoon was cloaked.

I lowered my barriers and listened. Max was issuing orders to Rake, who, in turn, issued orders to her platoon through their thoughts. Energy sizzled off of Max, causing the hairs on my arms to stand on end. She was made for this, thrived on this. If the enemy emerged from the jungle, she'd soon be wearing their blood as war paint.

Orion, the name wound through my mind.

Yes, I hear you, he replied, his voice echoing in my thoughts.

Don't put yourself in danger, I thought of him lying in a pool of his own blood in the kitchen of the old Sprinkles. He'd been Everett's clone then, and it had been heart-wrenching thinking of him dead.

I love you, too, I heard the smile in his thoughts, and I smiled in return.

But my smile vanished when I saw that whoever was cloaking themselves was advancing out of the jungle and toward the clearing. Rake ordered her platoon to prepare their weapons. Max reached behind her back and unsheathed the long, thin blade she so skillfully used on many an enemy.

In the blink of an eye, the platoon was rushing forward, weapons at the ready, trained on their target. At the point of impact, both groups dropped their camouflage, and Rake's platoon clashed with another platoon of my Royal Guard.

It was a brilliant display of war games— one they'd been long used to practicing. However, to their Queen, it seemed as though all hell was about to break loose.

Max turned and flashed a wicked smile at me then dove into the fray.

Orion held his own but needed some help from Max who stayed close by his side. I sunk back onto the bottom step of the pyramid and watched, as my alien father had done on so many occasions, in awe as a special breed of genetically-altered soldiers practiced battle techniques with each other.

A sudden lightning storm brought the skirmish to a halt, and only I knew, at that moment, that it was Orion who'd had the final say. He'd always loved creating a good storm. It was a gift he'd been born with as the son of Ash. My heart sank as I wondered what mine and Ash's children would have been like ... what powers they would have possessed. But they'd died, and I would never know.

"The weather patterns on this planet are erratic," Rake greeted the leader of the other platoon.

"It is a very strange place," Kin answered. They gripped each other in a half-armed hand shake.

Kin was the oldest member of the Royal Guard. He'd been chosen by my alien grandfather. His strength was strategy, and he was respected by every member of the Guard because of his age and his skill. Even-tempered and level-headed, he was a favorite on our alien world among the royal families at court.

Max, I focused my thoughts on her. She immediately turned to face me. Max and Orion were standing in the middle of the clearing, and she'd been explaining the war games to him.

Yes, my lady? she replied in like kind.

Please have them set up their tents. I will greet them later. I was tired and wanted a little time to myself.

As you wish, my lady, Max bowed her head, then carried out her orders.

The pyramid grounds were abuzz with activity. Tents were being raised, and a small hunting party was dispatched. Thirty-five soldiers would require a lot of food, and I knew Max would make sure everything was taken care of.

I needed a little peace and quiet to think. Max had said Xi would arrive within forty-eight hours' time. That would mean he and the remaining fifteen members of the Royal Guard would soon be assembling at the foot of the pyramid.

Would he actually have Ky with him? I wondered what he would be like now in his hybrid human body. I slipped into the shade of the jungle behind the pyramid. Cool leaves brushed against my arms and shoulders as I followed the sound of trickling water.

A small rivulet wove around tree roots and smooth stones, its water clear and shallow. I kicked my boots off and relished the cool water as it flowed over my feet. It occurred to me that it had been a while since I'd had a bath. So, I picked up my boots and walked in the stream, following the direction of the water to where it gathered in a deep, clear pool.

Clumps of ferns and moss grew at the edges of the pool, and overhead vines clung to the broad trunks and arching branches of ancient jungle trees. Colorful birds chirped and darted among the leaves, and I smiled when I saw the fluttering of butterfly wings overhead.

I removed my clothes and tossed them over a large rock at the edge of the pool. They were dirty, and I wished I had my backpack so I could have a fresh change of clothes. Surely, Xi would bring it with him when he arrived.

Another flutter of butterfly wings welled up in my stomach. Things that had been set in motion centuries ago were about to come together. I slipped beneath the cool water and brushed my hands over my shoulders and arms, then hugged myself.

What am I doing? The question bounced around in my head and heart. *I'm no alien princess or queen. I'm human. Only human, flesh and bone.* I lifted my hands out of the water. Droplets trickled from my fingertips and broke the water's surface, sending ripples traveling outward toward the mossy edges of the pool. I turned my hands over, examining them ... my human hands.

I'm human, my family is human, my boyfriend is human, I thought as I lowered myself into the water until my nose hovered just above the surface. A jolt of adrenaline pulsed through my bloodstream. My heart pounded against my ribs. Just beyond the jungle's edge, a group of dangerous alien soldiers were setting up tents and getting ready for evening to set in.

Kicking my feet, I twirled in the water, looking for a route of escape. There was none ... I knew this. Max would be on my heels in nothing flat. I plunged into the water, swimming down, down, down until I reached the bottom of the pool where smooth pebbles tiled the bottom and provided a place for grasses and other water plants to root and grow.

The cool water enveloped me. I exhaled, and a column of bubbles rose toward the surface, and I sat on the bottom of the pool and watched as the bubbles floated upward until they broke the surface of the water.

All the things that make me human are what brought me to this place and time, I thought, straining against the need for air. *Love ... pain ... loss,* I grasped my chest, holding my breath.

My body urged me to inhale. Still, I held my breath, laid back on the bottom of the pool, and wondered how I will ever be forgiven for all I'd done ... all the pain I'd caused to bring this plan about. *And it's not over yet,* I covered my face with my hands. *Who else will suffer or die before my plan comes to fruition? Who else will be lost so that I can be happy?*

Every human cell in my body screamed for oxygen. I kicked against the smooth stones at the bottom of the pool and traveled up, up, up and burst through the water's surface, gasping for breath ... for freedom.

My fingers dug into the thick moss at the water's edge as I struggled to catch my breath. I felt as though I'd been pretending for the last couple of days ...

pretending to be in control ... pretending to be what I didn't fully feel— an alien queen.

"But you're not pretending."

I gasped, nearly jumped out of my skin. I whirled around, splashing water and wildly searching for whose voice had broken my silent conversation with myself. Andrew knelt at the edge of the pool, near my clothes. It had been weeks since I'd seen my big brother, and I'd never been so glad to see anyone in my life.

"Andrew!" I swam to him. "How did you find me?" I reached up to take his hand.

"I was following a weird trail I found. Looked like a large group of soldiers of some sort, but not human soldiers ... damn that sounds weird!" he shook his head. His hair had gotten even bushier than when I'd last seen him, and he looked even more like Dad. Except for that hair. Dad never had big hair like Andrew's.

"Not as weird as you think," I answered, slipping down into the water until my chin was under the surface.

"Are you gonna stay in there all day? I'm hungry, and I smell barbeque," he held his hand out for me. I started to take it and let him pull me out, but I remembered I was sans clothes.

"Well, I need a little privacy," I motioned toward my clothes piled on the edge of the pool.

He stood and turned his back to me. I looked around to see if anyone else was watching, then grabbed hold of a root near a clump of fern fronds and pulled myself out and quickly put on my clothes. They smelled bad, and I hoped, again, that I'd see my backpack soon.

"Done yet, slow poke?" Andrew asked, his back still to me.

I paused a moment, remembering the enormous scar I'd seen on his back the night I'd spied on him. It had looked like a massive claw mark, and I had the immediate longing to ask him about it. But then he'd know that I knew he was in agony over losing my trail that night, and I'd done nothing to stop it.

"Yep!" I looped my arm through his.

"What's with those thoughts I overheard?" he pulled his arm away and looked me in the eye.

"Huh?" For a moment, I'd forgotten what I was thinking. I was just so glad to see him.

"That you were ... what was it? 'Pretending' to be in control, among other things?" He made the quotation marks around the word *pretending.*

"Oh," I shrugged. What else was there to say? He'd heard my complete conversation with myself, and I had nothing to add to it.

"Know what I think?" he asked but didn't give me a chance to answer. "Before this is all over, you're going to surprise yourself with what you're capable of."

"I don't know about that. Seems like I'm more capable of getting people involved in danger than anything else ..." I wanted to say more, to mention the scars on his back, Mom's disappearance, the death of my alien parents and babies.

"We can sort all that out after we've eaten something," he said, turning back toward camp where a wild boar was roasting over the campfire. Then he paused a moment, without turning back to me, and said, "Just don't disappear again, okay, Sis? I've already lost one sibling. I don't think I can bear losing another."

I nodded and tried to hide the frown that threatened to cross my features. His eyes had changed. They were still the same brown eyes he'd always had ... much like Dad's. Now they looked like they'd seen many horrors, things a person of his age from Willis, Texas would never have had to witness.

"So, is that Everett doing the barbequing?" Andrew started toward camp again, and I realized I would need to do some sort of introductions so Max wouldn't do to him what she'd done to the mercenaries.

"Andrew, wait!" I grabbed him by the shirtsleeve and pulled him back. "You can't just go tromping into that camp unannounced."

"What's going on, Sis?" alarm crossed his face.

I wanted to explain it all to him. But if he hadn't already picked up the details from fishing around in my brain, there wasn't enough time to fill him in. It was already late afternoon, and my Guard would soon be looking for their Queen.

"I can't explain it. I'll just have to show you," I grabbed his hand and led him toward the pyramid, stopping at the tree line and turning to say, "Just follow my lead, okay? And don't freak out or anything."

"What do you mean 'freak out'?" he asked just before I shushed him.

We reached the back corner of Lightning's corral just as Max's voice echoed around the corner of the pyramid, issuing orders to find and protect me. I put my finger to my lips to motion for Andrew to remain quiet and let me do the talking. He nodded, eyes wary, and with his free hand reached for something beneath his backpack … no doubt a weapon.

Before I could stop him, Max rounded the corner, followed by Jex and Mal, just in time to see Andrew, standing behind me, pulling his machete out of his backpack. I moved to lift my hands to motion for them to stop, but they were so quick that the air around and behind them blurred into streaks of smudged blues, greys, and greens.

In the time it took me to turn around, Max had lifted Andrew into the air by his throat and pressed the tip of her long, silvery blade into his belly. A small bead of blood dripped and ran down the flesh beneath her blade, and my brother gasped for breath, gripping Max's hand to keep from choking to death. His machete had fallen to the ground at Max's feet. I saw all this from the small space between Mal and Jex, who'd put themselves between Andrew and their Queen.

Max cocked her head to the side, and a wicked smile crossed her lips. I knew what she planned to do next.

"Stop!" I shouted at the top of my lungs. My heart pounded against my ribs and a strange wave of heat flooded up my back and neck. Everything turned red, and flames erupted through my skin, licking around me in tendrils of fire and heat. "Put him down at once!" my voice was an octave lower than usual and resounded in a bizarre twist of echo and voice.

Red light from the flames reflected against the three Guards' shimmery skin and uniforms and lit their eyes, turning them an iridescent red. Max dropped Andrew and quickly knelt on one knee, bowing her head. Jex and Mal followed suit.

Andrew rolled over on his side, gripping his throat and gasping for air. I called for Rake, my voice still sounding alien, and flames still winding around me in tendrils of heat and light. She appeared at my side, alarm crossing her face, and eyes reflecting the red flames that lapped around me.

"My lady," she bowed her head once.

"Tend to this man. He is very special to me," I pointed to Andrew. I wanted to tend to him, myself. But I couldn't take the chance of setting him on fire.

With one hand still at his throat, Andrew held his other arm up to defend himself from Rake. But she gently placed her large hand on the top of Andrew's head and tried to assure him she meant him no harm.

Of course, he couldn't understand what she was saying, because she spoke in my native alien language, and though my brother had some alien traits, he was not a true full hybrid. He'd not been recreated as I had.

"Andrew," I said, hating the look of confusion and fear on my brother's face caused by my weird alien voice. "Don't be afraid. Rake will help you." With that, Rake scooped Andrew up in her arms and carried him toward camp.

"My lady, I meant only to protect you. I did not know this man was special to you," Max said, her head still bowed. I examined my family crest inked across the shimmery skin on her scalp.

"I know, Max. Please rise," I signed, glad that my voice was turning back to normal again. "You were merely doing your job. I will meet with you later to inform you of others who are special to me so you'll know not to … disembowel them and eat their brains, or something." I merely motioned for Jex and Mal to stand. The conflagration I'd just ignited had drained me, and I needed food and recharging.

"Men, take the Queen back to camp. She is in need of food," Max ordered Mal and Jex, and they complied by lifting me to sit on their shoulders as they walked side-by-side back to camp. I felt like one of those women in those old black and white movies about Egyptian queens.

By the time I'd recharged and eaten, Andrew was sound asleep. Rake had given him something that knocked him out and had installed him in a tent next to mine. I didn't know whether or not I should worry about him being drugged, but hoped it would help his crushed throat and the shallow slice across his stomach heal. Most of all, I hoped his mind would calm down from what had just happened to him.

Daylight was ebbing, giving way to night. A few of the brighter stars appeared in the darkening sky, and several of the soldiers discussed the strange constellations that were so alien to them in the night sky of this alien planet.

It was apparent that I was the bridge between our two races. I was the half-human, half-alien, hybrid queen who would do as my human father had said in the letter he'd left in the locker for me to find. I would protect the people on this planet, my human people. But I'd also protect those I'd brought here with me. Somehow, some way, I'd have to find a balance.

A round of laughter broke my thoughts, and I glanced over at Kin's platoon. They were grouped around another campfire a few tents away, playing some sort of game that reminded me of dice. I'd never learned games that weren't considered fit for a princess in my former alien life, so there were some things my Royal Guard did that were alien to me in every sense of the word.

My eyes stopped on Kin's. He was watching me, observing me in my human-hybrid skin, and I realized that I'd never greeted them. No doubt, he was wondering why. I smiled and nodded at him, attempting to keep an air of authority about me. However, Kin was older than anyone I'd ever known. He was battle-hardened and wise.

I stood and walked over to their camp fire. Immediately, they stopped talking and stood to greet me. I thanked them for their loyalty and service and promised them a proper greeting as soon as Xi arrived with the rest of the Royal Guard with him. This seemed to relax Kin, who, I realized as I attempted to snoop around in his thoughts, had thought he'd displeased me somehow.

After a few rounds of playing their dice game with them, I realized they were all intentionally losing so that I would win. That took all the fun out if it for me, but I wouldn't dare let them know I felt that way. They would feel I was displeased with them. They all bowed their heads as I stood and thanked them for teaching me their game.

Without my realizing, Max had stayed nearby, guarding her Queen. *Xi must have given her orders to do so,* I thought as I acknowledged her with a nod. Night had covered the jungle in darkness, and the sky was full of stars.

Max's attention darted past me, to the edge of the jungle, where the trunks of ancient trees had been severed from their hold on the earth. I turned to follow her line of sight to where an infinitesimal movement alerted us that something or someone was there.

I held up my hand to Max, motioning for her to stay still. Then, I focused my mind on searching the surrounding forest. As my thoughts wound their way around the figure at the edge of the jungle, I realized it was a human. A female. *Could it be Mom?* I gasped. Whoever it was, she was too far away for me to identify her.

"Max, I need to go meet that person. Follow me at a safe distance. But be ready to attack if I signal for you." I turned to look up into her wide, slanted eyes and saw myself reflected back in them. My own eyes were solid black, in night vision mode. I'd gotten so used to my alien abilities that they no longer seemed out of the ordinary to me.

"Yes, my lady," Max answered, motioning for Mal and Jex to come with her.

I began walking the vast expanse from the camp to where the mystery woman stood. No doubt, her eyes would not see us until we were much closer. The moon wasn't out, and the clearing was very dark.

We trudged along through the growing brambles of jungle plants until it was obvious we were in her line of sight. She dipped back behind a tree, into the shelter of the shadows, and my heart sped up hoping, silently praying that it was Mom. My heart wasn't the only thing that sped up … so did my steps.

"It's okay to come out. We mean you no harm," I made sure to speak in English instead of my native alien language when we reached the edge of the jungle, near where we'd seen Mystery Woman standing.

A few crackles of sticks breaking and leaves rustling gave away that she was still there, hiding in the tangles of vines and branches. A bundle of emotions rolled off her. She was fierce, frightened, angry, and lonely. She was looking for someone.

"Bring her to me," I said to Max, speaking in my native tongue. I allowed a flaming orb to leap from my fingertips, lighting my surroundings.

A moment later, the jungle wall ripped apart after a blur of light and shadows where Max and the other two swiftly moved to follow my orders. Then a scream pierced the darkness, and a minute later Max stood in front of me, holding the woman still by gripping a fist full of fiery red hair.

It took a few moments to recognize who she was. She was so familiar, yet I'd never met her. I'd seen her, though, I realized. It was the night I'd spied on Andrew. She'd come out of the darkness of the jungle and comforted my brother. This was the flame-haired girl Andrew had told us about in the truck the night of the Rodeo Gala.

"Angelica?" I asked, stepping closer to her.

She flinched, turning her face away from me as if I were about to strike her. Max pulled her hair, and she yelped in pain.

"Max, release her," I stepped closer to her, holding out my hand to show her I meant no harm.

"What ... are ... you?" she gritted her teeth and clutched her scalp. No doubt she'd lost a few hairs.

For a moment, I was at a loss for words and wondered why she would ask me that question. I could understand why she'd ask that about Max and the other two. But didn't I look just as human as she did?

"Oh!" I closed my eyes and turned away. She'd been freaked out by my solid black eyes. I didn't blame her. They *were* freaky. I turned back around, opened my eyes, and motioned for the orb to hover above us.

"Who are you, and how do you know my name?" Angelica jerked at the hem of her shirt, straightening it into place. It was a movement I'd seen Mom do a lot of times when she was frustrated and upset.

It was a good thing Max didn't understand a word she'd said … there was no telling what she'd do. I looked up at Max, who watched my every move, with her head cocked to the side and a wicked look of bloodlust across her face.

"I think I know who you're looking for." I extinguished the orb a split second before I switched my eyes back to night vision. *Max,* I spoke in my thoughts. *Carry her back to camp.*

Angelica screamed and kicked her feet as Max tossed her over her shoulder, which only caused Max to grip both of her ankles with one of her large hands. Guilt spun around my heart as we made our way back toward the campfires that seemed so small in the distance. Hearing Andrew's girl saying the Lord's Prayer over and over didn't help matters much. I didn't blame her. If I'd have been in her shoes, I'd have done the very same thing.

Just before we approached camp, the rest of the Guard lined up to greet us, their silhouettes blocking the flames of the campfires and forming an eerie wall of dark figures. I walked past them without explanation, to Andrew's tent where Angelica was roughly deposited by Max.

"What did you do to him?" her voice wavered as she placed her hand on his forehead. The light from the campfire flashed across a thin gold band on the ring finger of her left hand, and I couldn't stop my mouth from dropping open.

"You two are married?" I knelt down by her, next to Andrew. He was sound asleep, and I was sure he hadn't slept that well in years.

Angelica brushed her thumb across my brother's forehead and nodded. She was pretty ... not like *Natalie* pretty. Her beauty seemed to come from the inside. She had a quiet strength. But with hair the color of fire, I was sure she could be a warrior if she had a mind to.

I watched as she cooed to Andrew, kissing his cheek and telling him that she was there, and everything was going to be okay. She had a small, athletic frame. Yet, she was feminine. Her nose was narrow and turned up a bit at the tip. And her lips were full. Freckles sprinkled across her shoulders, arms, and cheeks. And a thick braid of fiery red hair looped over her shoulder.

She removed the small backpack she wore and retrieved a canteen of water, which she held to Andrew's lips. He was so out of it that the water merely trickled down his cheek.

"What do you plan to do to us?" she asked, still looking at Andrew.

"I don't plan on doing anything to you," I answered, feeling hurt. "Don't you know who I am?"

"I know exactly *what* you are … what he's been hunting and destroying so his family will finally be safe." She lifted her eyebrows as she turned to look at me.

"Well, Sister-in-Law, I *am* his family," I felt my nostrils flare, my top lip lift into a snarl as I spoke those words. And I didn't stick around to enjoy the shock that crossed her face. I turned and walked away, before the tears came, and headed toward the pyramid steps where I ascended into darkness.

Heat still radiated off the stone seat atop the pyramid. I curled up in a ball and leaned my head against the back of the seat, feeling all alone. The world had become crazier than I'd ever imagined it could.

I could handle it, because I was made of tougher stuff. But that didn't mean that my heart wasn't longing for my own true love … the only one who would make me feel right and whole again.

Andrew had found his other half, and I was glad for him. He'd been miserable for so long that I'd forgotten what he was like before … before Aaron and Dad were murdered. But now he had someone to love him and watch over him.

Angelica was, I could tell, a good person. Andrew had chosen well. I hugged my knees and wondered how I would choose between Ky and Everett. Whichever one I ended up with would make at least half of me happy.

I sighed and turned around in the stone seat, facing the camp below. Firelight shined half-way up the stone steps, lending me the privacy of darkness. Two silhouettes on the steps below revealed Max and Orion were keeping watch.

They sat close together just inside the line of darkness. She was, of course, taller than him, but that hadn't mattered to Orion. He'd heard stories all his life of the Royal Guard from Ash and me. To him, she must appear magnificent. She tucked a lock of his windblown hair behind his ear and kissed him on the cheek. It was an oddly intimate and tender thing for such a vicious warrior to do.

At the foot of the pyramid, the campfires blazed, casting long streaks of light across the dark ground. Kin's platoon was practicing strategy games. The old leader stood as tall as his men, but he had a certain curve to his back that gave the impression he'd carried a heavy load for a very long time. And perhaps he had.

I felt the weight of a heavy load, too. It bore down on my shoulders every second of the day. Of course, it was a load I'd willingly put there myself so that I'd be reunited with the one I'd wanted to pair with in my alien life. And now things had become even more complicated …

The next few hours would prove just how complicated things would become. Xi would be arriving at any time, and he'd promised to bring me what I'd asked him to bring. I drew in a deep breath and pulled myself up by the proverbial bootstraps.

Whatever or whomever, as the case may be, came to me, I'd face it head-on. I'd soon be reunited with my chosen Other.

This was sure to be a wild night.

CHAPTER TWENTY-ONE

A WILD NIGHT

A light in Andrew's tent caught my attention. Angelica was moving around inside the tent as if she was getting her bed ready for the night. I yawned and stretched my arms over my head. My own tent was calling me to come release my tiny galaxy and let it lull me to sleep.

The stone seat was cooling down now, and a chill shivered through me. So, I decided to go sit by one of the fires for a while and wait to see if the night brought anything new before I headed off to bed.

As soon as the sole of my boot made contact with the top step, a movement on the opposite side of the clearing caught my eye. And I wasn't the only one who'd noticed it. Max was immediately on her feet, and the head of every member of the Royal Guard around the fires below snapped in the same direction.

Quick as a flash, a barrier of Royal Guard formed at the base of the pyramid. Weapons were at the ready, swords and guns were drawn, and a long, thin, silvery blade glistened a few steps below me where Max knelt, one foot a step lower than the other. Orion came to stand next to me at the top step.

Andrew, the name wound through my thoughts as I looked at Orion.

He'll be safe, he answered. *Max knows he's special to you.*

I nodded, worry crossing my heart, and turned my attention to the area of the clearing where a shadow moved toward the fires of the camp below ... their cracking flames like tiny gunfire were the only sound in the clearing. The platoons stood as still as statues; even their breaths were shallow and quiet.

A list of enemies quickly formed in my mind. If it was the Hunters, then my Guard will be meeting our mortal enemy face-to-face tonight. If it was the human alien Hunters, then they'll be no match for my soldiers ... unless they have some new form of technology.

What if it's The Resistance? I gasped, causing Max to flinch ever-so-slightly. I knew absolutely nothing about them. They were so secretive that even Everett didn't reveal anything about the shadowy organization he'd joined. *No, it's not The Resistance. Everett would protect me from an attack from them.* I took a deep breath, trying to calm myself down.

"What day is it?" I whispered to Orion.

"I believe it's June the twenty-fifth," he answered, keeping his eyes on the shadow that had now drawn close enough to make out multiple individuals.

"It's Ash!" I gasped, keeping my voice to a whisper. "I've missed the Summer Solstice!"

Orion squinted and shook his head, "That's not father."

Max slowly turned to look out of the corner of her eye at Orion. Apparently, she'd never been informed that she was in the initial steps of the pairing ritual with the son of the General. Then it occurred to me that the only member of the Guard who'd known I'd separated myself from Ash was Xi.

And that's when I saw him.

His massive form towered at the front of the formation, which followed him in a triangle like a flock of geese follow their leader. They marched, keeping step, behind the head of the Royal Guard … the most dangerous man in our race. Xi.

The hilt of his sword glistened from its place behind his shoulder. A wide sash crossed his chest, fitted with knives and ammunition, and a massive gun was strapped behind his other shoulder. Aside from their footfalls, Xi's platoon was silent. Some had shields, some carried backpacks full of supplies and other things I could never imagine.

"The Commander approaches!" Max shouted, and the rest of the Royal Guard below came to attention. When Xi's platoon heard Max's voice, they fell in with their own marching chants. Max descended the steps and came to stop next to Kin.

Firelight glistened on Xi and his men as they entered the circle of light around the camp, and I did what I'd always done best ... in this human life, anyway. I stood on the sidelines. I watched. Ancient soldiers reunited with each other at the bottom of the pyramid, and I stepped back and lowered myself into the stone seat. Orion sat next to me on a stone seat lower than mine. It had evidently been created for someone of lesser rank

Backpacks fell to the ground, weapons came to rest next to stacks of tents and bedrolls, and friends greeted friends. Xi pulled Max aside. I focused my mind on their thoughts, but even I couldn't break through their barriers.

Xi motioned toward the dark jungle forest behind the pyramid where I'd gone skinny dipping that morning ... *had it been the same day?* It was hard to believe. I shook my head to clear my thoughts and continued watching them.

Max pointed toward the top of the pyramid where Orion and I watched from the darkness. Xi nodded and then began ascending the steps.

Oh, God ... this is it! I tried to steady my breath. Xi's boots pounded each step, and my heart pounded against my ribs. *There's no going back now ...* I swallowed the lump in my throat and longed for my big brother to wake up.

Orion squeezed my hand once and smiled reassuringly. I pushed myself back into the stone seat and tried to look as noble and royal as possible for an eighteen-year-old cowgirl from Willis, Texas.

Then Xi reached the top few steps, and Lore's memories took over. I remembered him fondly, his strong shoulders that had once carried me as a child wherever I'd willed him to go. His huge arms that had torn the Hunter to pieces after it had killed Ky in our laboratory. His strong facial features that had frowned the day I'd been forced to pair with Ash. The cheek where that one tear had streamed down to fall from that strong jaw.

"My lady," he knelt on one knee before me, bowing his head to reveal my alien family's coat of arms tattooed across his iridescent skin. "It feels as if it has been an eternity."

"It *has* been an eternity," I shrugged. "We've got a lot of catching up to do, Xi."

"Yes," he answered, head still bowed.

"Please … let's go get something to eat," I stood. "You and your men must be hungry."

"Yes," he stood, towering over his Queen, a massive figure who blotted out the stars overhead. "But, first, my lady …" he paused and motioned to someone behind him. A female. A human. Light from campfires below formed a halo around her light brown hair as she slowly, warily stepped onto the pyramid platform.

"Blair? Sweetheart, is that you?" her voice was the sweetest sound I'd ever heard.

"Mom!" I wrapped my arms around her and hugged like I never wanted to let her go. She was shorter than me now since I'd changed. No doubt it seemed odd to her, but still she gripped me tightly with a desperation only a mother could feel.

Fatigued weighed her shoulders down, and she smelled of sweat and dirt. I had no idea what she'd been through, but as I took her face in my hands, I'd never been so glad that I'd awoken my Royal Guard. Then anger flashed through my body when I saw the cuts and bruises on my mother's beautiful face.

"Who did this to you?" I fought to keep the flames inside of me ... the same flames that had erupted through my skin when Andrew was almost disemboweled earlier that same day. I turned to look at Xi, but Mom's hand touched my cheek, and I turned back to look at her once more.

"It wasn't him," Mom attempted to smile, but her eyes were hollow. She'd been traumatized by whatever had happened to her. "It was Luke's men," she said just before a sob wrenched in her throat.

"Mom, I'm so sorry. I'm so, so, so sorry ..." I hugged her tight against me. Her head lobbed over onto my shoulder. She felt so small and frail in my arms. "You're safe now. Nothing can happen to you here ... not ever again."

Xi's eyes met mine, and I mouthed the words thank you in our native language. He nodded once, and a small smile turned up one corner of his lips.

Rake tended to Mom's wounds and gave her the same medicine she'd given Andrew, which knocked her completely out. She slept safe and sound in my tent while I sat near the campfire and finally officially greeted my Royal Guard as their Queen.

Once I'd made eye contact with each one, speaking his or her name, I thanked them for their service to me and the royal family. This, I noticed, caused shoulders to become broader, pride to brighten each pair of wide, slanted eyes, and hearts to fill with love for their new Queen. This greeting was an ancient one, a rite given only to the Royal Guard.

"We have begun a new phase in the existence of our kind," I tried to sound like I knew what I was talking about ... like I was really wise enough to lead these elite soldiers into a new life here. "Things will be much different than you are used to. However, my Royal Guard is capable of handling any task, no matter the time and place." I paused long enough to let them know they could now speak if they wished. It was something I'd observed my alien father do on many occasions.

"My lady," Kin spoke first. "Your message to us at the pod spoke of our planet being destroyed. Is it really true?"

"Yes," I nodded, recalling that distant day. Truthfully, it felt sort of like it was a scene from an emotional movie to me. "Our ship escaped orbit moments before the Hunters released their weapon and destroyed our planet." *Our planet,* I thought how strange that sounded as I glanced down at the dying campfire. "The King and Queen decided to stay behind."

"And the other ship?" Kin asked, attempting to hide the devastation he felt.

"Damaged so that my sister's Royal Guard would've had to take control and repair it. She and her Other ..." I shook my head, recalling the image of the gaping hole filled with flames where she and her Other would've been seated.

Kin looked down into the fire, no doubt recalling friends and loved ones now long lost. To him, and the rest of the soldiers, the loss was new. To me, it was an ancient recollection. The older soldiers grew somber and still. But the younger ones, Mal and Jex, felt that the loss merely provided them more opportunities.

"Where is General Ash, my lady?" Jex's eyes were bright with curiosity. "Surely, you could not be standing here with us if he had died."

"You'll recall the message I left at the pod for you all," I searched for the correct words. "I found a way to separate Others so that we don't die in pairs. It is a way to preserve our people."

No one moved a muscle. This was something they were interested in knowing more about. I glanced at Max who had a somber expression on her face as she looked at Orion.

"This is, of course, a decision each person has the freedom to make with his or her Other, birth or chosen. No one will be forced," I smiled, noticing Max's expression soften, her shoulders relax. She placed her hand on top of Orion's.

"I chose to separate from the General ... for reasons that are my own," I turned and walked around the fire to the other side where Xi sat. "However, Ash does not wish to remain separated from me. This may or may not cause us trouble ..." At the word 'trouble' each soldier sat straighter, more alert. "But I believe ... hope ... that, in the end, the General will remain loyal to the royal house and will follow my commands as his Queen."

I realized how ridiculous I must look, standing there talking to a group of elite alien soldiers. Me, with my human body and dirty clothes. How was I going to convince them that I ... Blair Reynolds ... could lead them? I felt like a little girl pretending to be a princess.

"We will serve you, protect you, and defend you, my lady. Even if it means our own deaths," I turned to see Kin kneeling in front of me.

A broad smile crossed Xi's face. He was proud of his group of soldiers. He nodded at me as if to say, *See? They will follow you to the ends of the universe.*

Instead, he turned to his men, and his voice rang out loud and clear, "Who will show their allegiance to the Queen this night?" As if they'd practiced it over and over, they all fell in line, kneeling before me, each with one arm crossing his or her chest, and holding a fist over each beating heart.

"Tonight, we start anew!" Xi's voice rang out. "Tonight we pledge our lives to the service and safety of Queen ..." he glanced at me, eyebrows raised, inquiring what name I wished to be called.

They'd all known me as Lore. Two of them, Xi and Kin, had been present at my royal naming ceremony when the Holy Men and Women had pounded the drums and sang the sacred songs of our people. I'd been named in honor of their religion ... their Lore.

However, I was a different girl now. I'd grown up in a country Baptist church where I'd memorized the Ten Commandments and the Golden Rule in Vacation Bible School. My brother had thought he'd be a youth pastor someday. My name was given to me by a mother who loved me.

"Blair," I said, lifting my chin, proud of my human name.

"Queen Blair!" their loud voices reverberated to my core.

They shouted it over and over, lifting me high on their shoulders, I spun round and round, like a rock star body-surfing her fans. When, finally, I reached Xi's grasp, he carefully lowered me to the ground. My smile was so broad, it felt like my face would split in two.

Xi dismissed the soldiers and whispered that he needed to speak to me alone. What now? I wondered but kept that thought to myself.

"Meet me up there in ten minutes," I motioned toward the pyramid, then turned to look for some food. I was famished. But instead of a roasted pig, I saw Andrew and Angelica standing hand-in-hand. Angelica looked confused and frightened. Andrew looked confused, but well-rested.

"How do you feel?" I asked, unsure of how he would react given the events of the day.

He looked himself over and, with a goofy smile, said, "Pretty damned good, actually!" I couldn't help but rush to him and hug him tight. "So, you two have met?" he released me and looked back and forth at Angelica and me.

"Yep," I crossed my arms over my chest. "And it was kinda awkward."

"Your trained monkeys man-handled me," her nose flared, her eyes flashed, and her hair glowed warning-red in the light of the campfires.

"Never, ever insult my soldiers, Angelica," I was shocked by the foreboding in my voice as I stepped toward her. "We are family now. But they are also my family. I will fight to the death to protect them ... and you, too, if the need arose."

Her mouth fell open, and another emotion replaced the anger in her eyes. Was that respect? Awe? Acknowledgement of kindred spirits? I couldn't tell and really didn't have time to try. Xi needed to talk to me, and I was really curious about what he had to say.

"Andrew," I grabbed a handful of his shirt and led him to Mom's tent. She was snoring softly, no doubt regenerating while sleeping. "Look," I said as I pulled the tent flap back.

"Oh, my God! Mom!" he rushed inside and knelt beside her. "Is she okay?"

"She's resting like you did. She'll feel a lot better when she wakes up," I frowned as I looked at poor Mom lying on the floor of the tent. The cuts and bruises that Luke's men put on her were quickly fading thanks to Rake's medicines. But I knew there would be other wounds even more painful that would take much longer to heal. "Luke's men did it. My soldiers rescued her."

"Luke and his men are gonna pay for doing this to her," Andrew said through gritted teeth.

"Oh, yes. They will," I said. "Enough of that for now. Angelica told me how you met. Now, tell me about your pairing … um … wedding ceremony."

"We eloped," he shrugged. Then he showed me a couple of cell phone pictures of their small ceremony. One with Angelica standing by a large wooden cross at the edge of the jungle. She'd had her hair braided and had tucked flowers in her hair. I blinked back a few tears when I saw the selfie of them kissing as husband

and wife. And then I punched him in the arm for getting married without the family being there.

"Ouch!" he rubbed his arm. "You've gotten strong!"

"And don't forget it," I grinned. "Oh, text me those pics, too, or I'll punch you again."

A small smile crept across Angelica's lips, and I knew we were going to end up being friends ... so long as she didn't insult my soldiers or my human family. She turned and stepped into Mom's tent, and Andrew followed.

I left them to tend to Mom. On my way toward the pyramid steps, I grabbed a bite to eat from the pile of roasted meat. Rake handed me a package of dried fruit from the pod, and I munched on it as I headed toward my meeting with Xi.

There were torches at the top of the pyramid. Xi was standing by the stone seat on the pyramid platform. He looked very official, and I had to wonder what on earth was going to happen now.

Couldn't I just get a good night's sleep? I thought as the sole of my boot reached the top step.

"My Queen," he bowed.

Oh, gosh. It's going to be bad ... I couldn't hide the disappointment on my face as I climbed into the stone seat and gripped the rough, weathered armrests.

"I found the hidden room ... the laboratory you built here." He sat next to me, then softened his voice a bit, "I watched the video."

My shoulders slumped under the weight of what was coming next. There were so many important bits of information in that video. There were images he'd not seen, because he'd been in stasis when much of it happened.

"You suffered a long time, but you still focused on the future of our people. You will be a great leader," he placed his huge hand on my forearm. "My lady, you suffered in silence over the death of your royal babies."

It had been a devastating blow to me in my alien life. I'd wanted those babies very much, even if they weren't Ky's. But I'd never gotten to hold them in my arms. A centuries-old frown crept across my face and heart.

"You wished to awaken me. You needed me, but the General kept you from coming to the pod," Xi's voice was filled with something that sounded much like regret.

"I did what I had to do to survive," my voice, the voice of Lore, sounded small in the darkness. "Until I could revive Ky and make everything right again …"

"The General will watch as I eat his heart," Xi's tone changed from comforting to deadly. "He will pay for the death of the royal children and for the misery he dealt to my Queen."

"It was a long time ago, Xi. I know it feels like yesterday to you, but to me," I shrugged, blinking away a tear. "Ash will be given orders to bring the other ship here so our people can be reunited."

"That is a wise decision," he nodded. "Bringing the other ship here will give our people a chance to escape extinction. "Any of my men can retrieve the other vessel. And I can rid you of the General ... it would be my greatest pleasure." His giant hand clenched into a fist.

"Would my father, the King, want the General to die? He saw fit to force me to marry him ..." It was an honest question, and I wondered what Xi's take on it would be.

He sighed, "No. He would not wish him to die." Xi stood and stepped to the edge of the pyramid platform. "He would put the General's skills to use for the good of his people. Just as you have decided to do." He almost sounded like a proud father when he spoke about me like that.

"Then, it's decided." I thought of Ash and how persuasive he could be. "Xi, I will need your support when I give him his orders. He *will* resist."

Xi turned to face me, a wild look in his eyes that spoke of a thousand conquests. "And I will resist the urge to tear him in half!" then he laughed, and I couldn't help but join in. Though, even his laughter was intimidating.

"He expects me to return to him, Xi. I made him a promise that I don't intend to keep," I said, taking a deep breath, so I could tell him the whole story of my deal with the devil to save an angel. "The date has passed, and he will be coming for me soon."

"You've awakened your Royal Guard, my lady," Xi's voice softened. "You can trust me to take care of certain things for you. This is one of them." Those were probably the most welcome words I'd ever heard. I had to wonder how many more things would happen to make me glad that I'd gone to the pod and awoken Xi and his soldiers.

"Since we are speaking of Ash …" I motioned for Xi to come sit by me again. "I don't know how he will react to Max and Orion's agreement."

"Max and the General's son?" Xi gasped. Then he tossed his head back, and his laughter boomed so loud it echoed down the stone steps and into the dark jungle forest below. "My lady, please allow me to be present at the announcing."

I rolled my eyes and nodded, which caused him to burst out laughing again. Apparently, he'd never considered Max the romantic type. Of course, he'd seen her do things I'd never imagined. But I'd also seen a tender side of her … when she didn't know anyone was watching. She genuinely cared for Orion. And this made me happy.

"There must be a chosen one for each of their birth others. Who will pair with Rake so that Max can separate and pair with her chosen one? Has Rake chosen someone?" Xi asked. He was really getting into this whole match-making thing. I couldn't laugh at it, though. Because he saw his soldiers as his family.

"Not that I know of. But I was sort of hoping Rake and Orion's birth Other, Nyx, might be instantly attracted to one another," I shrugged again. Really, I had no idea what to do about the whole thing. I couldn't even fix my own dilemmas when it came to my love life. "Well, that's all I've got to discuss right now," I stretched and yawned. "I think I'll head off to bed now. It's been a long day."

But Xi didn't budge. He sat there, looking at me with a big smile on his face. Grandma would've said that he looked like the cat who ate the canary.

"What?" I couldn't help but smile.

"I have brought what you requested," Xi said, his deep voice full of pride.

"I know! Thank you! I can't tell you how pleased I am that you found my human mother, Xi," I smiled.

Xi smiled a sort of confused smile, then, "I'm happy to please you. But that is not who I mean."

And it hit me. This was it. I swallowed hard, my heart pounded against my ribs, and a swirl of butterflies arose in my belly.

"Is it him?" I could barely choke the words up my throat.

He nodded, beaming.

And the distant memory returned, full force. We were in the laboratory. I'd wanted Ky to be proud of me ... I'd wanted to prove my worth as a scientist. But the monster had done his worst, and Ky laid in my arms, dying, his breath growing weaker and weaker as I'd begged him not to leave me. But his injuries were too severe. I'd captured his essence in a vial. And Xi had torn the monster to pieces.

I felt the sadness, the loss, right behind my breastbone, next to my heart where the deep dark dread had lived for so long. My bottom lip quivered, and a well of tears blurred the torchlight.

Could it be? Could it really be that he's here? I looked into Xi's wide, slanted eyes.

Yes. And he's waiting for you down there. His thoughts mingled with mine as he pointed to the path in the jungle that led to the pool where I bathed earlier that day.

"Look at me," I gasped, glancing down at my dirty, tattered clothes. "I don't have anything clean to wear."

Xi reached behind the stone seat and retrieved my backpack. I grabbed it and thanked him as I tore the zipper open and fished out one of the outfits Natalie had bought for me. Then I remembered that they'd been purchased with Everett's money. I glanced up at Xi, wishing I could describe how torn I felt inside over Ky and Everett.

"I will turn my back as you change, my lady," the tone in his voice relayed that he knew I was fighting a battle in my heart.

He turned his back to me and crossed his arms over his chest. And I slipped back into the shadows of the stone pavilion and changed into a pair of capris cargo pants and a tank top that had a hoodie on it. I examined the hoodie and shook my head. Natalie and her fashion. She'd dress me like a Barbie doll if I'd let her.

After I changed into the clean clothes and slipped the box with my tiny galaxy into my pocket, I reached down into the backpack and found my hair brush. I wanted to whoop and holler like a cowgirl, but I kept it to myself as I brushed my tangled hair. It had grown so long that it was now waist-length. I thought of how Everett would love to see it that long and suppressed the thought before it reached my heart.

"I'll be ready in a minute," I told Xi just before I shoved my toothbrush into my mouth and rinsed with a bottle of water I'd packed away before I'd lost my backpack.

"There's no rush, my lady," Xi answered.

"Oh, yes, there is! I've been waiting for this moment for centuries!" I stepped out from the stone pavilion, ready to see my truest of loves.

He was the biggest secret of all … the reason I'd set all of this into motion so long ago. The reason I'd made myself forget so no one would find out about him before it was time. And the time was now.

"He's waiting for you," Xi smiled. "You'd better go before he disappears."

I rushed down the steps, pausing at the bottom when I saw Mom and Andrew hugging. Angelica's eyes met mine, and I waved once before I headed around the right of the pyramid base. Turning the corner, I smashed into Max and Orion, who were obviously in the throes of a passionate make-out session. Max had pinned Orion against the stone wall, holding him high enough that they seemed to be the same height.

She started to bow her head and apologize. But I simply didn't have time for formalities. I looked from Max to Orion. The only way I could describe the expression on Orion's face was that he looked happy and drunk.

"Carry on, Max. Just ... don't hurt him," I gasped, already a bit winded. "Orion, it's time. Xi found him. I'm going to him now," then I turned and left before he could ask any questions. Lightning neighed and stamped her hooves as I passed her makeshift corral. I paused only a second to tell her I'd be back, that I was going to see someone special. Then, I headed for the forest.

The path punched a dark hole into the thick wall of jungle. My eyes immediately adjusted to the darkness, but still, the path was dark as night. Ahead, though, some sort of light shined down from the tree canopy.

A few steps further, and I was greeted by the sound of trickling water echoing from the small stream. The mysterious light sparkled on the ribbon of water, reflecting spots of light onto the surrounding trees and heavy moss that clung to the edges of the stream.

My heart fluttered behind my ribs as my eyes followed the golden ray of light upward, into the canopy overhead. Monarch butterflies of various shapes and sizes flitted among the branches and into the glimmering light. I sighed. It was pure magic.

It reminded me of something Everett would create.

But I'd gone into the jungle to meet Ky, not Everett. My heart was torn in two, and there was nothing to be done. I had to finish this part of the mission and meet the man who'd been the whole reason for all the secrets that surrounded my loved ones and me.

Everett will forgive me. He'll understand, I thought as I clutched my chest, feeling the charm on Grandma's necklace beneath my shirt. I thought of Grandma and how she'd always said 'do what's right, and it will all work out.'

I stepped into the glimmering beam of light, and warmth washed over me. It reminded me of the beam of light that had lowered me from the figure-eight-shaped UFO the night Everett returned me home from my first experience in dream-traveling. I tried to swallow down every thought and memory of Everett that flooded across my heart.

"Pssst!" the sound startled me. It was coming from somewhere above me.

"Where are you?" I asked, my voice barely above a whisper. Nerves gripped me around the throat like stage fright.

"Up here," he answered, speaking just as quietly. Then a hand appeared in the golden beam of light, reaching out of the bushy canopy. "Come to me."

Without a second thought, I leapt up, up, up. He caught my hand, and I squinted through the edges of the light, searching for his face. And I was hit with a déjà vu … or was it a dream I'd had? I'd dreamed of floating in the tree canopy, reaching for Everett. His name kept arising to the surface of my heart. I blinked away the tears, and swallowed hard. I'd deal with that loss another day.

"Close your eyes," he whispered.

I clamped my eyes closed and held on as he pulled me into the canopy. Leaves caressed against my face and arms and tugged at my hair. Suddenly, my feet landed on something sort of flat. It moved and gave way a little. But it was firm and steady.

"Sit, but keep your eyes closed," he whispered, a smile tinting his voice. I did as I was told, smiling in return and biting my bottom lip.

"Can I open them now?" I asked as he released my hand.

He answered by tenderly pressing his lips to mine, and everything, heaven and earth, jungle and sky, burst into millions of sparkles of light. My lips parted, and memories of my alien life flooded in like an ocean of images. All of them happy. All of them with Ky.

And nothing else and no one else in the universe mattered anymore. I'd finally, after centuries of mourning, of waiting, of desperately longing … finally, I was in his arms. His hands gently grasped tendrils of my hair, pulling me to him. My own hands gripped his shoulders, determined to never, ever let him go again.

He pulled his lips far enough away from mine to say, "Open your eyes, Firefly."

I gasped. My eyes flew open, and the world stopped spinning. "Everett?" I clasped his face in my hands.

"The one and only," he smiled broadly. "Well, maybe I should say the two and only. I'm all your true loves wrapped up in the body of a nerd."

"You're Ky?" I squealed, shoving him backward. He bounced back against the canvas trampoline-like-thing he'd hung between the trunks of several trees, no doubt another piece of cool equipment he'd gotten from The Resistance. I straddled him, pinning him down by his shoulders, and looked him over. It really was Everett … *my* Everett.

He nodded, a small smile at the corners of his lips. Then he was suddenly in my head, sharing a memory I'd clung to for so long. But it was from his point of view. We were on the beach, and he was roasting a wild bird for our dinner. I saw his reflection in my wide, slanted eyes. In a bounding flash, we were back in the tree canopy, him beneath me.

"Oh, how I wanted it to be you!" I fell on him, kissing him, loving the feel of his arms wrapped tight around me.

Then he flipped us over so that he was lying next to me, hovering over me, pressing me into the canvas. It was too good to be true, and I wanted to pinch myself. *But what if that made all of this go way?* I shook my head. *What if I lose him again, forever this time?*

His lips met mine once more, and we were taken away, again, to the distant past … to the day Ky died.

With both of our perspectives blended into one, we were like bystanders watching the whole ugly thing unfold. I cried out as we watched Ky take his last breath, and Everett gasped and shuttered, remembering the moment Ky's essence left his alien body and slipped into the silver engagement vial he'd given Lore.

"I'm so sorry," I whispered, pulling my lips from his, and with another blast of energy, we were back in the tree canopy, and I was in Everett's arms.

"Shhhh…" he cooed, pressing his finger to my lips. But I couldn't be silenced.

"Forgive me … forgive me …" my lips brushed against his as he tried to kiss away my sobs.

"There's nothing to forgive," he whispered, pulling me into his shoulder and cradling me close to him.

"You died because of my foolish decisions. Then things happened that you don't know, and they were all against my will. I had no other choice, but I never forgot you." I pressed my face against his chest, listening to the strong beat of his heart. "I never stopped loving you."

"I know what you had to do …" he pressed his cheek against the top of my head. "I saw the video you left for yourself."

I froze. My mind went back to the tunnel, the secret laboratory I'd created, and the work Orion had helped me with … and the fresh set of footprints I'd seen imprinted in the dust of the cave floor. "How?"

"Take a guess," he pulled away from me and looked into my eyes, his expression soft and sweet.

And it hit me like a lightning bolt …

We'd hidden the Cicada … Orion … in Everett's bug room at Bobby's Climate Controlled Storage Units. Everett had insisted on saving him and taking him there and nurturing him. I'd always assumed it was because of his love of bugs and creepy crawly things.

"He told you, didn't he?" I looked up into his bright blue eyes.

"Not until he gained his strength after leaving his cocoon," he answered.

"He chose to clone you, because he knew I would rather him protect you than me … that if something happened to you again, I would die." My heart was racing as all the puzzle pieces began falling into place.

"It really freaked me out seeing my clone crawl out of that slimy shell in my bug room," he fake-cringed.

"It freaked us all out!" I giggled. "That was the first time I ever heard you use the 'F' word." We both laughed at the memory that seemed ages old. "Wait!" I stopped giggling. I had to know. "So that's what's written in your notebook, isn't it … everything Orion told you while he was recuperating in your bug room?" I thought back to the night we were going to Everett's bug room at Bobby's Climate Controlled Storage Units. He'd shown me a few paragraphs of his notes he'd recorded in a battered old composition book. But he'd refused to let me read further, saying that it was for my own safety. He'd known who ... what I was before I had.

"Yeah," Everett looked like he'd been found out. "Poor guy was pretty much figuring things out while he went."

"He was sent by Ash to clone me," I nodded. Poor Orion. I'd put a huge responsibility on his shoulders by getting him involved. I decided to find a way to reward him someday soon. "So, what happened to the notebook? I thought it was in the box, because when we buried it, there wasn't anything metallic inside."

"I came back and switched it out with your armband and burned the notebook. I had to find Orion to get the armband from him. You'd left it for him in your secret laboratory," he answered, twirling a lock of my hair around his finger. "A piece was missing, so he decided to move it for your protection."

"Ash," I sighed. "He must have found it and disabled it so he could be in control of my immortality."

"It's all behind us now, babe," he hugged me tight.

"I wish we could have gone on like we were. Just kids growing up in a small town," I toyed with a lock of his dark hair and thought back to our home town. Everyone there was going on with their lives oblivious to the weird things that have happened.

"You made sure we grew up with good families ... that we had a happy human childhood. We got to know each other naturally, like we did before. I wouldn't change it for anything," he kissed my forehead and brushed my cheek with his thumb.

"Everett?" my heart sank again, remembering the video in the secret laboratory and the familiar woman on the gurney. Of course, now I knew who she was.

"Hmmm?" he mumbled, kissing my neck just below my earlobe.

"I'm sorry about what I did to your mother," I bit my lip, afraid that would be the end of his forgiveness.

"I didn't know her," he said, leaning over me again, looking into my eyes. "She died when I was born."

"I know, and I'm sorry. I think it had to do with my experiments," I frowned. "Forgive me. For everything."

"Lore," his tone changed a little, and it was at that moment that I realized we'd been speaking in our native alien language. "It's me – Ky. You did what you had to do to save me. You did this because you love me. And do you know what?" he raised his eyebrows.

"What?" my voice sounded so tiny in the back of my throat.

"I love you more than anything in this universe," he said, smoothing my hair away from my face.

"Tell me, Ky," I cradled his face in my hands. "Tell me you forgive me. I need to hear it."

He sighed, and I heard his thoughts. He didn't feel there was anything to forgive. That he understood everything I'd done and why. But he also understood my need for hearing his words of forgiveness. The need came from my human side, and it called to his human side to fill my need.

"Not that there's anything to forgive," he said, just before pressing a quick kiss on my lips. Then he paused, looking deep into my eyes, my soul, and gave me what I needed. "I forgive everything."

Then he pulled me to him again. He covered my lips with his as my body melded with his. Electricity sparked from us, pushing us off the canvas and upward through the canopy and into the starlit sky, spinning, whirling, kissing, caressing, whispering each other's name.

My hair lifted out in tendrils, each seeming to have a mind all its own. Winds whipped around us, tugging at the collar of his shirt, blowing through his short, black hair. No more did the tribal drums need to draw us together as I'd so carefully programmed my body to do when I found him in this human life.

I thought my face would split in half from smiling so broadly. Everett smiled back at me and then threw his head back and laughed. We spun around and around, enveloped in a wispy cloud that threaded round us like a gossamer ribbon.

"This is your wedding veil," Everett said, twirling his hand and spinning a strand of cloud around my head.

"Yes! The answer is yes!" I shouted over the wind.

"I haven't asked you the question yet!" he laughed.

"You asked me centuries ago!" I smiled again, placing a quick kiss on his lips.

"Oh, no, Firefly! We're doing this right!" he said just before he pulled me tight against him and spun us down, down, down so fast that I thought we'd smash into the ground.

Then we slowed just before we touched down at the top of the pyramid. My head was spinning, and I wavered a bit before I was able to stand still and straight. Everett grabbed my hand and led me to the top of the pyramid steps.

"Hey, everybody! I need your attention!" he shouted, alerting everyone below, and causing a stir among the soldiers, who started to advance before I held up my hand to stop them. Mom had been sitting by the fire with Andrew and Angelica. They all stood up and walked toward the pyramid steps, stopping when they saw the two of us at the top.

Everett took both of my hands in his and then knelt down on one knee. "Blair Reynolds, you are Queen of my heart … my reason for living and breathing. Without you, I'm only half a person. Make me the happiest nerd in the universe tonight. I love you. Please say you'll marry me." He reached into his pocket and retrieved the vial and wrapped it around my wrist the way he'd done so long ago on the beach on our home planet.

Something clinked against the side of the vial. I looked closely and discovered an engagement ring dangling from a piece of string tied to the chain. He snapped the string loose and a brilliant diamond star glistened in the torchlight as he slipped the platinum ring onto my finger, over my brand of a butterfly.

"Yes," I nodded. "A million times yes!"

He stood and twirled me around and around, holding me tight in his arms. Then lowered me down and kissed me once more. I slipped the engagement vial over his head ... two engagement traditions melded into one union. The first of its kind. We turned to the gawking soldiers and family members below, who cheered and clapped. Orion was beaming. He'd helped the only mother he'd ever known achieve happiness.

Happiness that will last forever now, I sighed, wishing on the diamond star on my finger. I leaned into Everett's side as we began to descend the steps.

We don't always get what we wish for ...

A blast of wind followed by a massive explosion blew us backward onto the pyramid platform. Below, Xi shouted orders over the melee of flaming bits of jungle trees that rained down over the camp.

"Xi, protect my family!" I shouted, pointing to Mom, Andrew, and Angelica, who were running toward the pyramid. He turned and nodded to me.

To the left of the vast clearing, the jungle had been laid bare by the blast, and plumes of smoke arose from hundreds of small fires caused by the explosion. Everett pushed me behind him as soon as they came into view. Dozens and dozens of soldiers, their hi-tech armor dull in the smoky light of the fires, were battling *them* ... the Hunters.

"Those are human soldiers!" Max shouted, standing in front of Orion. Kin nodded at her and ordered his men into battle formation.

A platoon of Hunters marched out of the clearing, heading for camp. Any resistance given by the human soldiers did nothing to stop them. These were the elite soldiers of their royal house. They were coming for me ... for vengeance.

"Protect the Queen at all costs!" Xi's voice rang out. Immediately, two Guards were at my side.

"You must come back to our pod, my lady," Jex bowed.

"There are other humans among them!" Mal interrupted, stepping to the edge of the pyramid platform. "I don't understand," he turned and looked at me. "Why are there humans on opposite sides of this battle?"

"Mercenaries," I said, gritting my teeth, feeling the flames building inside me. "No doubt Luke's men are on the side of the Hunters." My mind immediately flashed to Mom and what they'd done to her. I looked down at the camp in time to see Orion leading them into the forest. Rake was directly behind them. "But I have no idea who those soldiers are fighting against the Hunters."

"That's The Resistance," Everett answered. I wanted to know more, like how they knew about the Hunters and why they weren't fighting against us, too. Or were they? But Jex interrupted.

"My lady, we really must get to you safety," Jex said, gently touching my arm.

"He's right," Everett turned to me. "Go with them."

"I'm not leaving you!" I shook my head. "I'm not losing you again!"

"I'll be right behind you," he kissed my cheek. "Now, go!"

Kin's men were marching out into the clearing to meet the foe. Plumes of black smoke darkened the battlefield, making my Royal Guard look even more menacing. Max let out a battle cry. She'd be wearing blood across her face and body soon, and she was looking forward to it. The Hunters were close now, their armor heavy and dark. Their weapons drawn. Their leader shouted orders to his men.

And I sent up a quick prayer for protection for my men and women before following Mal and Jex down the steps and around the pyramid base, toward Lightning's corral. I blasted a section of the corral fence away and whistled to my horse. She trotted to me, wide-eyed and afraid. I grabbed her reins and led her behind me.

Judging by the clash of metal, and blood curdling screams of the Hunters, my Guard had entered the battle. My heart pounded against my ribs. This was nothing I could've ever imagined. Not even in my darkest memories of fleeing our planet during Ky's funeral did I feel the fear that flowed through my veins. This was too real.

"Jex, I don't know the way to the pod from here," I was already winded, but adrenaline pumped through every atom of my being, spurring me onward. I wasn't usually one to run, but it seemed I had no choice.

"Follow me, my lady!" Jex took the lead, jogging ahead of me, slaying bush and limb, vine and tree with his sword. Mal followed behind me, taking Lightning's reins and pulling her behind him. She kept her head down and followed without any resistance.

"Where is my family?" I asked, fighting to keep my breath. I needed to recharge, to dig my hands into the earth and absorb its energy.

"We'll meet them at the pod, my lady," Mal answered.

"Can't we get there some other way?" I thought of flying with Everett.

"We could be tracked and trapped, my lady," Jex answered over his shoulder. "The Commander ordered us to reach the pod this way, for your safety."

Another loud explosion behind us shook the ground, reminding me of the day we fled our home planet. And now I was fleeing again, to an ancient alien pod hidden in the side of a hill.

When will history stop repeating itself? I thought, wondering where Everett was and when we'd run into Ash again.

We came to a wide section of river. Jex went out ahead of us, testing the depth of the water. It came up to his waist, which would put it at near shoulder height for me. It would be treacherous, but there was no other choice.

He took my hand and led me into the rushing water. I glanced back over my shoulder to see Mal leading Lightning into the water. Then my eyes looked up above the tree canopy behind him and saw a blaze of billowing, growing, boiling cloud of fire heading toward us, devouring the forest.

"Jex! Run! Get us out of here!" I shouted. My boot slipped on a stone, and I plunged under the rushing water and lost my grip on Jex's enormous hand.

I clambered over the flat, slippery river rocks but couldn't regain my step. A flash of red reflected across the surface of the river. I opened my mouth and tried to scream, but only muted sounds and a column of bubbles came out.

Something pulled me upward to the surface and shoved me to the bank on the other side of the river, where smoke filled my lungs. Jex pulled me into the jungle on the other side. Mal and Lightning followed behind us.

"What happened?" I asked, coughing and gagging on the smoke.

"The humans have caught our trail," Mal answered, his voice sounding more menacing than I'd ever imagined a young handsome soldier could sound.

Jex motioned for us to stop. "My lady, forgive me, but the Commander ordered me to do this, for your safety." He quickly retrieved a wicked-looking syringe from his belt.

"What is that?" I heard the skepticism in my voice as I stepped back, looking at the syringe in his hand that reminded me so much of a bovine tranquilizer dart I'd once used on one of the Hunters.

"It contains a tracker," Jex held it out for me to see. "If we are separated from you, we will be able to find you quickly, so long as your armband remains undamaged." He pointed to the raised, woven band that circled my upper left arm.

Mal flashed an encouraging smile, "It is true."

"We must hurry, my lady," Jex tried to hide the disappointment he felt in knowing his Queen doubted his loyalty.

"I trust you," I tried to smile, then held out my left arm and steeled myself.

Jex grasped my arm with his large hand and quickly plunged the thick needle into my arm, releasing the tracker into the flesh just beneath the bend of my arm. I gritted my teeth and suppressed the scream that wanted to burst out of my chest. It hurt. Bad.

"I'm sorry, my lady," Jex quickly bowed his head. Then he pushed a button on a device on his belt, and a dim light glowed where the tracking device was embedded beneath my skin. "It's working. Now, let's go."

We're being followed, Mal's voice wound through mine and Jex's thoughts.

I know, Jex answered, his eyes scanning the surrounding jungle.

Dawn would arrive soon, and I hoped it would bring an end to this. However, it seemed that the smoke from the fires would keep the sun hidden behind the death and destruction that came with the Hunters.

My lady, if we fall, you must travel due east from here, Jex's voice spun through my head. He drew his sword again, and behind me, Mal's gun powered up. *Just remember to send up lanterns for us.*

What? I stifled a gasp.

We are surrounded, Mal's voice entered my thoughts. He slapped Lightning on the rump, sending her running into the forest. *By Hunters and humans, both.*

I didn't have my gun or any other weapon. I looked at the weapons on Jex's belt and had no idea how any of them worked. Closing my eyes, I reached out into the forest with my thoughts.

Two Hunters. I can't count the humans, I answered, trying to contribute some small bit.

Where are the Hunters? Jex asked, pulling me down to the ground as he and Mal knelt.

I motioned to where I'd sensed them, and Mal fixed a scope on his gun. *I see them,* his voice sounded like a whisper as it entered my head.

Send them to oblivion! Jex's voice was so loud in my head that I startled.

Even though Mal's gun made no sound, it tore a hole through the jungle and incinerated the two Hunters who had been sent to capture the Queen.

Then, my two brave young soldiers positioned themselves back-to-back and cloaked themselves, which also cloaked me. I crouched down low between them and wished I had Max's poncho. I'd been forced to flee so quickly that I hadn't had time to grab anything.

Jex released a tiny beacon into the sky. It flickered against the blood red clouds of smoke before it disappeared on the other side of the thick veil of destruction that threatened to suffocate us all.

Everything turned to slow motion as several mercenaries appeared from the smoke-filled jungle around us. From my perspective, all I could see was their black military boots and the camouflaged pants they wore with them. They slowly walked past us, unable to see us, their boots crunching the leaves on the loamy forest floor.

I hoped they would say something, so I could figure out their plans. But it seemed that they were communicating with hand signals. These weren't like the bumbling fools I'd encountered in the jungle cantina. These were the real deal, probably ex-military.

Then the enormous, black, scaly boot entered my vision. I imagined its face, much like the Hunters we'd killed in the building. No doubt it had the same vertical mouth lined with jagged teeth and strange reptile-like eyes.

A moment later, a thin line of light shone on the forest floor near us. It widened as the horrid creature scanned for cloaked soldiers, moving the end of its detection device back and forth until the line of light came within inches of Jex's boot.

Both of my soldiers stiffened, flexing muscles, getting ready to spring into action. My hands began to power up. I couldn't stop them. It was pure instinct that drove the energy down my arms and into my hands.

One more wide stroke of the detection device, and the line of light stopped on the tip of Jex's boot, revealing us. My soldiers leapt to their feet, weapons drawn, sword slashing, gun silently blasting, and me still kneeling behind them as they fought to protect and defend me at all costs.

The Hunter tossed his head back and laughed. He'd hunted us down and planned on returning with the heads of my soldiers as his prizes ... I picked up that image from his primal brain. I glanced up at the two young, handsome soldiers who were so loyally, valiantly risking their lives for a cowgirl from Willis who happened to be their Queen.

And the thought of the Hunters killing them really pissed me off.

I blinked once, and everything was covered in a blue haze. Looking up, I focused my mind and energy on the weather while digging my fingers in to the loamy jungle floor. Lines of electricity flowed through the soil and up my arms, and circled the band around my left bicep.

As guns blazed around me, the clouds overhead swirled in an increasingly darkening vortex as though a tornado would touch down at any moment. Although it was now early morning, the circling clouds overhead turned the jungle dark as the sky became a deep purple.

Quick as a flash, I stood and motioned for a lightning bolt. The clouds didn't fail my request. Down came the gleaming, blinding current of energy. With my other hand, I pointed at the enormous Hunter who'd come to collect me for his king.

"No!" shouted Jex, warning me not to use my powers.

Too late. The lightning bolt hit the Hunter right in the chest, sending him reeling backwards, and tumbling to the ground. The enormous energy seared the plants around his feet and melted the soil where his boots had been. Even my two soldiers were shocked at my ability to affect the weather, but that didn't stop them from fighting for their Queen.

What it did, however, was set off several snares that had been set as booby traps. Nets made of energy sprung out from the jungle on both sides. Mal shoved me hard, sending me flying backward into the underbrush behind him. He glanced back at me, brows low over his menacing eyes, ripped his shirt off, and flung it at me just before the sizzling mesh encircled my two brave Guards.

Run! his shout rang out in my brain.

For a split second, which seemed like an eternity, I remembered Dad explaining the instinct of fight or flight. If it's too dangerous to stand and fight, the wise thing to do is to take flight and save fighting for another day. I took off running through the underbrush, leaving my loyal Guards behind to fight.

CHAPTER TWENTY-TWO

FLIGHT

Clutching Mal's uniform shirt in my hand, I ran as fast as my legs would carry me, weaving around the trunks of enormous jungle trees, leaping over ancient fallen logs, my boots kicking up chunks of soil behind me while overhead the storm grew angrier.

I ran, for I don't know how long, until I came to a small clearing where a small village once stirred with life. The jungle was beginning its job of reclaiming, leaving the village dilapidated and its dwellings falling to the ground. But there was still enough of a break in the forest to attract a beautiful horse. Lightning stood in the center of a patch of grass as if she was waiting for me.

I whistled, and she trotted to me and nudged my shoulder while I hugged her neck. Then, I pulled Mal's uniform shirt over my head, climbed into her saddle, and looked around for my next route of escape.

The shirt was enormous on me. I quickly tied a knot at the waist and looked around to get my bearings. I had no idea where I was. However, it seemed wisest to go in the general direction my soldiers were taking me in hopes I could find the pod.

Lightning and I traveled for a while through the jungle unhindered until an arrow flashed past me, tearing a few strands of my hair from my head and stabbing into the tree behind me. Instinct turned my head to see that one of the mercenaries had spotted me. The arrow, no doubt, had a tranquilizer in the tip. I sent up a prayer of thanks that he missed me, then dug my heels into Lightning's ribs.

"This way!" I heard the jerk shout to his fellow jerks.

"Go, girl, go!" I bent over the saddle and hoped this horse was as good at barrel racing as my Daisy had been.

She proved her talent as she wove in and out of trees. Several more arrows struck nearby trees, missing their target as we dashed left, then right, then left. Suddenly, there was one of the jungle people, just ahead, he pointed to the right where there was a small hole in the forest leading to a clearing. I nodded to him as I steered the brilliantly fast horse toward the escape.

Bending low over the saddle, I missed the low-hanging branches by inches. We entered the clearing, the horse and I, in a rush of adrenaline-fueled speed. Overhead, the clouds still swirled, creating a startling contrast of rage against the rest of the sunlit sky, splitting it in half. Dark against light.

I wondered what was happening to Jex and Mal. They'd risked their lives for my safety when they could've easily escaped. But I had no idea how those nets would work on them. The Royal Guard were, after all, centuries old.

I slipped my hand into the narrow pouch at the neck of Mal's shirt, fished the hood out, and pulled it over my head. Then I pressed the tiny button inside the front of the shirt and the fabric shimmered and cloaked the top half of me.

What if the Hunters have been spending all that time creating new technologies to kill the rest of my people? I brought the long end of the reins down in a snap on Lightning's rump. *My people,* I thought. *Both human and alien-kind.*

Grandpa used to tell me to keep my mind from straying when I was about my work, that I could cause myself to get hurt. I heard his warning in my head just as I realized that the row of low shrubs I was about to guide the horse to jump was actually at the edge of a cliff. I pulled her reins with all my strength, digging my heels into the stirrups, and leaning back in the saddle.

But there wasn't enough time or distance.

Lightning tried, but the laws of inertia were against us. The horse stopped. But I tumbled out of the saddle, and got a clear view of the river below ... far below. I managed to grip one of Lightning's reins with one hand and grabbed a root with the other just before I slammed into the cliff wall.

There was nothing beneath my feet. I kicked and struggled to get a strong foothold. But all I did was loosen rocks and chunks of dirt, sending them splashing into the river. My arm muscles quivered under the strain.

"Pull me up, girl!" I shouted to the horse.

She snorted and started backing up. For a moment, I thought the plan would actually work. Until a mercenary appeared over the top of shrubs at the edge of the cliff, smiling. I was going to make him a good amount of money. The triumphant thought was swirling around and around in his mind.

I wouldn't make Jex's and Mal's sacrifice be in vain by giving myself over to a mercenary who had no idea that the Hunters would soon kill everyone on this planet if we let them. I shook my head *no*, then looked over my shoulder at the river far below. The fall was going to hurt like hell, but it would be a better choice than going with him.

"Come on. Don't be a fool. No one can survive a fall like that," he said, stretching his hand out to me. He was about Dad's age. I wondered if he'd ever known him as I looked into his green eyes. His face was clean-shaven and his hair shorn close to his head. Sweat beaded on his brow. *I bet he's even got a kid my age at home,* I thought as I looked him in the eyes one last time.

"I'll take my chances," I said, realizing how flat and resigned my voice sounded as I open my hands and felt the reins slip from my fingers.

He scrambled to the edge of the cliff, grappling for my hands. I pulled them away and kicked against the cliff wall. *This is really gonna hurt,* I thought as I fell down, down, down toward the river, tumbling head over heels.

About half way down, instinct kicked in and I tried to stop my fall as I'd done so many times before. True to what I'd feared, using my powers triggered a booby trap, and a dart with a line attached to it ejected from a nearby clump of trees and sliced through my shoulder. I yelped in pain, and began falling again. A stream of blood followed me like a red liquid rope.

Covering the gash with my right hand, I sent up a short prayer that this would all be over quick and that I'd be with Dad and Aaron. I opened my eyes just before I plunged into the shallow water at the river's edge and slammed into a very large, smooth rock. For the second time in one day, I screamed out under water. Only this time, I gulped in the water, and lost my breath just before everything went dark.

Green grass, as far as the eye could see, gently swayed in the lazy summer breeze. I didn't know how long I'd been napping, but I felt very rested as I pushed myself up on my elbow and plucked a tiny white wild flower and put it to my nose. It smelled as sweet as honeysuckle. I sat up and surveyed my surroundings. It looked like the west pasture at the ranch where Grandpa sometimes planted rye grass in the winter.

"Sleep well?" Dad's voice startled me. He was sitting next to me, knees bent, ankles crossed, and handing me a cold bottle of water.

"Daddy?" I lunged into his arms and hugged him tight. "What are you doing here?"

"I might ask you the same question," he kissed me on the cheek.

I shook my head and shrugged. Then a vague realization of something pecked at the back door of my brain. "I don't know. I must have been taking a nap."

"You've got to go back, Princess," he said, placing his hand on mine. "You're not done yet."

"Huh?" my brows drew together as I searched his face.

"I love you. Do you know that?" he brushed a lock of my hair away from my face.

I nodded and smiled. "Of course, I know that. And I love you, too." Then I had the vaguest feeling of deep heartache, but I didn't know why.

"Aren't you thirsty?" he held the bottle of water out to me again, and I took it from his hand. I unscrewed the top and lifted it to my lips. Right before I took a drink, he stopped me. "I'll see you again someday. Just remember, in order to beat them, you've got to surprise them. It's your only chance." I started to ask him what he meant, but he lifted my hand holding the bottle to my lips.

The cool water crossed my tongue and flowed down my throat. At first it was just a sip. But suddenly, it was a gush, filling my mouth, and choking me. "Long live the Queen," Dad's voice whispered in my ear.

Gasping ... choking ... coughing ... I lifted my head out of the shallow water at the river's edge. Pain sliced through my arm like a jagged piece of metal. I was weak, waterlogged, and nauseated. My head felt like it was spinning.

Something nudged me from behind, and I scrambled to my feet, stumbling, and confused. I turned, expecting it to be the mercenary. Lightning shook her head and neighed. Mal's shirt was still in cloak mode, and the hood was still over my head. I had no idea how she found me, but I was glad.

On wobbly legs, I leaned against her shoulder and thanked her for finding me. The pain in my arm was so intense that everything in my stomach came up at once. Cold chills flashed across my skin, and I threw up once more.

Finally, the stomach spasms ceased, and I was able to bring myself to look at my left arm. It dangled at my side like dead weight. The skin had turned dark purple and red. My bottom lip quivered as I slowly moved my eyes up my arm until they stopped where the woven band circled my bicep.

A black, splintered bone protruded through my flesh, severing the strands of the silver band embedded around my arm. An image of Everett laying strapped to the gurney in the building flashed across my mind ... the Hunter slicing his arm open, looking for a skeleton the color of carbon. It'd thought I'd been the one who'd cloned Everett to hide myself.

Lightning stamped her hooves and snorted as if to hurry me up. But I knew I had to do something about the bone protruding from my arm before infection set in. After a few tries, I was able to take Mal's shirt off. Then I removed mine and slipped back into the uniform shirt.

Intense pain stabbed through my arm sending tremors through my entire body, and a few times I felt as though I'd pass out. It took everything I had in me to keep that from happening.

Using Lightning to keep me from falling, I forced one foot to move in front of the other until I made it to the edge of the river where a tree had taken up root in the fertile river bank. My left hand was turning darker and swelling. I pried my engagement ring off my finger and stuffed it in my pocket.

"Don't leave me girl," I whispered to Lightning. "I've gotta try and set this before it gets so bad that I can't. I'm probably going to scream, but don't be scared."

With my bottom lip quivering and my stomach threatening to lurch again, I took a deep breath, pulled myself up by the bootstraps, and placed my right hand over the splintered bone. Before I could chicken out, I slammed against the tree, using the force of my body to push the bone back in place and my hand to keep the bone from being further damaged by the tree bark.

I screamed, but no sound escaped my throat. The pain was nearly too much to bear. The elements heard my silent scream, though. Rain poured out of the sky as clouds rolled and boiled out of thin air. Bolts of lightning struck time and time again, pounding the earth, and shaking the forest. Then the hail came.

The ground fell out from under me, or at least that's the way it seemed, as my knees gave way. After a few moments of catching my breath and fighting the blackness that threatened to pull me under, I managed to pull myself up using Lightning's saddle.

Natalie's shirt became a make-shift cast for my broken arm, wrapping it tight to stop the bleeding. I hugged Lightning once more, glad for the company, then managed to pull myself up into her saddle. Without my armband, I couldn't recharge … I'd become mortal again, and it seemed like gravity had tripled.

Hail pelted down on the horse and me as we made our way along the riverbank, looking for a way out of the canyon that sliced through the jungle. We finally found one where the jungle people came down to the river to fish. It was steep, but not too steep for a horse like Lightning. She carefully picked her way up the sharp incline until we were able to enter the forest once more by an often-used path.

Finally, the safety of the jungle encompassed us. I had no idea where we were, because I'd floated far downstream from where I'd fallen. No doubt the mercenaries would be looking for me. The rain would surely hide my path and give me a chance to escape their trackers.

To keep myself from passing out, I let my mind wander once I'd steered Lightning in the direction I thought was the way back to the pod. Hopefully, I'd run into one of my Guard soon. They wouldn't be able to track me now that my band was destroyed. But at least they had an idea on a starting point.

Everett was still alive, that much I knew. If something would've happened to him, I would have felt it in my heart and soul. I wondered where he was, if he'd joined ranks with the Royal Guard or if he'd gone to the aid of the soldiers in The Resistance.

Something perplexed me, picking out details in my distant memories. *Why were Everett's bones the color of a human's?* I bit my lip as I puzzled over it. Mine are black like those of my alien people. Then I realized the reason. It struck me like a lightning bolt.

My essence *and* my actual DNA had been melded into Mom's body. Only Everett's essence had been injected into his mother. So, while he's a hybrid, the lack of his alien DNA had required that he be formed with fully human tissues. I was proud that my science had worked.

But what good was it doing me at this very moment? I sighed. If I didn't get my thoughts off of Everett, I'd likely start bawling like a baby. So, I allowed my mind to wonder what had happened to Jex and Mal. The thought of the Hunters displaying their heads on spikes was almost too much, so I pushed that out of my mind and prayed they'd find a way of escape.

Xi crossed my mind. If he'd known I was missing, he would tear down the whole jungle. So, I doubt he knew yet ... unless he'd fallen to the Hunters. *Surely he hasn't,* I thought as I lowered my head, allowing the rain to pour off Mal's hood in rivulets.

I thought of the mercenary who'd tried to convince me to take his hand so he could pull me up over the edge of the cliff. He'd looked about Dad's age, and something ... a small part of the human in me ... had wanted to trust him and take his hand. And that led me to the thing I was avoiding ... my dream of Dad.

Had it really been a dream? I bit my lip and a rain drop trickled into my mouth. *Or had it been real? Had I died and returned? Did he save my life?* I nodded, resolved that he had. That I'd really died in that fall and had been sent back to finish what I'd started so very long ago. He'd even whispered something to wake me up.

"I love you, Daddy," I whispered, keeping my head down against the onslaught of rain. In my heart of hearts, I knew he'd heard me.

I knew something else, too. I'd had a long enough flight. Now, I needed to rest and rejuvenate. Surely, a safe refuge would present itself soon.

CHAPTER TWENTY-THREE

REST

At some point, I passed out. When I came to, Lightning had stopped walking and had found refuge for us under a heavily-laden tree. Vines, limbs, and leaves formed a perfect hiding place. It even kept the rain off of us.

I had no idea how long I'd been slumped over the horn of the saddle. But one thing was certain … I barely had the energy to move. My legs were stiff and achy, but they weren't the only part of me that was. In fact, there wasn't an inch of my body that wasn't in pain.

The ground looked so far away, but I knew I couldn't stay in the saddle and get any amount of real rest. Getting out of the saddle was going to be painful, that much was sure. Vines formed several loops that hung down from an arching branch. I slipped one under my good arm, gritted my teeth, slid out of the saddle, and slumped to the ground.

A mound of leaves formed a sort of cushion. Still, the shock of the fall jolted through all my bones, and I couldn't stop the yelp that escaped my lips. I curled into a ball between two large roots where the tree trunk made me feel a little safe. And the alien side of me began to whisper that it was time to form a cocoon.

Then everything went black.

I awoke once more. Lightning was nearby, munching on some grasses at the base of a tree. It was time to move, to travel to a different part of the jungle, so I wouldn't be found. But without my armband to help me recharge, my injuries were too much.

My left arm was swollen and extremely painful. I touched it with my good hand, and felt a sort of slimy membrane. When I examined my good hand, I realized that my skin was turning transparent the way the Cicada's had been.

Maybe it's for the best, I thought, giving in. Grandpa had told me that there are some things in life we have no control over. This felt like one to me.

Wincing, I rolled over onto my back and looked up at the jungle canopy. The rain had stopped, and drops of water glistened in the brilliant moonlight on the leaves overhead. Far above the jungle canopy, a cloud moved aside, allowing a silver moonbeam to pierce the treetops and shimmer down to dance in brilliant spots of light along the jungle floor.

I gave in. Resting in a cocoon wouldn't be the worst thing in the universe. Many of my alien people had done it so many times before. As soon as I came to terms with what I needed to do, a rush of fluttering wings filled the night air.

Flashes of color passed through the beam of moonlight, and my eyes followed the brilliant gathering of hundreds of Monarch butterflies. They came to light on me, covering every inch of me, their wings moving and weaving, forming the opaque shell that would soon separate me from the world.

Hours later, I awoke again. I'd dreamed about Ky and me, ages ago, dancing together at a ball. He'd held me in his arms, and I'd felt safe and loved. In this life, I'd felt the same way in Everett's arms. If I rested here, it may take years for me to be found ... if ever.

Clear slime filled my cocoon part of the way, just reaching my nose as I lay on my side. *How can I help him find me?* I wondered, going through everything in my mind, searching for options.

I thought of my tiny galaxy and slipped my good hand into my pocket. The little box tumbled out and snapped open. Sparkles of light reflected on the shiny walls of the cocoon as the tiny galaxy traveled around the confined space. It came to hover around my face as if to see if I was okay.

For some reason, a random thought of Mom came to mind. She was standing in her sparkling new Sprinkles. Her arms were crossed over her chest. She had a dish towel in her hand, and I'd just embarrassed her with a joke about her kissing Everett's dad.

Then my mind went to Christmas a year ago. I was just beginning to realize the pull between Everett and me. I'd given him a kiss as a Christmas present. Later, as our kitchen filled with guests and Andrew began singing *Deck the Halls* really loud, I'd turned around and saw Everett's broad, goofy smile.

Another memory flashed across my mind. It was the night of the Rodeo Gala. Everett had captured one of the tiny galaxies and had given it to me and said that now, he'd always be able to find me.

"Listen to me, Blair Reynolds," I said, deciding that I needed a pep talk. "You've never been a quitter, and you're not going to quit now. You've got people counting on you," my voice was scratchy and weak, but it did the trick.

My little galaxy hovered close to my face, bumping against my cheek and spinning off to hover over my lips. I have no idea what made me do it … but I opened my mouth, and the tiny, sparkling jewel dropped inside.

It sparkled on my tongue and then down my throat, where a well of energy grew and grew until my heart pounded so fast I thought I'd die. *Whoom!* A rush of energy burst through my chest wall, passed through the opaque cocoon shell, and rushed through the forest like a tidal wave.

Well, that's it, I guess, I thought. *Either someone will come for me, or that was a waste of a good galaxy.* Then, I closed my eyes and welcomed sleep again … the only thing that saved me from the immense pain.

A strange tugging and scraping awoke me some time later. The bark of the tree scraped against the outside of the opaque shell as the cocoon inched its way up the side of the tree. It was a very slow process that would end once the cocoon reached the appropriate height. Just like the Cicada's cocoon had. But it had gotten smashed under the top of a tree. *Or had it? Perhaps that had been orchestrated by Orion so that we'd find him,* the idea whirled around my brain until I dipped back down into darkness.

Sometime after that, I was awoken by the sound of leaves and sticks crunching under footsteps. They weren't the sounds of Lightning's hooves on the loamy forest floor. It was a human. Shifting onto my side was made easier by the slime that was accumulating. I turned toward the footsteps and waited.

A single light pierced the darkness of the jungle. Someone placed their hand on the side of my cocoon, and I placed my good hand on the slimy wall and pressed my face against the shell, hoping to identify the interloper.

First a muffled voice, then a few quick movements. Then a knife blade pierced the cocoon shell and sliced it open. The slime oozed out of the gash cut along the side of the shell, and I slipped out with it.

And landed in Everett's arms.

My love had found me, and now it was time to literally come out of my shell and plunge back into the fray.

CHAPTER TWENTY-FOUR

OUT OF MY SHELL AND INTO THE FRAY

"You found me," my slimy head lobbed over onto Everett's shoulder.

"I'll always find you," he pulled me tight against him and then began running.

I sighed and kept my eyes closed as I pressed my face against his neck, vaguely wondering if the feel of my skin grossed him out just before falling back under the veil of darkness.

Sometime later, I emerged above the surface of unconsciousness to discover that I was laying on the forest floor. Nearby, the sound of trickling water danced between the tree trunks like tinkling chimes. I opened my eyes to discover sunshine glinting on the surface of a narrow stream.

The skin on my good hand was beginning to look more human again, but not much. At least the coat of slime was gone. Still, my veins and tissues were visible through my skin. *That would really freak Natalie out,* I thought.

It was during that odd thought that I heard two people quietly talking nearby. I couldn't make out what they were saying, but they were both male. One of them cursed, and I immediately realized Andrew was talking. Probably to Everett.

A sudden chill ran down my body, and my teeth began to chatter a bit. I had a fever. I was on the ground in the middle of the jungle. My arm was severely broken. I couldn't recharge and regenerate. And I was being hunted.

Dad had once told me, "Never, ever ask if it can get worse. Because that's the exact moment that it will." Of course, I wish I would have remembered that before I managed to roll over onto my back and mumble, "Could it get any worse?"

Dad was never wrong.

Suddenly, Andrew and Everett were kneeling next to me. Andrew had Dad's knife in his hand, and Everett was holding a tiny ear bud in his ear, listening to something. He nodded, then slipped the ear bud into a small pocket on his black cargo pants. He was back into his uniform from The Resistance.

"We're surrounded," he whispered to Andrew.

"I know," Andrew answered, "I can sense them."

"All human?" Everett asked.

Andrew nodded.

"What's going on?" I asked, trying to keep my voice quiet.

Andrew patted me on the good shoulder. "Hey, Sis. We need you to keep very quiet and still. Okay?"

I nodded. Just past Andrew, I noticed Lightning drinking out of the stream. She wasn't tied to anything. I figured she must have followed us here.

Everett quickly pulled a square out of his pocket. At first, I had no idea what it was until he unfolded it into a large rectangle of very thin material. He covered me with it, and I thought it must have been one of those metallic shock blankets that paramedics carry in ambulances. Then he bent over me and planted a small kiss on my lips.

"I've got to cover you completely with this. It'll camouflage you. Just stay very still and quiet, okay?" His brows were drawn together, and worry pulled at the corners of his lips.

"Okay," I whispered so quietly that even I couldn't hear it.

He paused a moment more, then pulled the thin fabric over my face, and I disappeared. He and Andrew disappeared, too, behind some nearby trees. The cool thing about the fabric was that I could see through it. Ky … Everett … had developed the material centuries ago on our home alien planet. I figured he must have gone to the pod vessel looking for me and must have gotten it there. *Or had he recreated it in the laboratories of The Resistance?* I put the thought out of my head.

My thoughts were interrupted by the sound of crunching leaves and twigs. There was more than one person. In fact, it sounded like quite a few people, and they were coming from more than one direction.

And I was completely vulnerable.

I tried to make my breaths shallow. My heart pounded so loud in my ears, that I was sure that everyone in the world could hear it. Slowly, carefully, I turned my head to the other side. Several mercenaries crouched behind a large clump of undergrowth while one of their trackers looked for signs of us. He knelt on the ground examining something on the loamy forest floor, then turned to the others and nodded once.

Crap! They know we're nearby! The thought rang out loud and clear in my brain.

Then, the group of mercenaries moved from behind the undergrowth, and the first one to step out was none other than Luke. I bit my lip to keep me from swearing out loud. *Would the man never get a life and leave me alone?*

His blonde hair was pulled back in a neat braid. While the rest of the mercenaries had camouflaged hats and paint on their faces, he had none. He wanted me to know who he was when I saw him. He wanted me to be afraid.

Right at the very moment, it was working. The only protection I had was my teenage brother and boyfriend. I counted fifteen mercenaries. How could they fight them all off? Without my powers, we were all doomed.

And with booby-traps throughout the jungle waiting to be set off by my powers, we were doomed with them. *Damned if you do, damned if you don't,* I frowned.

Everett's and Andrew's backs were to the mercenaries, who were so close now that they didn't dare budge. From my perspective, I could see the whole thing unfold in front of me, and I couldn't do a thing about it. The tracker turned to the others, and using some sort of military hand signals, motioned to where Andrew and Everett were hiding.

Luke motioned for several men to move in on them. I had to warn them. I tried to scream out in my thoughts, but it wasn't working. I wracked my brain, but got nothing. There was only one thing for me to do.

"They're coming up behind you!" I screamed at the top of my lungs, trying to remain as still as possible, hoping no one would discover my hiding place.

And all hell broke loose.

Several men rushed Andrew and Everett, who fought like Spartans. Everett shot one of the men in the leg while Andrew slashed another across the cheek with Dad's knife before punching him in the throat.

Apparently, Everett had learned martial arts in The Resistance, and he was very good at it. He took a few more shots at several of the mercenaries with his handgun before engaging with another one in hand-to-hand combat.

Luke made it into Andrew's line of eyesight but didn't stay there long. Because Andrew's great at knife-throwing, and Dad's blade plunged into the tree inches next to Luke's head. Too bad he missed.

With a mere motion of his hand, Luke signaled for another group of armed men. They came out of the trees behind Andrew and Everett. One of them slammed my brother on the head with the butt of his rifle. Andrew's knees buckled, and he slumped to the ground.

He lay with his face toward me. He couldn't see me, of course, but he knew where I was. Blood trickled down the side of his head and across his face. Then he closed his eyes to give the illusion of unconsciousness.

They bound Everett's arms behind him, and one of them kicked him in the back of the legs, knocking him to his knees. I thought back to Christmas, when Ash had discovered Luke in my bedroom and choked him. Andrew had roughed him up, too, and threatened him to stay away from Mom. Luke was clearly enjoying getting revenge.

"Where is she?" Luke bent over Everett.

"Who?" Everett asked, playing dumb … something the very opposite of what he was.

"You look like a nice kid who's gotten into the wrong crowd," Luke knelt in front of Everett. "I'm with the Army, and this guy and his sister have been linked to some bad stuff. Just tell me where she is, and I'll let you go."

"Why don't you tell me what you think they're involved in?" Everett asked.

"This loser here," he jabbed Andrew in the shoulder with the barrel of his gun. "He's a known drug smuggler. The girl is a prostitute wanted for …"

Everett head-butted Luke so hard that I heard his nose crack. Blood poured down over his mouth and chin. He reeled backward, landing on his butt, and growled as he covered his nose with his hand.

Luke's sidekick grabbed Everett by the collar and roared, "Tell us where she is!"

"I don't know who you're talking about," Everett answered.

Luke motioned to his sidekick, and he slammed a Taser against Everett's neck, sending him into spasms and convulsions, and the sounds he made were almost unbearable. I wanted to scream out, to tell them to stop. I wanted to set them all on fire. But Andrew shook his head no. It was a very small movement, but he was still looking at me, his eyes open half-way.

Finally, it stopped. Everett lay still, face down on the ground, with his hands bound behind his back, and coughing. If there was ever a hell on earth, this was it. Watching them torture my brother and my Other was almost too much.

Luke knelt over Everett again, "Look, I know you've hidden her somewhere around here. Just tell me where she is, and I'll let you go."

"Go to hell!" Everett shouted between coughs.

"Have it your way, then," Luke said, standing and wiping the blood from his face. His nose was swollen and crooked, and dark circles were forming beneath his eyes. Everett had gotten a good blow in on him.

"Come on out, and I'll spare them!" Luke shouted out into the forest, looking up into the canopy, searching for me hiding among the branches and vines. I didn't look at Andrew, because I knew he'd motion for me to stay still. However, I knew in my heart of hearts that if I didn't reveal myself to Luke, he'd kill Andrew and Everett. And this time, I'd have no way of bringing anyone back.

"I'll count to three. If you don't come out, then I'll put a bullet in their heads." Luke held the barrel of his rifle just above the back of Everett's head.

My breath quickened, and my heart pounded against my ribs. A Queen was about to surrender. My alien royal house had never surrendered. Even my alien father and mother had stayed and faced the enemy to their own deaths.

"One …" Luke's voice rang out, echoing in the forest. His eyes combed the surrounding trees and canopy overhead. Little did he know that I was only feet away from him. "Two! Maybe you don't care about these two, after all. Maybe seeing them take a bullet for you won't bother you at all."

He waited a moment, looking … listening for any sign of me. "Have it your way."

He cocked his rifle and rammed it against the back of Everett's head. "Thr…"

"Stop!" I screamed as loud as I could, my voice still weak.

Luke and his men looked around, searching for me. Some of them looked really freaked out at having heard a disembodied voice. "Show yourself, or this one gets it first," Luke said, stepping closer to Everett.

Andrew was shaking his head, motioning me to stay still. But I couldn't just lay there and watch them both die. I would rather be the one who left this earth than see the two of them murdered because of me.

I grabbed the camouflage fabric with my good hand and slipped it off of me. Only one person saw me magically appear. I'd seen him before. He'd been the one who'd tried to pull me back over the edge of the cliff. I could have sworn that I saw a twinge of regret cross his face as he took in how broken I was ... how alien I looked.

"Luke," he said, kneeling next to me. His green eyes took in all my wounds. No doubt, he was imagining his own kid in the same predicament.

"Well, well, well ... the bitch has a heart after all!" Luke sneered, as he kneeled next to my face. He grabbed a fistful of my hair and twisted it hard. "You'll make excellent bait."

I yelped in pain, and Andrew tried to attack him. But one of the other men kicked him in the stomach, and he folded over on the ground, cursing Luke with every foul word known to mankind.

"I shouldn't have sent those bumbling idiots to carve up that horse of yours. I should have done it myself and made you watch," Luke sneered, looking down at me. "Pete, carry this garbage back to camp," Luke said, dropping my head against the forest floor.

I closed my eyes, fighting back the tears, thinking of the suffering poor Daisy had gone through. But they found their way from behind my eyelids.

"You're burning up," Pete said, scooping me up in his arms. Every inch of me cried out in pain. "You should've taken my hand. Now look at the condition you're in."

"Like you give a damn," my mouth was dry, and my throat hurt, but I managed to get the words out. "You'll all pay for this."

"What are you kids gonna do ... tell your mommy and daddy?" Pete obviously had no idea who and what he was dealing with. "Just look at what the drugs have done to your skin. Those kids are a bad influence on you."

I suddenly realized that Pete had absolutely no clue who he'd been hunting. I wondered how many of these mercenaries knew who and what I was and who was going to eat their hearts and wear their blood as war paint when all was said and done.

Luke's sidekick probably knew who I was. I could tell by the way he looked at me out of the corner of his eye every once in a while as we trudged through the jungle. He was all spit and shine. I had a feeling that he'd spent his military days behind a desk.

"If you knew what was good for you, then you'd help us get out of this," I spoke in low tones so only Pete could hear me. "This isn't what you think it is. I'm not on drugs, and my parents didn't hire Luke to find us."

"Riiiight," Pete stretched the word out. "So if you're not on drugs, what's wrong with your skin?"

"Can you keep a secret?" I asked, feeling my energy ebb away.

"Okay, let's hear it," he actually sounded interested.

"Your life depends on keeping it a secret," my voice was getting weaker by the second.

"Cross my heart," he said, slowing his steps a little to let the other men move on ahead.

"I'm not human," I said just as I opened my eyelids, revealing my solid black eyes. "And if you allow these men to injure us, you'll die a bloody death … possibly death by cannibal."

Pete stumbled and almost dropped me. My head snapped back, popping my neck, and causing me to yelp out in pain. Luke shouted at him, threatening him with loss of pay if he dropped me. Judging by the swearing he was doing under his breath, I didn't think it was Luke's threats that made him cradle me tighter in his arms so I wouldn't tumble to the ground.

I spent the last ounce of energy chuckling at his fear.

"Here, you need to drink this," someone spoke to me, awaking me and holding an aluminum cup to my mouth. Her arm was behind my shoulders, bracing me up so I could swallow without choking.

"Where am I?" my voice sounded paper-thin, even to me. I was too weak to switch my eyes to night vision. I'd used my last bit of energy on freaking Pete out. It was dark, but I didn't feel like I was outside in the jungle anymore.

"Take a sip of this," she urged me again.

I swallowed a gulp of the warm, stale coffee she held to my lips. It actually tasted good. I took another drink and welcomed the jolt of energy from the caffeine. Then, I motioned with a nod that I was done.

A strike of a match flashed, illuminating the stone walls of the small room. Some sort of canvas tarp was being used as a makeshift door. It moved slightly as the breeze blew it inward from outside. She lit a candle. Its warm glow illuminated the edges of her silhouette, making her look as though she was a holy relic.

Then Angelica turned around and placed a damp cloth on my forehead. She was dressed like a nun. I'd grown up a Baptist, but I knew nuns didn't marry. I opened my mouth to ask her what was going on.

She put her finger to her lips, and shook her head. She tiptoed to the open doorway and listened for a moment. Then she appeared back at my side, pulling a pouch from inside the sleeve of her habit. Her gold wedding band glimmered in the candlelight.

"I need you to listen carefully," she placed the pouch next to me and unrolled it, exposing two syringes.

What's with all the needles lately? I frowned.

"I've got to get you dressed," she pressed the cloth to my forehead once more and looked me in the eyes. "But, Blair, you're very sick. Your arm ..." she shook her head. "I don't know if anything can be done about it."

She tried to stop me, but I pulled the cover back with my good hand. My arm was black and green, and it looked like a fat sausage. I knew what gangrene looked like. I'd learned about it in Grandpa's clinic.

"Nobody's cutting off my arm," I gritted my teeth, refusing to cry.

She shook her head to let me know she wasn't planning on sawing my arm off. Then she began prepping one of the syringes. "This will numb your arm. You'll need to keep your wits about you."

I nodded, turning away and wincing as she made several injections into my swollen flesh. "How do you know all of this medical stuff?" I winced again as she made an injection near my wrist. Suddenly, my complete arm was numb. It was the first time I'd had any relief in several days. I could actually breathe ... and think clearly.

"I'm a med student. That's how Andrew and I met," she said, helping me rise to a sitting position. "I was here working with some missionaries. It was love at first sight," her voice wavered a bit.

I wanted to tell her how they made a perfect match ... that she was his perfect Other. That he'd told me about her before Christmas, and that I knew the family would love her. But she pulled me off of the cot and onto one of those things that royal people like Cleopatra were carried around on. We'd learned about them in history class. The teacher had called it a 'litter.'

"What's this thing for, Angelica? What's about to happen to me?" I asked, watching her pull some sparkly clothes out of a bag.

"You're going to go out there and save Andrew's life. Everett's out there, too." She slipped an odd costume-looking-thing over my head and smoothed it down over me. By the time she was through, which wasn't long, I looked like a gold-laden sacrifice to an ancient god.

"There's not much time, so listen," she held the second syringe up for me to see. "This has twice the amount of what I've just given you. If you inject it into your own bloodstream, it will stop your heart. But if you want to disable someone else, this could do the trick."

I wasn't a noob when it came to tranquilizer darts, which was what the syringe essentially was. I nodded, understanding the fullness of what she was telling me. She slipped it under a fold of the absurdly gaudy fabric that was now wrapped around my body. It was just beneath where I placed my good hand. In the event that I needed it, I'd be able to grab it fast.

"Is the bait ready?" Luke asked a guard outside the door opening.

"I heard them talking in there, but I don't know for sure." That voice was familiar, but I couldn't quite place it.

A frown tugged at the corners of Angelica's lips. She scurried around hiding the pouch and empty syringe. Then the weirdest thing happened. Music started playing, and it sounded like an outside concert.

Angelica paused a moment, then removed her necklace and wrapped it around my good wrist. A silver cross dangled from it. I kissed it. Then she slipped a golden mask over my face just before Luke pushed the canvas back and burst into the room.

That's when I saw the other man. It was the guy from the camp where Xi and Max had killed the bumbling idiots. Lee had been the one who'd been sitting at the campfire and had pulled the tarp off my Royal Guard, revealing them to Gordo and The Coward. He'd lived, because of fight or flight. I wondered if he even had the guts to fight as I looked at him through the crooked eyes of the mask.

Luke had put camouflage paint on his face, and I wondered why he'd done it now that he'd found me. He ordered Lee to lift the two poles at the front of the litter while he lifted the back, putting Luke closer to me. I placed my good hand over the lump in the fabric where the syringe was hidden. My heart was pounding behind my breastbone as the two men carried me out of the opening and down a short hall of sand and stone.

Was it MGMT singing Electric Feel? I wondered as the surreal music echoed up into the hallway. For a moment, I thought that maybe this was all a really, really bad dream. That hope was dashed as soon as Luke braced the litter with his knees while he tied a gag around my mouth, underneath the hideous mask.

I wasn't sure what kind of bait I was or what Luke intended to catch. Whatever he was planning, I knew one thing for sure as the two men carried me out onto a platform of an ancient stone building.

There was going to be some sort of sacrifice tonight.

CHAPTER TWENTY-FIVE

SACRIFICE

The balmy jungle night was alight with torches placed at intervals on the great pyramid steps. The pyramid, itself, was draped in golden light, reminding me of days long ago when Ash had this very same stone temple pyramid rubbed down with gold dust.

This was the very same location to which I'd dream-traveled the night Everett had been trapped beneath the rubble in the Queen's city. Tonight, the plaza was abuzz with music, roasting pigs and lambs over several large fires, and lots of people decked in colorful fabrics dancing at the base of the pyramid.

I couldn't see very well through the eye holes on the flimsy gold mask, and I couldn't cry out for help, either. Because my armband was broken, and I was so weak, I couldn't conjure up a storm or set anything on fire.

Finally, we made it to the center of the courtyard where the dancing crowds moved back on both sides, creating a clear path to the long narrow staircase that led to the top of the pyramid. The only thing going through my mind over and over was how weird the whole thing was. I couldn't reconcile my mind with the reality of it all.

But as soon as Lee began ascending the stairs, I slumped back and got a glimpse of the pyramid platform. On the right, there was a large cage made of bamboo and bound together with rope at the sides and corners. It was like a cage from centuries ago ... the kind that humans were kept in for sacrifices.

There were two people in that cage, but due to the ill-fitted mask, I couldn't see who they were. I tried moving my face around, hoping to be able to see around the sides of it. But it didn't work.

As soon as Luke's feet hit the steps, the whole litter lurched back, and I got a clear view of the pyramid platform. And my breath caught in my throat. There was no escape. *Oh, God, oh, no. I'm trapped!* The panic rang out in my head.

There he was, in all his glory. Covered in gold dust and decked in plumes of thin, colorful feathers was Cloud. My ex. Ash, the powerful General who'd been my protector in the beginning after Ky fell to the Hunters. He stepped to the edge of the platform, and stared down the long staircase. MGMT was singing about getting turned on by some girl's electric feel. It was like a song right out of Ash's head.

"Look at that bastard," Luke muttered under his breath. "He'll burn with the rest of you."

I wanted to shout out and warn Ash … I didn't want him to die. I just wanted to be free to be with Ky. But if Ash knew that Luke was trapping us … that he was in cahoots with the Hunters, he'd break his neck.

Ash's broad smile looked menacing. All he was wearing were plumes of feathers in his flowing hair and round his biceps and ankles … and a loincloth. He looked like a sex god. *Oh, hell, he thinks we're going to complete the pairing ceremony tonight and start over,* I thought as I slumped back against the litter seat.

Someone shouted my name. I barely heard it over the blare of the MGMT singing about getting shocked like an electric eel.

"Blair! Up here!" Everett called. He and Andrew were trapped in the sacrificial cage, their hands bound behind their backs.

My mind went back centuries earlier when Ash had conquered a city where so many poor, innocent jungle people had lost their lives as sacrifices. He'd had his soldiers sacrifice the king and his Holy Men to Ash as punishment. *Would he do it to Andrew and Everett now?* I cursed my weakness. *How could I possibly save them now?*

If I could alert Ash and somehow let him know that it was Luke that was behind me, wearing camouflaged paint on his face, then maybe that could buy Andrew and Everett time to escape.

"We found what you hired us to find!" Luke shouted over the music as he pulled the litter to a halt, keeping me on the horrible incline. It reminded me of the time Andrew and I were riding a roller coaster at Six Flags, and it got stuck.

"Bring her to me, and show me her beautiful face," Ash called back, flashing his brilliant, terrifying smile.

"We're not taking another step until we see our payment," Luke called back.

A million things went through my mind, and none of them good. *What if Luke doesn't like the payment? Will he dump me down the staircase right in front of Ash?*

I looked up at the sacrificial cage. Everett was pressed against the side, gnawing on the rope, trying to escape to save me. *I have to do something now, even if it means sacrificing myself.* I wracked my brain for something … anything … that would work.

"This should cover it," Ash tossed a burlap bag just beyond Luke's reach. The bag landed on the stone steps and burst open. Ancient gold coins spilled out, jingling and bouncing down the steps. "Now, bring me my bride!" Ash's voice rang out into the night air.

The litter lurched as Lee and Luke turned to look at the massive amount of ancient gold shining in the torchlight, their eyes drawn to the gold like moths to the flame. And that gave me an idea. With my good hand, I yanked the mask off my face, uncovered my bad arm, and then drove the syringe into Luke's thigh, pushing the plunger down before he could yank it out.

I only had a split second to look up at Ash, but that was all I needed to see his smile replaced by the vicious face of a warrior. He leapt the great distance from the top step, landing just in front of Lee, sending glimmers of gold dust and ancient coins spinning into the night air.

"What have you done to her?!" he shouted in our alien language this time. Lee and Luke had no idea what he'd said.

The litter lurched backward and slammed against the steps as Luke's leg crumpled beneath him. He tumbled backward a few steps, managing to stop beside the sack of gold. Lee struggled to hold on to the two front poles on the litter, but he was losing his grip.

I tugged the gag out of my mouth with my good hand. "It's a trap, Ash!" I spoke in our native language.

"Yes, Princess. I know," he answered.

"They killed Daisy!" I managed to get the words out just before all hell broke loose.

Lee took the opportunity to run. Suddenly, I was sliding backward, resolved that I was about to meet my maker ... that I'd lived all the years I'd been allotted. That I'd see Dad again. The littler flipped upside down, and I tumbled off. A loud snap rang out in my ears, and everything from my neck down turned numb.

Strewn across the stone steps, I was positioned in such a way that my face was pointed toward the top of the pyramid where Everett and Andrew were screaming my name over and over as they struggled to escape the cage. Tears poured out of my eyes as I looked up at

Everett, hoping my sacrifice would free him so that he could have a long life.

Suddenly, I was moving upward. I thought I was being taken to heaven ... that Dad would be waiting for me. But my head lobbed sideways, and I found myself looking directly into Ash's aquamarine eyes.

"You will not die!" he shouted, his voice breaking. "I will not allow it!"

Up, up, up the steps we flew as he rushed me to the room at the top of the pyramid, to the mattress and pillows he'd prepared for completing the paring ritual. Candlelight washed the walls of the ancient room with golden light. But I paid no attention to all the decorations he'd placed in the room. All I could think about was how I was going to get my next breath.

He placed me on the fluffy mattress and immediately lowered himself to hover just above me. Waves of energy flowed over him in rings of white. But they would not pass over into my skin to heal me.

"This must work, it has to work ... please work," he chanted over and over. To no avail. I was going, and nothing he could do would save me. He was no longer my Other. And that's when I knew I needed Everett. Only he would be able to sustain me until Rake could fix me.

"Father!" Orion's voice rang out somewhere near the doorway. "She needs Ky!"

"What?!" Ash blurted, veins bulging in his forehead and neck.

"Ky, Father!" Orion knelt next to us ... the only parents he'd ever known. "She needs her chosen Other."

"Ky has been dead for centuries," Ash answered, his face turning red from straining to force the energy to flow into me and save me.

"It's a long story ..." Orion stammered. "But he's alive, and he's in the cage."

"Is this true?" Ash whispered as he looked into my eyes. His hair draped around my face, and for a moment, it felt like we were all alone in the universe.

Of course, I couldn't speak, nod, or signal anything. Everything beneath my chin was numb, and my lungs were slowing by the second. I blinked once, sending a tear out of one of my eyes and into my hair, hoping he would understand. He placed a tender kiss on my lips, then pulled away, and knelt next to me.

"Bring him," Ash said, keeping his eyes on mine. As soon as Orion was out of the room, he brushed a lock of my hair away, pressed a gentle kiss against my forehead, and whispered, "This changes nothing. Your father gave you to me. You are mine, and I love you."

Shouts rang out over the band that continued to play for the dancers in the courtyard below. I heard Andrew cussing and ordering Orion to untie his hands. Everett was asking about me as they burst into the room.

"Blair!" Everett shouted, his voice squeaked a little the way it used to. He fell to his knees next to me and took my hand in his. The effect was immediate. Waves of light flowed from his hand and crossed over into mine, moving up my arm.

"She needs a doctor," Andrew sounded broken. But then his face lit up with an idea, and he rushed out of the room, shoving Orion aside.

"Breathe, baby. Come on, breathe," Everett whispered as he laid down at my side, pulling me close to him. "I love you so much, Lore. Please, please don't leave me here all alone..." his breath brushed across my hair.

The hum of electricity filled the room and reverberated off the ancient stone walls. It coursed through my veins, and circled around the broken vertebrae in my neck, but it stopped at my arm where my dying flesh was still numb from Angelica's shot.

"I will kill every one of them who hurt you," Ash spoke through gritted teeth, his eyes glowing with anger.

"You," I managed to whisper. It was almost inaudible, but he heard and leaned forward. "You paid them to do this to me … to bring me to you."

A sudden rush of wind toppled over several objects. I was too woozy to immediately connect what was happening until I realized Ash was hanging in midair with the enormous hand of Xi around his throat.

"You did what to my Queen?" Xi's voice lowered an octave and became a menacing alien growl. "I will eat your heart and grind your remains into dust!"

Xi was dressed in some sort of disguise. A hood covered his head, and a cloak fashioned of the colorful fabric of the jungle people covered the rest of him. If we'd have been in another time and place, I would have wanted to laugh. However, when he glanced down at me, his Queen, he remembered our discussion at the top of the pyramid. He remembered that I'd said I didn't want Ash killed. So, he dropped Ash and knelt next to me.

"Rake is here?" I muttered into his enormous shoulder as he lifted me into his arms.

"We are all here, my lady," Xi cradled me gently against his chest.

"Mal and Jex, too?" The memory of them fighting to protect their Queen would forever be engraved on my heart.

"No. They have not been found," Xi's voice dropped. "They fulfilled their oath to you by risking their lives. If they have fallen, we will remember them. If they have been captured, then we must heal you so that their suffering isn't in vain." He pulled me to him in a gentle hug.

I wanted to thank him, to tell him that I loved him for all he'd ever done for me ... that he was more like family to me than a body guard. But drawing air into my lungs was extremely difficult, even with Everett's energy flowing through my veins. He kept a hold of my hand as Xi walked out of the room and down the pyramid steps.

Ash followed us out onto the pyramid platform. My head lobbed back, giving me a view of his glorious face, rubbed with gold dust, his aquamarine eyes filled with regret. All manner of emotions rolled off him as he followed behind Xi, longing to be the one who was my hero. Then movement on the steps caught his eye.

Luke gripped his numb leg, struggling to stand up. He motioned for some of the other mercenaries to come help him. The ones who hadn't already left made for the jungle. He nodded to his second-in-command who was talking into some sort of handheld communication device. I'd seen one before, but couldn't place it. Sweat rolled down Luke's face, smearing the camouflaged paint, and revealing his identity.

"You!" Ash stretched out his hand. Golden electricity surrounded Luke, lifting him off the steps, and holding him in the air. "I should have killed you the first time we met. Now, I will make you a sacrifice to my bride Queen!"

Luke answered by laughing. It was a sort of maniacal laughter, very unnerving. He had something up his sleeve. I glanced back at his second-in-command, who'd put the device away and was looking into the dark jungle. He turned and looked to the other side. He was waiting for something ... for back-up.

Xi ignored it all and continued carrying me down the steps to Rake who would fix me up. At that moment, I was his sole priority. Everett followed along, continuing to hold my hand tightly in his, feeding me energy that kept me alive and breathing, if only barely.

Then I remembered. It came out of the blue. Natalie and I had seen one of the Hunters outside the building that night. He'd been using one of those communicators to talk to more of them.

Xi, this is a trap ... Luke's working with the Hunters, I strained to think the words into this mind, looking up into his wide eyes.

How do you know this? he asked, his words weaving around my thoughts.

I just know. We've got to prepare the others. Now! I tried to sound like I was issuing orders, but even my thoughts sounded like a sick cat.

Xi turned to take me to where Rake was waiting to tend to my wounds. As we disappeared into a cloaked triage tent, I looked over my shoulder to see Ash placing Luke into the sacrificial cage.

"Soldiers!" Ash's voice boomed over the revelries in the courtyard, "Prepare yourselves! The Hunters are nearby!"

Max slipped in sideways. "The General has awakened his soldiers," Max said, looking at Xi. When she saw me, she dropped to her knees. "My lady! I was so worried. I've thought of nothing else but your return to us."

"Thank you, Max," I said, my voice wavering from sickness and from emotion. "I'm glad to be back among my family ... my Royal Guard."

Max kissed my hand, bowed her head, and stood to leave.

"Max," I focused on keeping my voice from wavering.

"Yes, my lady?" she stood ready to carry out anything I asked of her.

"Whose blood are you wearing?" I asked, looking at the streaks of blood she'd smeared across her face.

"The one called Lee," she straightened her back, proud to have vanquished one of her Queen's foes.

"Good," I blinked, letting her know it was okay for her to leave now. She had other people she'd like to cannibalize or disembowel.

Xi followed Max to the door of the triage tent then turned to Rake, who was examining my wounds. He and Max clinched their fists when they observed the fullness of my injuries as Rake removed the hideous costume.

"Who is responsible for your injuries, my lady?" Xi could not contain his anger.

The man named Luke. He's in the cage ... I swallowed as the words wound through my mind. I was too weak to speak anymore. My head lobbed back into Rake's arms. Two angry members of my Royal Guard left the tent. One angry member of the Royal Guard remained, examining my wounds. And Everett knelt beside me, continuing to hold my hand.

"You have suffered greatly," Rake said, while laying out several wicked-looking medical implements and syringes. "And your neck ... it is broken."

Make me well, Rake. Do whatever you must do to fix me. Just don't saw off my arm. I closed my eyes tight and clenched my jaw, bracing for the worst.

"Why would I do something like that, my lady?" she asked just before stabbing one of the syringes into my arm. It was a good thing that everything beneath my chin was numb, because I could still feel the medicine as it flowed into my dying flesh.

My neck bones snapped together as soon as the accelerant reached the broken vertebrae. My head no longer lobbed loose and wobbly. Tears streamed out of my eyes and into my hair as the feeling returned to my body, except for my arm.

She began working on the wound where the bone had pierced my skin. I winced as she mended torn, damaged flesh. Before I knew it, she'd put on a pair of magnifying goggles of some sort and was working on the wires of my arm band.

Each thing she did brought a little more life back into my hybrid human-alien body. Every once in a while, she stopped to give me a sip of water and a bite of ancient dried food from our home world. The smoky tang of the meat brought my taste buds to life, and I savored the essence of our ancient sun as I rolled the spicy flesh of the dried fruit across my tongue. Each sip of water soothed my sore, parched throat.

As soon as the last strand of wire was melded together, streams of light formed across the ground and radiated up the legs of the cot, and through my skin.

Energy sprung back into my body, flowing through my veins, and feeding my cells.

"Yes!" I hummed.

Rake smiled as she continued working on me, injecting medicines into my veins. As soon as the accelerator reached my wound, my bone snapped together. I yelped, then smiled. Soon, my arm was whole again. I lifted it and moved my fingers, watching as the last few blotches of purple ebbed away.

The only mark left on my hand was my branded butterfly. I released Everett's hand and fished my star ring from out of my pocket and handed it to him. He slipped it on my now normal-sized finger.

"My beautiful Butterfly!" Everett gasped.

"Ky, kiss your Queen," I said, smiling. He complied without a moment's hesitation.

Then I stood. My body buzzed with energy. This was the way it felt to be Lore. I never wanted it to stop. But there was something that I *did* want to stop. That was what was going on outside the triage tent. Anything that came between me and my happy ending was about to come to a grinding halt.

"What is going on out there?" I asked, looking toward the tent door. "Ky, my love, let's end this so we can begin again."

"I'll go help Xi," Everett said, smiling a broad, goofy smile. "I love you, Lore," he said just before he left the tent.

My clothes were filthy. They'd suffered the river, the mud, the slime, blood, and other things I couldn't even remember. *How am I going to look menacing wearing this?* I thought, looking down at myself.

So I did the only logical thing I could think of.

I stripped down bare-naked, wearing only the symbols that once again glowed beneath my flesh. They wove down my arms and legs, up my torso, shoulders, and neck. I could even see hints of them near my eyes. With every intention of facing my foes down naked as a jaybird, I started to leave the tent.

"Wait," Rake lifted a long, narrow box. As the lid slid away, what lay inside made my heart speed up.

My own personal armor glimmered as Rake lifted it out and held it out for me. It was my coming-of-age gift from my alien father. I'd loved it then as I loved it now. Rake fastened it to me. It covered me up to my throat in layers and bands of silvery metal, unlike anything on earth. She pressed a button inside the neck of my armor, and it came alive, melding to my human-alien hybrid body.

I quickly wound my hair into a tight braid down my back. Then Rake, as if holding a holy relic, lifted my crown out of the box. It matched the thin braided loop embedded in my arm and the glowing symbols and swirls alight beneath my skin. She placed it on my head, and it, too, came alive and melded against my scalp, becoming the perfect fit for my head.

"Thank you, Rake," I said, looking up into her wide, slanted eyes. "Now, let's go kick some ass."

"My lady, what is your plan?" Rake asked.

"I'm going to rein in the General, then conquer the Hunters," I answered, moving my hands over my armor. Weapons were hidden throughout the torso and some on the legs of the silvery metal armor.

"May I suggest that while you deal with the General, I will meet with the Commander and tell him your wishes?" she asked.

"That is a good idea," I nodded and pulled open the flap of the triage tent.

"Yes, my lady," she bowed, then began strapping her weapons over her shoulders.

I turned back to her, "It's time the Hunters learned first-hand the theory of Survival of the Fittest." I lifted my chin, feeling even taller than I was before. And perhaps I was after Rake's care. "It's time for them to learn that we are the fittest."

Confusion flashed across Rake's tattooed face, her brows pulling together over her wide, slanted eyes. There wasn't time to explain. Sometimes, the best way to learn something is to live it.

CHAPTER TWENTY-SIX

SURVIVAL OF THE FITTEST

"Survival of the Fittest was Darwin's explanation of Natural Selection," Dr. Boyd had explained to my dual credit Biology class at Montgomery College. "The struggle for life in which those best hybridized to existing conditions survive and multiply." He'd actually used the word "adapted" instead of "hybridized." But I liked my version better.

The flap of the triage tent slipped aside as I stepped through. It was a bit disconcerting leaving the silence of the tent and stepping into the raucous melee outside.

A live band still played atop a lower stone structure to the left of the pyramid, and the courtyard was still filled with dancing people clad in colorful fabrics, their heads covered with hoods. Roasting meat filled the air with a smoky aroma that made my stomach growl.

"Blair?!" Andrew ran toward me, dragging Angelica behind him. They both looked confused, yet glad that I was healed. "How? Who?" he'd gone to get Angelica in hopes that she could help me.

"Rake and Everett," I answered. "Everett kept me alive until Rake could doctor me back to health. Alien medicine at its finest," I smiled, and something told me that I looked terrifying. "Angelica helped me, too," I smiled. "Thanks sis-in-law."

"You're welcome," her voice sounded small as she clung to Andrew and looked me over from head to toe. "You look … magnificent."

"Thanks," I nodded, "But now, I've gotta go kick some ass. Bro, get ready for a battle. The Hunters are coming."

"Oh, shit," dread tinted his voice.

But I didn't stay to console him. He had Angelica, and she could do that. I turned and headed toward my other family members. My Royal Guard was cloaked in their camouflaged skin and uniforms. Xi appeared at my side out of thin air as I strode toward the pyramid temple. Ash was nowhere to be seen, but he was still there … I could sense him.

I stretched my hand out, and a small twister formed in front of me, clearing a path through the courtyard, flinging debris into the air. As I crossed the courtyard, the dancers stopped and turned to face me. Several of them fell to their knees, heads bowed. I paid them no attention.

"Ash!" I called, my voice echoing up the pyramid steps.

"I'm here," Ash answered, stepping out of a doorway at the top of the pyramid. He'd changed from his jungle wear. Now, he was wearing his own armor. His was made of a metal that shone in gold tones. The armor of his soldiers would be the same. Only I wore the gleaming silver of the Royal House. "I see you've crowned yourself," he smiled.

"I *am* the Queen, after all, General!" I lifted my chin and straightened my shoulders. "It is time for this all to come to an end." I hoped he'd comply willingly. For I had no real urge to kill him.

"And it's time for you to pay for giving this man coin in exchange for the capture of the Queen!" Xi's voice boomed next to me. Anger boiled off of him, and I could sense that he still wanted to kill Ash. It had become very personal to him now.

"Ah, Princess, your guard dog likes to growl," Ash tilted his head forward, flashing a dangerous smile. His thoughts were clear to me ... calling me *princess* should remind me that I'd been given to him as a bride by my father the King.

Even now, as I strode up the stone steps of the ancient stone pyramid, I could appreciate Ash's glory. His hair flowed in the night breeze, and gold dust still gleamed across his skin. His aquamarine eyes flashed in the torchlight. His physique had been legend on our home world. Nothing had changed.

"Don't make me sic him on you, Ash," my voice changed a little, sounding more alien than human. "I'll have Ky and no other," I said. "What was between us is now over."

"You'd choose a mere mortal over a god?" Ash cocked a crooked smile and swaggered toward me.

"He is no mere mortal, and you are no god," I pushed him aside and strode toward the cage where Luke pressed himself into the back corner, as far from me as possible. Disbelief covered his face as he took in the fullness of my recovery. I blasted the door away and held my hand out, willing him to come forward. He had no choice in the matter. I reined him in with a rope of electricity around his neck. "He's yours to deal with as you will," I said to Xi.

"He should be sacrificed to my bride," Ash's voice rang out.

"I am not your bride!" I shouted, whirling around on Ash, my voice changing again. Blue tinted my vision, casting a haze on everything. Energy pumped through my veins, and I felt stronger than I'd ever felt in my long life.

"You'll always be my ..." Ash stopped mid-sentence and looked past me into the darkness of the jungle.

I turned, following Ash's line of sight, toward the dark jungle beyond the light of the torches. There were whispers ... I heard them in my thoughts. The Hunters had found us. The time had come to prove who'd become the fittest.

The music stopped. I glanced down at the courtyard to see Ash's soldiers removing the colorful clothing they'd been wearing over their armor. I'd had no idea they were his soldiers. I glanced back at him, and he cocked a crooked smile and shrugged. Even at the dawn of battle, charm oozed off him. I made a mental note to find him a bride as soon as our people were reunited. I was resolved to order him to stay true to her, too.

"Xi, it's time to end this once and for all," I looked up into Xi's battle-scarred, tattooed face. "Let's kill them all."

"Ash, I order you to work with my Royal Guard. United we stand, divided we fall," I looked Ash square in the eyes. "Do not disobey the order of the Royal House, General."

"Never," he said, smiling proudly. And then he bowed his head. I thought my jaw would drop to the ground.

As Xi and Ash planned their strategy, I took a moment to look out over the courtyard where I'd first set foot on this planet in my alien life, where I'd first laid eyes on Nyx and Orion, where I'd been willing to give up my life with Everett in return for his safety. Here was the place where it would all end.

Something caught my eye to the left of the courtyard, on the opposite side from where the Hunters were gathering. He stepped out of the clearing, his dark hair flowing around his shoulders. Nyx stood just inside the ring of torchlight. I'd watched him grow up in this very place, and I would recognize his form anywhere. Orion ran to him, and they greeted each other in a brief embrace.

The soles of my armor barely touched the steps. I ran faster than I'd ever imagined toward my adopted sons. They saw me coming and turned to greet me. Bright smiles crossed their faces as I ran into their arms, nearly knocking them over with the weight of my armor and my newfound strength.

"Mother!" Nyx said pressing his face into my hair. I was immediately drawn back to the distant past ... to when they were both young boys who were as swift as the wind and as terrible as any storm.

"Son," I kissed his cheek and hugged them both tight against me.

"You're crushing us," Orion chuckled, still hugging me.

"Boys, I want you to leave. It's about to get dangerous, and I can't bear anything happening to either of you," I pulled away from them.

And that's when I realized that Nyx was dressed in a black t-shirt and fatigues like Everett wore ... the clothes of The Resistance. I glanced behind him to see countless soldiers in the same garb. They stood among the shadows, waiting for some order or command. My hands instinctively went to my weapons. Nyx stopped me by gently putting his hand on mine.

"It's okay. They're with me," he flashed a reassuring smile. He was beautiful, a mixture of the jungle people and Ash's genes. He looked like a Native American god. So did Orion.

"I don't understand," I stammered. "Have you joined The Resistance, too?" I was hurt, heartbroken, that he would join a group of militia who would fight against his own kind ... his own parents.

"Mother," Nyx said, straightening his shoulders and smiling, "I *created* The Resistance to protect our kind ... to protect *you*." He glanced at his brother then back at me. "I told you Orion wasn't the only one looking out for you."

I was speechless. Dumbfounded. Another puzzle piece snapped into place. Nyx had known my parents, the sheriff's son, maybe even my grandparents. My mouth gaped open as I looked at my two handsome adopted sons. They'd made me proud, they'd looked out for me and our kind. They'd been loyal, and I would reward them somehow, some way.

"All I need is your love, Mother," Nyx answered, hearing my thoughts. I'd forgotten how in-tune to me they'd always been.

"You've both got that and more," I said, reaching for them again and pulling them into another hug.

We were interrupted by someone clearing his throat. I turned to see Everett standing nearby, a sheepish smile across his face. He'd known all along and hadn't told me. No doubt, Nyx had sworn him to secrecy. Behind him stood Rake, towering over him. Max stood next to her. She was covered in even more blood than before.

"Max, you've been busy," I said, motioning to the streaks of blood she'd smeared down her arms and across her chest. "Whose blood is that?"

"The one called Luke. The Commander gave him to me and told me what he'd done. I didn't give him time to scream," she bowed her head once, then smiled a terrifying smile.

"That's so damn sexy," Orion said, just before Max tossed him across her shoulder and spun him around.

I suddenly noticed that Nyx and Rake were staring at each other. Everett motioned with a tilt of his head for me to introduce the two. I smiled a moment, glad that all my wishes were coming true, then cleared my throat.

"Rake, this is the General's son, adopted by me and very special to me. His name is Nyx," I said, catching her eyes only briefly, for she had great difficulty tearing her gaze from him. She smiled and gave a quick bow of her head.

"Nyx, this is Rake. She is very special to me," I said these words with great pride. She'd saved my life and deserved my praise.

Their attraction was immediate and very apparent to everyone. I wished there was more time for them to grow their attachment, but Ash's army was forming in the court yard, and Xi was signaling for his soldiers to muster.

"We must go," Max said, setting Orion down. "Come, Rake," she touched her sister on the shoulder in such a way that I sensed Max's regret in having to interrupt the attraction between Rake and Nyx.

"Take this with you," Nyx said with earnest as he tugged a necklace over his head. Various charms and beads he'd collected over the years dangled from the braided cord. Rake blushed as she took it and wound it around her wrist. Then she smiled a brilliant, terrifying smile before turning to leave with Max.

"She's beautiful," Nyx's voice was filled with wonder.

"She saved my life," I said, wanting him to know I approved. "She is ready for pairing, just so you know."

"Love is in the air," Everett said as he twined his fingers with mine.

Just as I was entertaining the thought of all my alien kind becoming hybrids and building a long, happy life here in the safety of the jungle, a shout interrupted my reverie.

"Protect the Queen at all costs!" Xi's voice boomed.

I turned to see the Hunters emerging from the jungle's edge on the opposite side of the courtyard. Ash was at the head of his army, all of them gleaming in golden armor. My Royal Guard was in battle formation, ready to slay anything that came across their path.

Nyx gave an order, and his own army emerged from the shadows of the jungle. All of them were dressed in black, wearing dull black armor. Everett nodded to several of them. No doubt he'd gotten to know many of them during his training days.

I glanced at him, his handsome features outlined in the golden torchlight. My hand found its way up his arm to his bicep, where his own braided band was embedded beneath his skin. I'd always assumed it was Orion who'd applied it, but now I realized it had been Nyx.

"Love you, Ky," I whispered as Nyx handed him a set of armor.

"Love you, too, Firefly … Monarch of my heart," he said just before pulling me to him and kissing me full on the lips. Then he released me, and began putting his armor on. "Let's get this over with so we can all start our new lives."

"I second that!" Nyx said, buckling a black breastplate across his chest.

"Be careful," I fought the frown that threatened to cross my face. "I can't bear life without any of you."

"Mother, we want this to be over just like you do," Orion said while strapping on some armor, "So, we'll do our best to survive."

"Good!" I smiled. "Let's kick some ass, boys!"

"One more thing," Nyx said, just as I was turning to join the battle. "We've disarmed all the booby traps in this part of the jungle. So, it's safe to use our powers here."

"We?" a familiar voice came from behind us. My heart filled with warmth. Mom strode out of the jungle, suited in the dull black armor of The Resistance and the handle of a samurai sword peeked up over her shoulder. Her hair was shorn close to her head around the sides and back, leaving hair at the crown of her head long. It hung over to one side, touching just her jawline. The tattoo at the nape of her neck was now clearly visible. I'd never in a million years imagined my mother could look so ... well ... bad ass. "In all honesty, it was Nyx's idea. But I'm the one who did the dirty work. Anything for my kids!" Her smile was a strange juxtaposition to her new hair and clothing ensemble.

"Mom, I'm so weirded out right now," I admitted, looking her over once more. "Andrew'll be shocked."

"Imagine how weirded out I am! My daughter is suddenly taller than me, she's got glowing symbols all over her body, and she's hanging out with a bunch of extraterrestrials in the woods!" she put her hands on her hips, and I got another glimpse of the mom I was familiar with.

"Mother," Nyx interrupted us. "I have taken care of everything. All we need to do is go support the soldiers and end this."

I tossed a flaming orb into the air and motioned for it to circle above my head. "I'm so proud of you." I smiled at his surprise, then spun toward the courtyard-turned-battlefield.

"This is where the fittest survive," I said, squaring my shoulders and steeling myself for the fight ahead. Just as I was about to strut across the battlefield, I saw Lightning trotting toward me. She neighed and stamped her hooves, and I hugged her neck before climbing into her saddle.

I steered Lightning toward the battlefield, and like a true queen on her steed, I urged her forward. With the flaming orb still circling my head, I imagined I must have been an odd sight. I patted Lighting on the shoulder and said, "This is where it ends."

CHAPTER TWENTY-SEVEN

WHERE IT ENDS

"Keep an eye on my mother, Nyx," I glanced down at him. He'd caught up to me as I rode Lightning across the courtyard. "I guess that makes her your grandmother!" I blurted, realizing how weird it sounded.

"She'll be fine," Nyx answered. "Especially now that Luke is gone."

I nodded, turning toward the looming battle ahead of us. The Hunters were entering the courtyard. An inaudible gasp rushed through my Royal Guard as soon as they saw their two youngest soldiers being led in shackles by the enormous King of the Hunters.

My knuckles turned white from gripping Lightning's reins so hard. Mal and Jex had risked their lives for my safety. I had to do whatever it took to free them. However, I didn't want to disrupt Ash's and Xi's plans. I glanced to Kin. Though his aging features were stoic, his eyes were examining the battlefield as if it were a chessboard. It was clear he was working his strategy, testing move against move.

"Give yourself over to us, and we will release these two!" the enormous Hunter bellowed. He jabbed Jex in the shoulder with something that resembled a cattle prod, and he fell to his knees, but remained silent. Jex wouldn't cry out no matter what was done to him. But I wasn't going to sit idly by and watch my men get tortured to death.

"Let us call a truce and go our separate ways!" I answered, surprised at how loud my voice was. This was the voice of Lore. It was alien and lower than my human voice. "Many years have passed and much blood has been shed ... you have taken our home world from us. Now leave us in peace!"

The monster threw is head back and bellowed in laughter. "The only peace you will know are the pieces of you that will litter this ground and the pieces of this planet floating in the void of space!"

I paused a moment, observing the monster and his army, which was outnumbered by my own. I wondered how that could be so, since they'd killed all but those of my kind on earth and the sister ship somewhere out in space. *What had dwindled their numbers so much that they hadn't overcome us already? Was there disease among them?* I chewed my lip as I noted how age had done its deed on the Monster King of the Hunters.

"You have no young soldiers among you!" I shouted as Lightning pranced beneath me. "Where are your females?"

He didn't reply, but the answer was obvious. They had never learned to grow and adapt the way my kind had. They'd forever remained the ruthless killers and warmongers, never valuing science or knowledge. Their females had always fought alongside their males, much like my kind had. But there were no females among them this night.

"When you took my son, you took the future of our people! We have survived to get vengeance. That is all that matters!" the monster pounded his chest.

Ash and Xi were looking at me now, realizing that I was right. This was a dangerous foe, to be sure. But they were ailing ... something was wrong with them ... something that had not been affecting them just a short time ago.

We've grown stronger here, developed powers we didn't have at home, Ash's voice threaded through my thoughts. *Perhaps the opposite has happened to them.*

I nodded and thought back to nature walks with Dad. He'd described Mother Nature as a force to be reckoned with. *The earth was made for mankind,* he'd said as we'd walked barefoot in the narrow creek that wound through the woods near our house. *If we take care of her, she'll take care of us.*

This planet fights against destruction, I answered Ash. *The Hunters are destroyers. We are builders.*

Maybe they've been poisoned by some of the jungle fruit or have contracted a disease from the water. Maybe it's the gravity here or the UV rays of the sun. It could be any number of things.

"You could've spent all those centuries rebuilding your people. Yet you've hunted us to your own extinction!" I shouted, angry that we were even having to deal with this ... wishing that they'd have just died out before we'd had to fight them.

"We will rebuild here, on top of the bones of your people!" the Monster roared, and his soldiers drew their weapons. "This place will become ours!"

I glanced at Ash and Xi, then to Nyx. They waited for my signal. I gave it to them when I turned back to the Monster King and shouted, "Come and take it!" just like a true Texan.

With that, I drew a weapon from the waistband of my armor. It slid smoothly out of its holster then hummed with electricity as I swung it over my head and brought it down to the ground beside me with a loud *crack.*

The electrified whip had been designed by Xi. Long ago, he'd trained me in its use, as well as all the other weapons hidden within my armor. A small fire ignited in the grass where the tip of my whip connected with the earth, melting the soil and stones into a solid pane of glass.

A split-second later, Ash was sounding the call to charge. His soldiers, male and female, gleamed golden in the firefight. Max's battle cry could be heard over the melee of boots pounding the earth, weapons sliding from their holsters, curses of vengeance for our lost world that filled the night air with centuries' worth of rage.

My Royal Guard fell back to shield their Queen. I looked around at my men and women, willing to give their lives to protect mine. But someone was missing. Kin was gone from the platoon. Apparently, my soldiers were aware he was missing. One of his soldiers stepped into his place.

I scanned the battlefield as Ash's and Nyx's soldiers rushed forward, filling the gap between friend and foe. As the ones on the front line crossed the midway point, the Monster King lifted a wicked sword high into the air with the intent of bringing it down on the back of Jex's neck. Killing one of the pair, would kill both.

"No!" I shouted, urging Lightning forward.

However, Xi caught the horse by the harness just as Kin appeared out of nowhere, blocking the broad stroke of the Monster's sword with his own. Sparks erupted as blade met blade. Both of the young soldiers leapt to their feet, struggling to help Kin overcome the Monster King.

A quick swing of Kin's sword snapped Mal's restraints, who, in turn tossed Jex over his shoulder and disappeared into thin air, cloaking them both. The sequence was lightning-fast, as unreal as watching a movie. For a moment, I thought my soldiers would all return to me unharmed.

But only for a moment …

Kin turned to follow the two young soldiers he'd just saved, but he wasn't quick enough. The Monster King's blade pierced him through his back, and burst through the tattoos across his chest. With a level of bravery unimaginable, Kin turned to face his killer.

Staggering, the oldest member of my Royal Guard swung his sword, slicing a wicked wound across the Monster King's face before another Hunter blasted him with a weapon, sending him reeling backward into the middle of the charging soldiers.

"Release my horse, Xi! I can save Kin's essence!" I shouted, tears streaming down my face.

"No, my lady," Xi looked up at me, somberness had replaced the battle rage he'd worn seconds earlier. "This was Kin's wish – to die for his Queen so that the younglings would know the importance of this life."

"What?!" I screeched, looking back to where Kin had fallen. He was hidden by the onslaught of soldiers. But a wispy ribbon of light wound upward into the night air from where the old soldier had fallen. His essence reached up, up, up into the night sky, searching for his ancestors.

And I feared we'd be sending up lanterns for more than Kin tonight.

What had begun only minutes earlier had seemed to last for hours. Though the Hunters were weakened, they were still lethal. I sat astride my horse and watched the horror that was the ending of something I'd begun so very long ago when I'd ordered Xi to bring me one of them. And now more lives were being endangered because of me.

I could no longer sit on the sidelines, watching others suffer for my own choices. And as soon as I saw Everett enter the battle, I slipped out of Lightning's saddle, gripped the handle of my whip, and strode toward the enormous free-for-all.

"Blair Reynolds, where do you think you're going?" Mom's voice cut through the night air, stopping me in my tracks. I turned to see her behind me, her samurai sword drawn, and hanging at her side.

"I'm going to kill the Monster King!" I shouted over a sudden burst of gunfire.

"Well, you're gonna need help with that," she answered.

"Let's get it over with," I nodded. "You look like an '80s punk rock chick with that hair. What's Mr. Forster gonna say?"

"Oh, he'll like it," she said, running a hand through the long section of hair that fell over one side of her face. "You know how those nerds are!"

Before I could answer, an enormous explosion rocked the entire jungle and lit up the skyline behind the Hunters. Then the wind and heat came, bursting through the trees and knocking most of the Hunters on their faces.

Loose leaves and chunks of trees flew past us by the force of the wind from the explosion. Something flew just over my head, snagging a section of my hair. Then a loud squawk and flapping of wings was followed by Andrew cussing ... again.

"What the hell is this?" he held the flapping, squawking bird up to Mom and me as if it belonged to us.

We both shrugged, and he tossed it into the air, sending it flying to the safety of the jungle behind us. His hair was ginormous, flapping and fluffing in the wind, with a feather from the bird stuck among the tangles. I started to say something, but several other people I'd never met joined us.

"It's a bird, dude," one of the other guys said.

A smaller blast made us duck, and I really wanted to join my soldiers. But I wanted my family to stay out of it. I simply couldn't bear losing any of them. I realized one of Andrew's companions was staring at me like a star-struck teen, oblivious to what was going on around us.

"Andrew, I've got to get back to my people," I wanted to cringe as soon as the words came out. They were *all* my people, except for the Hunters. "You and Mom stay out of the fight, okay?"

"Sis, we've come here to help you end this. Who do you think poisoned those suckers?" Andrew saw the feather and plucked it out of his hair.

"Yeah, hottie," one of the other guys said, "We've killed more of them than you could imagine in that pretty head of yours." A crooked smile cocked the corner of his mouth up, and I quickly realized that Ash wasn't the only womanizer on the battlefield.

"Can you explain all of that to Xi?" I asked Andrew, ignoring Mr. Suave.

"Sure," Andrew shrugged.

"So, are y'all responsible for that blast?" I asked, motioning to the glowing red and green smoke in the sky.

"Yes, we are," I startled at the sound of Mal's voice.

"My boys! My sweet, sweet boys!" I answered them in our native language.

"Sweet? Ha!" Jex answered, a weary smile crossing his face. Kin's death would wear on them for a very long time. "That's the last word to describe us, my lady. We've just blown up their mother ship containing their women and children."

"Good," I knew it wasn't a Christian thing to say in such a circumstance, but it was the truth. And it was the only way to stop the monsters from killing us all and ruining this planet I now called home.

"We've placed Kin at the top of the pyramid, my lady. We are far from home, and we wanted to make sure the ancestors will see his lanterns and pyre." Sadness washed across Jex's young face.

"We'll honor him," I nodded my head once, as I'd seen my alien father do in such situations, "For now … let's avenge him."

"The Commander ordered us to keep you from the battle," Mal stepped between me and the raging storm ahead.

"And who commands the Commander?" I raised my chin and lifted my eyebrows.

"Please, my lady," Jex interjected. "We need our Queen if we are to start over on this strange planet."

"I know," I placed my hand on his forearm. "But a good ruler doesn't let her people do her dirty work. It's for me to kill the king of the Hunters."

"My lady, please …" Mal started to protest. I held my hand up and cut him off.

"With your help, I will kill him. Agreed?" I offered a bargain they couldn't refuse.

When I turned around to order my human family to stay out of the fight, the first person I saw was Angelica. She was tucked under Andrew's arm, her head on his shoulder. She reached into her bag and retrieved something and held it out to me.

"Andy said this is your weapon of choice," the firelight glistened on her red hair, making it even brighter.

"Andy?" I asked, holding back a smile while taking the object into my hand. "A bovine tranquilizer dart!" I gasped. "How'd you get your hands on this?"

"I have my ways," she flashed the kind of smile that made me believe it.

The plan was to lure the Monster King into a clearing where there was no fighting. I would pretend that I was unguarded and afraid. When he approached, I would pretend to cower at which point Jex and Mal would advance on him. I would attack from the front with the tranquilizer dart and my handy whip. Together, we'd take him down.

By now, one would think I'd realize things don't always go as planned ...

I tucked the tranquilizer dart into a chink in my armor and gripped the handle of my whip firmly in my palm as I headed toward the clearing. The rest of the group went to their appointed spots to lay in wait for the Monster King's approach. I'd ordered Mom, Andrew, and Angelica to stay behind. But as soon as I neared the edge of the battle zone, my attention was immediately drawn to the center of the battlefield by the loud voice of the King of the Hunters.

"Look what we've captured!" his voice rang across the fray, breaking through the sounds of swinging of swords and rounds of gunfire.

He had her by the throat, her feet high off the ground. Angelica's face was purple, and she was kicking wildly against the Monster King's chest and clawing at his hideous hand trying to free herself.

The plan shattered to pieces, and everything around me warped into shades of blues and purples. With a flick of my thumb, the electric whip sprung from the handle in my hand and wound round and round in the air, searching for its target.

"Release her now!" my voice rang out, drawing the attention of many of the soldiers, both friend and foe. For this was the angry voice of Lore, and it was inhuman, low, and alien.

"Come and take her from me!" the Monster King challenged, his gravelly voice echoing across the battlefield.

I whirled the snaking whip over my head and brought it down on one of the Hunters in a blinding blaze of light and deafening blast of thunder. Its skin sizzled and shrank away from its skeleton as the monster was seared alive from the inside out.

With my teeth bared, my eyes blazing, and flames looping around me in ribbons of red and blue, I brought the whip down again and again as I advanced toward the Monster King. Even my Royal Guard stepped back with awe-filled faces as I strode across the field taking out the enemy, both human and Hunter-kind, with my whip and flames.

"Put her down," I growled as I came to a stop in front of the Monster King.

He dropped my sister-in-law, and she crumpled to the ground. With a quick flip of my wrist, a wave of energy bounded out of my fingertips and lifted her off the ground. She tumbled through the air and fell softly at the edge of the jungle, out of harm's way. Andrew would be at her side in a moment, I knew. I could feel his presence as he ran, full-blast, across the clearing.

Xi was at my side in an instant, just beyond the reach of the ribbons of flames that looped and wound through my body, forming a blazing barrier around me. Then, there was Everett ... Ky, my truest of loves, the whole reason I'd brought us to this very moment in time, stepping behind the Monster King, carefully, stealthily.

The Monster King was too busy growling and striding toward me to see me slip the bovine tranquilizer dart from my armor. It felt familiar in my hand, taking me back to the building when we'd rushed in and saved Everett. How fitting ... a tribute, memorial ... a perfect ending to a centuries-long tragedy.

Ash was watching me, waiting for a signal. Xi was sensing each infinitesimal movement I made. And Everett was doing something I hadn't seen him do since the barbeque at the ranch, when he'd picked up his sunglasses with a tiny bolt of lightning. Yes, he was powering up his hands. Electric sparks crackled into the night from his fingertips, and I felt the draw between us like the gravity between the moon and the earth.

It was time to end this thing so we could have our new beginning.

Without warning, I lunged forward, running in swift long strides. Everything around me turned to slow motion as I leapt into the air, tugging the tip of the tranquilizer dart loose with my teeth, and coming down on the Monster King's chest in a clash of good versus evil.

He didn't immediately feel the needle plunge into the thick, scaly skin where his shoulder and neck met. My thumb came down on the plunger, sending the serum coursing through his veins, and his eyes flashed wide open as he roared and gripped me tight, squeezing me like a python.

Everett was immediately on the massive Hunter's back, his dagger plunging and slicing deep into the flesh of the Monster King. And my flames seared the Hunter's flesh, making it impossible for him to continue holding me in his death-grip.

Ash blasted the monster with a blinding flash of electricity, hitting him in the face. The Monster King screeched in agony. And my Royal Guard killed any Hunter who tried to come to the aid of their king.

My eyes were wide with victory, as I bounded out of the Hunter's grip and stepped back to allow Xi to move in with his sword. The Monster King staggered sideways, flailing his arms, trying to remove Everett from his back. But the tranquilizer was doing its work, and Everett was too agile and cunning to be caught.

Everett's smile was fierce, his own eyes gleaming and glowing a bright iridescent blue as he plunged his dagger into the Monster King once more. Another blast from Ash, and the giant Hunter staggered backwards. Xi advanced, his sword gleaming as he gripped it tightly with both hands, swinging it over his shoulder, and slicing the air as his blade came down on the Monster King's neck.

In that split-second, Everett leapt backwards, and Xi's blade sliced through the Monster King's scaly flesh, lobbing his head off, sending it tumbling through the air, and finally hitting the ground in a loud *thud* before rolling to the center of the battlefield. Then, his massive body fell to the ground like a tree hitting the earth.

Silence filled the night as the remaining Hunters looked at the massive heap of dead flesh that had once been their king. Their raspy breaths filled the silence, disbelief dawning on them. They were reaping what they'd wanted to sow upon my people so long ago— complete extinction.

"No!" the Monster King's second-in-command shouted, running toward me. I turned, ready to use my whip, but someone jumped in front of him. At first, I didn't know who the Hunter struck with his massive mace-like weapon. When Orion's body spun sideways from the blow, I knew ... in an instant ... I knew my adopted son had been fatally wounded.

"Orion!" Max bellowed as she ran toward him, shielding him from another blow, and vanquishing the Hunter by opening an enormous gash across his abdomen, spilling his entrails, and then snapping his neck

Ash dropped to Orion's side. It was the first time any of our people had ever seen defeat weighing down on the never-defeated General. Lore's heart broke inside my chest, but there was something I could do. But it had to be done quickly, before it was too late. I yanked the tiny, silvery vial from around Ash's neck and fell to my knees next to Orion, whose breaths were ragged and shallow.

"Mother," he said, then coughed.

"Yes, son. You know what I will do," I bent over him and kissed his forehead.

Max knelt next to me and lifted Orion's hand to her chest. "I cannot live without my Other," she whispered, tears streaming down her tattooed face.

"I love you, Max," Orion stammered, a weak smile at one corner of his mouth. Then a rivulet of blood rushed out of his mouth and down the side of his face, streaking his hair with ribbons of crimson. He gasped for air, and glanced at me, his eyes turning solid black and his skin turning ashen grey the way they had in Sprinkles the night he'd saved Everett's life for my sake.

"I will see you again soon, Son," my own voice wavered as I held the tiny vial next to his lips.

With one last jagged gasp, he fell limp in Ash's arms. I blinked the tears away so that I wouldn't miss the thin ribbon of blue light that wound up his throat and across his lips. I had to be quick to capture it, before Orion's essence escaped into the night sky.

The glistening wisp of light of Orion's essence poured into the silvery vial, and I quickly corked it and clasped it to my chest, unable to swallow down the sobs that escaped my throat in growls of anger and grief.

"Kill them all! Slaughter them!" my voice rang out across the field. And my Royal Guard obeyed with a ferocity never seen on this planet, for they felt Max's keen rage of revenge as it filtered through the entire group of soldiers.

Nyx, disbelief covering his face in a mask of loss and grief, ordered the soldiers of The Resistance with shouts and hand motions. Weapons blasted, lighting up the pre-dawn with brilliant flashes and rounds of deafening ammunition.

His thoughts shouted out loud enough for them to echo in my brain. He knew he shouldn't still be standing, alive and breathing, with his birth Other lying still and breathless on the ground. And he also knew that I'd worked a sort of magic, somehow saving Orion to live another day.

My whip did its work on every enemy within its reach, scorching, searing, and burning from the inside out, as I took out every ounce of grief and frustration on them. I turned in search of more to kill but saw Ash carrying Orion's body up the steps of the pyramid ... the same pyramid that Orion and Nyx had called 'home' in their childhood.

I thought back to Orion's chubby fingers gripping my hands as he learned to walk in this very courtyard where he'd just taken his last step. I thought of his bright eyes shining when he'd walked the first time ... and how those same eyes had turned dark when he'd fallen just moments earlier.

A loud call snapped me out of my dark thoughts. I spun around to see Max, covered in blood, standing on a pile of bodies, shouting the victory cry, her tears mingling with the blood that was smeared across her tattooed skin. Every one of the enemies, both alien and human, lay strewn across the field.

Countless columns of smoke rose from the fires that had been ignited by the tip of my whip. My eyes watered and throat burned as I took in the desolation around me. Smoldering heaps of alien and humankind, alike, were strewn across the battlefield, mingled among each other as a gory testament of what centuries of hate and revenge could cause.

It was over. The battle was won. Lore's heart leapt in my chest, unable to believe that her age-old plan had finally been accomplished.

And just like a scene from a movie, a Queen turned to see her horse trotting toward her through veils of smoke. I swung myself into Lightning's saddle, blinking the burning smoke from my eyes, and got a different view of the battlefield.

My Royal Guard had all survived. They'd gathered at the heap that had once been the King of the Hunters and were greeting each other. When they saw their Queen astride her horse, crown gleaming in the glow of the firelight, face smudged with smut and blood, cheeks stained with tears over the loss of a royal son, they each covered their chest with a fist in salute. Then Xi held the severed head of the Monster King high into the air, and his cry of victory echoed through the jungle and filled the waning night.

My reply was a loud hoot and holler of a cowgirl from Willis, Texas. Lightning lifted her front legs off the ground, and I had to wonder what a sight we must have been ... me in gleaming alien armor, my hair loosened from its braid and flowing in the smoky night air with a silvery crown woven through its tangles, astride a beautiful chestnut horse on a victorious battlefield. This was a sight my alien father would have been proud of.

At that moment, my eyes lit on my mother's face. She was just as covered in smut and blood as I was and was standing with Angelica who was checking her for wounds. Mom smiled at me and nodded once. I had no idea how long she'd known this battle would one day happen, but the relief that it was over showed in her eyes.

Andrew and his group of rag-tag alien Hunters were poking and prodding at the bodies of the Hunters, making sure we'd finished them all off. He nodded and smiled as he looked up at me.

"It's finished, Sis," he smiled. It was the first time I'd seen that kind of a smile on his face in longer than I could remember. His hair was huge, and one side of it had been singed. It must have gotten too close to the fire. He noticed me looking at it, and he shrugged, then tossed his head back and laughed.

Giggling, I tugged Lightning's reins and spun around and around, searching for Everett. Every direction revealed more death and destruction. *Could it be finally over?* I wondered as a wild smile crossed my face. *Could this* really *be the way it ends?*

I should've known the answer before the question even crossed my mind.

CHAPTER TWENTY-EIGHT

IS THIS THE WAY IT ENDS?

Is This the Way it Ends? My hope for a final ending was dashed as soon as I turned the horse around once more. A loud electrical current caught my attention. After all the horrid events of the night and glory of a battle won, I couldn't believe my eyes.

Everett was suspended in the air, encapsulated in a bubble of energy, and unable to move. Hovering in front of him, arms held out, and hands blasting him with electricity, was Ash. A snarl of anger pushed his lip up, exposing his bared teeth.

"Put him down!" I ordered, "Now!" The last word was more of a growl ... a threat.

"Oh, no, Princess," Ash's voice was filled with a mixture of anger and resentment, and his face twisted with grief. "You're not forsaking me for a hybrid half-breed!"

"I'm your *Queen*, and you will obey me at once, General!" I shouted, my voice warping into Lore's.

"And I'm your Royal Consort, appointed by your father!" Ash answered, unaccustomed to a challenge he couldn't master. "I won't lose what's mine to this mere mortal." He lifted Everett higher into the air. "I will kill him first."

"I will kill you if you harm even a hair on his head!" I gritted my teeth. My heart pounded against my ribs, and that dark dread lifted its ugly head ... winding its tentacles around my ribs. The thought of being without my true love after all of this would be my ending. "He will be my Royal Consort, and you will retrieve the other ship and bring the others back here."

"This whole plan of yours is the reason my son is dead," Ash's voice broke. "You owe me another child, Lore! You *owe* me this!"

"I owe you *nothing!*" I shouted as I steeled myself for what I was about to do. "Where are my daughters, General? *Where?*"

He looked at me, pain slashing across his handsome face as if I'd clipped him with my whip. For a split-second we were back on the ship together, centuries in the past, and our twin daughters were gone. A second later, we were back in the present, and he was glaring at me, holding my true love hostage.

"I *will* retrieve the other ship," he nodded after a long pause ... his tone eluding to a hidden meaning behind that one sentence.

"Blair, get away from him!" Andrew shouted as he ran across the battlefield toward me. He'd sensed more than I had. For I was so distracted with the possibility of losing Everett that I didn't pick up on Ash's thoughts.

Ash knew how to draw me closer. He closed his hands into tight fists, forcing the energy bubble to collapse around Everett, sending him into convulsions. I brought the end of the reins down on Lightning's rump with a snap and dug my heels into her ribs, ignoring Andrew's warnings and shouts from Mom and Xi.

Then, as I'd learned to do for a rodeo show once, I lifted myself to stand on Lightning's saddle, trusting her to take me where I needed to go. As usual, the horse knew my intentions and ran straight ahead, toward the bizarre spectacle of two men levitating.

When I got close enough, I kicked off the saddle and leapt through the air, casting my own electrical net over Ash. He released Everett, allowing him to fall to the ground. A quick glance back revealed that Everett was struggling to stand, coughing as the air entered his lungs once more. Xi knelt to check him out, then glanced back up at me.

"Do as you're told, Ash. Don't make me your enemy," I warned gritting my teeth and strengthening my net around him.

"Gotcha!" Ash smiled broadly as if he'd just said "check mate." He cast a snare of blazing blue light around me.

Like a butterfly caught in a net, I struggled to free myself from his grip. As if catching me was as easy as pie, he held me captive with the energy from one of his hands while he used the other to press a series of commands into a small screen on the sleeve of his armor.

A rumble grew deep in the earth. The ground shook and cracked beneath us like a movie about a cataclysmic earthquake. The quaking loosened the ancient pyramid stones. They lost their grip on one another, slipped free, and scattered across the battlefield like giant dice tossed by pagan gods of old.

Then the deafening sounds of engines whining and the fumes of ancient jet fuel shot from the underground hangar. Ash had built it beneath the foundations of the stone pyramid. This was the storage place of the pod containing the captain's quarters … the part of the ship we'd lived in for centuries while we'd traveled through deep space.

Two gigantic doors slid away, and the nose of the pod ship emerged from deep beneath the ground. I'd never wanted to step foot on that ship ever again. It had been my prison while we'd sought a new home until I'd gone into stasis and slept away my grief over the loss of my tiny daughters.

Ash twirled us around and lowered us to ground-level so that we faced the silvery ship as it rose out of the hangar. Rivulets of dirt shook from its hull revealing the high gleam of a ship capable of fully cloaking itself. I struggled to free myself from his snare as the main hatch opened and the light beam readied itself to pull us inside the ship.

"Let me go, Ash!" I ordered, blasting him with bolts of electricity from my hands. "I *order* you to release me!"

His armor absorbed the energy and increased the strength of his hold on me. I was trapped and couldn't free myself, because his power was feeding off of mine. I needed someone or something to intervene.

"We *will* be happy again, Princess," he moved closer to me, pushing me toward the light beam.

"I was *never* happy with you!" I shouted, straining every inch to push away from him. I looked down at Mom. She was reaching toward me, and I felt like a small child again. Everett and Andrew were planning something, but I had no idea what it was.

My Royal Guard was helpless to do anything. I was trapped in an endless loop of energy. Ash's snare fed off of mine. Xi held a large weapon on his shoulder, but if he blasted Ash with it, he'd likely hit me, too.

I was inches from the light beam, and I looked back at my loved ones one last time. It would be years before I'd see them again, if ever. Some of them weren't hybrids like Everett and me ... they'd likely be very old or gone by the time we returned with the other ship.

Xi had dropped his weapon and was working with Andrew and Everett on some sort of strategy. I couldn't read their thoughts through the energy bubble around me. I'd never felt so helpless in my whole life. It seemed like a real check mate after all.

History was about to repeat itself with me being trapped with no one but Ash for centuries until we found the other ship. I would release myself into the void of space before I let him touch me ever again. If I couldn't be with Everett, then my people would be left without a Queen.

The outer shell of Ash's snare slipped away as a bright beam of light shot from his hands. It pulled me toward him so that he'd be holding me in his arms when we were pulled into the hatch. I tried to knee him in the groin, but he blocked me and smiled.

I spun away from him, putting a few feet between us, but it only spurred on his hunter's instinct. This was all a turn-on for him. If I could've killed him in that moment, I would have. And I desperately wished I'd let Xi do it when he'd had the chance.

The ship was fully powered up and straining to exit our atmosphere. The only thing holding it still was the button on the command screen on Ash's armor sleeve. He reached for me again, releasing the tractor beam to draw us into the ship together.

In that split second, Everett blasted Andrew in his back, sending him into the bubble between Ash and me. Andrew had something in his hand, but everything was happening so fast, I couldn't make out what it was.

Murphy's Law was in full swing. At the precise moment Andrew slipped between Ash and me, I saw one of the Hunters move. We'd thought they were all dead. We were wrong. He lifted his hand just long enough to aim and fire a weapon, igniting the energy bubble in an intense flash of light that vanished in an enormous clap of thunder that rolled through the jungle.

The enormous blast threw me backward onto the ground. Then, suddenly, everything was silent. The only sounds to be heard were the rustling wind in the trees and the nearby whooshing of a waterfall. All else had hushed.

I staggered to my feet, dazed, and partially deafened by the high-pitch ringing in my ears. My skin felt scorched like I'd spent too long in the sun, and my sight was dimmed as if I'd been staring into a bright light.

"No!" someone sobbed nearby. "Oh, God, no! No … no … no …"

What is it? I desperately asked myself as I spun around. What's happened?

I saw Rake snap the neck of the Hunter who'd shot at us. Jex ran him through with his sword for good measure. I turned again to see Xi coming toward me, saying something … his lips were moving … but I couldn't register his words.

Another turn, and Everett was there, dark remorse washed across his face and tears welled up in his brilliant blue eyes. I wanted to reach for him, but I was so confused and shaken that I spun once more, stumbling in my tracks, and saw Mom holding Angelica in her arms. Angelica was reaching toward the ship but, when I turned to see, the ship was gone. Ash was gone.

Andrew was gone.

"Andrew!" I shouted, staggering forward, my eyes scanning the demolished courtyard. "Answer me, damn it!"

Silence.

"AN-DREW!" I shouted again as loud as physically possible. Tears poured down my face and rolled down the front of my armor. Two strong, gentle arms embraced me from behind, cradling me as I sobbed, shaking my head ... refusing to accept what my eyes were telling me.

There was nothing where Ash had snared me, where the ship had hovered awaiting its passengers ... where Andrew had lunged between us just as the Hunter had discharged its weapon.

The only thing left was a pile of smoldering clothes ... a pair of khaki cargo pants, t-shirt, and a pair of boots that looked as though they'd been tossed high into the air and allowed to land wherever they may.

I fell to my knees and crumpled into a ball. I wanted to disappear, never to be seen again. Everett knelt next to me, keeping one hand on my side, and issuing orders for my soldiers to search the area. But I knew what they'd find. Nothing.

Andrew, my big brother, was gone.

"Is this the way it ends?" I asked Xi, searching for wisdom in his wide, slanted eyes.

"There is no other way for it to end now, my lady," he answered, helping me out of my armor. I nodded, accepting the painfully inevitable.

The sun was high in the sky, and the courtyard looked nothing like it had before. The pyramid was gone, strewn in giant stone blocks across the clearing. Nyx wandered the courtyard in meandering lines where he and his birth Other had grown from babies to men. He'd never lived apart from Orion. I clasped the silver vial that held Orion's essence and held it over my heart.

"We have defeated the enemy. This day will be remembered for all time among our people, my lady." Xi said proudly, tenderly, as he packed my armor away. "It has been written in blood, and we will remember."

I nodded, recalling the old way of my alien people. Tonight, the pyres would burn and the lanterns would reach the sky. "We don't have enough time to awaken the Holy Men and Women for the funerals."

"No, we do not," Xi shook his head. "Where do they await us?"

I pointed to the edge of the jungle where the entrance of the Queen's city was hidden by a massive overgrowth of roots and vines. The entrance had caved in the night I'd traded myself for Everett's life. Then Ash had blasted the stones away to save him. He'd resealed it for the safety of our people. That was one thing I was glad of.

"The containment quarters of the ship were turned into an underground city," I explained, etching a crude drawing into the dirt with the tip of Xi's sword. "A few of our people decided not to rest underground again after I'd left them to become a hybrid. They're hidden in cocoons throughout the jungle." I didn't explain to him that Dad and Andrew may have had a hand in the murder of some of them.

"Many of our people were never awakened and remain in stasis below this very ground." I felt hollow inside, talking about a distant past, which held plans that ended in the loss of my brother. "That's where the Holy Men and Women are."

"We will manage, my lady," Xi answered.

There was no pyre to be made for Andrew. All that was left of him were his clothes. I gave them to Mom and insisted she and Angelica leave with Andrew's friends. Besides, he would have wanted a Christian memorial service ... not an alien one. I tried to swallow down the enormous lump in my throat as they disappeared into the jungle. But it was impossible.

So, I did the only thing I could. I rushed into the shadows of the jungle and threw up.

Xi debriefed Ash's band of soldiers while Nyx released his men and women of The Resistance to go back to their compound with orders to remain there until he returned to them. He was a natural leader, and I was very proud of him. I'd been very proud of his brother, too.

Max built the pyre for Orion's body. It was intricately carved with promises they'd made to each other, and it also had the coat of arms of the royal house whittled into the bark where his head would lay. She hadn't spoken to anyone all day but went about her work in honoring her beloved.

Mal and Jex built the pyre that would hold Kin's body. They'd been silent all day, as well. Kin's sacrifice for them and their Queen had been a great honor and a huge blow to both of the young soldiers. Though, the pyre they'd built for Kin hadn't been as elaborate as Orion's, it was still done as creatively. They'd carved the stories of Kin's conquests into the logs that built his pyre so his ancestors would know the stories.

Everett let me be as I processed it all. I loved him even more for it. So many alien and human emotions pumped through my veins that I felt as though I'd explode and fly away on the wind like so many ashes from a burning funeral pyre. He'd made himself busy all day making the lanterns that would be used for the funeral services.

At midday, he took me by the hand and led me to a spot of shade at the jungle's edge. Rake had insisted that he make me eat. So, he placed a handful of rations into my hand and gave me a sip of water from his canteen.

"I remember my funeral," he said, his voice sounding a bit distant.

"What?" I turned to look at him.

"Not the actual funeral, itself, but the ache in your heart. I felt it ... or at least my essence did." He touched the vial that hung around my neck. "I never stopped being Ky, and I never stopped longing to be with you."

My sobs rang out across the battlefield as I fell into Everett's arms causing my soldiers to come to attention long enough to see that I was okay. Then they went back to their duties. It had been a long time since the wish crossed my mind, but I found myself longing for the old days back in Willis. I wanted my innocence back. But it was long gone.

I'd fallen asleep in Everett's arms and dreamed of a quiet, normal day back home on the ranch. Nothing spectacular or scary happened in my dream. Just the everyday workings of the ranch and lunch in the kitchen with Grandma.

A loud blast of a horn jolted me awake. My heart pounded hard against my ribs, and I struggled to catch my breath as I sat up and clutched my chest. Xi was sounding the Call to the Pyres. It was time for goodbyes.

"It's okay, Babe. It's only Xi," Everett cooed as he hugged me gently to him.

"I know," I nodded and reached up to kiss his cheek.

"Let's get this over with," he stood and helped me to my feet.

Overhead, an endless sky of deep navy velvet was strewn with twinkling stars, like diamonds on a royal canopy. It was a natural thing, years later, for my royal banners to be patterned from the star-strewn sky in tribute to a night that marked both endings and beginnings for my alien people and me.

There were no drums to beat, no Holy Men and Women to chant the sacred words. There was only a band of soldiers, their Queen, and her Consort. Everett's lanterns lifted into the air, flickering with candles inside them. They drifted up, up, up into the night sky, toward the ancestors.

But I felt that the two on the pyres deserved holy words spoken for them. So, I stepped between them and cleared my throat so that the words rang out loud and clear into the night. They were the words that were spoken at Dad's and Aaron's funeral.

"The Lord is my shepherd, I shall not want," tears flowed down my cheeks, and my Royal Guard and Ash's soldiers hung on my every word. "He maketh me to lie down in green pastures; He leadeth me beside the still waters." The words rolled off my tongue from memory. Vacation Bible School had been where I'd memorized the 23rd Psalm and the Ten Commandments. But these were new words to these battle-hardened alien soldiers who listened so intently. "He restoreth my soul; He leadeth me in the paths of righteousness for His name's sake."

I paused a moment and looked down at Orion's broken body, then up into Max's tear-filled eyes. "Yea, though I walk through the valley of the shadow of death, I shall fear no evil; for thou art with me; Thy rod and thy staff they comfort me." A lump filled my throat, and I couldn't continue. Not only was my adopted son lying broken and dead on his funeral pyre, but my heart was broken for Andrew. I opened my mouth again to continue, but I couldn't form the words.

"Thou preparest a table before me in the presence of mine enemies; Thou anointest my head with oil; my cup runneth over," Everett's voice rang out into the night. "Surely goodness and mercy shall follow me all the days of my life; and I will dwell in the house of the Lord forever. Amen." He took my hand and led me away from the pyres. With his arm wrapped tightly around my shoulders, we stood at the point where the darkness met the line of light from the torches.

Mal and Jex lit Kin's pyre, saluting the old soldier as his ashes spiraled high into the night sky to his ancestors. Max looked at me for permission, and I nodded, feeling my bottom lip tremble.

"Farewell, my love," she said just before placing the flaming torch into Orion's hands.

I glanced up at Everett's handsome face. The firelight lit the lines of his profile as he gazed up into the night sky. *The ancestors will have to wait a while longer for Orion,* I whispered into his thoughts.

I know, his answer wove through my thoughts, and a slight smile turned up the corner of his lips.

Max doesn't know yet, I responded.

Don't tell her 'til it's done. We still have to find suitable parents, his voice whispered in my thoughts.

I already have, I answered, smiling up at the night sky. Suddenly, everything felt as though it would be alright.

Who? Everett turned to me, brows knit together. *Not us, right?*

Don't be absurd, I shook my head.

Relief flooded his face as he turned back toward the burning pyres. Max's shoulders were slumped with heavy grief. She'd lost everything when Orion had fallen while protecting me. I squeezed Everett's hand, then stepped away and motioned for Max. She was at my side in an instant.

"It was the highest honor for you to speak the holy words, my lady," Max said, starting to bow her head. I waved off the formalities and nodded.

"It was my honor to speak them," I answered, guiding her away from the others. "But I have something I need to tell you."

"What is it, my lady?" she asked, trying to keep her eyes from going back to the burning pyre.

"Orion isn't gone," I blurted the words out. "I saved his essence the same way I saved Ky's."

"What?" I had her full attention. Her wide, slanted eyes, swollen with tears of grief now sparkled with possibilities.

"I captured his essence in this vial," I held the precious ornament in my palm for her to see. "I'd like for you to wear it for a while. He'll feel your thoughts." I lifted the chain over my head and placed it in her hands. "It'll give you some comfort until I leave."

"You're leaving us?" Max held the vial gently to her chest. The silver chain dangled through her fingers and shimmered in the firelight.

"No, I'm not leaving my people. But I have to go tend to some ... business. While I'm there, I will begin the process of Orion's rebirth." It was my turn to glance back at the pyre.

"Will I recognize him, my lady?" Max's voice sounded unbelievably small.

"I will ensure that he looks exactly the same. But you'll need to prepare yourself to wait until he's grown," I placed my hand on her arm.

"I would wait forever for my Other, my lady." A tear slowly trailed down her cheek, across the tattoos on her shimmery skin.

"I know the feeling," I answered.

My Royal Guard had set up camp with tents and fires. Mal and Jex hunted for some meat that now roasted on the central fire in the camp. My tent was at the center, next to the fire, with my soldiers' tents situated around mine, forming a protective barrier. Ash's soldiers arranged their encampments in a circle around the outer perimeter.

"I need to go home," I whispered, pressing my cheek against Everett's chest. I was stiff and sore as I lay in his arms in the privacy of my tent. Every joint ached and cried out for a hot bath and a year-long nap. So much had been sacrificed, so many had died ... all for the sole purpose of me having my happily-ever-after.

"I know," he answered, toying with a lock of my hair.

"Things have gotten so weird," I lifted my face to look into his eyes. "I need to reconnect with my human half ... and to do other things."

"Other things sounds interesting," he smiled.

"I'm ready for my happily-ever-after now, Mr. Forster," I smiled in return and kissed him lightly on the lips.

"Me, too," he said just before flipping us over, pressing me against the soft mattress and slipping a hand into my hair, holding my lips tightly against his.

CHAPTER TWENTY-NINE

HAPPILY EVER AFTER

"My lady, who will protect you?" Xi asked, concern awash across his tattooed face.

"Everett will look out for me," I placed my hand on his enormous forearm. "I'll be back soon. And I've still got my tracker in my arm, so you'll know how to find me."

"As you wish, my lady," he bowed his head, "But I do not like this."

"I know, old friend," I took him by surprise when I hugged him.

I turned to the rest of my loyal soldiers and thanked them all for their service and promised to return to them as soon as possible. They'd already received their instructions to rebuild the pyramid and prepare the area for my return and the arrival of the other ship.

In the weeks following the funerals, Xi and Max had moved their pod ship into the hangar beneath the pyramid foundation. From there, they'd diligently searched for Ash's ship. They'd been unsuccessful, so far, in finding it. So had Nyx, who'd been obsessed with finding his lost father.

Max placed the silver vial and chain into my palm, and bowed her head. I promised her that by the time my city was rebuilt, and the other ship returned to us, she would have her Other back. She promised to tend my horse and keep her safe and healthy.

Then Everett and I disappeared into the shadows of the jungle with backpacks full of provisions and other things we would need. The trek to my old laboratory took two-and-a-half days. By the time we reached the hidden tunnel, we'd managed to gather a large amount of the prickly, sweet fruit like the monkey had handed to me on our bus ride into the jungle.

We spent another couple of days working in the laboratory, preparing Orion's essence, programming it so that he'd look exactly the same as he had before. We also distilled the fruit into a clear, tasteless liquid.

Once those things were completed, we sealed my laboratory and headed for the bus station where Dad's locker had been. It was another four-day journey through the jungle. We passed the tree where I'd spent the first few nights in my cocoon. I showed Everett where the jaguar had plunged over the mossy cliff, and he pulled me to him both proud of me and angry at how close he'd come to losing me.

Nothing about the jungle bus station had changed. The gravel parking lot still looked the same. Even the people looked the same milling about, selling their wares, or awaiting their bus. There was even a goat tied to the bench near the front door. I doubted it was the same goat as before, though.

The bus was much the same as the one we'd ridden the day our plane had nearly plunged into the depths of the jungle. We were just as jostled by the ride once we reached the small airport as we'd been that first day in the jungle.

That day seemed like a million years ago, I thought as I stumbled off the rickety over-crowded bus and looked around for a payphone to call David. I'd seen too much, heard too much, done too much to ever feel like the same person again.

Even twenty-four hours later, as we stepped off our plane at the George Bush Intercontinental Airport in Houston, I still felt like an alien in a human's skin. Which is exactly what I'd become.

Natalie and David were holding a sign with our names scrawled across it in colorful letters cut out of construction paper ... I could tell it was created by a future kindergarten teacher.

I gripped Everett's hand tight and looked up into his eyes for reassurance. With as much regret crossing his face as washed across my heart, he flashed me a half-smile and a reassuring nod. I swallowed hard and returned his nod.

Natalie squealed and hopped up and down when she saw us. David merely smiled and waved. Some things never change. They were living proof that opposites attract and were obviously still very much in love.

They were the perfect couple.

"Welcome home, Little Sis," David said while hugging me tight. "I'm real sorry about Andrew," his voice broke, and he cleared his throat to hide it. "I feel like I've lost a brother." What could I say to that? Nothing without breaking down and sobbing for the millionth time. So I merely hugged him back and relished the smell of Texas on him.

"I spy something sparkly!" Natalie immediately saw my engagement ring and a brilliant smile crossed her pink, glossed lips.

"Isn't it pretty?" I held my hand out. "I think he did good," I said, smiling at Everett.

"Heck, yeah, he did! How many carats is that?" Natalie gasped, grabbing my hand and pulling it toward her.

"Four carats. It's a one-of-a kind," Everett said, forgetting he wasn't wearing his black rimmed glasses and pushing his finger up the bridge of his nose. I giggled and hugged him, so glad that at least one of us had kept something from our humanity.

"Are y'all hungry?" David asked.

"Starving!" Everett and I answered at the same time. We hadn't eaten on the plane, and it had been a long flight. Thick, humid heat clung to us as soon as we stepped outside into the coming night.

"Whew! It's a different kinda heat," I said fanning myself as we walked through the parking garage. Exhaust from passing vehicles made both Everett and me cough. The air had been so much cleaner in the jungle.

"I almost forgot how hot August is," Everett said as we climbed into the back seat of David's truck.

"It's been a really hot summer this year," David answered, cranking the truck engine and putting the air conditioning on full blast. "But it's been good for the construction business."

"Good thing you're planning a Christmas wedding," I smiled at Natalie, remembering her humongous wedding dress and thinking about how hot that thing would've been on a smoldering summer day.

"Well," she drew the word out. "Considering everything that's happened ... we just felt like ..." she stammered for the words, but I knew what she meant. Losing Andrew had been a horrific blow to all of us. "Life's just too darn short to put off the good stuff!" she smiled brightly and bounced in her seat as she said that last sentence.

"I couldn't agree more," I replied. A different kind of feeling was growing behind my ribs. It wasn't the dread I'd once known so well. It was plain ole guilt.

"Good, 'cause we're getting married in two days!" she squealed. "It's a good thing I did those clothing measurements on you before you left. Your maid of honor's dress is *gorgeous!*"

"What?" I gasped and glanced at Everett, then back to Natalie.

"Yep! But we decided on a small wedding so we could have a nice honeymoon and then have some money to start out our lives with," she said, beaming at David. Judging by the lift in his profile, he was smiling, too.

"That's … awesome!" I tried to sound excited. I was happy for them, but such short notice was cutting into a lot of plans Everett and I had already made.

A quick change of plans, huh? Everett's voice whispered in my thoughts.

Yeah, I sighed and leaned my head on his shoulder. *Guess we better do it tonight.*

I hope they'll forgive us one day, he answered, and I could feel his guilt mingling with mine.

So do I, I pressed my face into his neck, wishing I could hide from what we were about to do.

"Does Pizza Shack sound okay?" David interrupted our silent conversation.

"Oh, my gosh, yes!" my stomach immediately growled at the thought of a hamburger and mushroom pizza.

"Can we get it to go?" Everett asked. I wondered what plans he was hatching.

"Uh, sure ..." David answered, the glow of the dash light cast an eerie contrast of light and shadow across his features as he glanced at us in the rearview mirror. Natalie turned to look at us, resting her chin on her hand.

"It's just ..." Everett stammered, "Kinda hard for Blair to face everyone asking about Andrew."

"Oh, dude! Why didn't you say so?" David relaxed. "That's understandable. There was a lot of talk ... a lot of people loved Andrew ..." his voice trailed off.

"His memorial service was really nice. The whole town was there ..." Natalie reached for my hand and squeezed it. The lump filled my throat again. My chin quivered and tears streamed down my face. I couldn't stifle the sobs that inched up my throat.

"He was just ... gone!" I blurted, sobbing and snuffing my nose. "One second he was there. The next ... all that was left was a pile of clothes."

"Damn it," David said under his breath. I could sense that he was thinking if he'd have been there, it never would've happened.

We rode in silence for a long time, heading north on Interstate 45 toward home. As we passed through The Woodlands and then through Conroe, I was struck by how everything looked the same. But when we rolled to a stop at the red light at FM 1097 in Willis, I realized just how much I'd changed.

Nothing about Willis had changed since we'd struck out toward Brazil. It seemed that time had stood still in my small, inconsequential southeast Texas home town.

People were going about their lives and routines unaware of a secret alien invasion that was here to stay.

Bright lights sliced into the darkness of the night. My eyes weren't accustomed to light brighter than a campfire at night anymore. I squinted against the onslaught of manufactured light from the giant new Kroger store across the highway as we turned the opposite direction toward the Pizza Shack.

"I'm sure glad I didn't have to sack groceries and pull buggy duty at *that* monster store!" Everett snorted. We all had a good laugh at that, but fell silent at the mention of Andrew doing wheelies in the parking lot of the old Kroger.

We practically attacked David and wrenched the pizza out of his hand when he climbed back into the truck. It smelled so good and tasted even better. David parked the truck in our favorite stall at the Sonic and ordered some cokes.

"This is where we were when it all began," Everett said.

We all just sat staring straight ahead at the dark, empty lot across the street where the building had sat ... where the new Sprinkles had blown to smithereens. It looked as though the city had filled the giant crater in with dirt.

I clamped my eyes closed at the thought of Andrew looking back at me, reassuring me that it was just an old building ... that it would be okay to check it out. I shook my head, trying to remove the guilt that reminded me it was all my fault he was gone. I dropped my pizza and covered my face in my hands.

"Let's go somewhere else," Natalie whispered to David.

"Anywhere we go is gonna remind us," Everett said, pulling me close to him. "Maybe just away from all these bright lights?"

Of all places on earth, we ended up out at the back gate at the ranch. Natalie was a little freaked out, but Everett assured her that nothing was going to happen out there ever again. Oh, how I wished that were true.

Fifteen minutes later, both of our friends were laid out, unconscious, in the truck bed. It was so immoral, so unethical. Just so wrong on all levels known to mankind. But Everett and I weren't members of mankind. Not really.

It wasn't my first time to abduct a human with the purpose of doing reproductive procedures. However, it *was* my first time to do it to a close friend ... someone I loved ... someone who trusted me.

I reminded myself over and over again that I was also doing it for someone else I loved ... someone who'd given his life for me. He'd been a beautiful child, a brilliant teen, and he'd make them proud of him with good grades and his athletic abilities. The Willis WildKats would be a winning team with Orion playing ball. I smiled at that thought.

Of course, they'd be having twins. There was no getting around that. But at least one of their children would be a normal human ... hopefully. In retrospect, I realized that my procedures on Mom had produced multiple twin births, one of them ... Andrew ... had been a true telepath.

All that mattered, at this point, was that Orion's essence had been properly transferred into Natalie, and she'd be a wonderful mother to him. The next few years would be very interesting. It wasn't guaranteed that her first birth would produce the alien I'd just injected into her reproductive system.

Hopefully it will, I thought as I buttoned her shirt and smoothed it down over her stomach.

A shooting star etched a streak of sparkles across the star-filled sky overhead. Everett and I made a wish and then stood in each other's arms for a while, looking at the sky. The earthy scents of the pasture mingled with the late summer night air. Everything was coming full-circle now. Everything was being set right.

When David and Natalie began to show signs of waking up, Everett and I lay down and pretended to be asleep, too. The fruit serum had been so potent that they were extremely groggy. I was glad that Natalie hadn't woke up screaming like Mom and Everett's mother had. She'd never remember a thing.

That's the way it should've always been.

And that's the way all future hybrid implantations would be.

The wedding was lovely. It was a small church wedding, and Natalie beamed as she walked down the aisle to violin music. Her ebony hair hung in ringlets pinned with pearls. She was beautiful. David, wearing a black tux with a white vest and bowtie, teared up as his beautiful bride held out her hand for his. Everett filled in for Andrew as best man. Looking at him during the vows made me long to hurry our own wedding plans.

I wanted my happily-ever-after. I'd waited long enough.

After the cake was cut and the couple left in a flurry of handfuls of birdseed and shouts of well-wishes, I looked up into Everett's eyes. He nodded, then got everyone's attention and announced a wedding at the ranch tomorrow.

"Be there or be square!" he snorted just before he pulled me into his arms and kissed me in front of God and everybody.

Grandma and Mom would be up all night getting things ready. Mr. Forster smiled brightly as he glanced at Mom, and I got the feeling that he was planning on popping the question to her sometime really soon.

"Well, I'll be John Brown, son!" Grandpa said over all the whooping and hollering. "When were you gonna ask my permission to marry my granddaughter?"

"Right now," Everett said, beaming from ear to ear as he walked into the church with Grandpa who would undoubtedly give him his blessing. But us Texans like our traditions. And so do us aliens.

Which led me back to the problem with our wedding. We couldn't just show up back in the jungle, married. My alien people had to witness the ceremony. It was an important part of our society and had been for longer than anyone could remember.

For some strange reason, my mind went back to last Christmas when Ash had said, "Ceremonies and rituals are important. They mend broken hearts and spirits and bind individuals together in community." That was a true statement when it came to both alien and humankind alike.

So there was only one solution.

We had to have two weddings.

CHAPTER THIRTY

TWO WEDDINGS IN ONE DAY

Grandma's wedding dress was my "something old." It fit me perfectly. In retrospect, I realized that she'd had a build almost identical to mine when she was young. I'd remembered placing her carefully on the muddy bank of the river so she'd be found by her fellow humans. I'd stood over her and thought that one day, my human hybrid form would favor her in looks. I'd hand-picked her to be my grandmother.

I shook my head to clear my thoughts.

"Hold still!" Mom smiled as she tucked flowers into my hair. If Natalie had been there, my make-up would've been perfect. But she was on her honeymoon on a sandy beach in Hawaii. She'd already texted us a few pictures and had promised that she wasn't mad about our last-minute wedding plans.

Grandma's butterfly necklace hung around my neck as my something blue. It had needed some polishing and cleaning after months of me wearing it in the jungle and all I'd gone through ... not to mention all that goo it had suffered through when I'd been curled up in my cocoon.

The pearl earrings that dangled from my earlobes were my "something new." Grandpa had gone to town and gotten them for me and had blinked back tears when I'd opened them. Worry had aged him since I'd been away ... and, of course, the loss of Andrew had taken a huge toll on him. Still, he was strong and agile. I hated the thought of leaving him to work in the clinic alone now. But my future had a different path.

"I don't have a 'something borrowed'," I said, looking at Mom in the mirror. "It has to be just the right thing." We all started looking around the room. Mom and Grandma looked at their jewelry. Just as Mom was about to take off her bracelet, there was a knock at the door.

"May I come in?" Mr. Forster's eager voice was muffled by the door. "I have a surprise for my soon-to-be daughter."

"Say *please*," mom opened the door just a crack and smiled flirtingly.

"Please," he slipped his hand through the crack and stroked her cheek with his thumb.

My Mom, who'd shaved the sides and back of her hair off, exposing her tattoo, which marked her as a member of The Resistance, who'd fought alongside my soldiers with her samurai sword and had been splattered with the blood of those she'd killed, melted like butter.

"Look out your window," Mr. Forster said, stepping into the room.

I ran to the window and pulled back the curtains. Out in the middle of Grandma's rose garden was my perfect "something borrowed." Lightning snorted and stamped her hooves as if to hurry me up.

Grandpa was holding her reins and smiling. He was all dressed up and wearing his good cowboy hat. He'd braided Lightning's mane and tail with ribbons. She looked beautiful. This was where she belonged. Grandpa would take excellent care of the horse I'd "borrowed" and never returned. She'd saved my life on more than one occasion, now she'd get her reward.

The music started playing out in the back where we'd set up a few rows of white chairs for our closest family and friends. It was late afternoon when Mr. Forster led me outside, with my arm in his.

I recognized the saddle. It had Daisy's name inscribed across the back. The Rodeo Club had given it to me as a gift for my years of service to the club and as a memorial to my beloved horse.

With Mr. Forster's help, I slipped the tip of my white cowgirl boot into the stirrup and sat side-saddle. Mom and Grandma fixed my dress and handed me a small bouquet of roses from Grandma's garden. We didn't have any bridesmaids or groomsmen. It was just going to be Everett and me standing before the pastor just as it would be the two of us standing before the Holy Men and Women that evening.

"Oh, Darlin', those boots look so cute on you! I just can't believe you're old enough to be getting married," Grandma's voice wavered as she lifted a handkerchief to blot away a stray tear.

"I love them, Grandma," I said, reaching for her hand, "But not as much as I love you," I smiled. I wanted to say something to distract her from crying, because this was a happy day ... a very happy day, which had been a long time coming. "Remind me to send a thank you card to Gail for helping you find these for me," I said. It worked. She nodded and smiled.

"Gail's here! She'll love seeing you wear them!" she gushed.

"Lilly, let's get this show on the road. There's a young man awaitin' at the altar," Grandpa said. I was so glad he'd intervened before Mom started crying. I didn't think I'd be able to stand that. However, when I saw Mr. Forster twine his fingers with hers, I knew she'd be okay when we left again.

As soon as Grandpa led Lightning around the corner, the wedding march started. But it wasn't the normal wedding march. Willie Nelson started crooning From *Here to the Moon and Back*. A moment later, Dolly Parton joined in.

Everett was smiling a broad, goofy smile. He looked glorious in his black tux and black bow tie. I had no idea where he'd gotten a perfectly-fitted tux in such a short amount of time. Maybe Gail had the tux in her dress shop in Montgomery. Natalie would have said something about him looking hot. I happened to agree.

Friends and family stood as Grandpa led Lightning down the aisle, with me in her saddle, while Willie and Dolly sang about everlasting love. It was the perfect song; every word seemed to be meant for Everett and me.

When we reached the altar, Grandpa helped me out of the saddle and spoke up when the pastor asked who was giving the bride away. "Her family and I are," he answered, tipping his hat to the pastor. Then he kissed me on the cheek and placed my hand in Everett's.

The sheriff took Lightning's reins and led her off to the barn so Grandpa wouldn't miss the ceremony. And everything else faded away as I gazed up into Everett's bright blue eyes.

I love you to the moon and back, his thoughts wound through my mind as the pastor gave everyone a chance to speak now or forever hold their peace.

I love you more! I answered back, smiling from ear to ear. This was it. This was what I'd been waiting for longer than anyone could ever imagine.

Impossible, he said, returning my smile.

We'd chosen to have traditional vows. As the pastor led us through the vows, we each placed our wedding rings on each other's hand. The band of platinum looked perfect around Everett's finger. I'd had the words "I am my Other's, and my Other is mine" engraved inside his band. It would be a nice surprise for him to discover on our honeymoon.

My wedding band matched my engagement ring. It was a band of platinum with diamond stars embedded all around it. He slipped it on my finger, and my heart sang. It seemed too good to be true that after all this time I'd gotten my wish.

"I now pronounce you husband and wife. Everett, you may kiss your bride," the pastor said.

Everett took me in his arms, and in a romantic dip like in the movies, he placed a tender kiss on my lips, and whispered promises of a wonderful wedding night wound though my thoughts. I wrapped my arms around his neck, twined my fingers in his hair, and returned his kiss and his promises.

Applause erupted from the small crowd of close friends and family, reminding us that we weren't alone yet. Everett lifted me to stand next to him. Holding my hand, he led me down the aisle while the pastor announced us as Mr. and Mrs. Forster.

I had to keep pushing back that old, tired feeling that something was going to go wrong to ruin my happily-ever-after. That some devastating event would happen to take away all the happiness and love that was filling my heart and soul.

"That's all behind us now," Everett whispered in my ear and gently kissed me on the neck as we stood next to the cake table, ready to receive our guests.

I still couldn't believe it was all real as we sliced our wedding cake and fed each other our first bite as husband and wife. The cake was modest, with just three layers stacked on top of each other, frosted in white buttercream. Written in white on the front of the cake were the words *Happily Ever After*, and on the top were our initials. Tucked between the layers were roses from Grandma's garden. Mom and Grandma had made it, and it was the loveliest cake I'd ever seen.

"Oh, that's good!" Everett said when I fed him his bite. "Here, taste it," he smiled as he placed a bite in my mouth.

"That's the best thing I've eaten in months!" I giggled.

We toasted each other with a glass of champagne poured in the glasses from Mom's and Dad's wedding. Then everyone had a slice of cake. Coffee and tea was served from Grandma's kitchen while Grandpa and the Sheriff finished up the barbeque and set up tables in the back yard.

Everett and I put on our getaway clothes as the sun crept behind the horizon. Outside, music played from Grandma's garden speakers, and the guests enjoyed plates of food made by my loving family. I watched for a while from the window in the hallway. I didn't hear him step up behind me. But as my new husband's arms wrapped around me from behind, I melted against him.

"I love you, Lore," he said, his breath brushing against my hair.

"I love you, too, Ky. Forever and always," I said, feeling so full of love that I could explode into tiny bits of light.

"Forever and always," he replied.

I turned to face him and lifted myself on my toes, awaiting a kiss. He lingered a moment, caressing my cheek with his thumb. Then pulled me tight against him and covered my lips with his. And immediate warmth grew between us until sparks erupted, catching the curtain on fire.

Everett ripped the curtain down and rushed into the bathroom with it. He tossed it into the bathtub while I cranked on the shower. Damp smoke twirled into the air as the flames quickly extinguished.

"Well, I didn't foresee that happening," Everett said.

I laughed so hard that I snorted, which caused him to start laughing. I shut off the water and led him out of the bathroom. "Come on, husband. They're waiting for us," I giggled as I dragged him down the stairs.

The lawn in the back yard had become a makeshift dance floor. A family friend named Rick was manning the stereo as our resident deejay. When we stepped out the back door, everyone stood and applauded us.

"Before we begin the festivities, Grandma and I have something for you," Grandpa said. He and Grandma were holding hands. "So, come on over here for a minute before Rick takes over."

Every eye was glued on us as Grandpa removed the white envelope from his shirt pocket. He held it in his hand for a moment, then said. "We all saw this day coming … you two seemed perfect for each other, and I couldn't be happier in your choice of a husband." Grandpa said, his voice trembling a little from emotion.

"Everett is now a member of this family, and we'll love him like one of our own." Grandpa cleared his throat. "Grandma and I have a wedding gift for the two of you. We hope it will help you start your lives out together," he handed the envelope to me. Inside the envelope was the deed to that old ranch I'd happened upon out on Rose Road. Grandpa and I had talked about it, and he'd said he'd check on it for me.

"Grandpa," I gasped, looking up into is old, blue eyes. "I'm speechless …"

"We love you, Sweet Pea. We want you to be happy," he cleared his throat again. "When you two have kids and settle down, you'll have a nice starter ranch to call home."

I hugged him, pressing my cheek against his shoulder. He smelled of Old Spice and smoke from the barbecue pit. Grandpa had been an anchor to me in the storm. He'd been my hero, and I'd never told him. I was about to when he slapped Everett on the back and drew him into a hug. It was a missed opportunity, but I promised myself that sometime soon, I'd tell him.

"It's time for the couple's first dance together!" Rick announced.

Everett nodded to Rick. Judging by Rick's expression, they'd had an arrangement between them about which song Rick would cue up for our first dance. I was right, because as soon as we stepped onto the center of the grass dance floor, Everett spoke up.

"I hope y'all don't mind that Rick's put together a soundtrack of songs I've picked out for my bride tonight. Everyone, give Rick a hand!" Everett smiled. The crowd applauded Rick and his musical prowess. "Now, if you'll indulge us, we'll have our first dance as husband and wife."

To everyone watching us, Everett's choice seemed like a strange song for a wedding dance. But for us, it was the perfect song. In fact, he couldn't have chosen a more fitting song for our dance. As Kyler England sang *When the World Stops Spinning*, it occurred to me that this was truly our song. It was the story of our lives, our history ... like it was specifically written for us. And I loved it.

The song started in the same manner as our story. Our home world being destroyed, the smoke of Ky's funeral pyre turning the sky to charcoal grey. Then the destruction and us leaving. But my love for him never stopped. Ever.

I put my arms around Everett's neck and sang the chorus of the song to my truest love. He pulled me to him, kissing me tenderly, and I couldn't stop the tears of happiness from spilling down my cheeks.

"I'll love you forever and ever," I whispered, looking up into his blue eyes.

"You are my heart, my soul. I'll love you always," he whispered in return, wiping away my tears with his thumbs as he cupped my face in his hands.

As the song ended, there wasn't a dry eye among our guests. Grandma was blotting away tears with her handkerchief, Mom was wiping away a tear with the back of her hand, and Mr. Forster had removed his glasses and was drying his eyes with a napkin.

"How about a line dance, everyone!" Rick shouted. "Stop yer caterwauling' and get out on the dance floor, y'all!"

The second song Everett had picked was *Flowers in Your Hair* sung by The Lumineers. Even Grandma and Grandpa got out and danced. Everett was really enjoying dancing, so was I! I was glad I'd already changed out of my wedding dress and into my miniskirt. However, I'd kept my white boots on. It had been a long time since I'd line danced. Whoops and hollers ended that dance.

But the next dance was the show-stopper. I'd stepped off the dance floor long enough to get a drink of punch. When the song started playing, I whirled around, remembering Everett dancing at the Rodeo Gala. I wasn't disappointed.

Wild Wild Love sung by G.R.L. and Pit Bull started playing. The first line started out with G.R.L. singing, and the other couples started dancing, but Everett just stood in the center of the dance floor swaying back and forth waiting for Pit Bull's part.

When Pit Bull started his part, Everett ripped his shirt open, sending buttons flying. My mouth flew open and everyone else was shocked as he danced like he was one of Magic Mike's friends.

His abs were ripped, and, my gosh, he knew how to thrust his hips. He mouthed the Spanish words while Pit Bull sang them. It was sexy as hell. When Pit Bull sang about how I needed it and wanted his wild love all over my body, Everett pulled his shirt back to reveal his tattoo of my name over his heart.

"My lands!" Grandma exclaimed. "Have you ever seen such a thing?"

"Nope. But damn, Lilly, your granddaughter just married a strange, sexy young man!" Gail said to Grandma just before she downed a glass of champagne.

I tossed my head back and laughed, then leapt into Everett's arms. He spun me around and around while singing the song to me. And I had to agree with the words. I wanted our wild love to live forever.

When the song ended, we took a break to get some barbeque and more cake. Everyone sort of looked at Everett like he'd become a whole different person than the boy they'd watched grow up. They had no idea just how right they were.

Just as I was taking a bite of potato salad, a hush fell over the crowd. Used to being on-guard for anything, Everett and I immediately looked around. But there were no monsters emerging from the darkness out by the back gate where the edge of light met the shadows.

What we saw was Mr. Forster standing alone in the middle of the dance floor.

"If I could have everyone's attention for a moment … I'd like to make a toast." Mr. Forster held up a cup of punch. "To my son, who's always made me proud. You'll always be my boy, and I love you. And to my new daughter-in-law, Everett could've searched the whole planet and never found a young lady as perfectly fit for him as you. I wish you both happiness, health, and wealth your whole lives through. Oh! And I'd like some grandchildren someday, too!" At that, everyone raised their glasses of punch or cans of soda or beer. I was about to stand and hug him, but he wasn't done talking.

"At the risk of stealing some of the bridal couple's spotlight, I'd like to ask Renee to come stand with me for a moment," Mr. Forster's voice wavered slightly, and I noticed him swallow hard. He was nervous about something.

"Okay," Mom answered, sounding unsure of what he had up his sleeve. When she stepped next to him, he awkwardly took her hand and turned to her.

"Renee, I fell for you the first time I met you … we bumped into each other at that little coffee shop on the corner. We were both very young, freshmen in college," he stuttered a bit, and it reminded me so much of the old Everett. Mom smiled and blushed. "Life took us on separate paths back then, but those paths later brought us back into each other's lives. I'd like to think that's more than coincidence." Then he dropped to one knee, and everyone gasped, including me. Mom covered her mouth with her hand as he removed a ring box from his pocket.

"I love you dearly, Renee. And I promise to love you and honor you for the rest of my days," he popped the ring box open, and I saw a sparkle of diamonds. "Sweetheart, will you marry me?" Mr. Forster looked hopefully up into Mom's eyes.

"Yes!" she blurted as she dropped to her knees and fell into his arms. He pulled away briefly to place the ring on her finger, then looked at Everett and said, "She said yes, son!"

Everyone whooped and cheered, including Everett and me. Then, Rick cranked up the stereo again, and Mom and Mr. Forster had their first dance as an engaged couple. *Could things really end up this perfect?* I wondered as I watched Mom dancing with my future stepfather while Landon Pigg sang *Falling in Love at a Coffee Shop.*

"That's the perfect song for them," Everett said, wrapping his arm around my shoulders.

"Yeah," I smiled and nodded, turning my head to look up into his eyes, longing to be kissed. "Should we join them for another dance?" I asked, not really wanting to.

"Better save some energy for our *other* wedding," Everett said under his breath as we sat down to eat, "And for after."

I blushed. I was sure my face was red enough to catch the whole universe on fire. Everett's shirt was open, and my fingers itched to trace the swirls of ink across his chest and over his shoulders and arms.

"I see your tattoos, too," Everett leaned close to me and whispered in my ear. His lips brushed against my earlobe, and a swell of butterfly wings fluttered in my stomach. I looked down to see symbols glowing beneath my skin, calling to my Other to complete the pairing ritual.

"We should probably get going," Everett said, putting down his fork. He looked as affected as I felt. Desire glowed behind his blue eyes, and I swallowed hard. All I could do was nod. My voice was caught in my throat.

Our luggage was already in the limousine that someone had decorated with streamers and balloons. A sign with "Just Married" was attached to the back and cans were tied to the back bumper. So all that was left was to say our goodbyes. We waited until Mom and Mr. Forster finished their dance. Then Everett motioned to Rick ... apparently they'd had the whole evening planned out. And it was perfect.

"Looks like it's time for the bride and groom to catch their flight," Rick announced.

Everyone met us out front. They'd formed a path for us to walk through. Instead of rice or birdseed, each person had a tiny bottle of bubbles. The night air was filled with shimmery orbs as we made our way to the limousine.

"Wait!" Mom called as I was climbing into the car. "I need to hug you," she pulled me tight against her, and for a moment, I felt like a small child again. "I love you, sweet Blair with the light brown hair," she cooed.

"Love you, too, Mom," I answered. Then I got a look at her ring. It was a single solitaire with a nice diamond. It was perfect for her. "You're next!" I smiled. "I'm so happy for you. Andrew would approve." Mom brushed my cheek with her hand and nodded, smiling a sad sort of smile.

"See you soon," I said, letting Everett guide me into the car.

We waved at everyone as the driver pulled the limo past the group of our closest friends and loved ones. They'd probably stay up partying for a long while. More than likely, the family would invite more people and keep themselves distracted from the sadness of me leaving again. I was glad they weren't alone. And, now, Mom had Mr. Forster, and that pleased me very much.

"Let's not think about what's behind us," Everett pulled me close to him. "Only happy thoughts from now on," he said just before kissing me.

And I forgot everything but him.

He pulled his lips away long enough to direct the driver to turn left onto the gravel road that led to the back gate of the ranch. I started to ask why we were going that way, but he kissed me again, and I forgot what I was thinking.

As the limo bumped along the gravel road at a snail's pace, I loosened a few buttons on Everett's shirt. His skin immediately heated beneath my fingertips as I explored his abs. Then, I splayed my hand across the fine dusting of hair on his chest and pressed a line of kisses up his neck and along his jaw.

"This is torture," he moaned as he pulled me to him and covered my lips with his while his hand followed my outer thigh upward.

"Is this it, Mr. Forster?" the driver asked, uncertainty tinting his voice as he pulled the car to a stop by the old rusty gate at the back of the ranch.

"Yes," Everett answered, gently pulling away from me and buttoning his shirt.

"Here?" I asked, wondering if he was planning on us camping out for our wedding night.

"Do you trust me, Baby?" he smiled, holding his hand out to me.

"Always," I stepped out into the night air. It was really dark, and the cicadas were singing in the woods on the other side of the clearing. Not the haunted woods, though. Because they were gone. Nothing remained of them but charred tree stumps from the night Ash had placed the band on my arm.

"You want me to leave you guys out here ... alone?" the driver stammered, thinking we were nuts.

"Yeah, it's okay," Everett answered, handing him a tip.

"Dude, this is the weirdest thing I've ever seen," the driver said, stuffing the cash in his pocket. "Sure you'll be alright, ma'am?" he asked, looking at me with concern.

I smiled and nodded. Everett unloaded our two suitcases from the trunk.

"Alright! Well, you two nerds have fun out here in the dark," he said as he got into the limo. As the car drove away down the gravel road, the headlights glinted against something out in the pasture.

I waited until the limo was out of sight before I tossed a flaming orb into the air and directed it to hover around the area where I'd seen a glimmer of something metallic. And gasped. A UFO sat where the crop circle had once been imprinted into the lush pasture grass.

"Surprise!" Everett smiled, "My bride deserves to ride in style." Everett locked the gate behind us with a tiny spark of electricity from his fingers.

My new husband carried our luggage as we trudged across the dark pasture toward the magnificent piece of machinery that had ridden through space in the cargo hold of the main ship. Now that I was both Lore and Blair, flying that small craft would be as familiar to me as driving my old pick-up.

The only light in the pasture was hovering in a circle above the UFO. My flaming orb kept its course, drawing a golden halo above the small craft. Although it was ancient, it was still more advanced than anything made by human hands.

There were no windows, no seams or joints, and no lights ... just a silvery, smooth shell. Entry into the craft was through a hole in the bottom of the ship. When we stepped under the edge of the UFO, the light beam sliced through the darkness.

"Ladies first," Everett said.

I stepped into the beam of light. It pulled me upward, into the ship like the vacuum tube at the bank drive-through – only much smoother. When I stepped out of the beam and into the small craft, the internal lights and computer systems came online. The screens were like a pane of invisible glass. There was no need for a monitor. This was my own personal craft. It had been in storage for centuries.

The interior was solid white like the one Everett had flown the year before. But this one was top-of-the-line, a birthday gift from my alien father. The newest technology our people had was used in creating this vessel, and I'd loved it in my former life. I still loved it.

"Welcome aboard, Princess Lore," the computer's voice was the soft voice of a male. I realized it had been programed to sound like Ky before his death.

I gasped and turned to look at Everett as he stepped out of the light beam. A flash of confusion crossed his face ... like the voice had sounded familiar to him, but he couldn't quite place it.

"That's weird ..." Everett cocked his head to the side, and his brows drew together.

"Welcome aboard, Ky, Prince of the Princess's heart," the computer spoke again.

And we both remembered, then. We'd programmed it together the day we'd flown to the beach. The craft had been filled with the spicy scent of the red waves that lapped along the shore where the sand had been used for healing by our people for eons. It had been the day Ky had placed a flower behind my ear and had given me the pairing vial. We'd never gotten to use it, because he'd been killed days later.

I pressed the panel next to the pilot's seat. A small door slid back, and I reached inside. The vial was still there. So was the flower. Its dried petals crumpled as soon as my fingertips brushed across them. I gently lifted the chain and vial out of the compartment, careful not to destroy the rest of the long-dead flower.

"Look what I found!" I gasped, holding the silvery chain so that the tiny vial dangled in front of Everett.

"I wondered what happened to it," Everett's voice was full of surprise. "We'll be putting this to use tonight," he smiled while taking the chain and wrapping it around my wrist. It was a sign of engagement on our home world.

"I love you," I smiled, stepping closer to my new husband.

"I love you more," he answered just before placing a small, tender kiss on my lips. "We better get going." His lips hovered just above mine. It was a heady feeling having him all to myself in the privacy of my own craft.

"I'll drive," I smiled and sat in the pilot's seat.

"Figured you would," he sat next to me. "Too bad this thing doesn't have seatbelts," he joked, smiling broadly.

"Silly Bug Boy!" the nickname rolled off my tongue without my even thinking about it.

"I've missed that," he said after a long pause.

"Me, too," I smiled, then placed my hand against the transparent panel in front of me. "Hang on!"

The craft powered up and lifted off with such ease that I could barely tell we were flying. I started to enter our destination, but it had already been programmed in. I looked at Everett, thinking he'd done it over the course of the past few days. But he shrugged.

"Must've been Nyx. I'd messaged him and asked him to send us a ride. Guess he knew where you'd stored this beauty," he said, looking around the small pod.

"But would he have known how to program my craft?" I wondered aloud. Then shook my head and cleared my thoughts. It didn't really matter, anyway. All that mattered was that I was finally ... after so many centuries ... getting my happily-ever-after.

I tapped a symbol on the transparent screen, and the walls of the craft seemed to shimmer away, revealing the night sky outside. We were already over the Gulf of Mexico, and the waves sparkled far below us. Of course, the walls were still there, just as solid as ever.

But this was the new technology our scientists had developed just before the destruction of our world.

"This is the coolest thing ever," Everett said, reaching for my hand and wrapping my fingers in his. "It's almost as beautiful as my new bride." He paused a moment, then a goofy smile lit his face up just before he started singing Justin Timberlake's *Spaceship Coupe*. It was really hot hearing him singing those lyrics. I made a mental note to download that album as soon as we got back to civilization.

When we touched down at our destination, I was in Everett's lap with my arms around his neck, my fingers tangled in his hair, and my lips pressed to his in a passionate kiss. His hands were stroking my back, beneath my shirt. And the heat between us was so great I thought I would self-combust.

"I think we're there," Everett's voice sounded breathless. At first, I thought he'd meant that we were both at the point of no return. But I looked around and realized we'd landed at the far end of the courtyard, just beyond the reach of the torch light.

I'd cloaked my UFO, so none of the soldiers realized I'd returned. Xi would be miffed, because I hadn't given him fair-warning, so he could properly greet us. He'd know soon enough when we exited the ship. That was good enough for me.

Several large campfires burned brightly in the courtyard. Silhouettes of my Royal Guard and Ash's soldiers moved back and forth, preparing for the night's festivities. A thrill of butterflies fluttered behind my navel. My human wedding had been beautiful, it was important to me as a human to be married to my husband in front of God and our families and friends. But this was the real wedding ceremony ... the one that counted ... the one I'd been waiting for.

Then, I saw the Holy Men and Women. Xi had brought them out of stasis for the ceremony. No doubt they were extremely confused and disoriented. These weren't the same ones who'd paired me to Ash. These were the younger generation. The old ones had stayed behind with my alien father and mother. Nonetheless, these Holy Men and Women had been present at my forced pairing to Ash.

Their drums were sitting atop the newly-built pyramid, which was lit with many torches. The Holy Tapestries hung behind them. Embroidered across their colorful surfaces was the history of our people. Soon, a new page of our history would be added.

"It's beautiful," Everett said, standing beside me. The walls of my craft still appeared transparent. They weren't, of course. But the technology it had been built with had made it appear to be see-through, which made it really weird to be able to stand inside of the craft and have a 360° view of the jungle and courtyard.

"Yes, it will be a pairing ceremony fit for a Queen," I smiled. "I've been waiting centuries for this."

"Let's go," Everett picked up our luggage. "You've waited long enough. I want your every wish to be fulfilled tonight." He kissed me on the cheek just before I stepped into the beam of light that lowered me to the ground outside.

All five senses were greeted with green, earthy scents of the jungle mingled with the roasting spices over the fires ... flutes and strings playing songs from our home world ... colorful fabrics of the Holy Men and Women ... boisterous laughter of the soldiers ... a star-lit canopy overhead.

"It all brings back so many memories," Everett whispered. "It's hard to reconcile this kind of past with the life we've lived as humans.

"I know," I whispered in return. "I've been struggling with it for a while now, coming to terms with it."

"How do we come to terms with it?" firelight reflected in his eyes.

"We just accept it," I shrugged. "That's all we can do."

"You're starting to sound like me," he smiled.

"Well, I am Mrs. Bug Boy now," I giggled louder than I meant to.

"Uh-oh," Everett said, looking into the darkness near the jungle edge.

"Halt or die!" Max's voice rang out over the festivities.

Everything went quiet. A blur of movement, was followed by Max, Mal, and Jex. They were in full formal uniform, ready for the Royal Pairing, which made their drawn weapons look even more menacing.

"Whoa!" Everett dropped his luggage and held a hand out to them to calm them down.

"My lady," Max gasped as she put her knife away. The other's followed suit, dropping to their knees, and bowing their heads. "We meant no disrespect."

"Of course you didn't," I motioned for them to stand. "You were doing as I'd asked you to do."

They each insisted on kissing my hand, so I allowed it. It was so weird to my human half, yet it felt normal to my alien half. It was another thing I'd have to accept. This was a ritual important to them and the rest of my people. I dismissed Mal and Jex, but held Max. Her eyes looked hopeful.

"It's been done. Now we wait," I said, fishing Orion's empty vial out of my skirt pocket and placing it into her hand.

"Thank you, my lady!" Max closed her hand around the vial and lifted it to her chest. The chain dangled between her fingers and glimmered in the firelight. "How can I ever repay you?"

"You loving Orion is all the payment I need," I smiled. "Now show me to my tent. I'm ready for my pairing ceremony."

"My lady?" Xi's voice rang out across the courtyard. "If I'd have known when you were arriving, we would have greeted you properly." I knew he was going to be disappointed. But he'd known me long enough to know that I liked doing things my own way.

"It's alright, Xi," I replied, allowing him to kiss my hand. I'd forgotten how formidable he looked in his formal uniform. Shimmery fabric fit his body like a second skin. There was no need for medals, because rank was tattooed on the neck of any member of my Royal Guard. However, he wore a strap of silvery bullets that crossed his chest and looped over his right shoulder. One bullet for every ten enemy he'd vanquished. "I'm here now. Everything's okay. Any news?"

"None. We've sent up a probe to search for signals from the General's ship ship. We have received no communication. It may be that all's lost," he looked genuinely saddened.

"That's not entirely accurate," Nyx's voice startled both Everett and me. None of us had seen him approach. He'd always been good at sneaking around, even as a child. We hugged, and he held me a little longer. He'd missed me. "It's good to see you, Mother."

I didn't have the heart to ask him not to call me that anymore. I'd asked Orion that, and now he was gone ... sort of. And I regretted hurting him like that. What did it matter, anyway? I was the same person in a different body.

"It's good to see you, too, son," I said, pulling out of his hug and returning to Everett's side. "So, what's not accurate about the search results?"

"I've been doing my own search from The Resistance headquarters. We have found father's ship." He looked proud, standing there in his black fatigues. His silky ebony hair was pulled back into a braid, and he was so very handsome.

"Were you able to communicate with Ash?" Everett asked, and I realized for the first time that the two of them must have been working closely for a long time.

Nyx merely shook his head while a frown tugged the corners of his mouth downward. As if she'd sensed his sadness, Rake appeared next to him. Nyx perked up, standing a little straighter and taller. Rake had eyes only for Nyx. *This will be another good match*, I thought as I watched the two of them. They were, no doubt, exchanging a quiet conversation between the two of them.

"Did your sensors pick up any ... life signs on Ash's ship?" I asked, hoping ... praying he'd discovered two life forms on board.

"The ship is fully cloaked, so I could not get a passenger reading," Nyx tore his gaze from Rake. "One thing is certain. The explosion damaged the navigation system. Father will not be able to steer the ship until he has repaired it ... if he's still alive."

"Can you program your systems to navigate for him?" Xi had been silent, listening and weighing options.

"Yes, but what would be the point?" Nyx asked, sounding a bit exasperated.

"We have located the sister ship," Xi answered.

He had all of our attention now. Even Rake tore her gaze from Nyx. For a moment, I felt like I'd been pretending all this time … that I wasn't a Queen after all. I felt like a cowgirl in the wrong place at the wrong time. Everett sensed my internal battle and gently squeezed my hand, reminding me that I would just have to accept the fact that I am who I am.

"My soldiers can direct the navigation systems on the ship to rendezvous with the General's ship. We are able to detect that all life, except Your Majesty's sister and her husband, are alive and in stasis." Xi had known both my alien sister and her husband. He hadn't known of their deaths until he'd watched the video I'd left for myself in my secret laboratory, so it was still new to him.

"Is the ship repaired well enough to make it through our atmosphere?" I asked.

"Yes, my lady," Xi nodded. "And the Commander of your sister's Royal Guard left a recorded message in case we found them. She sends her allegiance and hopes we've found a home for our people."

"This is the best gift you could give me, Xi," I said, smiling. "Let's do what it takes to get the two ships together."

"As you wish," Xi bowed his head, pleased. "I will also leave a message for the sister ship with your instructions for them to work together to return to their Queen."

"Thank you, Xi," I inhaled a deep breath. I was exhausted, and we still had a busy night ahead of us. "We have brought things full circle. Now we can start over."

CHAPTER THIRTY-ONE

FULL CIRCLE

Boom boom-boom boom! Boom boom-boom boom! The Holy drums resounded down the temple steps, across the courtyard, and into the dark reaches of the jungle. Everett stood at the top of the steps, dressed in the clothes of our alien people.

A cloak made of rich tapestry draped over one shoulder, across his chest, and under the other arm. One bold, silver pin held it together at the top of his shoulder. I would stand on that side, with his arm around me and his cloak around my shoulders. It was a part of the ceremony in which he would promise to honor and protect me forever.

The sun's warmth still radiated from the steps. It felt good on the soles of my bare feet as I climbed the steps, one-at-a-time, toward my truest love and my destiny. Unless some enemy emerged from the jungle or the sky, it seemed that I'd actually brought everything full-circle.

My wedding garments matched Everett's. My friends and I had woven the fabrics ourselves as was tradition when an engagement had been arranged. But when my hopes had ended at the hands of a Hunter, I'd packed them away. Now my dreams were coming true. Now, the wrongs have been made right.

Rake and Max were the only other females to help me with my makeup and dress aside from the Holy Women, who really weirded me out. Rake took great care to apply the black swirls over my eyelids and at the edges of my face. Max wasn't the kind to wear makeup, so she helped with the heavy tapestry garments and brushed my hair. My crown completed my pairing trousseau.

The closer the stairs took me to Everett, the hotter the soles of my feet became until flames were circling around me in flickers of yellow, orange, and blue. Centuries of mourning were replaced with a flaming passion. I was Lore reborn. And as I ascended the last step and stood before Everett, I was looking into the eyes of Ky.

He took my hand and guided me to stand beside him as he placed the edge of his cloak around my shoulders. Flames began to erupt through his skin to meld with mine. But this wasn't the kind of fire that burned things into destruction. These were the flames of rebirth.

I couldn't stop the tears of happiness from flowing down my cheeks as I looked up into Everett's brilliant blue eyes while the Holy Men and Women pounded the drums. Both mine and Ash's soldiers watched their Queen and her new Royal Consort.

When the drums halted, the jungle was silent. There wasn't a sound from the courtyard or far beyond the waterfall where a large village of jungle people lived. Even the sky seemed to hold its breath as I opened the front of my garment to reveal my stomach and smiled at Everett.

He uncorked the vial with his teeth and poured the thin ribbon of blue iridescent light out into his hand. Electricity crackled and sparked out from us as he placed his palm to my belly and rubbed the serum into my skin. Then he covered my lips with his as the flames and sparks of energy enveloped us.

We must have looked as though we were burning alive, but there was no heat to the flames. They were only mirroring what our hearts were feeling. After all those centuries of waiting, true love actually won out.

One more round of the drums, and he placed the chain that held the vial over my head, looping us both together as one. Then the drums halted and the Holy Men and Women announced the Queen was bound to her Royal Consort for all time.

Everett lifted me in his arms and carried me down the steps, and I rested my head on his shoulder. Being in his arms was the best place on earth, and the effects of the serum only magnified the pull between us.

Xi led the way as Everett carried me through the audience of Ash's soldiers and my Royal Guard. The

Holy Men and Women followed us with the holy lights in their hands. We entered a newly cleared path into the jungle. More holy lights hung from the tree branches, lighting the path and blessing us as we walked beneath them.

I'd paid no attention to them when Ash had carried me to his chambers centuries earlier. My eyes had been swollen with tears, my heart broken with loss, and my mind fogged with mourning. I quickly pushed that memory out of my mind and tightened my arms around Everett's neck.

He pulled me against him and whispered, "Put those unhappy thoughts behind you. I'm here now, and we'll never be apart again." I sighed and smiled.

The wedding march came to a halt, and I turned to see that my Royal Guard had built a honeymoon hideaway for us. A sort of domed ceiling had been carved out of the thick tree canopy. My cocoon tent was nestled between the limbs. Everett's trampoline was suspended between the tree trunks, providing a place for us to lounge outside the tent. Smaller holy lights glittered among the leaves, creating an effect of fireflies. It was very romantic.

Once the Holy Men and Women chanted their blessings over our union, Xi led them out of our secret grotto. But I knew he and his soldiers would be nearby, keeping watch over their Queen. This was their duty, and it didn't bother me a bit.

"Ready?" Everett asked. I nodded, and he leapt up, up, up and landed us on the canvas platform in front of my cocoon tent. We didn't bounce as I'd thought we would. But it was a soft landing that barely jostled the shining tray of food and drink left for us by my Guard.

Sleeping bags and pillows had been placed inside my cocoon tent. No doubt Max and Rake had tried to make it as romantic as possible using whatever extra supplies they'd had stowed in their pod. It made my wedding bed even more special.

Everett carried me into the tent and placed me on a pile of covers, then zipped the door closed behind us. Even though the flames had subsided on our way down the path, the symbols and swirls glowed brighter beneath our skin. And the passion began to grow between us again, drawing us to one another ... husband and wife ... chosen Others.

Later that night, the jungle sparkled with tiny galaxies— twirling, spinning, and casting dazzling glimmers of light on the leaves around us. Everett caught one for me and put it inside a small container on the food tray. I'd missed my tiny galaxy. Now it had been replaced with a new one.

"Thank you for saving me, for making this wonderful life possible," Everett kissed me on the forehead. I snuggled against his bare chest beneath the thin sheet of fabric that lay across us as we lounged on the canvas trampoline outside the cocoon tent.

"It was all because of you that I did it. I couldn't face forever without you," I closed my eyes and relished his scent.

"Do you realize how amazing you are?" he stroked my hair, causing it to drift down over my shoulder and across my bare back. "You found a way to become reborn so that you could grow up with me."

"Guess that makes me like a Queen ... a Monarch butterfly coming out of her chrysalis," I smiled, tracing one of his tattoos with my fingertips.

"No, not something so temporary," I heard the smile in his voice as his breath brushed across my hair. "You're a beautiful phoenix. You've come back from the ashes with a burst of flames and light. And you've brought us and our people back around full-circle." He placed a tender kiss on my lips, then smiled, "I love you, Lore."

I placed my cheek against his chest. His skin was hot against mine. And I wondered if he sensed that we weren't alone ... that there were now two more hybrids growing behind the glowing swirls of light across my belly. "I love you more, Ky ... more than anything in the world."

EPILOGUE

ANGELICA

My boots and socks were soaked, and my clothes clung to me. I chopped one last branch out of my way using Andy's machete. It felt like my chest clinched together, keeping me from breathing each time his name crossed my mind, which was at least once a minute.

The past few months had been a living hell. I wasn't at home anywhere without him. He was my home. *I grew up in an orphanage. I have ... had no one but him,* I thought.

"*Have*, Angelica," I said aloud once again. I refused to accept any other reality than that.

That's the reason I returned to the jungle where I last saw him. I felt that if he came back, it would be at the same place where he'd disappeared. At any rate, I had nowhere else to turn.

It was a smoldering, sunny day. Blair must have been really happy, because the sun always shined brightly when she was. I stepped out of the shade of the jungle and into the sunshine. It would only take about ten minutes for me to turn bright red on a day like this.

I didn't get too far into the courtyard before I heard one of her freaky alien guards sound the alarm. In the blink of an eye, two of them were standing in front of me, scaring the crap out of me.

What would I have to lose if they killed me? I placed my hand on my swollen belly. *Everything.*

The way they cocked their heads and looked at each other, I could tell they were communicating telepathically. If Andy had been with me, he would have heard their thoughts. My chest clinched again, and I swallowed hard.

"You must be tired and hungry," Rake said.

"Yes," I answered, blinking back the tears.

The enormous she-alien led me across the courtyard, to the colorful pavilion that now flapped in the breeze at the top of the pyramid. The last time I'd seen this place, it had been a battlefield strewn with death and destruction.

A shining marker etched with strange symbols lay flat against the ground. It was the place where Andy had disappeared. My chest clinched again as I knelt and brushed a few grains of sand from its surface.

"Angelica?" Blair called from the pavilion. "We weren't expecting you! But I'm so glad you've come to visit!" She descended the steps, and I immediately noticed how different she looked. And it kinda freaked me out. I hadn't been expecting to see her looking less human and more ... alien.

"I had nowhere else to go," I said, hating myself for sounding so helpless.

"Nonsense," she said while hugging me. It felt really good to be hugged. I'd been alone in the jungle for weeks and weeks. Andy would have wanted me to come to her. I placed my hand on my chest, willing the spasm to stop. "I miss him, too," she whispered, just before letting me go.

I swallowed hard again and tried not to be creeped out by how her skin had turned opaque and shimmery like her Royal Guards' skin. Her eyes had grown a bit wider and sort of slanted. She reminded me of the ethereal elves in the *Lord of the Rings* movies, without the pointed ears. I could tell she hadn't spoken English in a while, because she now had a sort of strange accent.

"It's good to see you," I managed to say.

"I'm glad you came. But if you'd have just called, we would have picked you up and saved you a lot of trouble," she said, sounding a little more like herself. That relaxed me a bit. "I bet you're hungry and tired. Come on, let's get you taken care of."

She led me into a massive underground system of caves. I wasn't expecting them to be so busy with activity. Andy had said she was from another world, but actually seeing so many alien humanoids going about their work was ... staggering.

Her quarters were brilliantly decorated like a fancy apartment in New York City. The flooring was white carpet. I kicked my boots and socks off at the door and wiped my feet on the mat.

"Sorry," I shrugged, embarrassed of my filthy state. "I haven't bathed in a few days."

"I know how that feels!" Blair giggled. "Come on, girl. Let's get you into a bath."

After bathing and towel-drying my hair, I changed into some of the clothes she'd said Natalie had gotten for her when she'd first come to the jungle. The sundress was a bit long for me, but it was loose enough to cover my growing belly. I felt like a new person as soon as I got some food into me.

"This is so good!" I grunted and stuffed another bite of a hot buttered roll into my mouth.

But a kick in my side startled me, and I covered my belly with my hand and smiled. That was the first time I'd felt any movement at all. Maybe it was the food or maybe it was the place. Or maybe it was Blair. I had no idea. All I knew was that I was glad my baby was still alive and growing.

"How far along are you?" Blair asked, smiling. "Can I feel it?" she spread her fingers out over my swollen belly and smiled. A thin layer of joyful tears filled her eyes as she looked into mine. "You're carrying twins!" she gasped.

"How can you know that?" I asked, reeling from the thought of raising twins without a father. I swallowed hard once more, willing the tightness in my chest to go away.

"I can sense them," she said, cocking her head to the side. "You know about Andrew, right? That he's a hybrid ... not quite like me, but not all human."

"He told me," I nodded. "That's why I came to you. I didn't know where else to go. Your mom's busy with her own life, and I ... I needed family."

"Well, you've come to the right place," Blair smiled. She placed her hand on her own belly and said, "They'll have cousins to grow up with. But I haven't told Everett, yet. So don't say anything to him when you see him."

"Of course, I won't! It's been a long time since I've felt happy," I smiled, genuinely glad that I'd come to her. Perhaps everything really would be okay, and I would have her to help me raise my strange, beautiful children. "Oh, I forgot to tell you. Natalie sent you a message," I pulled the sealed envelope out of my backpack and handed it to her.

She opened it and pulled out a sonogram photo. I couldn't make out what it was, but I could tell that there were four separate images on it. Blair turned it over, and the words "Quadruplets!!!!! Can you believe it?" were neatly written across the back in blue ink. Blair's mouth fell open. She covered it with her other hand and held the picture to her chest like it was a cherished photo. Maybe it was, for all I knew.

"I've gotta tell Everett," she said, her voice full of a strange sort of wonder.

"Tell me what?" he asked, pulling the door closed behind him. He'd changed, too, in the same ways Blair had. And it was freaky to me. But he still looked like Everett ... sort of ... so I didn't turn and run screaming into the jungle.

"Natalie and David are having *quadruplets*," she said, holding the photo up for him to see.

"Well, that was something I wasn't anticipating," he replied, turning the picture different directions, trying to make out the shapes. He'd gotten even cuter than the last time I'd seen him ... in a weird alien-dude sort of way. I noticed he had that same slight accent Blair had developed, too. "This is a happy development," he smiled and handed the picture back to Blair. "Are you going to tell Max?"

"I think I should, don't you?" she replied, looking up at him like he was the only person in the universe. The bond between them was nearly tangible. It made me miss Andy even more. I clutched my chest again and bit my lip.

"My lady, excuse the intrusion. But I have urgent news. I think you should see this," I startled when the giant he-man-alien named Xi called her on a hi-tech communicator. I wondered why he was speaking in English.

"He wants to be able to speak both my languages," Blair shrugged, answering my thoughts. It seemed she'd developed the same ability that Andy had ... *has*, I corrected myself again.

I followed them further underground to the hangar where the other ship had once been. At one end, there was a newly-built control room behind a thick wall of glass. When we entered the room and turned around, the glass wall no longer appeared transparent.

It now showed a large image of outer space. I recognized the ship as the one that had come out of that very hangar the night Andy disappeared. That was when I noticed the guy they'd called Nyx. He was sitting in the corner, leaning back in his chair, looking completely relaxed and comfortable in his skin.

"We've received a transmission from the sister ship," Nyx said, a cocky smile tugged up the corner of his mouth into a smile. I had the feeling he took after his father in some ways. "Our attempts at awaking the Royal Guard were successful."

"Let's see it!" Everett said, a goofy smile crossed his face. He seemed to be friends with Nyx. There was an obvious easy rapport between the two of them.

It was a written transmission in a language I would never be able to understand. But Blair translated it into English for me. "Communication received. My lady, my soldiers and I cannot express our excitement at being reunited with you and the rest of our people. We are ready to rendezvous with the General's ship and will return to you with all haste. Please send our regards to our brothers and sisters in your Royal Guard. We eagerly await being joined with them in your service."

"That's fantastic, son!" Blair said. "Xi, this is excellent work. Thank you both."

"Still no word from Ash's ship?" Everett asked. I knew there'd be no love loss for him if Ash had died. But I had the feeling he was eager to find out about Andy.

"No," Nyx shook his head. "Father has a limited amount of resources on board that ship. So, it will likely take him a while to repair the communication system.

"Were you able to detect life forms aboard?" Blair asked the question that was screaming inside my head.

Nyx merely shook his head and frowned.

"The cloaking field is on, my lady. It was also damaged in the blast," Xi explained. "It was designed to hide a ship and its passengers. It's doing what it was designed to do. Do not lose heart."

I was struck by how much Xi cared for Blair. He almost sounded like a father or uncle in the way he cared for her. The warmth in his voice actually filled me with hope. The fact that they were using technology far more advanced than anything NASA had made me feel like I might actually see Andy again.

I hugged myself and followed them out of the hangar. Tonight they would celebrate their success. Tonight I would celebrate my new home and look forward to the time when Andy would come home to me again.

NATALIE

A lingering dream haunted me during my sleep and spilled over into my waking hours. It involved Blair and Everett. I couldn't make out what was happening, because it seemed like mine and David's minds had been separated from our bodies and trapped in a dark room together.

On the other side of the dark wall, we could hear Blair and Everett whispering. But we couldn't understand what they were saying. Then our minds were suddenly jolted back into our bodies and we woke up in the pasture where the crop circle had been. Just like what had happened that weird night we'd gone out with them.

We'd awoken in the bed of David's truck. Blair and Everett had both seemed to have been asleep, too. But I hadn't felt like I'd been asleep, and neither had David. We'd felt drugged and sick. My stomach had felt like I'd spilled my coke all over the front of my clothes. My skin was ice cold, but my clothes were dry.

When I'd mentioned it to Blair, she'd only shrugged and looked away. Her reaction had hurt my feelings, and there was some deeper emotion brewing in my gut. It's weird, I know. And I have no reason to have even felt it ... but I'd felt betrayed by her, as if she'd violated me in some way.

Those weird feelings had followed me for weeks. When I'd started getting sick and throwing up, I'd thought I'd just had a virus or something. So, I'd made the doctor appointment. But Dr. Dubose told me that I was pregnant, and I couldn't believe my ears.

I'd made her do a second test just to make sure. It had given the same result: positive. That was when I'd tried to chalk my weird dreams and feelings up to hormones. Finally, I'd just pushed them aside and tried to forget them.

The next appointment, I took David with me. He was really uncomfortable at first. He even got woozy when the doctor squished the gel on my belly before doing the sonogram. But when the doctor pointed out one ... two ... three ... four little growing babies, he was so excited that he had a big, dumb smile on his face the rest of the day.

"How am I going to be a teacher with all these babies?" I asked him that night while we sat in the lounge chairs near the trampoline swing he'd made for me.

"We'll make a way," he answered, still smiling.

I watched him for a moment. The firelight from the fire pit lit his handsome face and highlighted his blonde hair. I was still as crazy about him as I'd been in high school. David had been the biggest, best football player the Willis WildKats had ever had. He could've had his pick of any college and gone on full scholarship.

However, there were things that were more important to him. And those things made me love him even more. His business had grown by leaps and bounds. Now, he planned on adding more rooms to the house he'd built for us. He was going to be a great daddy.

"Whatcha thinking about, Little Mama?" he put his hand on mine. It felt strong and safe. We were going to have a long, happy life together.

"Just how lucky I am," I climbed into his lap. "Oh, my gosh!" I gasped, putting my hand on my belly. It felt like one of the babies was doing summersaults.

"He'll be a football player," David smiled and put his hand next to mine on my belly. "Just think of all the things we'll be doing with them as they grow up."

"I think this one is going to keep us busy!" I gasped again at the activity going on in my belly.

"We'll just have to run faster to keep up with him," David said, still smiling.

I had no idea what life held in store for us. But I did know that we will be a content family with a normal life. Our kids would have a good childhood. Our home would be filled with laughter and wonderful memories.

And that was plenty for me.

DAVID

"Andrew, I'm going to be a father," I placed a Sonic burger, fries, and coke by the memorial stone with his name chiseled in it. "Doc says we're having quadruplets. I guess that makes me a he-man!" I laughed out loud.

"I sure wish you were here, dude," I said, putting my half-eaten burger down on the tailgate of my truck. "Nothing's the same without you."

I sat in silence for a while, looking around the old cemetery at the other stones families had put in place to remember their loved ones. A lot of them had been busted up and repaired. I'd remembered Blair telling me about what had happened to her the day she'd first realized she had freaky alien powers.

"I wish none of this had happened to any of us," I said, looking at the engraved image of Andrew on his memorial stone. "I wish everything would have stayed normal and we'd have all gone on with our lives and never found out about all that alien shit."

I tried to imagine what he'd say. Probably something about fate or religion … at least the old Andrew would've. The new Andrew would have probably started cussing. I laughed about that and blinked away the stupid tears that wanted to well up in my eyes.

"Natalie says she wants to name one of the babies after you," I said, distracting myself from crying like a sissy. I thought of the sonogram that showed one of the little guys moving all over the place in Natalie's belly.

"One of 'em is an active little booger … always moving around and kicking. I think he's gonna be a handful." I tried to smile like I'd been doing for days. "We skyped with Blair and Everett the other day … Blair made us promise to name him Orion."

I scratched my head and thought about what a weird name that was for a boy from Willis, Texas. But, hell, what wasn't weird around here anymore? Blair and Everett had even started looking weird. When we'd skyped with them, I couldn't believe my eyes. I took another bite of my burger and wished I could say all this out loud to Andrew.

I missed my best friend so bad. I wasn't ready to lose the closest thing to a brother I'd ever had. And now he was gone. Everyone who'd known Andrew had felt his loss. How could I tell my kids what a great guy he was? How can I tell them about everything we went through together?

I can't. It's a secret. All of it. And I don't want any of my kids even knowing about it, much less getting involved in it. Natalie and I had decided that we'd never mention any of it to them.

I spent a few more minutes in the cemetery until the sun was far enough behind the trees that the place started looking creepy. Then I picked up the food I'd brought for Andrew and drove back to town, passing all the places we'd frequented while growing up.

This little town was the perfect place for our kids to grow up. They'd have friends and make memories of their own. They'd have a nice, normal, human life.

EVERETT

I knew I loved Blair Reynolds the first time I laid eyes on her. It was the day of the school science fair. Andrew stuck up for me against the bullies who'd killed my giant beetle.

We fought side-by-side that day against that gang of thugs. I knew that day that there was something special about Andrew. I just didn't realize just how extraordinary he was until the secrets all started unraveling.

The day we got into that fight, we had to stay after school for detention. Afterward, we stopped by Sprinkles for something to eat. And there she was, standing behind the counter. Her hair was pulled up in a ponytail, and she was wearing a T-shirt that said, "Sweeten Your Morning with Sprinkles."

She smiled at me, and in that moment I felt like I'd known and loved her forever. We held each other's gaze for a long time until Andrew interrupted us and ordered a whole pie. She handed me a drink, and when my fingertips touched hers, I felt the sparks fly. She did, too, and blushed. After that, there wasn't an hour that passed when she wasn't in my thoughts.

We had so many great memories of our time in Willis, Texas. Four-wheeling, horseback riding, barbecues … too many to name. We both grew up with loving parents and had the chance to know good people and make great friends.

Can I really be so lucky to have a second chance at a life with her? I brushed a lock of hair off her cheek as she slept next to me.

I thought about how all my memories of my past alien life were now mixed in with my human memories. Now, it seems normal to have all those memories categorized in my head. But I remember how odd it felt to be awakened at once ... when all the memories and realizations burst through the floodgates and filled my brain with a storm of mixed up memories.

The Cicada ... Orion ... told me things ... clues ... that meant nothing to me until the night he saved my life in the kitchen at the old Sprinkles. As his energy flowed into me, so did all the secrets he carried. He filled my head with the truth of who and what I was and how I'd come to be alive as a human-alien hybrid.

Then it all made sense.

So I followed his instructions and went to be trained by his brother, Nyx, in The Resistance. It cut me to the core to leave Blair behind that day. Seeing her cry as I left made me feel like I was leaving half of myself behind. But I needed to know more, so I could help her when she was awakened.

It was worth it ... all of it, I thought as I examined her beautiful face while she slept sweetly next to me. She still had her features as Blair, but was beginning to look more and more like the Lore I'd loved for centuries.

She'd started calling me Ky more often. It didn't matter what name she called me so long as it was me she wanted.

Truthfully, I had no idea what our future held. Certainly, we'll have a family. One of the children would be named Andrew ... we both agreed on that when we received word that Ash had said he was alone on his ship.

One thing about our future is certain. When Ash returns, we'll have a problem on our hands. He'll be here sooner than we think. The sister ship will be intercepting his ship and towing it back with them. He'll be angry when he thaws out, but who cares? The deed's done. It's all been made right. We've come full-circle, and now we can move forward.

"I love you, Babe," I whispered as I kissed Lore on the forehead.

"Mmm ... love you more," she muttered, sleep heavy in her voice. Out of instinct, her hand moved to cover her belly. I noticed her doing it often, and I played along and pretended not to know the last secret she thought she was keeping to herself.

I thought of visits to Willis with the twins, showing them all the places we grew up. Taking them to the Sonic and later to the ranch to ride the horses or four-wheelers. *Christmases will be fantastic,* I smiled, thinking about two beautiful children tearing into presents under the tree with a big happy family around them. We even had our own ranch we would use as a sort of vacation property, thanks to Blair's grandparents.

There'd be limited visits to public places, to be sure. Neither of us looked the way we had in our human lives. We would stand out unless we hid behind sunglasses and clothes that hid our iridescent skin.

Of course, I had no idea how our children would be as toddlers. The last thing Willis needed was another massive blast and enormous fire. If our kids were anything like Nyx and Orion had been, that could be a problem.

It didn't matter what their temperament would be or how much we had to camouflage ourselves. Going home to visit would make my new wife happy. I planned on spending the rest of my long life doing just that.

I gently pulled Lore, my beautiful phoenix, into my arms and fell asleep next to my Other in our quarters underground in the Queen's City where we planned on rejuvenating our race and raising our family.

Life is good.

BLAIR

I'd been a bystander to this story. I didn't want to get involved. I stood on the sidelines. I saw. Can you keep a secret?

Once upon a time, centuries ago, light years away, I started a chain of events that would follow me across the universe to a planet called Earth ... to a small, inconsequential Southeast Texas town called Willis.

Only a handful of people had known my secret, and none of them had been human until recently. They'll keep the secret, because it involves them now ... all of them. And who would believe them, anyway?

But the biggest part of my secret isn't known by any human. Only a select few of my kind know that I'm the one who orchestrated all these things just so I could have my happily-ever-after.

Wouldn't you do the same, if you were in my shoes?

So that's why I ask again, can you keep a secret? If not, throw away this story. Burn it. Tell no one what lies between the covers of these books. But if you can keep a secret, take a trip to Willis and look for a family with quadruplets. The one who makes the sky fill with dark clouds and lightning when he cries is ... well, you know who he is.

While you're there, get some flowers at the Kroger and place them at Andrew's memorial stone. He'd had that sort of sixth sense, and no doubt wherever he is, he'll know someone was thinking about him. I just hope he's in the arms of our ancestors ... that he's with Dad and Aaron.

Soon, the last remnant of my kind will arrive. Some will choose to remain as they are, and some will choose to become human-hybrids. We'll integrate into the human population and both our races will be stronger for it. It's already happening.

The new serum Everett and I developed increases birthrates, making it possible for two pairs of Others to be hybridized simultaneously in one human birth mother. Natalie will be held in high esteem by my alien people for her contribution to my science and our continuation as a race here on this planet we now call home.

I thought of Orion and how good it will be to see him again. I was sure that, at some point, Natalie and David would realize what we'd done ... that one of the children she now carried is not human. They won't be able to love him, because he will be wild and alien. Natalie will insist on sending him to me, and then she'll have her normal life back in Texas.

Our friendship will be over. She'll never forgive us, and I couldn't blame her. I would feel the same way. But I had no other choice. Orion's life depended on it. Besides, deep down, I had to admit that I'd wanted to be the one to raise him again as his mother. I was so glad I was able to bring him back.

So far, I'd only been able to capture the essence of my alien kind in two ways: as it left the body or by distilling it. Distillation had only been accomplished once when my essence had been inserted into Mom.

I hoped to perfect the procedure to include humans one day with hopes of either extending the length of human life or give humans the option of becoming alien hybrids by choice. The options could be endless.

The universe is vast and there are many races hidden among the stars. We'd encountered them on our home planet. Some were friend, and some were foe. My science will strengthen our chances of survival from any foe that may find our small planet. My people, both human and alien-kind, will be like me ... like the phoenix. We will be reborn, renewed and stronger than before. Of that, I'm sure.

ASH

"She'll come back to me. I know she will," I said aloud while prying the panel off the navigation system. The heat from the blast had nearly welded it closed. Inside, the wires were burnt and melded together. "Damn it!" I snarled and threw a wrench across the room, shattering a glass panel that housed some of Lore's scientific equipment.

I stood and paced the room. The pod was a mess. Wires hung down between the ceiling panels. Black marks from fire and smoke looked like giant strokes of charcoal across the white walls and ceiling. It had taken a while to put out all the flames and expel the smoke into the void of space. But I'd done it. I'd survived to win another day.

And that's exactly what I intend to do. I'd never lost a battle before this one ... and I've resolved to win this war. Her father gave her to me in marriage, and I'd sworn on my life that I would protect her forever. I don't care whether she's Queen or not. She's *mine*.

"General, can you hear me?" a garbled voice startled me out of my thoughts. *The communication systems are working!* I rushed to the screen and entered my code.

"Yes, I am here. Can you hear me?" I answered, unable to hide the happiness in my voice. "I repeat— I am here. Can you hear me?"

"General, if you can hear this message, please be aware that we have received your coordinates and have locked onto your ship. We have adjusted our trajectory to rendezvous with you."

The screen flickered, blurring in and out due to interference from damage to the navigation system. Out of frustration, I slammed my hand against the screen. For a moment, a clear picture of the leader of the Royal Guard on our sister ship came through. Judging by her expression, she'd received the image of me, too. Though, I doubted I looked as spit and shine as she did.

My hair had been singed from the explosion. Though I'd healed quickly, I still had a long slash from my shoulder down to my ribs. It had been a deep wound and still hurt. But I'd had worse injuries, and I was no sissy. The thing I hated worst about it was that there'd likely be a nasty scar. Even I knew I was too damned handsome for that.

"Yes, I read you loud and clear, Commander," I hoped she could hear as well as see me.

"The Queen has ordered an account of passengers you are carrying," Commander Lex said.

"Passengers?" I snorted. "What does she think this is, a luxury ship?"

"Answer the question, please, General. I'm only following orders," Lex said. She was about as dry as her counterpart, Xi. I'd tried to convince Lore's father that the Royal Guard should have to answer to me as well as the Royal House. But he'd disagreed. Now look what I was dealing with.

"What do you think, Commander? Do I look like I'm entertaining guests? This ship is falling to pieces because of an idiot who discharged his weapon at the wrong time, over-heating the transport system, and burning out every wire in this damned ship!" I slammed my fist down on the console, infuriated that I was being forced to report to a glorified bodyguard.

Lex crossed her tattooed arms over her chest and looked at me, waiting for the answer she was requesting. I knew she was wanting a "yes" or "no" and was enjoying making her practically beg for it. At least I could still get one of our women to beg me for something, even if it wasn't the pleasure of my company.

"No," I said, cocking my famous smile. She showed no emotion, which made me wonder if she even liked men. Every woman liked me, wanted me.

"The Queen also sends this message …" the screen blurred and the sound garbled. I slammed my hand against the screen again, and Lex was back. "She orders you to secure the ship and then place yourself into stasis at once."

"What?!" I growled, leaning over the console, ensuring my angry face filled Lex's screen. She was not intimidated. That ticked me off even more. "I'm Royal Consort to the Queen! I'll decide when and if I go into stasis!"

"The Queen orders that you secure the ship and place yourself into stasis at once to ensure your chances of survival until we rendezvous with you," Lex continued calmly. "She has also informed me that you and she are no longer bound. She has revived Ky and has paired with him. Royal children will be awaiting our allegiance when we arrive at our new home." Lex lifted one eyebrow as if to say, "Check mate."

"Children?" I hated how weak my voice suddenly sounded as I slumped down into the chair in front of the screen.

"General, do we have an understanding of your orders?" Lex repeated.

"Yeah," I nodded, resolved to turn this around in my favor ... somehow, some way. Lore was all I had ... this was all some sort of misunderstanding. We could surely find some way to start over. *She's just trying to make me jealous*, I told myself as I straightened my shoulders. "We have an understanding, Commander. And I'd like you to relay a message to my *Other*. Tell her this: It's not over."

ANDREW

Searing, burning bolts of icy-hot pain shot through my body. It felt as though I was lying on the cold, hard floor somewhere. I couldn't remember anything but the all-encompassing pain. I lifted my hands up in front of my face. They were charred and red; the skin between my fingers was burned away exposing the tender, raw flesh underneath. The pain was maddening.

I blinked away the wash of tears that filled my eyes and tried to get my bearings. From somewhere nearby, came the sounds of someone shouting and things crashing and breaking. Protecting my hands, I rolled over onto my knees and slowly stood, wincing against the onslaught of a new wave of horror. I was completely naked, except for a melted, warped gold band on my left hand.

I had no idea where I was or what had happened to me. All I knew in that moment was that every nerve in my body was on fire and that some other person sounded as if he were suffering as much as I was.

Carefully inching toward the corner, I peeked around to see that the person shouting and breaking things was none other than that bastard Ash. He tossed a beaker-looking-thing across the room, crashing a glass panel. It looked like it wasn't the first thing he'd broken. The place was a wreck. Black streaks of smoke smudged the walls that must have been shiny and white once. I shook my head to clear my thoughts.

Am I in a UFO or something? I focused on trying to clear the fog that had taken up roost in my brain.

Ash started talking to the auto-control module of the computer system. At first, I thought he'd gone as crazy as he looked. I'd never seen that dude look as ramshackle as that. His hair was fried, he had bruises on his face, neck and side. And he wasn't all calm, cool, and collected now as he'd been every other time I'd seen him.

But he hadn't lost his mind, and I was glad. I had no idea how I'd be able to fight him with my arms and hands burned to a crisp, and I had no idea how to fly a UFO. The computer started talking to him, answering his questions as he went through some sort of checklist. Finally, the computer confirmed that the ship was secure and safe to travel in stasis mode.

He paced the room a few more times, talking to himself about someone named Lore, then slammed his hand onto the side of a medical-bed-looking-thing with a glass bubble over it. The glass bubble slid back, revealing a bed.

He crawled into it and lay down with a huff and stayed like that for a few moments, muttering to himself about the ridiculousness of having to do as he was told and something about how he'd been worshipped as a god, and now he was reduced to obeying orders.

"I should have never let her find a way to separate Others," Ash muttered.

His thoughts spoke the opposite of what he was saying. It was like I could hear his inner-most feelings, and it felt both familiar and weird at the same time. He closed his eyes and recalled some ancient image of a king with flowing grey hair and dressed in fine robes and jewels.

"Son, you will someday meet a battle that you cannot … will not win. We all do," the old king said has he placed his hand on Ash's shoulder. Ash must have loved that king like a father. The pain and regret that flowed through him was proof of that. "When it happens, and it will, you'll have to learn from it and move on."

"You were right, My Lord," Ash whispered aloud as if the old man in his memory could hear him. Loneliness rolled off him and seemed to fill the entire room. He was probably the loneliest bastard in the universe at that moment. "And I will move on. Hell, I could have any one of those starlets in Hollywood. And that's exactly what I intend to do."

Then he pressed a large green button inside the pod, and the bubble closed over him. A few moments later, a thin layer of frost covered the inside of the bubble. Then the computer announced that the ship was entering stasis mode and that life support systems would soon work at a minimum.

"Shit!" I looked down at my damaged hands and arms. I had to find some medicine quick and figure out how to get myself into stasis, too.

On the other side of the room, there was a darkened hall. I tiptoed through the broken glass, trying to miss as many shards as possible. When I got to the hallway, a dim row of lights came on, illuminating the hall which led to only two rooms.

One of them was a sort of Captain's Quarters. The other was a laboratory. Many of the things in there had been smashed, too. There was a sort of first aid kit attached to the wall that had made it through his tirade. I found some sort of ointment and some bandages and doctored my arms and hands as much as possible.

More of the ship's systems shut down, and it started getting really cold *really* fast. When I whirled around to head back to the other stasis pod next to Ash's, I stopped dead in my tracks. On the far end of the laboratory was a huge, round window.

All I could see was a million pinpoints of light … stars. It was both beautiful and terrifying. My hearted pounded hard in my chest as I gazed out into the vastness of space. Frost quickly formed across the large window, and the cold ebbed across the floor. My feet … not to mention the other exposed parts of me … would soon freeze if I didn't do something.

The only thing I could do was rush back to the empty stasis pod next to Ash. I pressed a button on the outside of it to open it, but nothing happened. I cussed, then pressed a few more until I finally hit the right one.

When the glass bubble slid back, I scrambled into the pod and said a quick prayer. "Lord, if I make it through this alive, I promise to go to seminary when I get home. Amen." The lights went out, and the pleasant female voice of the computer system announced that the ship was now in stasis mode.

I pressed the large green button next to my head, and the bubble closed over me. My body shivered uncontrollably from both the cold and out-right fear. First, I heard a whooshing sound, then a blast of warming air calmed my quivering and soothed the goose bumps that covered every inch of my naked body.

But it wasn't real warmth, only a sensation of warmth and something that made me feel very sleepy. I blinked my eyes a couple of times, fighting the urge to close them and fall asleep for fear I would never wake up.

"*If* I ever get home ..." I said, aware of how far away my own voice sounded.

A flash of a memory looped around my thoughts of a familiar, old cowboy ... perhaps my grandfather, I couldn't recall. His cowboy hat was tilted slightly to the side, and one corner of his mouth drew up into a small grin beneath a well-trimmed mustache.

He winked and bit down on the cigar stub he'd obviously been chewing for a while, then said, "Sometimes, son, the ending is really just the beginning of something new."

A stronger whoosh of air flowed over my body. I could no longer fight the urge to sleep, so I clamped my eyes closed, and hoped I'd wake up alive someday. Then I drifted off into darkness and dreamed of spending the rest of my life with a girl who had hair the color of fire and a passion to match it.

ABOUT THE AUTHOR

Belle was raised in deep East Texas. She now resides somewhere north of Houston, Texas in a small inconsequential town with the smallest, most inconsequential name. There, in the shady reaches of the pines, elms, and oaks, she daydreams adventures and secrets she weaves throughout her stories. She studied literature and history at University of Houston where Beowulf, Shakespeare's works, and the history of the Vikings were her favorite topics. Belle is positive her readers and fans are the best in the universe.